The Skiver's Guide

The Thirteenth Enchanter

Howl's Moving Castle

A Tale of Time City

Chair Person

Wild Robert

Hidden Turnings (editor)

Castle in the Air

Black Maria (USA: Aunt Maria)

A Sudden Wild Magic

Yes, Dear (picture book)

Hexwood

Fantasy Stories (editor)

Everard's Ride (short stories)

Stopping for a Spell (short stories)

The Tough Guide to Fantasyland

Minor Arcana (short stories)

Deep Secret

Believing Is Seeing (short stories)

Dark Lord of Derkholm

Puss in Boots (retelling)

Mixed Magics (short stories)

The Year of the Griffin

The Merlin Conspiracy

Unexpected Magics (short stories)

The Game

House of Many Ways

Enchanted Glass

Earwig and the Witch

FIREBIRD
Where Fantasy Takes Flight™

The Blue Girl	Charles de Lint
The Blue Sword	Robin McKinley
Dogsbody	Diana Wynne Jones
Dragonhaven	Robin McKinley
Eon	Alison Goodman
Eona	Alison Goodman
Fire	Kristin Cashore

Firebirds:
  An Anthology of Original
  Fantasy and Science Fiction
	Sharyn November, ed.

Firebirds Rising:
  An Anthology of Original
  Science Fiction and Fantasy
	Sharyn November, ed.

The Game	Diana Wynne Jones
Incarceron	Catherine Fisher
Magic or Madness	Justine Larbalestier
The Safe-Keeper's Secret	Sharon Shinn
Sapphique	Catherine Fisher
Singing the Dogstar Blues	Alison Goodman
Snow White and Rose Red	Patricia C. Wrede
A Tale of Time City	Diana Wynne Jones
Tam Lin	Pamela Dean
The Tough Guide to Fantasyland	Diana Wynne Jones

DIANA WYNNE JONES

Fire and Hemlock

Introduction by Garth Nix

FIREBIRD

AN IMPRINT OF PENGUIN GROUP (USA) INC.

FIREBIRD

Published by the Penguin Group

Penguin Group (USA) Inc., 345 Hudson Street, New York, New York 10014, U.S.A.

Penguin Group (Canada), 90 Eglinton Avenue East, Suite 700, Toronto, Ontario, Canada M4P 2Y3
(a division of Pearson Penguin Canada Inc.)

Penguin Books Ltd, 80 Strand, London WC2R 0RL, England

Penguin Ireland, 25 St Stephen's Green, Dublin 2, Ireland (a division of Penguin Books Ltd)

Penguin Group (Australia), 250 Camberwell Road, Camberwell, Victoria 3124, Australia
(a division of Pearson Australia Group Pty Ltd)

Penguin Books India Pvt Ltd, 11 Community Centre, Panchsheel Park, New Delhi – 110 017, India

Penguin Group (NZ), 67 Apollo Drive, Rosedale, Auckland 0632, New Zealand
(a division of Pearson New Zealand Ltd.)

Penguin Books (South Africa) (Pty) Ltd, 24 Sturdee Avenue, Rosebank, Johannesburg 2196, South Africa

Penguin Books Ltd, Registered Offices: 80 Strand, London WC2R 0RL, England

First published in the United Kingdom by Methuen Children's Books Ltd, 1985
First published in the United States of America by Greenwillow Books, 1985
Published by Firebird, an imprint of Penguin Group (USA) Inc., 2012

The essay "The Heroic Ideal—A Personal Odyssey" first appeared in
The Lion and the Unicorn, Volume 13, Number 1, June 1989.

Excerpts from "Burnt Norton," "East Coker," "The Dry Salvages," and "Little Gidding," from FOUR
QUARTETS by T.S. Eliot. Copyright 1936 by Houghton Mifflin Harcourt Publishing Company; © renewed
1964 by T.S. Eliot. Copyright 1940, 1941, 1942 by T.S. Eliot. Copyright © renewed 1968, 1969, 1970
by Esme Valerie Eliot. Reprinted by permission of Houghton Mifflin Harcourt Publishing Company.
Excerpt from *Dogsbody* copyright © Diana Wynne Jones, 1975
Excerpt from *A Tale of Time City* copyright © Diana Wynne Jones, 1987
All rights reserved.

3   5   7   9   10   8   6   4   2

Copyright © Diana Wynne Jones, 1985
Introduction copyright © Garth Nix, 2012
"The Heroic Ideal—A Personal Odyssey" copyright © Diana Wynne Jones, 1988
All rights reserved

LIBRARY OF CONGRESS CATALOGING-IN-PUBLICATION DATA IS AVAILABLE
ISBN 978-0-14-242014-0

Set in Minion
Design by Tony Sahara

Printed in the United States of America

To Laura

CONTENTS

Introduction
by Garth Nix

FIRE AND HEMLOCK

"The Heroic Ideal—
A Personal Odyssey"
an essay by Diana Wynne Jones

Introduction
Garth Nix

It is a difficult task to write an introduction to a novel by the incomparable Diana Wynne Jones, because all the introduction required is, "I really think you should read this book."

Go on. Then, if you still want an introduction, you can come back here later and read the rest of this. Or go and pick up another Diana Wynne Jones novel that also won't need an introduction.

It doesn't matter *which* novel. There are very few authors about whom I could happily say, "read any book, they're all good, and many of them are not only good, they're great," but Diana Wynne Jones is certainly among that select number.

Her novels are also often great in different ways, so that when it comes to recommending particular works of Diana's, I will change my recommendation based upon the prospective reader, their current mood, the weather, and the phase of the moon. If I am actually lending a book, I also consider how recently I read it and whether or not I can bear to see it leave my library before I get a chance to read it again.

If greatly pressed, I guess there is a particular charmed circle of Diana Wynne Jones books that are my particular favorites, books that I return to time and time again. This "best of the best" list, in no particular order, includes *Power of Three* (the first Diane Wynne Jones I ever read, at age thirteen), *Archer's Goon*, *Dogsbody*, *Eight Days of Luke*, *Charmed Life*, *Enchanted Glass*, *Howl's Moving Castle*, and of course, *Fire and Hemlock*.

I was twenty-two when *Fire and Hemlock* was published. I bought it immediately when it was released, having been a committed Diana Wynne Jones reader for almost a decade. At the time I was studying writing and literature at what is now the University of Canberra, happily working on my own first novel, and not very happily deconstructing numerous classic novels. Very few of those books have stayed with me the way *Fire and Hemlock* has lingered on in my head.

It is the mark of a very good book that not only does it resonate for years, you can also reread it and enjoy the reminiscence of your past readings and younger self (or selves), while at the same time having an entirely new reading experience.

Fire and Hemlock is just such a book, rewarding each rereading, whether it be a year or five years or a decade on, with new nuances of story and character, with new understandings and a rearrangement and enlargement of the thoughts that it once inspired.

I think the first time I read *Fire and Hemlock*, I saw only Polly's story, and I mean "saw," because the book was so vivid in my head. The others to my mind were a brilliant supporting cast, but it was Polly's story. Or so I thought, until the next time I read it, a few years later, and I saw things a little differently and Thomas Lynn came into closer focus. Later still, I found myself interested in Polly's grandmother, and in the sadness of her mother, and in the musicians of Tom's quartet.

The story that ties all these characters together is typically imaginative and multi-layered. Though the plot is inspired by the ballads "Thomas the Rhymer" and "Tam Lin," the novel is not a "retelling" of these legends. As always when Diana Wynne Jones takes a piece of mythology, she brings her own unique perspective and inventive skill to it, creating a story that no one else could tell.

One particular talent she has is the gift to take the commonplace, the suburban and ordinary, and make it rich and strange—while still retaining its normality, so you can believe it without any difficulty at all. Whether it is Norse gods inhabiting a pool hall (as in *Eight Days of Luke*), or the Queen of the Fairies dividing her time between a suburban mansion and a city flat, Diana manages to make it both believable and fantastical at the same time.

Fire and Hemlock was way ahead of its time when it was published in 1985. It is a coming-of-age story, but one that even now would be considered ambitious, tracking the life of Polly Whittacker from the age of around ten to the age of nineteen, framed by the older Polly trying to remember a past that has been magically erased and altered. Within that frame there is the Thomas the Rhymer plotline of a man destined to be sacrificed unless his true love can save him, but woven around that are numerous other story-lines, embellishments, and adornments. *Fire and Hemlock* is a quest story, a love story, an adventure story, a coming-of-age story, a dysfunctional family story, a story *about* stories, a school story, a family saga, a mystery story, and a whole host of other kinds of stories—all worked together so wonderfully well that you will never find a stitch, or even think to look for one.

Before I wrote this introduction, I naturally read the book again, for the seventh time, maybe even the eighth. I hadn't read it for six years, a figure I easily established by a form of archaeology, as after fruitlessly searching my shelf of Diana Wynne Jones books, I had to unstack book boxes in my shed until I came to the layer of boxes packed for the move to my current house. Once again I read it in a single sitting, late at night, and again noticed new things, as well as relishing the old.

I also read it with my writer's eye more active than I ever have done before, but I came to no newer conclusion than one I arrived at all those years ago as a student writer. It is a conclusion that I think has been shared by many other writers.

I hope one day I will be able to write a book even half *as good as this one.*

I wrote the introduction above before the terrible news of Diana's death on March 26, 2011. I still find it difficult to believe she's gone, because for a while it seemed her strength of character, eccentric optimism, and just sheer magical nature might beat the cancer she had been fighting for some time. But she lives on in her books, and so is Everywhere and Nowhere, gone but never forgotten.

Garth Nix
Hunsdon House (just visiting), 2011

Fire and Hemlock

CONTENTS

PART ONE
NEW HERO
allegro vivace

1

PART TWO
NOW HERE
andante cantibile

135

PART THREE
WHERE NOW?
allegro con fuoco

223

PART FOUR
NOWHERE
presto molto agitato

319

CODA
scherzando

411

PART ONE

NEW HERO
allegro vivace

1

A dead sleep came over me
And from my horse I fell

TAM LIN

Polly sighed and laid her book face down on her bed. She rather thought she had read it after all, some time ago. Before she swung her feet across to get on with her packing, she looked up at the picture above the bed. She sighed again. There had been a time, some years back, when she had gazed at that picture and thought it marvellous. Dark figures had seemed to materialise out of its dark centre—strong, running dark figures—always at least four of them, racing to beat out the flames in the foreground. There had been times when you could see the figures quite clearly. Other times, they had been shrouded in the rising smoke. There had even been a horse in it sometimes. Not now.

Here, now, she could see it was simply a large colour photo-graph, three feet by two feet, taken at dusk, of some hay bales burning in a field. The fire must have been spreading, since there was smoke in the air, and more smoke enveloping the high hemlock plant in the front, but there were no people in it. The shapes she used to take for people were only too clearly dark clumps of the dark hedge behind the blaze. The only person in that field must have been the photographer. Polly had to admit that he had been both clever and lucky. It was a haunting picture. It was called *Fire and Hemlock*. She sighed again as she swung her feet to the floor. The penalty of being grown up was that you saw things like this photograph as they really were. And Granny would be in any minute to point out that Mr. Perks and Fiona were not going to wait while she did her packing tomorrow morning—and Granny would have things to say about feet on the bedspread. Polly just wished she felt happier at the thought of another year of college.

Her hand knocked the book. Polly did not get up after all. And books put down on their faces, spoiling them, Granny would say. It's only a paperback, Granny. It was called *Times out of Mind*, editor L. Perry, and it was a collection of supernatural stories. Polly had been attracted to it a couple of years back, largely because the picture on the cover was not unlike the *Fire and Hemlock* photograph—dusky smoke, with a dark blue umbrella-like plant against the smoke. And, now Polly remembered, she had read the stories through then, and none of them were much good. Yet— here was an odd thing. She could have sworn the book had been called something different when she first bought it. And, surely, hadn't one of the stories actually been called "Fire and Hemlock" too?

Polly picked the book up, with her finger in it to keep the place in the story she was reading. "Two-timer" it was called, and it was about someone who went back in time to his own childhood and changed things, so that his life ran differently the second time. She remembered the ending now. The man finished by having two sets of memories, and the story wasn't worked out at all well. Polly did not worry when she lost her place in it as she leafed through looking for the one she thought had been called "Fire and Hemlock." Odd. It wasn't there. Had she dreamed it, then? She did often dream the most likely seeming things. Odder still. Half the stories she thought she remembered reading in this book were not there— and yet she did, very clearly, remember reading all the stories which seemed to be in the book now. For a moment she almost felt like the man in "Two-timer" with his double set of memories. What a madly detailed dream she must have had. Polly found her place in the story again, largely because the pages were spread apart there, and stopped in the act of putting the book face down on her rumpled bedspread.

Was it Granny who minded you putting books down like this? Granny didn't read much anyway.

"And why should I feel so worried about it?" Polly asked aloud. "And where's my other photo—the one I stole?"

A frantic sense of loss came upon her, so strong that for a moment she could have cried. Why should she suddenly have memories that did not seem to correspond with the facts?

"Suppose they *were* once facts," Polly said to herself, with her hand still resting on the book. Ever since she was a small girl, she had liked supposing things. And the habit died hard, even at the age of nineteen. "Suppose," she said, "I really am like the man in the story, and something happened to change my past."

It was intended simply as a soothing daydream, to bury the strange, pointless worry that seemed to be growing in her. But suddenly, out of it leaped a white flash of conviction. It was just like the way those four—or more—figures used to leap into being behind the fire in that photograph. Polly glanced up at it, almost expecting to see them again. There were only men-shaped clumps of hedge. The flash of conviction had gone too. But it left Polly with a dreary, nagging suspicion in its place: that something *had* been different in the past, and if it had, it was because of something dreadful she had done herself.

But there seemed no way to discover what was different. Polly's past seemed a smooth string of normal, half-forgotten things: school and home, happiness and miseries, fun and friends, and, for some reason, a memory of eating toasted buns for tea, dripping butter. Apart from this odd memory about the book, there seemed no foothold for anything unusual.

"If nothing happened, then there's nothing to remember," she told herself, trying to sound philosophical. "Of course there's nowhere to start."

For some reason, that appalled her. She crouched, with her hand growing damp on the book, forgetting her grimy shoes tangling in the bedspread and the suitcases open on the floor, staring into her appallingly normal memories: a Cotswold town, London, a shopping precinct somewhere, a horse— "That's absurd. I don't *know* any horses!" she said. "It's no good. I'll have to go back to the time before it all started, or didn't start, and get in from that end." That was when she was how old? Ten? What was she doing then? What friends had she?

Friends. That did it. From nine years ago came swimming the shape of Polly's once-dear friend Nina. Fat, silly Nina. Granny used to call Nina a ripe banana. And Polly was so attached to Nina that Granny had agreed to have Nina along with Polly, that first time Polly came to stay with Granny. That would be back around the time there was first a question of divorce between Polly's parents. Back too to when Polly's favourite reading was a fat book called *Heroes* that had once been Granny's.

At that, Polly raised her head. "The funeral!" she said.

2

In those days people who did not know Polly might have thought she chose Nina as a friend to set herself off by comparison. Nina was a big, fat girl with short, frizzy hair, glasses, and a loud giggle. Polly, on the other hand, was an extremely pretty little girl, and probably the prettiest thing about her was her mass of long, fine, fair hair. In fact, Polly admired and envied Nina desperately, both Nina's looks and her bold, madcap disposition. Polly, at that time, was trying to eat a packet of biscuits every day in order to get fat like Nina. And she spent diligent hours squashing and pressing at her eyes in hopes either of making herself need glasses too, or at least of giving her eyes the fat, pink, staring look that Nina's had when Nina took off her glasses. She cried when Mum refused to cut her hair short like Nina's. She hated her hair. The first morning they were at Granny's, she took pleasure in forgetting to brush it.

It was not hard to forget. Polly and Nina had been awake half the night in Granny's spare room, talking and laughing. They were wildly excited. And it was such a relief to Polly to be away from the whispered quarrelling at home, and the hard, false silences whenever Mum and Dad noticed Polly was near. They did not seem to realise that Polly knew a quarrel when she heard one, just like anyone does. Granny was a relief because she was calm. Nina's wild, silly jokes were even more of a relief, even if Polly was hardly awake the next morning. The whole first day at Granny's was like a dream to Polly.

It was a windy day in autumn. In Granny's garden the leaves whirled down. Nina and Polly raced about, catching them. Every leaf you caught, Nina shrieked, meant one happy day. Polly only caught seven. Nina caught thirty-five.

"Well, it's a whole week. Count your blessings," Granny said to Polly in her dry way when they came panting in to show her, and she gave them milk and biscuits. Granny always made Polly think of biscuits. She had a dry, shortbread sort of way to her, with a hidden taste that came out afterwards. Her kitchen had a biscuit smell to it, a nutty, buttery smell like no other kitchen.

While Polly was sniffing the smell, Nina remembered that today was Hallowe'en. She decided that she and Polly must both dress up as High Priestesses, and she clamoured for long black robes.

"Never a dull moment with our Nina," Granny remarked, and she went away to see what she could find. She came back with two old black dresses and some dark curtains. In an amused, uncommitted way, she helped them both dress up. Then she turned them firmly out of doors. "Go and make an exhibit of yourselves round the neighbourhood," she said. "They need a bit of stirring up here."

Nina and Polly paraded up and down the road for a while. Nina looked for all the world like a large, fat nun, and the dress held her knees together. Polly's dress, apart from being long, was quite a good fit. The neighbourhood did not seem to notice them. The houses—except for a few small ones like Granny's—were large and set back from the road, hidden by the trees that grew down both sides, and not a soul came to see the two High Priestesses, even though Nina laughed and shrieked and exclaimed every time her headdress flapped. They paraded right up to the big house across the end of the road and looked through the bars of its gate. It was called Hunsdon House—the name was cut into the stone of both gateposts. Inside, they saw a length of gravel drive, much strewn with dead leaves, and, coming slowly crunching along it towards them, a shiny black motor-hearse with flowers piled on top.

At the sight Nina shrieked and ran away down the road, trailing her headdress. "Hold your collar! Hold your collar till you see a four-legged animal!"

They ran into Granny's garden where, luckily, Granny's black-and-white cat, Mintchoc, was sitting on the wall. So that was all right. They could use both hands again. "Now what shall we do?" demanded Nina.

Polly was still laughing at Nina. "I don't know," she said.

"Think of something. What do High Priestesses *do*?" said Nina.

"No idea," said Polly.

"Yes you have," said Nina. "Think—or I shan't play with you any more!"

Nina was always making that threat. It never failed with Polly. "Oh—er—they walk in procession and make human sacrifices," Polly said.

Nina shrieked with gleeful laughter. "We did! We have! Our corpse was in the hearse! Then what happens?"

"Um," said Polly. "We have to wait for the gods to answer our sacrifice. And—I know—while we wait, the police come after us for murder."

Nina liked that. She ran flapping and squawking into Granny's back garden, crying out that the police were after her. When Polly caught up with her, she was trying to climb the wall into the next garden. "What are you doing?" Polly said, hardly able to speak for laughing.

"Escaping from the police, of course!" said Nina. With a great deal of silly giggling, she managed to scramble to the top of the wall, where her black robe split with a sound like a gunshot. "Oh!" she cried. "They got me!" Whereupon she swung her legs over the wall and vanished in a crash of rotting wood. "Come on!" said her voice from behind the wall. "I won't be your friend if you stay there."

As usual, the threat was enough for Polly. It was not really that she was afraid Nina would stop being her friend—though she was, a little. It was more that Polly could not seem to break out of her prim, timid self in those days, and be properly adventurous, without Nina's threats to galvanise her. So now she boldly swung herself up the wall and was quite grateful to Nina when she landed in the middle of somebody's woodshed on the other side.

After that, the morning became more like a dream than ever—a very silly dream too. Nina and Polly scrambled through garden after garden. Some were neat and open, and they sprinted through those, and some were overgrown, with hiding-places where they could lurk. One garden was full of washing, and they had to crouch behind flapping sheets while somebody took down a row of pants. They were on the edge of giggles the whole time, terrified that someone would catch them and yet, in a dreamlike way, almost sure they were safe. Both of them lost their curtain headdresses in different gardens, but they went on, quite unable to stop or go back, neither of them quite knowing why. Nina invented a reason in about the tenth garden. She said they were coming to a road, because she could hear cars. So they went more madly than ever, across a row of rotting shed roofs that creaked and splintered under them, and jumped down from the wall into what seemed to be a wood. Nina ran towards the open, laughing with relief, and Polly lost her for a few seconds.

When Polly came out into the open, it was not a road after all. It was gravel at the side of a house. There was a door open in the house, and through it Polly caught a glimpse of Nina walking up a polished passage, actually inside the house.

"The cheek Nina has!" she said to herself. For a moment she almost did not dare follow Nina. But the dreamlike feeling was still on her. She thought of the threats Nina would make if she stayed hiding in the wood, and she sprinted on her toes across the space in a scatter of gravel and went into the house too, into a strong smell of polish and scent. Cautiously, she tiptoed up the passage.

Here it was completely like a dream. The passage led into a

grand hall with a white-painted staircase wrapped round the out-side of it in joints, each joint a balcony, and huge, painted china vases standing around, every one big enough to contain one of Ali Baba's forty thieves. A man met her here. As people do in dreams, he seemed to be expecting Polly. He was obviously a servitor, for he was wearing evening dress and carrying a tray with glasses on it. Polly made a little movement to run away as he came up to her, but all he said was, "Orangeade, miss? I fancy you're a bit young yet for sherry." And he held the tray out.

It made Polly feel like a queen. She put out a somewhat grubby hand and took a glass of orangeade. There was ice in it and a slice of real orange. "Thank you," she said in a stately, queenlike way.

"Turn left through that door, miss," the servitor said.

Polly did as he said. She had a feeling she was supposed to. True, underneath she had a faint feeling that this couldn't be quite right, but there did not seem to be anything she could do about it. Hold-ing the clinking glass against her chest, Polly walked like a queen in her black dress into a big, carpeted room. It was dingy in the gusty light of the autumn day, and full of comfortable armchairs lined up in not very regular rows. A number of people were standing about holding wineglasses and talking in murmurs. They were all in dark clothes and looked very respectable, and every one of them was grown up. None of them paid any attention to Polly at all.

Nina was not there. Polly had not really expected her to be. It was clear Nina had vanished the way people do in dreams. She saw the woman she had mistaken for Nina—it was the split skirt and the black dress which had caused the mistake—standing outlined against the dim green garden beyond the windows, talking to a high-shouldered man with glasses. Everything was very hushed and elderly. "And I shan't look on it very kindly if you do," Polly heard the woman say to the man. It was a polite murmur, but it sounded like one of Nina's threats, only a good deal less friendly.

More people came in behind Polly. She moved over out of their way and sat on one of the back row of chairs, which were hard and upright, still carefully holding her orangeade. She sat and watched the room fill with murmuring, dreamlike people in dark clothes. There was one other child now. He was in a grey suit and looked as respectable as the rest, and he was rather old too—at least fourteen, Polly thought. He did not notice Polly. Nobody did, except the man with glasses. Polly could see the glasses flashing at her uncertainly as the lady talked to him.

Then a new stage seemed to start. A busy, important man swept through the room and sat down in a chair facing all the others. All the rest sat down too, in a quiet, quick way, turning their heads to make sure there was a chair there before they sat. The room was all rustling while they arranged themselves, and one set of quick footsteps as the high-shouldered man walked about looking for a place. Everyone looked at him crossly. He hunched a bit—you do, Polly thought, when everyone stares—and finally sat down near the door, a few seats along from Polly.

The important man flipped a large paper open with a rattle. A document, Polly thought. "Now, ladies and gentlemen, if I have your attention, I shall read the Will."

Oh dear, Polly thought. The dream feeling went away at once, and the ice in her drink rattled as she realised where she was and what she had done. This was Hunsdon House, where she and Nina had seen the hearse. Someone had died here and she had gate-crashed the funeral. And because she was dressed up in a black dress, no one had realised that she should not be here. She wondered what they would do to her when they did. Meanwhile she sat, trying not to shake the ice in her glass, listening to the lawyer's voice reading out what she was sure were all sorts of private bequests—from the Last Will and Testament of Mrs. Mabel Tatiana Leroy Perry, being of a sound mind et cetera—which Polly was sure she should not be hearing at all.

As the lawyer's voice droned on, Polly became more and more certain she was listening to private things. She could feel the way each item made sort of waves among the silent listeners, waves of annoyance, anger and deep disgust, and one or two spurts of quite savage joy. The disgust seemed to be because so many things went to "my daughter Mrs. Eudora Mabel Lorelei Perry Lynn." Even when things went to other people, such as "my cousin Morton Perry Leroy" or "my niece Mrs. Silvia Nuala Leroy Perry," the Will seemed to change its mind every so often and give them to Mrs. Perry Lynn instead. The joy was on the rare occasions when someone different, like Robert Goodman Leroy Perry or Sebastian Ralph Perry Leroy, actually got something.

Polly began to wonder if it might even be against the law for her to be listening to these things. She tried not to listen—and this was not difficult, because most of it was very boring—but she became steadily more unhappy.

She wished she dared creep away. She was quite near the door. It would have been easy if only that man hadn't chosen to sit down just beyond her, right beside the door. She looked to see if she still might slip out, and looked at the same moment as the man looked at her, evidently wondering about her. Polly hastily turned her head to the front again and pretended to listen to the Will, but she could feel him still looking. The ice in her drink melted. The Will went on to an intensely boring bit about "a Trust shall be set up." Beside the door, the man stood up. Polly's head turned, without her meaning it to, as if it were on strings, and he was still looking at her, right at her. The eyes behind the glasses met hers and sort of dragged, and he nodded his head away sideways towards the door. "Come on out of that," said the look. "Please," it added, with a sort of polite, questioning stillness.

It was a fair cop. Polly nodded too. Carefully she put the melted orange drink down on the chair beside hers and slid to the floor. He was now holding out his hand to take hers and make sure she didn't get away. Feeling fated, Polly put her hand into his. It was a big hand, a huge one, and folded hers quite out of sight under its row of long fingers. It pulled, and they both went softly out of the door into the hall with the jointed staircase.

"Didn't you want your drink?" the man asked as the lawyer's voice faded to a rise and fall in the distance.

Polly shook her head. Her voice seemed to have gone away. There was an archway opening off the hall. In the room through the archway she could see the servitor setting wineglasses out on a big, polished dinner table. Polly wanted to shout to him to come and explain that he had let her into the funeral, but she could not utter a sound. The big hand holding hers was pulling her along, into the passage she had come in by. Polly, as she went with it, cast her eyes round the hall for a last look at its grandeurs. Wistfully she thought of herself jumping into one of the Ali Baba vases and staying there hidden until everyone had gone away. But as she thought it, she was already in the side passage with the door standing open on the gusty trees at the end of it. The lawyer's voice was out of hearing now.

"Will you be warm enough outside in that dress?" the man holding her hand asked politely.

His politeness seemed to deserve an answer. Polly's voice came back. "Yes thank you," she replied sadly. "I've got my real clothes on underneath."

"Very wise," said the man. "Then we can go into the garden." They stepped out of the door, where the wind wrapped Polly's black dress round her legs and flapped her hair sideways. It could not do much with the man's hair, which was smoothed across his head in an elderly style, so it stood it up in colourless hanks and rattled the jacket of his dark suit. He shivered. Polly hoped he would send her off and go straight indoors again. But he obviously meant to see her properly off the premises. He turned to the right with her. The wind hurled itself at their faces. "This is better," said the man. "I wish I could have thought of a way to get that poor boy Seb out of it too. I could see he was as bored as you were. But he didn't have the sense to sit near the door."

Polly turned and looked up at him in astonishment. He smiled down at her. Polly gave him a hasty smile in return, hoping he would think she was shy, and turned her face back to the wind to think about this. So the man thought she really was part of the funeral. He was just meaning to be kind. "It *was* boring, wasn't it?" she said.

"Terribly," he said, and let go of her hand.

Polly ought to have run off then. And she would have, she thought, remembering it all nine years later, if she had simply thought he was just being kind. But the way he spoke told her that he had found the funeral far more utterly boring than she had. She remembered the way the lady she had mistaken for Nina had spoken to him, and the way the other guests had looked at him while he was walking about looking for a seat. She realised he had sat down on purpose near the door, and she knew—perhaps without quite understanding it—that if she ran away, it would mean he had to go back into the funeral again. She was his excuse for coming out of it.

So she stayed. She had to lean on the wind to keep beside him while they walked under some ragged, nearly finished roses and the wind blew white petals across them.

"What's your name?" he asked.

"Polly."

"Polly what?"

"Polly Whittacker," she said without thinking. Then of course she realised that the right name for the funeral should have been Leroy or Perry, or Perry Leroy, or Leroy Perry, like the people who got the bequests in the Will, and had to cover it up. "I'm only adopted, you know. I come from the other branch of the family really."

"I thought you might," he said, "with that hair of yours."

"And what part of the family are you?" Polly said, quickly and artificially, to distract him from asking more. She took a piece of her blowing hair and bit it anxiously.

"Oh, no part really," he said, ducking his head under a clawing rose. "The dead lady is the mother of my ex-wife, so I felt I ought to come. But I'm the odd man out, here." Polly relaxed. He was distracted. He said, "My name's Thomas Lynn."

"Both parts surname?" Polly asked doubtfully. "Everyone's so double-barrelled in there."

That made him give a little crow of laughter, which he swallowed hastily down, as if he were ashamed of laughing at a funeral. "No, no. Just the second part."

"Mr. Lynn, then," said Polly. She let her hair blow round her face as they walked down some sunken steps, and studied him. Long hair had its uses. He was tall and thin and walked in a way that stooped his round, colourless head between his shoulders, making his head look smaller than it really was—though some of that could have been distance: he was so tall that his head was a long way off from Polly. Like a very tall tortoise, Polly thought. The glasses added to the tortoise look. It was an amiable, vague face they sat on. Polly decided Mr. Lynn was nice.

"Mr. Lynn," she asked, "what do you like doing most?"

The tortoise head swung towards her in surprise. "I was just going to ask *you* that!"

"Snap!" said Polly, and laughed up at him. She knew, of course, by this time, that she was starting to flirt with Mr. Lynn. Mum would have given Polly one of her long, heavy stares if she had been there. But, as Polly told herself, she did have to distract Mr. Lynn from thinking too deeply about her connection with the funeral, and she did think Mr. Lynn was nice anyway. Polly never flirted with anyone unless she liked them. So, as they edged their way between two vast grey hedges of uncut lavender, she said, "What I like best—apart from running and shouting and jokes and fighting—is being things."

"Being things?" Mr. Lynn asked. "Like what?" He sounded wistful and mystified.

"Making things like heroes up with other people, then being them," Polly explained. The tortoise head turned to her politely. She could tell he did not understand. It was on the tip of her tongue to show him what she meant by telling him how she had arrived at the funeral by being a High Priestess with the police after her. But she dared not say that. "I'll show you," she said instead. "Pretend you're not really you at all. In real life you're really something quite different."

"What am I?" Mr. Lynn said obligingly.

It would have been better if he had been like Nina and said he would not be friends unless she told him. Without any prodding, Polly's invention went dead on her. She could only think of the most ordinary things.

"You keep an ironmonger's shop," she said rather desperately, To make this seem better, she added, "A very *good* ironmonger's shop in a very nice town. And your name is really Thomas Piper.

That's because of your name—Tom, Tom, the piper's son—you know."

Mr. Lynn smiled. "Oddly enough, my father used to play the flute professionally. Yes. I sell nails and dustbins and hearth-brushes. What else?"

"Hot-water bottles and spades and buckets," said Polly. "Every morning you go out and hang them round your door, and stack wheelbarrows and watering cans on the pavement."

"Where passers-by can bark their shins on them. I see," said Mr. Lynn. "And what else? Am I happy in my work?"

"Not quite happy," Polly said. He was playing up so well that her imagination began to work properly. Down between the lavender bushes, the wind was cut off and she felt much calmer. "You're a bit bored, but that doesn't matter, because keeping the shop is only what everyone *thinks* you do. Really you're secretly a hero, a very strong one who's immortal—"

"Immortal?" Mr. Lynn said, startled.

"Well nearly," said Polly. "You'd live for hundreds of years if someone doesn't kill you in one of your battles. Your name is really—um—Tan Coul and I'm your assistant."

"Are you my assistant in the shop as well, or just when I'm being a hero?" asked Mr. Lynn.

"No, I'm me," said Polly. "I'm a learner hero. I come with you whenever you go out on a job."

"Then you'll have to live within call," Mr. Lynn pointed out. "Where is this shop of mine? Here in Middleton? It had better be, so that I can pick you up easily when a job comes up."

"No, it's in Stow-on-the-Water," Polly said decidedly. Pretending was like that. Things seemed to make themselves up, once you got going.

"That's awkward," Mr. Lynn said.

"It is, isn't it?" Polly agreed. "If you like, I'll come and work in your shop and pretend to be your real-life assistant too. Say when I found out where you lived, I journeyed miles from Middleton to be near you."

"Better," said Mr. Lynn. "You also pretended to be older than you are, in order not to be sent to school. But that sort of thing can easily be done by the right kind of trainee-hero, I'm sure. What's your name when we're out on a job?"

"Hero," said Polly. "It *is* a real name," she protested, as the tortoise head swung down to look at her. "It's a lady in my book that I read every night. Someone swam the sea all the time to visit her."

"I know," said Mr. Lynn. "I was just surprised that *you* did."

"And it's a sort of joke," Polly explained. "I know a lot about heroes, because of my book."

"I see you do," said Mr. Lynn, smiling rather. "But there are still a lot of things we need to settle. For instance—"

As he spoke, they pushed out from between the grey hedges into a small lawn with an empty sunken pool in it. A brown bird flew away, low across the grass as they came, making a set of sharp, shrieking cries. The wind gusted over, rolling the dry leaves in the concrete bottom of the pool, and a ray of sun followed the wind, travelling swiftly over the lawn.

"For instance," said Mr. Lynn, and stopped.

The sun reached the dry pool. For just a flickering part of a second, some trick of light filled the pool deep with transparent water. The sun made bright, curved wrinkles on the bottom, and the leaves, Polly could have sworn, instead of rolling on the bottom were, just for an instant, floating, green and growing. Then the sunbeam travelled on, and there was just a dry oblong of concrete again. Mr. Lynn saw it too. Polly could tell from the way he stopped talking.

"Heroes do see things like that," she said, in case he was alarmed.

"I suppose they do," he agreed thoughtfully. "True. They must, since we both are. But, tell me, what happens when the call comes to do a job? I'm in the shop, selling nails. We each snatch up a saw—or I suppose an axe would be better—and we rush out. Where do we go? What do we do?"

They walked past the pool while Polly considered. "We go to kill giants and dragons and things," she said.

"Where? Up the road in the supermarket?" Mr. Lynn asked.

Polly could tell he thought poorly of her answer. "Yes, if you like, if you're so clever!" she snapped at him, just as if he were Nina. "I know we're that kind of heroes—I know we're not the kind that conquers mad scientists—but I don't know it *all*. *You* do some of it, if you know so much! You were just pretending not to know about being things—weren't you?"

"Not altogether," Mr. Lynn said, politely holding a wet lump of evergreen bush aside for Polly. "It's years since I did any. Beside you, *I'm* the learner. I'd really much prefer to be a trainee-hero too. Couldn't I be? You could happen to be there when I kill my first giant—and perhaps it could be thanks to you that I didn't get squashed flat by him."

"If you like," Polly agreed graciously. He was so humble that she felt quite mean to have snapped.

"Thank you," he said, just as if she had granted a real favour. "That brings me to another question. Do I know about my secret life as a hero while I'm being an ironmonger? Or not?"

"You didn't at first," Polly said, thinking it out. "You were awfully surprised and thought you were having visions or something. But you got used to it quite quickly."

"Though at first I blundered about, utterly bewildered," Mr. Lynn agreed. "We both had to learn as we went on. Yes, that's how it must have been. Now, what about my life selling hardware in Stow-on-the-Water? Do I live alone?"

"No, I live there too, when I get there," said Polly. "But of course there's your wife, Edna—"

"No there isn't," Mr. Lynn said. He said it quietly and calmly, as if someone had asked him if there was any butter and he had opened the fridge and found none. But Polly could tell he meant it absolutely.

"Well—there *has* to be," she argued. "There's someone—I know her name's Edna—who bosses you round, and makes your life a misery, and thinks you're stupid, and doesn't allow you enough money, and makes you do all the work—"

"My landlady," said Mr. Lynn.

"No," said Polly.

"Sister, then," said Mr. Lynn. "How about a sister?"

"I don't know about sisters!" Polly protested.

They wandered round the overgrown garden, arguing about it. In the end, Polly found she had to give way about Edna and make her a sister after all. Mr. Lynn was just quietly adamant over it, and he would not budge. He gave in to Polly on most other things, but not on that.

"Must I kill dragons?" he said, rather pleadingly, as they came up to the house from the back somewhere.

"Yes," said Polly. "It's what our kind of heroes do."

"But most dragons seem to have rather interesting personalities— besides probably having quite good reasons for what they do, if only one could understand them," Mr. Lynn objected. "And almost every dragon-slayer I ever heard of came to a sticky end in the end."

"Don't be a coward," said Polly. "St. George in my book didn't come to a sticky end."

"I'm nothing like St. George," said Mr. Lynn. "He didn't wear glasses."

This was true, even though Polly had always imagined St. George as tall and thin like Mr. Lynn. He seemed so unhappy that she relented a little. "We'll keep the dragon to the end, then, for when we're properly trained."

"That's a good idea," Mr. Lynn said gratefully. "Now come over here. There's something I think you'll like."

He led the way up the lawn, against the gusts of the wind, right up to the house. Three stone steps there led up to a closed door. On either side of the steps there was a short stone pillar with a stone vase on top of it. Mr. Lynn stretched his arms out so that he had a hand on each stone vase. "Are you looking?" he said, standing in his bowed way between them. Like Samson in my book, Polly thought, getting ready to pull the temple down.

"Yes," she said. "What?"

"Watch." Mr. Lynn's hand moved on the right-hand vase. The vase began to spin slowly, grating a little. Two, three heavy turns and it stopped. Now Polly could see there were letters engraved on the front of the vase.

"HERE," she read.

"Now watch again," said Mr. Lynn. His big left hand spun the other vase. This one went round much more smoothly. For a while it was a grey stone blur. Then it grated, slowed, and settled, and there were letters on it too.

"NOW," Polly read. "NOW—HERE. What does that mean?"

Mr. Lynn spun both vases, one slowly, grinding and groaning, the other smooth and blurring. They both stopped at exactly the same time.

WHERE, said the one on the left. NOW, read the right-hand one.

Upon which, Mr. Lynn spun them again. This time when they stopped, the vases read NO and WHERE.

"Oh I see!" said Polly. "NOWHERE! That's clever!" She moved sideways to look round the curve of the vases and found they still said NOWHERE, though this was because the left-hand vase now seemed to say NOW and the right-hand one HERE from where she had moved to. Both vases really said NOWHERE, but the letters were so arranged on them that you could never see the whole word at once on the same vase. Polly made sure, by going right up to them, ducking under Mr. Lynn's arm, and putting her head sideways to read the letters round the other side.

"Yes that's right," Mr. Lynn said. "They both say NOWHERE really." He spun them again, the slow grinding one and the fast smooth one, and this time they came up with HERE—NOW.

"Heroes see things like that," he said.

"It's obviously an enchantment of some kind," Polly agreed, humouring him.

"It must be," he said. It sounded as if he was humouring her.

Here, they both looked round, Polly was not sure why. The boy who had been at the funeral was standing behind them, still very smooth and neat in spite of the wind. Maybe he had snorted. At any rate, he was looking very scornful.

"Oh hello, Seb," Mr. Lynn said. "You got out at last, then?"

"Only because it's over," the boy said contemptuously.

"Is it? Thank goodness for that!" Mr. Lynn said.

Instead of answering, the boy simply turned round and walked away. Mr. Lynn's face, Polly thought, showed just a trace of hurt feelings.

"What a horrible, rude boy!" Polly exclaimed, hoping it was loud enough for the boy to hear as he walked. But he walked very quickly and was out of sight round the corner of the house before she had finished saying it. "What relation is he?" she asked.

"Son of Laurel's cousin—distant enough," Mr. Lynn said. He stood looking the way the boy had gone, in an absent, unhappy way that made Polly uncomfortable. But when he looked down at her, he seemed quite cheerful. "I think we could risk going back in again now," he said. "They tell me I'm allowed to choose some of the old lady's pictures. Would you like to help me choose?" He held out his hand to Polly and smiled.

Polly almost took hold of it. Then she backed away. Mr. Lynn stayed with his hand awkwardly stretched out, and the smile died off his face, leaving it perplexed and a good deal more hurt than he had looked over Seb's rudeness. "What's the matter?" he asked.

It made Polly feel mean as well as dishonest. "I'm not a relation," she blurted out. She could feel her cheeks stinging as they turned red. "I came in by mistake. I thought Nina was in there—being silly, you know."

"I had an idea it was something like that," Mr. Lynn said rather sadly. "So you're not coming?"

"I—I will if you want me to," Polly said.

"I'd be very much obliged if you would," said Mr. Lynn.

His hand was still stretched out. Polly took hold of it, quite extraordinarily glad to have told him the truth, and they went on round the house the way Seb had gone.

"So my first giant is to be in the Stow-Whatsis supermarket," Mr. Lynn said as they turned the corner.

"Quite a small one, or he wouldn't fit," Polly said consolingly. This side of the house was the grand front. There was a large space of gravel with cars parked in it. These must have been the cars they had heard which had made Nina think they were coming to the road. Polly wondered where Nina was, but she was far too interested in her own adventures to worry about Nina. Numbers of people, dark-dressed and sober from the funeral, were drifting out of the open front door of Hunsdon House and wandering about on the gravel. Some seemed to have come out for fresh air. Some were getting into cars to leave.

Polly and Mr. Lynn went along the side of the house to the front door. "Even a small one would get into the local papers," Mr. Lynn said. "What do we say to the reporters?"

"Leave all the interviewing to me," Polly said grandly.

Perhaps it was a strange conversation. Perhaps this accounted for the unfriendly looks they got from the people round the front door. Some pretended not to notice Polly and Mr. Lynn. Others said, "Hello, Tom," but they said it in a grudging sort of way, and raised their eyebrows at Polly before they turned away. By the time she and Mr. Lynn had edged their way inside into the grand hall again, Polly was sure this had nothing to do with their conversation. The people crowding the hall, she could somehow tell, were the most important members of the family. Every one of these gave Mr. Lynn a disapproving look—if they bothered to notice him at all—before turning away. Before they had pushed their way halfway across to the stairs, Polly did not wonder that Mr. Lynn had wanted her to keep him company indoors.

The one person who spoke to Mr. Lynn was a man Polly did not like at all. He turned right round, in the middle of talking to someone else, in order to stare at Mr. Lynn and Polly. He was a big, portly person with a dark, pouchy piece of skin under each eye.

"Slithering off as usual, are you, Tom?" he said jovially. It was not nearly as jolly as it sounded.

"No, I'm still here, Morton, as you see," Mr. Lynn said, ducking his head apologetically.

"Then stick around," the man said, "or you'll be in real trouble." He laughed, to pretend it was a joke. It was a deep, chesty laugh. Polly thought of it as a fatal laugh, the way you think about a bad cough. The man turned away, laughing this chesty laugh. "Laurel told me to tell you," he said, and went back to talking to the person he had turned away from.

"Thanks," Mr. Lynn said to his back, and towed Polly on across the hall.

They had reached the foot of the jointed staircase when the servitor politely stopped them. "I beg your pardon, sir. Will you or the little girl be staying for lunch?"

"I don't—" Mr. Lynn began. He stopped and looked down at Polly, rather dismayed. He had obviously forgotten she was not supposed to be there. "No," he said. "We'll be leaving almost at once, thank you."

The servitor said, "Thank you, sir," and went away.

Polly did not blame Mr. Lynn for not doing what the laughing man had told him to do. "Who was that man?" she whispered as they went up the stairs.

"One of the caterers, I think," said Mr. Lynn.

"No, silly! The one with black poached eyes," Polly whispered.

That made Mr. Lynn utter a yelp of laughter, guiltily cut short. "Oh, him? That's Seb's father, Morton Leroy. He and Laurel are probably going to get married. The pictures are in here."

Polly had hoped that they would be going right up the stairs, round all the joints, so that she would have a chance to investigate the upstairs of Hunsdon House. But the room Mr. Lynn went into was off a half-landing, only one short flight up. It was a small, bare place. There were marks on the carpet where furniture had stood for a long time and then been taken away. The pictures were leaning against the walls to left and right, in stacks.

"Some of these, as I remember, were very nice," Mr. Lynn said. "Suppose we lean all the ones we think are worth taking against the wall under the window, and then consider which to take. I was told I could have six."

As soon as they started looking at the pictures, Polly discovered that the ones leaning on the left-hand wall were by far the most interesting. She left Mr. Lynn to sort through the ones on the other side of the room, and knelt facing the left wall, using her chin and stomach to prop the front pictures on while she leafed over the ones behind like the pages of a heavy book. She found a green, sunlit picture of old-fashioned people having a picnic in a wood, in a pile that was otherwise only saints with cracked gold paint on their halos. The next pile had a strange, tilted view of a fairground, a lovely Chinese picture of a horse, and some sad pink-and-blue Harlequins beside the sea. Polly put all these against the end wall at once. The one on top of the third pile she liked too. It was a swirly modern painting of people playing violins. Underneath that was a big blue-green picture of a fire at dusk where smoke was beginning to wreathe round the vast skeleton of a plant like cow parsley in front. Polly exclaimed with delight at it.

Meanwhile, Mr. Lynn. was saying, "I don't remember half these pictures. Take a look at this. Dismal, isn't it?"

Polly swivelled round to be shown a long brownish picture,

more like a drawing, of a mermaid carrying a dead-looking man underwater. "It's awful," she said. "They've got silly faces. And the man's body is too long."

"I agree," said Mr. Lynn, "though I think I may take it as a curiosity. Explain how you got into this house by mistake."

Polly got up and carefully carried the violin picture and the smoke picture to the end wall. "Nina started it," she said. "But I got just as silly." And she told him about the High Priestesses, and how they had climbed out of Granny's garden into all the others. "Then we had to hide behind some sheets on the washing line," she was saying, when she saw Mr. Lynn stand up and, in a flurried sort of way, brush at the knees of his suit.

"Oh hello, Laurel," he said.

The lady Polly had mistaken for Nina was standing in the doorway. Seen this close, she struck Polly as plump and quite pretty, and her black clothes were obviously very expensive. Her hair was rather strange, light and floating, of a colour that could have been grey or no colour at all. Polly somehow knew from all this, and most of all from a powerful sort of sweetness about this lady, that she was the one who had inherited almost everything in the house. And from the stiff way Mr. Lynn was standing there, she also knew that Laurel was the ex-wife he had talked about. She just could not think how she had taken her for Nina.

"Tom, didn't you know I'd been asking for you?" Laurel said. Then before Mr. Lynn could do more than begin to shake his head—he was going to lie about that, Polly noticed with interest—Laurel's eyes went first to the pictures and then to Polly. Polly jumped as the eyes met hers. They were as light as Laurel's hair, but with black rings in the lightness, which made them almost seem like a tunnel Polly was looking down. They had no more feeling than a tunnel, either, in spite of the sweet look on Laurel's face.

"When you choose your pictures, Tom," Laurel said, looking at Polly, "don't forget that the ones you can have are the ones over there." Light caught colours from her rings as her hand pointed briefly to the right-hand wall. "The ones against the other wall are all too valuable to go out of the family," she said.

Then she turned round and went out onto the landing, some-how taking Mr. Lynn out there along with her. They half shut the door. Polly stood by the window and heard snatches of the things they said beyond the door. First came Laurel's sweet, light voice saying ". . . all asking who the child is, Tom." To which Mr. Lynn's voice muttered something about ". . . in charge of her . . . couldn't just leave her . . ." She could tell Laurel did not like this, because she seemed pleased when Mr. Lynn added ". . . away shortly. I've a train to catch." One thing was clear: Mr. Lynn was very carefully not tell-ing Laurel who Polly was or how she got there.

Polly leaned against the window, looking down at the cars on the gravel, and considered. She was scared. She had thought it would be all right to come back into the house if Mr. Lynn asked her to. Now she knew it was not. Mr. Lynn was having to be artful and vague in order to cover it up. Laurel was frightening. Polly could hear her arguing with Mr. Lynn now, out on the landing, her voice all little angry tinkles, like ice cubes in a drink. "Tom, whether you like it or not, you are!" And a bit later: "Because I tell you to, of course!" And later still: "I know you always were a fool, but that doesn't let you off!"

Listening, Polly began to feel angry as well as scared. Laurel was a real bully, for all her voice was so sweet. Polly went over to the pictures on the other side of the room, the ones Mr. Lynn was allowed to have. Sure enough, as she had expected, they were nothing like as good as the ones on the left-hand side. Most of them were terrible. Since the argument was still going on, outside on the landing, Polly tiptoed back to the pictures she had leaned against the wall by the window. Back and forth she tiptoed, putting all the good, interesting pictures she had already chosen into the stacks against the right-hand wall, and a few, not so terrible, to lean on the wall by the window, to look as if they had been chosen.

Then, to make things look the same as before, she took terrible pictures from the right-hand wall to the left-hand stacks. They ended up a complete mixture. When Mr. Lynn came back into the room, Polly was kneeling virtuously by the right-hand wall, taking her mind off her evil deed by studying a picture called *The Vigil*, of a young knight praying at an altar.

"Do you think he's a trainee-hero?" she asked Mr. Lynn.

"Oh no. Put that back," he said. "Don't you think it's soppy?"

"It is a bit," Polly agreed cheerfully, and watched Mr. Lynn choose pictures through her hair while she slowly put *The Vigil* back.

That was how she got *Fire and Hemlock*, of course. When he sorted through the doctored stacks, Mr. Lynn picked out every one of the pictures Polly had chosen. "I didn't know this would be here!" he said, and, "Oh, I remember this one!" He was particularly pleased by the swirly one of the violins. When he came to the picture of the fire at dusk, he smiled and said, "This photograph seems to haunt me. It used to hang over my bed when I lived here. I always liked the way the shape of that hemlock echoes the shape of that tree in the hedge. Here," he said, and put it in Polly's hands. "You have it."

Polly was awed. She had never owned a picture before. Nor had she expected to profit from her bad deed. "You don't mean I can *keep* it?" she said.

"Of course you can," said Mr. Lynn. "It's not very valuable, I'm afraid, but you'll find it grows on you. Keep it instead of a medal for life-saving." At this, Polly tried to say thank you properly, but he cut her short by saying, "No, come on. I think your Granny may be worried about you by now."

Mr. Lynn had to carry the picture, along with his five others. It bumped against Polly's legs as she walked, which threatened to break the glass. The other funeral guests were having lunch by then. Polly could hear the chink of knives and forks as they hurried through the empty hall. Polly was glad. She knew, if they met Laurel on the way out, Laurel would know at once that Mr. Lynn had all the wrong pictures.

Thinking of Laurel, as she trotted beside Mr. Lynn down the windy road, caused Polly, for some reason to say, "When I come to work as your assistant in your ironmongers shop, I'm going to pretend to be a boy. You pretend you don't know."

"If you want," said Mr. Lynn. "As long as that doesn't mean cutting your lovely hair."

The lovely hair was blowing round Polly's face and getting in her mouth and eyes. "It's *not* lovely hair!" she said crossly. "I hate it. It drives me mad and I *want* it cut!"

"I'm sorry," said Mr. Lynn. "Of course. It's *your* hair."

"Oh!" said Polly, exasperated for no real reason. "I do wish you'd stop *agreeing* all the time! No wonder people bully you!" They came to Granny's front gate then. "You can give me my picture now," Polly said haughtily.

Mr. Lynn did not reply, but he looked almost haughty too as he passed the picture over. The silence was all wind blowing and leaves rattling, and most unfriendly. But Granny had clearly been looking out for Polly. As Polly hitched the picture under her armpit and managed to get the gate unlatched, the front door banged open. Mintchoc came out first. For some reason, she put her back and tail up and fled at the sight of them. Granny sailed out second, like a rather small duchess.

"Inside, please, both of you," she said. "I want to know just where she's been."

Polly and Mr. Lynn stopped giving one another haughty looks and exchanged guilty ones instead. Humbly they followed Granny indoors and through to the kitchen. There sat Nina, over a half-eaten plate of lunch, staring wide-eyed and full-mouthed. By heaving a whole mouthful across into one side of her face, Nina managed to say, "Where did you go?"

"Yes," said Granny, crisp as a brandy-snap. "That's what I want to know too." She stared long and sharp at Mr. Lynn.

Mr. Lynn shifted the heavy pile of pictures to his other arm. His glasses flashed unhappily. "Hunsdon House," he admitted. "She—

er—she wandered in. There's a funeral there today, you know. She—er—I thought she looked rather lost while they were reading the Will, but as she was wearing black, I didn't gather straightaway that she shouldn't have been there. After that, I'm afraid I delayed her a little by asking her to help me choose some pictures."

Granny's sharp brown stare travelled over Mr. Lynn's lean, dark suit and his black tie and possibly took in a great deal. "Yes," she said. "I saw the hearse go down. A woman, wasn't it? So Madam gate-crashed the funeral, did she? And I'm to take it you looked after her, Mr.—er?"

"Well he *did*, Granny!" Polly cried out.

"Lynn," said Mr. Lynn. "She's very good company, Mrs.—er?"

"Whittacker," Granny said grimly. "And of course I'm very grateful if you kept her from mischief—"

"She was quite safe, I promise you," said Mr. Lynn.

Granny went on with her sentence as if Mr. Lynn had not spoken. "—Mr. Lynn, but what were *you* up to there? Are you an art dealer?"

"Oh no," Mr. Lynn said, very flustered. "These pictures are just keepsakes—for pleasure—that old Mrs. Perry left me in her Will. I know very little about paintings—I'm a musician really—"

"What kind of musician?" said Granny.

"I play the cello," said Mr. Lynn, "with an orchestra."

"Which orchestra?" Granny asked inexorably.

"The British Philharmonic," said Mr. Lynn.

"So then how did you come to be at this funeral?" Granny demanded.

"Relation by marriage," Mr. Lynn explained. "I used to be married to Mrs. Perry's daughter—we were divorced earlier this year—"

"I see," said Granny, "Well thank you, Mr. Lynn. Have you had lunch?" Though Granny said this most unwelcomingly, Polly knew Granny was relenting. She relaxed a little. The way Granny was interrogating Mr. Lynn made her most uncomfortable.

But Mr. Lynn remained flustered. "Thank you—no—I'll get something on the station," he said. "I have to catch the two-forty." He managed somehow to haul up one cuff, and craned round the bundle of pictures to look at his watch. "I have to be in London for a concert this evening," he explained.

"Then you'd better run," said Granny. "Or is it Main Road you go from?"

"No, Miles Cross," said Mr. Lynn. "I must go." And go he did, nodding at Polly and Nina, murmuring goodbye to Granny, and diving through the house in big strides like a laden ostrich. The front door slammed heavily behind him. Mintchoc came back in through her cat-flap in the back door. Granny turned to Polly.

"Well, Madam?"

Polly had hoped the trouble was over. She found it had only begun. Granny was furious. Polly had not known before that Granny could be this angry. She spoke to Polly in sharp, snapping sentences, on and on, about trespassing and silliness and barging in on private funerals, and she said a lot about each thing. But there was one thing she snapped back to in between, most fiercely, over and over again. "Has nobody ever warned you, Polly, *never* to speak with strange men?"

This hurt Polly's feelings particularly. About the tenth time Granny asked it, she protested. "He isn't a strange man now. I know him quite well!"

It made no impression on Granny. "He was when you first spoke to him, Polly. Don't contradict." Then Polly tried to defend herself by explaining that she'd thought she was following Nina. Nina began making faces at Polly, winking and jerking and twisting her food-filled mouth. Polly had no idea what Nina had told Granny, and she saw she was going to get Nina into trouble as well. She said hurriedly that Mr. Lynn had taken her out of the funeral into the garden.

Granny did indeed shoot Nina a look sharp as a carving knife, which stopped Nina's jaws munching on the spot, but she only said, "Nina's got more sense than to walk into people's houses where she doesn't belong, I'm glad to see. But this Mr. Lynn took you back indoors again, didn't he? Why? He must have known by then that you didn't belong."

Granny seemed to know it all by instinct. "Yes. I mean, no. I told him," Polly said. And she knew it had somehow been wrong to go back into the house, even if she had not made it worse by rearranging the pictures.

She thought of Laurel's scary eyes, and the way Mr. Lynn had been careful not to explain to Laurel who Polly was, and she found she could not quite be honest herself. "He needed me to choose the pictures," she said. "And he gave me this one for my own."

"Let's see it," said Granny.

Polly held the picture up in both hands. She was sure Granny was going to make her take it back to Hunsdon House at once. "I've never *had* a picture of my own before," she said. Mintchoc, who was a most understanding cat, noticed her distress and came and rubbed consolingly round her legs.

"Hm," said Granny, surveying the fire and the smoke and the hemlock plant. "Well, it isn't an Old Master, I can tell you that. And Mr. Lynn gave it you himself? Without you asking? Are you sure?"

"Yes," said Polly. This was the truth, after all. "It was instead of a medal for life-saving."

"Very well," Granny said, to Polly's immense relief. "Keep it if you must. And you'd better get that old dress off you and some lunch inside you before it's time for tea."

Nina was on pudding by the time Polly was ready to eat, and Mintchoc came and stationed herself expectantly between them. Mintchoc had got her name for being frantically fond of mint-chocolate ice cream, which was what Nina had for pudding. But Mintchoc liked cottage pie too.

"It was a very respectable funeral," Polly explained as she started on her cottage pie. "Boring really."

"Respectable!" Granny said, plucking Mintchoc off the table.

"And I like Mr. Lynn," Polly said defiantly.

"Oh, I daresay there's no harm in him," Granny admitted. "But you don't go in that house again, Polly. What kind of respectable people choose to get buried on Hallowe'en?"

"Perhaps they didn't know the date?" Nina suggested.

Granny snorted.

Later that day Granny and Nina had helped Polly bang a picture hook into the wall and hang the picture above Polly's bed, where she could see it when she lay down to sleep. It had hung there ever since. Polly remembered staring at it while Nina clamoured to be told about her adventures. Polly did not want to tell Nina. It was private. Besides, she was busy trying to make out whether the shapes in the smoke were really four running people or only people-shaped lumps of hedge. She put Nina off with vague answers and, long before Nina was satisfied, Polly fell asleep. She dreamed that the Chinese horse from one of Mr. Lynn's other pictures had somehow got into her photograph and was trampling and rearing behind the fire and the smoke.

3

Abide you there a little space
And I will show you marvels three

THOMAS THE RHYMER

Polly forgot to take the picture home with her when she went back from Granny's. Granny did not remind her. Thinking about it nine years later, Polly wondered if it was not really because Granny disapproved of Mr. Lynn giving it to her. On the other hand, it could have been that Granny knew, as well as Polly did, that home was not a *Fire and Hemlock* sort of place.

Home had bright, flowered wallpaper with matching curtains. Polly thought, going to bed in her own room, that pulling the curtains was like pulling the walls across the windows.

When she did remember the picture, quite late that night, she opened her mouth to yell. Then she thought better of it. Mum was in one of her moods, stony-quiet and upright, and the slightest thing would send her off into one of her long grumbles. Polly knew this, although Dad was not there to say warningly, "Quiet—you'll have Ivy in her discontents again!" Dad had gone away on a course, Mum said. So Polly shut her mouth and did not raise an outcry at forgetting her picture.

School started again. Everybody was talking about fireworks and bonfires, except Nina, who had to be different. Nina went round claiming that she was being followed by sinister strangers. Nobody knew whether to believe Nina or not, least of all Polly.

"You mustn't speak to them," she said, thinking of what Granny had said.

"No fear!" said Nina. "I'm going to tell my Dad about them."

That made Polly wish *her* Dad would come home. She missed him. She spent a lot of time with Nina that week, round at Nina's house. Mum was still in the mood, not speaking much and not much company. Nina's house was much more fun. It was all lined with varnished wood inside and smelled of cooking spices. Nina's toys were allowed to lie about on the floor, just anywhere. Nina had cars and Action Men and guns and Lego and dozens of electronic machines. Most of the batteries were dead, but they were still fun. Polly loved them.

The irony was that Nina much preferred Polly's toys. By Friday evening she was sick of playing with cars. "Let's go round to *your* house," she said. "I want to play with your sewing machine and your dolls."

Polly argued, but Nina won by saying, "I shan't be your friend if we don't."

They set off. Nina's Mum shrieked after them that Nina was

not to be a nuisance and be back in an hour. It was getting dark by then, and streetlights were coming on. Nina's glasses flashed orange as she looked over her shoulder. "I am being followed," she said. It seemed to please her.

By this, Polly understood that it was a game of Nina's. She was glad, because the idea of being followed in the dark would have been very frightening. "How many are there of them?" she asked, humouring Nina.

"Two," Nina said. "When it's the man, he sits in his car pretending to be someone's Dad. The boy stands across the road, staring."

They walked on until they came to the pillar box on the corner of Polly's road. Nina knew Polly did not believe her. "I told my Dad," she said, as if this proved it. "He took me to school this morning, but the man kept out of sight."

He would, Polly thought, if he wasn't there anyway. All the same, it was a relief to rush up the path to her own front door and burst breathlessly inside.

Ivy met them in the hall, carrying a long, fat envelope. She handed it to Polly. She was still in her mood. "This came for you," she said in her stony mood-voice. "What have you been up to now?"

"Nothing, Mum!" Polly exclaimed, genuinely surprised. The envelope was addressed in Granny's writing, to Miss Polly Whittacker. At the back, somewhat torn where Mum had slit the envelope open, Granny had written: *Sorry, Polly. I opened this. It wasn't a mistake. You never know with strange men.* Inside was another envelope, fat and crackly, with a typed address to Polly at Granny's house. It was slit open too. Polly looked at it, mystified, and then up at her mother. "Why did you open it as well?"

Nina took a look at their faces and tiptoed away upstairs to Polly's room.

Ivy smoothed at her beautifully set hair. "It was from Granny," she said in a stony voice. "It might—I thought—It could have been something to do with your father." Two tears oozed from her eyes. She shook them away so angrily that some salty water splashed on Polly's mouth. "Stop standing staring at me, can't you!" she said. "Go upstairs and play!"

There seemed nothing Polly could do but climb the stairs to her room. There, Nina was busily setting out a dolls' tea party. Polly could taste salt still, but she pretended not to notice it and sat on her bed and opened her letter. It was typed, like the envelope, but not in an official way. Polly could see mistakes in it, all the way down the first page, some crossed out with the right word written above in ink, some crossed by typed slanting lines and *sorry*! typed before the right word.

The paper it was typed on was a mad mixture, all different sizes. The first page was smooth and good and quite small. The next page was large and yellowish. There followed two pages of furry paper with blue lines on, which must have been torn out of a notebook, and the last pages had clumps of narrow lines, like telegraph wires, printed across them. Polly, after blinking a little, recognised these pages as music paper. At this stage, delicately and gently, almost holding her breath, Polly turned to the very last page. The end of the letter was halfway down it, followed by an extra bit labelled *P.S.* She read, *With best wishes to my assistant trainee-hero, Thomas G. Lynn.* The name was signed in ink, but quite easy to read.

It really was from Mr. Lynn, then. Polly felt her whole face move,

as if there was a tight layer under her skin, from solemn to a great,
beaming smile. Polly, in those days, was slow at reading. Long before she had finished the letter, Nina had given up even threatening.
She played crossly on the floor by herself, and only looked up once
or twice when Polly laughed out loud.

```
Dear Polly,
After I had to run away so abrbubtly
sorry!—suddendly, I had quite a while to
sit on the train and think, and it
seemed to me that we still had a lot of
details to settle conconcerning our
secret lives. Most of the things are
questioneins—sorry!—I need to aks you.
You know more about thseses things than
I do. But one thing I could settle was
our first avdenture—sorry!—vadntrue—
sorry!—job with the giant. I think it
happened like this. Of course if you
think differntly, please say so, and I
shall risk your annoyance by agreeing
with you. Here goes.
    The first thing you must rememember
is that Mr. Thomas Piper is very
strong. He may look exactly like me—not
unlike and ostrich in gold-rimmed
glasses—but he has muscles which I, in
```

my false identity as a mere cellist,
lack. Every morning he lifts mighty
sin—sorry!—sun-blistered wooden
shutters, two of them, from the windows
of his shop and carries them away
indoors. He follows this by carrying
outside to the pavement such items as
rolls of chicken wire neither you nor I
could lift, piles of dustbins, graden
rollers neither of us could move, and
stacks of hefty white chamberpots that
we would have to take one at a time.
Every evening he takes it all in again
and brings out the shuterts. He could,
if he wished, win an Olympic Gold Medal
for wieght-lifting, but this has never
occurred to him.

In between customers, he idly
sharpens axes and stares out into the
street, thinking. Like me, he has an
active mind, but not having been given
the education which was thrust upon me,
his mind whirrs about rather. He buys
old books from junk shops and reads
them all. Most of them are horribly out
of date. His sister Edna, who, you tell
me, hates him to spend money on useless

things like books, tells him he is mad.
Mr. Piper thinks she may be right. At
any rate, on this particular morning
his thoughts are whirring about worse
than ever, because he has been reading
an old book called "Don Quixote," about
a tall thin man who had read books
until he went mad and fought some
windmills, thinking they were giants.

Mr. Piper is staring out between
dangling scrubbing brushes as he
sharpens his axe, wondering if he is
that mad himself, when the light is
blocked from the door, once, twice, by
something enormous going by. The fire-
irons round the door knock together.
Mr. Piper blinks. For a moment he could
have sworn that those were two huge
legs, each ending in a foot the size of
a Mini Metro, striding past his door.
"I _am_ that mad," he thinks. He has gone
back to sharpening his axe when he
hears crashing from up the street. Then
screams. Then running feet.

Edna calles from the back room. What's
going on, Tom?"

A girl Mr. Piper recofnises as Maisie

Millet from the supermarket checkout
goes running past, looking terrified.
"Something at the supermarket, dear,"
he calls back.

"Go and see!" Edna screams at him.
She is unbearably curious. She likes to
know everything that goes on in Stow
Whatyouma-callit. But she cannot go out
herslef because she always wears a
dressing gown to save money and never
takes her hair out of curlers.

Mr. Piper, still holding his axe,
goes out of his shop and stares up the
srteet. Sure enough, there is broken
glass, over the pavement in front of
the supermarket, and people are running
away from it in all directions,
shouting for help. A robbery, thinks
Mr. Piper, and runs towards it, axe in
hand. He pases the phone booth on the
way. The manager of the supermarket is
in it, white-faced, dialing 999. The
plate glass window of the supermarket
has a huge hole in it, with notices
about this week's prices flapping in
shreds around it. As Mr. Piper races
up, a white deep-freeze sails out

through the hole and crashes into a
parked car. Dozens of pale pink frozen
chickens drop like bricks and skid
across the road. People scream and
scatter.

One person does not run. This is a
small boy with rather long, fair hair.
As Mr. Piper stops and stares at the
slithering chickens, this ~~boy girl~~
person comes hopping through the mess
towards him.

"Thank goodness you've come, Tan
Coul!" this person calls. "Do hurry!
There's a giant in the supermarket."

This child suffers from too much
imagination, Mr. Piper thinks, looking
down at ~~her~~ sorry!—him. She—sorry!—he
is madder than I am. "There are no such
things as giants," he syas. "What is
really going on?"

Like an answer, there is a terrible
roar from inside the broken window. Mr.
Piper wonders if his glasses need
cleaning. A young man in white overalls
from the butchery departmnent leaps
through the hole in the window and runs
as if for his life. Something seems to

grab at him as he leaps. Whatever it is
is snatched back immediately, and there
is an even louder roar. It sounds like
swearing.

Mr. Piper is trying to convince
himself that he did not, really and
truly, see a huge hand trying to grab
the younf man, when the boy says, "See
that, Tan Coul? That was the giant's
hand. He cut his thumb on the window.
That's why he's swearing. Let's go in
quickly, while he's sucking it. There
may be some more people stuck inside."

Mr. Piper looks down the street,
where the supermarket manager is still
frantically talking into the
teolephone. There is no sign of police
or fire brigade yet. It is clear
something has to be done. Consoling
himself with the thought that there
must be a lunatic inside the
supermarket even more insane than he
is, he says, "Very well. Stay there,"
and crunches through the broken glass
to the window.

There is an awful mess inside.
Shelves of things have been pushed this

way and that. The floor is covered with
mounds of salt and washing powder,
broken jam jars and pools of cooking
oil. There are holes in the walls where
freezers have been ripped out. Toilet
paper has been unreeled across
everything. But the thing which causes
Mr. Piper to stop short by the checkout
desks is the huge bulk he can see down
at the far end. Something large and
round shines balefully at him from
there, surrounded by what seems to be
barbed wire.

Could that thing really be a giant's
eye, peering at him from a giant's
hair, behind a giant's doubled-up
knees?

"I don't <u>think</u> it's a windmill," he
murmurs doubtfully to himself.

"Of course it isn't," says a voise at
his elbow. He sees that the boy has
followed him inside. "The giant's
sitting down against the end wall, with
his knees up. He's too big to stand up
in here. That should make things easy.
You can just chop his head off with
your axe." Mr. Piper does not like

~~ve~~even killing flies. He is quite convinced that the huge thing down at the end is an optical illusion of some kind. He tucks his axe under his arm and takes his glasses off to clean. The giant—or whatever—dissolves into a blur, which makes him feel much happier. "I told you to stay outsude," he says to the boy.

"I wouldn't be much use as an assistant if I did that," the boy retorts. "I've come miles from Middleton to be your trainee, Tan Coul, and I'm not going away now."

"My name is Piper really," Mr. Piper says. "I keep a hardware shope. Is that why you keep calling me Can Tool?"

"Not Can Tool, Tan Coul, stupid!" says the boy. "The great hero—"

But at this moment the giant moves. The blur Mr. Piper can see produces a yard-long bent strip of white, unpleasantly like a glaoting grin. Something huge softly advances on them. Mr. Piper claps his glasses on his nose and sees an immense hand with a cut on its thumb reaching out to grab them.

Illusion or not, he and the boy dive
out of its way. The hand, with terrible
speed, snatches after them. The boy
dodges behind a zig-zag of loose
shelves. Mr. Piper is left out in the
open and only a pool of washing-up
liquid saves him. He slides in it,
falls flat on his back, and loses his
glasses. Somehow the boy pulls him
behind the shelves too. They crouch
there, panting, while the giant, as far
as Mr. Piper can tell, lumbers about
the shop on his hands and knees. The
giant is too big to see all in one
piece, even if he had not lost his
glasses. There are crashes, rendings
and sliding sounds.

"What's he doing?" pants Mr. Piper.

"Pushing some freezers and the cash
desks across the hole in the window,"
says the boy.

"Now he's put another freezer across
the door at the back."

"Oh," says Mr. Piper unhappily.

The giant begind to roar again. His
voice is almost too loud to hear, but
Mr. Piper distinctly catches the words

"fresh warm meat on legs!" and possibly
something about Fee-Fi-Fo-Fum too. He
does his best not to believe that he is
trapped in a supermarket with a hungry
giant. But the shelf they are hiding
behind tips and begins to move. Four
enormous fingers with dirty nails seem
to be gripping it by one end. The boy
and Mr. Piper get up and tiptoe
hurriedly behind the next lot of
shelves, skipping over smashed pickle
jars and trying not to crunch in
cornflakes. Mr. Piper has to do this by
smell and instinct, since he can hardly
see the floor.

"Kill him!" the boy whispers as they
tiptoe. "You're a hero. You <u>can't</u> be a
coward!"

"Oh, can't I just!" Mr. Piper
whispers back. The shelf they are now
behind gegins to move too. They tiptoe
on, through tins of dogfood and mushy
peas. "There are no such things as
giants," Mr. Piper explains as they go.
"This is some kind of illusion." The
latest shelf moves, and they scuttle
behind another.

Now a low rumbling begins, getting
gradually louder. If Mr. Piper were not
doing his best to know better, he would
swear it was the giant laughing with
triumph, because the giant is moving
his prey shelf by shelf into a corner
where the upended freezers spill out
squashed butter and squinched cartons
of yoghurt. They will be trapped in
that corner.

The boy sighs. "Do me a favour, Tan
Cou—er—Mr. Piper. Pretend there _is_ a
giant. Pretend we'll be dead in a
minute unless you do something."

Mr. Piper's foot slips in yoghurt. He
goes down with one knee in a pound of
butter. The giant's rumbles becomes a
roar. The boy's advice suddenly seems
excellent. Mr. Piper swings his axe
round in threatening circles as he
kneels.

The laughter stops. The blurred shape
of the giant, on all fours against the
windows, looks at them with its bushy
head tipped on one side. Then a vast
arm stretches. Mr. Piper scrambles
round on his knees and chops

desperately at the huge hand reaching
out at him.

"Throw tins at his face!" he gasps to
the boy. "Get him to stand up!"

"Good idea," says the boy. He picks
up a tin and hurls it, and another. His
aim is good, but he is not strong
enough to worry the giant, who just
comes crawling towards, them.

Mr. Piper throws a tin himself and
chops again with his axe at the reaching
hand. The giant gives a roar that
buzzes the windows. They snatch up tin
after tin and bombard the giant's head.
The giant, kneeling hugely opposite,
keeps on grabbing at them. Mr. Piper
chops at his fingers every time he
does, keeping him at bay. He feels
hopeless now. He can only see the
reaching fingers when they are almost
too close. He cannot see properly to
aim tins. The boy keeps hitting, but
this does not worry the giant at all.
On the rare occasions when Mr. Piper's
tins hit, they make him rear up and
bump his head on the ceiling.

"What's up there?" pants the boy.

"Anything that might help?"

As far as Mr. Piper knows, there is
the supermarket manager's flat up above.
He is hoping that there are iron girders
in the ceiling, on which the giant might
be induced to brain himself. But they
run out of tins just then. Mr. Piper
scrambles backwards to the nearest shelf
and seizes a packet off it at random.
Beside him, the boy hurls a large
cheese. It misses, because the giant
moves his bushy head aside. He moves it
into line with the packet Mr. Piper has
just thrown.

It turns out to be a packet of flour.
It succeeds beyond Mr. Piper's wildest
hopes. It hits the giant in the eye
and bursts all over his face. The giant
howls, so loud it hurts their ears. He
claps both fists to his face and, most
unwisely, rears up on his knees. The
great, bushy head goes straight through
the ceiling. The giant howls again and
falls over backwards, smashing two
sets of shelves underneath him. And
things begin to rain down on the giant
through the hole in the ceiling. First

comes a large sofa, then a television,
followed by a squad of armchairs.
While the giant is gasping from these,
there is a pause, full of sliding
noises. Then a kitchen table falls
on him, followed by a washing machine,
a big refrigerator, a dishwasher, and
finally a heavy gas oven. The gas
oven hits the giant in the stomach
and knocks the breath out of him with
a WHOOF that blows all the tiolet
paper into the air. Mr. Piper picks
his way among the fluttering streamers
of it until he is so close that even
he can see he is standing by a steep,
bushy hill of head, beside a monstrous
ear. He takes careful aim, swings
the axe with all his great strength,
and hits the giant with the flat
of it, just behind that enormous ear.

Everything goes quiet. In the qiet
Mr. Piper becomes aware of ~~sirnes~~
sorry!—sirens, and neenawing and
whooping. Flashing lights are arriving
outside the window.

The boy appears at Mr. Piper's elbow
again.

"You didn't kill him," he says
reproachfully. This is a very
bloodthirsty child, Mr. Piper thinks.
Does she—sorry!—he want me to cut the
giant into joints and pack him in the
freezers? He does not like to admit
that he cannot even kill flies. He
replies with dignity, "I never kill a
helpless enemy. Haven't you heard of
chivalry? What's your name, by the
way?"

"P—er—Hero," says the boy. "There are
police cars and fire engines outside.
What shall we tell them?"

"Nothing," says Mr. Piper. "We'll go
out of the back door. I'll move that
freezer as soon as I've found my
glasses."

"Here they are," Hero says, and puts
the glasses into Mr. Piper's hand. As
Mr. Piper fumbles them on to his nose,
Hero explains, "I picked them up and
kept them. I knew you'd manage better
if you didn't have to keep explaining
you weren't really seeing a giant."

Mr. Piper looks from the boy to the

giant. It is indeed, monstrously and hugely, a giant, snoring peacefully among the litter. He feels rather sick.

They leave the supermarket the back way as the police come through the front. Edna, by this time, has taken her curlers out, put on her best dressing gown, and arrived at the shop door. She is watching when the police make the mistake of asking the fire brigade to hose the giant's face to revive him for questioning. The giant hates this. He has had enough anyway.

Edna sees him burst out of the supermarket, shoving a police car one way and a fire engine the other. After which he rises to his full height of forty feet or so and runs away, shaking the ground as he goes. Edna is so amazed at this sight that she not only forgets to scold her brother for being covered with flour and yoghurt; she forgets to forbid him to take on a smart new boy assistant.

In this manner Mr. Thomas Piper and his assistant Hero began their careers

```
as trainee-heroes. At least, I hope you
agree that this is how it was.
                    With best wishes to
              my assistant trainee-hero,
                            Thomas G. Lynn

P.S. I seem to remember that all heroes
have a special weapon of some kind.
Don't I need to find a sword? And what
about a horse? I tried to be faithful
to your description of Edna. Did I get
her right?
```

Polly put the letter down with a sigh. She thought the giant ought to have been killed too.

"Finished?" Nina said rather sourly. She was standing by the window. "If you can spare the time, come over here and look."

"Why?" said Polly, still seeing broken supermarket in her mind's eye.

"Because," Nina said with awful patience, "one of the people following me is standing across the road."

That fetched Polly across the room. Funny thing, she thought, as she pressed her forehead against the window in order to see into the dark outside, real life trumps made-up things every time—if this *is* real, of course. "Where? I don't see anyone."

"Under that person opposite's big bush. There," said Nina.

Polly could see the figure now. It looked like a boy humped in

an anorak. While she looked, the person shifted, stamped feet, and
began walking up and down. He must have been cold standing out
there in the dark. He stopped before he got to the streetlight and
turned again, but at that end of his walk there was enough light to
show he had neat hair and a scornful set to his smooth face. And
Polly had sharp eyes. Her heart thudded rather. She said, "He's
called Seb. He was at the funeral."

"Why is he following me?" Nina whispered. "I'm scared, Polly."

Polly asked, feeling rather shrewd and detective-like, "Did the
man following you have two sort of black lumps under his eyes?"

Nina nodded. "He's the scary one. He sits in his car and stares."

"He's Seb's father," said Polly. "Mr. Morton Leroy. Is he here
now?"

"I told you!" Nina said irritably. "They take it in turns. But *why*?"

Polly had just been reading Mr. Lynn's letter. Mr. Lynn obviously thought she was bold and bloodthirsty, and she wanted to
prove he was right. "Lets go out and ask him," she said.

Nina replied with a shocked giggle. She could not believe Polly
meant it. "Never speak to strange men," she said. "Your Granny
said."

"He's not strange—I know his name," Polly said. "He's not even
a man."

"He's big, though," Nina objected.

At this, Polly took great pleasure in saying, "Nina Carrington,
stop being such a scaredy-cat or I won't be your friend any more."
It worked too. As Polly marched to the door and downstairs, she
heard Nina come stumbling after her, fighting her way into her

coat to disguise her lack of courage. They went out of the front door and crossed the street together.

As they went towards him, Seb backed away into the shadow under the bush. Probably he did not credit that they were actually on their way to speak to him. By the time they reached him, he was flattened against the wall beneath the bush. He stared at them, and they stared at him. He was a good foot taller than they were. If it had not been for Mr. Lynn's letter, Polly thought she might have run away.

"What are you spying on Nina for?" she said.

Seb's face turned from one to the other. "Which of you is Nina?"

"Me," Nina said in a scared, throaty way.

"Then I'm not," said Seb. "It's you with the fair hair I'm supposed to watch. Now get lost, both of you."

"Why?" Polly said. And Nina was indignant enough to add, "And we're not going till you tell us!"

Seb hunched his shoulders against the wall and slid his feet forward across the pavement. He laughed at the way they backed away from his feet as they slid. It brought his face nearly down to their level, giving them a full blast of the scorn and dislike in it. "I've a good mind to tell you," he said. "Yes, why not?" He nodded his chin at Polly. "You," he said, "took something when you came to our house, didn't you?"

"It was *given* me!" said Polly.

"So what? You took it," said Seb.

"I am not a thief!" Polly said angrily. "I didn't even break and enter. The door was open and I went in."

"Shut up," said Seb. "Listen. You didn't eat and you didn't drink, and you worked the Nowhere vases round first. Don't deny it. I saw you working them. And I haven't told my father that—yet. You owe me for that."

"I don't understand a word of this!" Nina said. "And it *was* me you were following, not Polly."

"You shut up too," Seb said, jerking his chin at Nina. "You only come into it because the two of you act like Siamese twins, trotting to her house, trotting to your house, trotting to school together. I didn't know even little girls could be that boring!"

"We're not boring," said Polly.

"Yes you are—boring as hell," Seb retorted disagreeably.

"Hell's not boring," Nina said smartly. She hated not being the centre of attention. "There's devils with forks and flames, and thousands of sinners. You won't have a dull moment when you go there."

"I'm not planning to go there," Seb said. "I told you to shut up. I'm planning *not* to," he said to Polly, "and I told you, you owe me."

Polly was puzzled and scared, but she said defiantly, "Laurel's not having it back! It's mine."

"Laurel doesn't know," said Seb. "Luckily for you. Have you seen or talked to a certain person from the house since the funeral?"

Polly thought of the varied sheets of Mr. Lynn's letter lying on her bed across the street, and her heart began bumping again. "Yes," she said. "I'm talking to you now." And she prayed that Nina had not chanced to notice who the letter was from—or, if she had, that Nina would have the sense not to say.

"Very funny!" said Seb. "You know that's not who I mean." Nina, to Polly's relief, looked puzzled to death. "All right," said Seb. "You haven't—and I should know, standing outside in all weathers, watching—"

"Don't you have to go to school at all?" Nina interrupted.

Seb sighed. "Yes I do, you boring little girl, but it's still half-term. Shut up. I'm talking to *her*." He stood himself up and turned round to face Polly. "Now see, you—this is a warning. Don't. Don't have anything to do with a certain person. Understand? Come on—promise. You owe me to promise."

Polly stared up at Seb's shadowy, orange-lit face. Since she could not pretend not to know what he was talking about, she thought rapidly for a way *not* to promise. She said rather vaguely, "It's very kind of you to warn me."

"Kind!" exclaimed Seb. He stamped about in disgust. Polly stood back, gently holding her breath. It looked as if he was distracted. "Who's kind? I don't do favours. I only told you because I'm sick of standing outside your beastly home and your boring school every day for a week! My feet are killing me. Yesterday I got soaked to the skin . . ."

He complained for quite a long time. Polly let her breath out and tried not to look smug. She could tell he was a selfish person. His own sufferings meant more to him than making her give promises.

All the same, Seb was not a fool. Having grumbled until Nina was yawning and shivering, he gave Polly a bad moment by rounding on her threateningly.

"Don't forget," he said. "If you break your promise, it won't be me who sees to you. My father's bad enough, but if Laurel gets to know, I wouldn't be you for a billion pounds!" Polly believed him. She shivered as hard as Nina.

"I won't forget," she said.

"And good riddance!" Seb said. Polly watched him swing round and walk away. She watched him turn the corner by the pillar box. He was gone. Remembering, she thought, is not the same as promising. Good. I've won.

For a moment she thought Seb was coming back round the corner, uttering shrieking shouts. But it was only Nina's Mum, come to see where Nina had got to. "I was worried, cherub. If somebody really *is* following you—"

"They weren't," Nina said crossly. "That was a mistake." Her glasses flashed at Polly, puzzled and conspiratorially, as she was towed away.

And that was a good thing too, Polly thought, as she went back across the road. Nina had not had time to ask things which it was beyond Polly to explain.

Her own Mum met her at the front door. "Polly, what have you been up to now?" she said tiredly. "Door open, no coat."

Polly looked up at her, remembering those angry splashes of salt. It was such a pity, when Ivy was so much better-looking than Nina's Mum. Polly thought, I am *not* going to be a selfish person like Seb. "Sorry," she said. "What's the matter, Mum?"

"Nothing's the matter," said Ivy, drawing herself up stony and still. "Why should there be?"

"You cried," said Polly.

"The idea!" exclaimed Ivy. "Go straight upstairs and don't give me those stories!"

Polly went upstairs, trying to shrug. Mum *was* in a mood, all right. It didn't do to get upset about it. To prove she was not upset,

Polly read Mr. Lynn's letter all through again. Then she drew the curtains—after all, Seb might come back—and fetched out her birthday writing paper with roses on, and her best pen. Kneeling on her bed, rear upwards, hair dangling, she wrote a reply to Mr. Lynn in her best writing. His letter deserved a good answer, but she wanted it to be good because of Seb, and because of Mum too, though she was not sure why.

Dear Mr. Lynn,

Your letter is good and funny but you are not like Mr. Piper reely. You should have killed the giant like you said I said. Now I will anser your questions. You are right heros always have a weapon but you do not need a sord, you have your axe. You need a horse. St. Gorge had a horse for killing draguns. You got Edna right only not nasty enuff. She nags. She is so upposed to Mr. Piper reading books that the pore man has to rap them in the cuvers of yusefull books called "A Short history of nales" for the big ones and "Iron list" for the small ones and read them secritally wile Edna watches the telly.

I hope you are well.

Polly was going to finish here, when she remembered Seb again. A new thought struck her. She sucked her pen a while, then wrote:

Mr. Piper has a nefue, Edna is his Mum, called
Leslie. He is a horrid boy and gets scaunfull
every time Mr. Piper is nice to him. Leslie is
ashamed of Mr. Piper, he thinks he is mad. He
did not see the giant.
   That is all. By for now.

                                        Polly

She put the letter into an envelope and addressed it carefully.
She went downstairs with it, intending to ask Mum for a stamp
from her handbag. But since Ivy was sitting at the kitchen table
pretending to read a magazine and showing no sign even of thinking of getting supper, Polly helped herself to a stamp and stuck it
on. She went back to the kitchen. Ivy was still sitting.

"Mum," Polly said softly, "shall I go and get fish and chips for
supper?"

Ivy jerked. "For God's sake, Polly, don't treat me as if I was ill!"

Then, as Polly was slithering away, sure that she had pushed
Mum from a mood into one of her discontents, she heard Ivy say
thoughtfully, "Chinese. I fancy Chinese. Or would you rather have
Indian, Polly?"

Polly did not like curry, nor the severe man in the Indian takeaway. "Chinese," she said. "Shall I get it?"

Instead of fussing, as she often did, about Polly going out alone
in the dark, Ivy simply said, "The money's in my bag. Cross the
road carefully."

Polly found some pound notes and hid those and the letter in a carrier bag. She went out cautiously into a drizzling night. There was no sign of Seb. Nevertheless, Polly smuggled the letter into the pillar box on the corner, looking round everywhere as she did it, as if it was the guiltiest thing she had ever done. She had no doubt she was breaking the promise Seb thought she had made. Then she went on her way to the Chinese takeaway, thinking she was probably quite heroic.

4

The steed that my true-love rides on
Is fleeter than the wind;
With silver he is shod before,
With burning gold behind.

TAM LIN

In those days Polly never quite believed that a letter you put in a pillar box really got where you meant it to go. She was astonished to get a reply to her letter a week later. She had almost forgotten Mr. Lynn by then, because she was so worried about Dad. Dad had been away so long that Polly knew he was not on a course. She thought he might be dead, and that somehow Mum had forgotten to tell her. The reason she thought this was that Ivy's mood seemed to be over and she was behaving the way she always did, but Polly could tell it was a disguise to cover the mood still going on underneath. Polly dared not ask her about Dad in case he really was dead. She almost dared not ask Ivy anything for fear of being told about Dad. But she had to ask about Mr. Lynn's letter. Mr. Lynn had scrawled it in big, crooked handwriting, and Polly could not read a word.

Ivy read the letter, frowning. "What's this? Asking you to drop in and have tea with him when you happen to be in London next. How old does he think you are? Things to discuss—what things? Who is he?"

Polly went skipping round the room. "He plays the cello in the British Symphony Orchestra," she said as she skipped. "Granny's met him. You can ring Granny and ask her if you like."

But Ivy did not seem to be getting on with Granny. She stood, stony and doubtful, holding the letter.

Polly jumped up and down with impatience. Then she stood still and did some careful pleading. "Please, Mum! He's ever so nice. He wrote me that big letter—remember? It's because he's a trainee-hero and I'm his assistant."

"Oh," said Ivy. "One of your make-believes. Polly, how many times have I told you not to bother grown-ups to pretend with you. All the same—" She stopped and thought. Polly held her breath and tried not to jig.

"I have to go to town anyway," Ivy said, "to see this lawyer I was told about. I was going to dump you at Nina's, but I think people are beginning to think you live there. If this Mr. Lynn really wants you, I could dump you there instead."

Ivy telephoned Mr. Lynn. While she was doing it, Polly remembered—with a jerk, like someone landing on her stomach with both feet—the promise Seb had thought she made, and his threats about Mr. Morton Leroy and Laurel. She was suddenly terrified that one of them could tap the telephone and listen in to Ivy talking to Mr. Lynn in her brisk, unfriendly telephone-voice.

But nothing seemed to happen. Ivy came away from the phone, saying, "Well, he sounds all right. Wanted to know what you like for tea. Now, don't let him spoil you, Polly, and don't be a pest."

This was the thing she went on saying, almost mechanically, all the next few days and all the way up to London in the train. Polly listened without really hearing. Now she had started being frightened, she was terrified. She was excited, but she was terrified too. They took a stopping train from Main Road Station, and Polly could think of nothing but Laurel's strange, empty eyes. It seemed no time before they were in King's Cross. Polly felt that Mr. Lynn must think very quickly to have made up the whole giant story on the way.

"Now, don't let him spoil you and don't be a pest," Ivy said as they got off. "Oh, come on, Polly, do! What do you keep looking round for?"

Polly was looking for Seb or Mr. Leroy. She was sure they were there somewhere, and that, even if they did not know where she was going, they would guess at once when they saw her all dressed up in her nice dress. The odd thing was that her very terror made her all the more determined to see Mr. Lynn. I must be quite brave after all! she thought.

Ivy took Polly's wrist and dragged her downstairs to the taxis. Polly's head was turned the other way the whole time. They took a taxi to Mr. Lynn's address because Ivy only knew that it was somewhere quite near the lawyer's. Polly stared out of the back window for other taxis following her with Seb in them. And for big, expensive cars with Laurel in them. Laurel, she knew, would have a chauf-

feur to drive. Laurel would be sitting beside him, wearing dark
glasses. She saw a lady exactly like that, and she thought she was
going to be sick. But it was a different lady entirely. Meanwhile, Ivy
kept repeating the lawyer's address and making Polly say it back to
her. Both of them talked like machines.

"And tell him to bring you there at five-thirty sharp," Ivy said
again as the taxi stopped. "Now, don't—"

"Don't let him spoil me and don't be a pest. I know," Polly said
as she climbed into the road. And she promptly forgot all that. She
was relieved to find herself in a quiet street, with no Seb, no Mr.
Leroy and, above all, no Laurel.

Mr. Lynn lived in a very Londony house, with steps up to the
door, regular windows, and a stack of bell-pushes beside the door.
Polly found and pressed the one labelled LYNN. The door was
opened almost at once by a very glamorous lady in tight jeans. The
lady had a baby bundled onto one tight denim hip and she grinned
so cheerfully at Polly that Polly was convinced she must be Mrs.
Lynn. But it seemed not. The lady turned round and shouted,
"Hey! Second floor! Visitor for Lynn!"

Mr. Lynn was hurrying down the dingy stairs, "Sorry to trouble
you, Carla," he said. "Hello, Polly—Hero, I should say."

"Not at all," said Carla. "I was just going out." She jerked a push-
chair from behind the front door and bumped away with it down
the steps, leaving Polly, just for a moment, not at all sure what to
say next.

The trouble was, she had been thinking of Mr. Lynn as a tortoise-
man, or as a sort of ostrich in gold-rimmed glasses, the way he had
described himself in his letter—anyway, as rather pathetic and

ridiculous—and it was quite a shock to find he was a perfectly reasonable person after all, simply very tall and thin. And it was a further trouble to realise that Mr. Lynn did not quite know what to say either. They stood and goggled at one another.

Mr. Lynn was wearing jeans and an old sweater. That was partly what made the difference. "You look nicer like that—not in funeral clothes," Polly said awkwardly.

"I was going to say the same about your dress," Mr. Lynn said in his polite way. "Did you have a good journey?"

"Yes really," Polly said. She was just going on to say that she had been afraid of Mr. Leroy or Laurel following her, when it came to her that she had better not. She was quite sure she should not mention them. Why she was sure, she did not know, but sure she was. She chewed her tongue and wondered what to say instead. It was as awkward as the first day at a new school.

But it was just like that first day. It seems to go on forever, and it is full of strangeness, and the next day you seem to have been there always. The thing Polly thought to say was, "Is Carla your landlady?" Mr. Lynn said she was. "But she's nothing *like* Edna!" Polly exclaimed.

"No, but Edna lives in Stow-Whatsis," Mr. Lynn said. Then it was all right. They climbed the stairs, both telling one another at once how awful Edna was, and in what ways, and went into Mr. Lynn's flat still telling one another.

Polly thought Mr. Lynn's flat was the most utterly comfortable place she had ever been in. It had nothing grand about it, like Hunsdon House, nor was it pretty, like home. Things lay about in it, but not in the uncared-for way they did in Nina's house, and it was not nearly as clean as Granny's. In fact, the bathroom was distinctly the way Polly always got into trouble for leaving bathrooms in. She went over it all. There were really only three rooms. Mr. Lynn had a wall full of books, and stacks and wads of printed music, a music stand that collapsed in Polly's fingers, and an old, battered piano. There were two great black cases that looked as battered as the piano, but when Polly opened them she found a cello nestling inside each, brown and shiny as a conker in its shell, and obviously even more precious than conkers. Polly was delighted to recognise the Chinese horse picture on the wall, and the swirly orchestra picture over the fireplace. The other pictures were leaning by the wall. Mr. Lynn said he had not decided where to hang them yet. Polly saw why. There were posters and prints and unframed drawings tacked to the walls all over.

"It's a very ordinary flat," Mr. Lynn said, "and the real drawback is that it's not terribly soundproof. Luckily the other tenants seem to like music." But he sounded pleased that Polly liked the flat so much. He asked her if she liked music. "One of the things we never got round to discussing," he explained in that polite way of his. Polly said she was not sure she knew music. So he put on a record he thought she might like, and she thought she did like music. Then he let Polly put on records and tapes for herself in a way Dad would never let her do at home. They had it playing all the time. Meanwhile, Polly toasted buns at the gas fire, and Mr. Lynn spread them with far too much butter and honey, which Polly had to be careful not to drip on her nice dress while she ate them.

She ate a great deal. The music played, and they went on discussing Edna. Before long they knew exactly the pinched shape of her face and the sound of her nasty, yapping voice. Polly said that the stuffing was coming out of Edna's dressing gown because she was too mean to buy another, and she only let poor Mr. Piper have just enough money each month to buy. tobacco. "He had to give up smoking to buy books," she said.

"I feel for him," said Mr. Lynn. "I had to do that to buy my good cello. What is Edna saving her money for?"

"To give to Leslie," said Polly.

"Oh, the awful Leslie," said Mr. Lynn. "From what you said in your letter, I see him as dark, sulky, and rather thick-set. Utterly spoiled, of course. Is Edna saving to buy him a motor bike?"

"When he's old enough. She gives him anything he wants," said Polly. "She's just bought him an earring shaped like a skull with diamonds for eyes."

"Shaped like a skull," agreed Mr. Lynn, "for which he is not in the least grateful. How does he get on with my new assistant?"

"We hate one another," said Polly, "But I have to be polite to Leslie in case he guesses I'm not a boy."

"And for fear of annoying Edna," said Mr. Lynn. "She'd have you out like a shot if Leslie told tales."

When they had settled about Leslie and described the shop to one another—which took a long time, because both of them kept thinking of new things—they went on to Tan Coul himself.

"I don't understand about him," Mr. Lynn said dubiously. "What relation does he bear to me? I mean, what happens when he's needed? Do I have to become Mr. Piper in order to become Tan Coul, or can I switch straight to Tan Coul from here?"

Polly frowned. "It isn't like that. You mustn't ask it to bits."

"Yes I must," Mr. Lynn said politely. "Please don't put me off. This is the most important piece of hero business yet, and I think we should get it right. Now—can I switch straight to Tan Coul or not?"

"Ye-es," Polly said. "I think so. But it's not that simple. Mr. Piper is you too."

"But I don't have to rush to Whatsis-on-the-Water and begin each job from there, do I?"

"No. And neither do I," said Polly.

"That's a relief," said Mr. Lynn. "Even so, think how awkward it will be if the call comes while I'm in the middle of a concert or you're doing an exam. How *do* the calls come, by the way?"

Polly began to feel a bit put-upon. "Things just happen that need us," she said. "I think. Like the giant. You hear crashing and you run there."

"With my axe," Mr. Lynn agreed. "Where do you suggest I keep my axe in London?"

Polly turned round, laughing. It was so obvious she hardly needed to point.

"In a cello case, like a gangster?" Mr. Lynn said dubiously. "Well, I could get them to make a little satin cushion for it, I suppose."

Polly looked at him suspiciously. "You're laughing at me."

"Absolutely not!" Mr. Lynn seemed shocked. "How could I? But I don't think you realise just how much that good cello cost."

It was odd, Polly thought then, and later, and nine years after that, remembering it all. She never could completely tell how seriously Mr. Lynn took the hero business. Sometimes, like then, he

seemed to be laughing at them both. At other times, like immediately after that, he was far more serious about it than Polly was.

"But I still don't understand about Tan Coul," he said thoughtfully, with his big hands clasped round his knees—they were sitting
at opposite end of the hearth rug. "Where is he when he—or I—do
his deeds? Are the giants and dragons and so forth here and now,
or are they somewhere else entirely?"

If it had been Nina asking this, Polly would have answered that
was not the way you played. But Mr. Lynn had already proved that
you could not put him off like that, and she could see he was serious. She pushed aside the empty plates and knelt up in order to
think strenuously. Her hair got in the way and she hooked it behind
her ears.

"Sort of both," she said. "The other place they come from and
where you do your deeds *is* here—but it's not here too. It's—Oh,
bother you! I just can't explain!"

"Don't get cross," Mr. Lynn begged her. "Maybe there *are* no
words for it."

But there were, Polly realised. She saw in her mind two stone
vases spinning, one slowly, the other fast, and stopping to show half
a word each. With them she also saw Seb watching, looking scornful. "Yes there are," she contradicted Mr. Lynn. "It's like those vases.
Now-here and Nowhere." The idea of Seb was so strong in her mind
as she said it that she felt as if she had also told Mr. Lynn how Seb
had tried to make her promise not to see him.

"Nowhere," repeated Mr. Lynn. "Now-here. Yes, I see." He was
not thinking of Seb at all. Polly did not know whether she was re-

lieved or annoyed. Then he said, "You mentioned a horse in your letter. A Nowhere horse, I suppose. What is my horse like? Do you have one too?"

"No," said Polly. She would have liked one, but she was sure she had not. "Your Nowhere horse is like that," she said, pointing to the picture of the Chinese horse on the wall.

They both looked up at it. "I'd hoped for something a bit calmer," Mr. Lynn confessed. "That one obviously kicks and bites. Polly, I don't think I'd stay on his back five seconds."

"You'll have to try," Polly said severely.

Mr. Lynn took it meekly. "Oh well," he said. "Perhaps if I spoke to it in Chinese—Now, how did I come to find this vicious beast?" They were thinking of various ways Mr. Piper could have met the horse, when Mr. Lynn happened to see his watch. "When does your mother want you back? Is she coming here?"

"Half past five," said Polly, and then had an awful moment when she seemed to have forgotten the lawyer's address. She had just not listened in the taxi. But, because Ivy had made her say it, it had gone down into her memory somehow. She found she could recite it after all.

Mr. Lynn unfolded himself and stood up. "Lucky that's quite near here. Come on. We'd better get going if we're to be there by five-thirty."

Polly got her coat. Mr. Lynn put on a once shiny anorak almost as worn-out as Edna's dressing gown, and they set off, down the hollow stairs and into the now dark street. Strangely enough, Polly forgot to look in case Mr. Leroy or Laurel were following her. The road was so busy and Londonish and full of traffic that she only thought how glad she was to be able to grab hold of Mr. Lynn's hand, and how grateful she was that he took her a shortcut down small streets where there were fewer cars and even some trees. The trees still had some shivering leaves clinging to them. Polly was just thinking that those leaves looked almost golden in the orange of the streetlights when the noise began in the street round the corner.

It was about seven different noises at once. A car hooter blared. With it were mixed the awful screech of brakes and a splintering, crashing sound. Behind this were angry voices yelling and several screams. But the noises in front of these, which made it obviously different from a simple car crash, were iron-battering sounds and a terrible shrill yelling that was the most panic-stricken noise Polly had ever heard.

Mr. Lynn and Polly looked at one another.

"Do you think we should go and see?" Mr. Lynn said.

"Yes," said Polly. "It might be a job for us." She did not believe it was for an instant, and she knew Mr. Lynn did not either, but it seemed the right thing to say.

They went round the corner. Mr. Lynn said, "Good Lord!" and a lot seemed to happen in no time at all.

The thing making the noise was a horse. It was loose in a narrow street with a rope bridle trailing off it, dodging and rearing as people tried to catch it—or the people might have been running away from it: it was not clear which. Slewed across the street behind the horse was a car with a broken headlight. A man was leaning angrily out of the car window, shouting. And the horse, a great, luminous, golden thing in the streetlights, slipping and crunching in the glass from the broken headlight, had just dodged someone's grabbing hands and was now coming battering towards Polly and Mr. Lynn, screaming more like a person than a horse.

There was just an instant, while Mr. Lynn said "Good Lord!" when Polly could see Mr. Lynn's eyes behind, the orange glow of his glasses, staring at her, wide and grey and incredulous. Then the horse was almost on top of them, and it reared.

Polly, to her everlasting disgust, did not behave anything like an assistant hero. She screamed almost as loudly as the horse and crouched on the pavement with her arms over her head. The horse was huge. It stood above her like a tower of golden flesh and bone, beating the air with its iron hooves, and screaming, screaming. Polly saw a big eye, a rolling bulge of blue-brown and white, shot with veins and tangled in pale horsehair, stuff like detergent bubbles dripping, and huge, square teeth. She knew the horse was mad with terror, and she screamed and screamed.

She heard Mr. Lynn say, "Here." Something hard and figure-eight-shaped was pushed into her fending hand. Polly's fingers closed round it without telling her what it was. She just knelt and screamed among flying shadows while the front hooves of the horse crashed down close beside her with Mr. Lynn's feet next to them. Then its back feet crashed. Mr. Lynn's hunched shoulder had hit the horse in its side as its back feet left the ground to lash at Polly, and swung it round just enough to miss her. After that, he managed to grab the rope trailing from the horse's nose.

There was furious trampling and squealing. Sparks that were pale in the orange light came from under the horse's feet, and the horse's head, twisting and flattened, more like a snake's than a horse's, darted at Mr. Lynn's arm and tried to fix the huge teeth in him.

Mr. Lynn said words which Polly, up to then, had thought only Dad and the dustmen knew, and pulled hard down on the rope. There was a further rush of feet and sparks, and the two of them were trampling away from Polly towards the crashed car. The horse stopped screaming. Polly could hear the things Mr. Lynn was saying quite clearly. Most of it was to the horse, but some of it seemed to be just swearing. She giggled rather, because Mr. Lynn was not behaving like a hero either. Nor did he look like one. As the horse stamped round in a half-circle in front of the broken car, with Mr. Lynn hanging on to the rope at the end of both long arms and his anorak up under his armpits, he looked more like an orangutan than anything else, or perhaps a spider monkey. His hair, which even the wind at the funeral had not done much to disarrange, was all over his face, and he seemed to have lost his glasses.

Here Polly's fingers told her again about the figure-of-eight object she was clutching. She looked down and found it was a pair of gold-rimmed glasses. She scrambled up and backed against a wall behind her, holding them very carefully. It would be awful if she broke Mr. Lynn's glasses. The horse was sliding about in the broken headlights. "Look where you put your bloody feet, you fool!" Mr. Lynn said to it. It looked as if he was going to make it stand still any second.

The motorist climbed angrily out of his smashed car. "I say!" he called out in a loud, hectoring voice. "Is this your damned horse? It could have killed me!"

That set the horse off again. It became all orange, rearing panic, high on its back legs, with Mr. Lynn frantically leaning on the rope. He swore at the horse, then at the motorist. "No, it is not my horse," he added, "Get out of the way!"

The horse managed to lash out with a hind foot before its front feet hit the road. The motorist bolted for his life. Mr. Lynn yelled at the horse that its grandfather was a donkey with venereal disease and told it to *Come off that!* And the two of them came rushing back up the street again. They trampled round in front of Polly, with Mr. Lynn practically swinging on the rope. Polly could feel waves of terror coming off the horse. She had to hold both hands, and Mr. Lynn's glasses, to her mouth to stop herself screaming this time. In front of her were huge, bent, golden hind legs, stronger than she could have imagined, and a tail that lashed her face like her own hair in the wind, only harder, smelling of burning. Someone's burned it! she thought. No wonder it's so upset!

The next thing Polly knew, the motorist was standing beside her, watching the horse and Mr. Lynn rush away down the street. "How was I to know it wasn't his bloody horse?" he said to Polly. "He's behaving as if he knows it."

"Be quiet," Polly said. Her voice was thick from screaming. "Mr. Lynn's being a hero."

The motorist did not seem at all grateful. "Well, he needn't have said *that* to me," he said.

When Polly did not answer, he gave her up and went to complain to some of the people further down the street. Polly could hear him, all the time Mr. Lynn was dragging the horse to a stand-still, telling someone that the horse had appeared out of the blue right in front of his car and that people shouldn't be allowed to own wild animals like that.

The horse stood still at last, orange flecked with detergent stuff, swishing its tail. Each of its legs seemed to be shaking at a different speed. Polly could see shivers chasing up and down them as she walked gently towards it. Mr. Lynn was rubbing its nose and calling it soothing bad names. "You cartload of cat's meat," she heard him say. "Mindless dog food. They'll eat you in Belgium for less than this."

Before Polly had reached Mr. Lynn, people at the sides of the road began crowding forward. "That'll be them," someone said. "Help at last!"

The horse shivered and stamped. "Keep back, can't you!" Mr. Lynn said over his shoulder.

Everyone, Polly included, prudently stopped. Two small, worried-looking men in greasy body-warmers slipped hurriedly round the broken car and came rather cautiously up to Mr. Lynn and the horse.

"Thank you, sir," said one. "Thought we'd never catch him."

"Kid let off a firework in his stall," said the other.

"I thought I smelled burning," Mr. Lynn answered. The horse answered too, in his way, by putting his head down and letting one of the small men feed him peppermint. Mr. Lynn passed the other one the rope.

This made it clear to the motorist and to all the other people that the horse belonged to the two little men. They crowded round—at a safe distance—and called complaints. "Wild horses like that! . . . Ruined my car! . . . Panicked the whole street . . . Really dangerous! Ought not to be loose! . . . Scared my old mother stiff . . . No end of damage . . . Police . . ."

In the midst of the babble Mr. Lynn somehow located Polly and stretched a long arm backwards to her. Polly put his glasses into his hand.

Mr. Lynn thankfully put them on. He took them off again quickly. "Can't see a thing. All greasy," he said. On one side of him, the motorist was trying to grab his arm. On the other, one of the little men was trying to thank him. Mr. Lynn was clearly embarrassed. Polly could see sweat shining on him. "Polly," he said. "Find the back door."

Polly looked round. There was more movement up the street, where a police car was coming whispering to a stop. "At last! The fuzz are never here when you need them!" someone said. Polly realised that she would never get to the lawyer's by five-thirty unless they went at once.

"This way," she said. "Quick." She pushed Mr. Lynn round the broken car and along the empty street beyond. Everyone's voices rose to a big babble and then faded as Polly kept on pushing Mr. Lynn. "The police are there now," she explained.

"Thanks!" said Mr. Lynn. He was trying to clean his glasses on a handkerchief. "Keep guiding me, or I shall be apologising to doorsteps and lampposts. I can barely see a thing without my glasses."

This was obviously true. Polly found she had to steer Mr. Lynn round three dustbins, some plastic sacks and a bicycle. His face looked odd with no glasses and his hair hanging down in front of it. It looked longer and smoother, more like a real face. But his eyes did not look fat like Nina's did. "How ever did you see the horse?" she said.

"It was a bit big to miss," he said in his most apologising way. Then he added in quite a different way, "But what an extraordinary thing, though! Just after we'd been talking about my horse! You'd almost think—"

"You would," Polly agreed. "But it wasn't the right colour to be the Chinese horse."

"Streetlights," said Mr. Lynn as she steered him round a doorstep.

His elbow was bony and quivering rather. Polly kept her hands on it to guide him and stared up at Mr. Lynn's bewildered, naked face. She wanted to say what she had to say before he put his glasses on again and could look at her. She took in a gasp of breath. "I didn't help at all. I was too scared."

"You aren't heavy enough to have stopped it," said Mr. Lynn. "You'd just have dangled." Polly thought that was very nice of him. He finished cleaning his glasses at the end of the street and put them on. He looked up at the street name, then at his watch, and set off again much faster, in the direction they needed to go. "If it's any comfort," he said, "I was scared stiff too."

"But you did something," Polly said, rather breathless from hurrying. They turned into another street before she got her second wind.

"How did you know what to do?" she asked. "You did know."

They swung round another corner, with Polly sort of swirling out on the end of Mr. Lynn's arm. "Laurel taught me about horses," Mr. Lynn said.

They were opposite a small park now. CLOWNS, CLOWNS, CLOWNS!!! said notices along the park fence. Coloured lights looped in the trees. JACK'S CIRCUS, read a canvas banner over the park gate. There was music, and a smell of squashed grass and of animals. Polly could just see the orange-white shine of the big tent above the entrance booth by the gate.

"*That's* where the horse came from!" said Mr. Lynn. "I wondered how—" He looked down at Polly. "Are you all right?"

"Oh yes," Polly said drearily.

Mr. Lynn slowed down and looked carefully at Polly. "Now, come on," he said. "You must know that, when heroes do their deeds in these modern times, there has to be a modern explanation. I can't have everybody guessing I'm really Tan Coul, can I? This circus is only a disguise."

Polly smiled gratefully, although she rather thought that it was not the circus that was the matter with her. It was the way Mr. Lynn mentioned Laurel. "Anyway," she said as they hurried on again, "you *are* a hero. Except for swearing. That may be a disguise too."

Mr. Lynn gave his guilty cut-off yelp of laughter. It was not just the way he laughed at funerals. He always laughed like that. "Call it a symptom," he said. "Expert heroes never swear."

"I shall be a hero too," Polly panted. "I'm going into training from now on."

By the time they reached the lawyer's, it was so late that Mum was standing in the street beside a waiting taxi. She was in such a state that she barely looked at Mr. Lynn. "Come *on*, Polly!" she said. "It's rush hour and I don't know *what* time we'll get home! Say goodbye," she added as she bundled Polly into the taxi. That was all the notice she took of Mr. Lynn politely holding the taxi door open for her. Polly was the one who remembered to call out "Thank you for having me!" as the taxi drove away. She was rather surprised that Ivy had forgotten to remind her to say it—usually she made such a point of it—but she could see Mum was in a real state.

Unfortunately, Ivy's state was a silent one. Polly was dying to tell her all about tea and Mr. Lynn's flat and, above all, about the horse, but Ivy sat fenced in silence as thick as barbed wire, and Polly knew better than to try to break in. The train was so crowded that Polly had to perch on Mum's knee, and Ivy's mood made that knee stiff and uncomfortable.

Ivy said just one thing on the train. She said, "Well, Polly, I've taken a step."

And so have I, I suppose, Polly thought with a kind of dismal excitement. I saw Mr. Lynn when they said not to. But all she could really think about was the unheroic way she had screamed and crouched on the pavement and given Mr. Lynn no help at all.

When they got home, instead of looking in the fridge or suggesting fish and chips, Ivy sat down at the kitchen table and talked to Polly. "I suppose I owe it to you to explain a bit," she said, sitting very upright and staring into the distance. "I went to talk to that lawyer about getting a divorce from your father. You may well ask why—"

Polly hurriedly shook her head. She knew now why she had

dreaded being told about Dad. But Ivy talked anyway. Polly listened in silence, hoping she would begin feeling honoured soon that Mum was confiding in her. She told herself she felt honoured, but in fact she mostly felt shocked and awed by the way tears came and went in Ivy's eyes without quite ever falling out and running down her face.

"You know what he's like as well as I do, Polly. Reg has no sense of reality. Money goes through his hands like water. And if I presume to say anything, he just laughs it off and spends more money on a present to soothe me down. Presents!" Ivy said bitterly. "I want a relationship, not presents! I want happiness and sharing—not just two people living in the same house. That's all we've been for years now—two people living in the same house. Your father's so secretive, Polly. On top, he's all smiles and laughs, but if I ever ask him what he's really thinking, it's 'Oh, nothing particularly, Ivy,' and not a word more will he say. That's not right, Polly. He's got no right to keep himself to himself away from me like that!"

This was already beginning to sound like one of Ivy's usual discontents. Polly had long ago learned to dread them. Later in her life she learned to dread them much more. This time, as usual, her feelings were hurt on Dad's behalf. She had to give up trying to feel honoured and tell herself she was being considerate instead. As Ivy talked on, she found herself thinking that Dad was *not* secretive. He just expected you to know what he was feeling by the things he said and did. It was Mum who kept herself to herself, locked away in moods.

"I know I have these moods," Ivy was saying, a long time later.

"But what can I do when I'm being rejected at every end and turn? It gets me that way. I know when I'm not wanted. It didn't use to be that way when Reg and I were first married. We shared then. But not now."

Polly listened, still trying to be considerate, and kept vowing privately that she would never, ever lock herself away from anyone. When she looked at the clock, she was surprised to find it was past her bedtime and Ivy was still talking. By now it was sounding just like her usual discontents.

"Well you know me—I've slaved and worked to make the house nice, gave up my job to have it all perfect. And I do think in return the least he could do is not walk muddy feet all over the carpets, and shut drawers after he's opened them, and tidy up a bit sometimes. Not a bit of it. When I mention it—and I'm not a nag, Polly—he laughs and says I'm in my mood again. Then he gives me a present. *Then* what does he do? He goes straight from me to that Joanna Renton of his!"

This was new, Polly thought dully. This must be what Dad had done.

"Joanna's not the first either," said Ivy. "But I was a fool before and didn't keep track of what he was doing."

"Is—is he with Joanna Renton now?" Polly broke her long, long silence to ask.

"Yes," Ivy said. She sounded tired. She too looked at the clock. "Oh, is that the time? Are you hungry at all, Polly?"

"No," Polly said considerately, though she was rather. "I had a big tea."

"Good," said Ivy. "I haven't got the energy to think of food, somehow. You hop along to bed, Polly. And remember when you get married not to make the mistakes I did."

"I don't think I will get married," Polly said as she stood up. "I'm going to train to be a hero instead." But she could tell her mother was not listening.

5

O see you not yon narrow road
So thick beset with thorns and briars?
That is the path of Righteousness,
Though after it but few enquires.

THOMAS THE RHYMER

D ad came back two days later. Polly had just got home from Nina's and she was in the hall when she heard his key opening the door. She rushed and hugged him. Dad greeted her with his usual half-shout and great grin, and hugged her back, just as usual. Polly felt the arms hugging her quivering ever so slightly. It reminded her of the quiver she had felt in Mr. Lynn's arm when she pulled him down the street after catching the horse.

The quiver stopped when Ivy came and stood in the living-room door, looking at them with her stoniest expression. Polly felt Dad's arms all hard as he looked up and said, "Now, what's all this, Ivy?"

"I've been to a lawyer," said Mum.

"You haven't!" Dad said blankly, and then tried to hide the blankness with a grin.

"That's right, laugh it off," Ivy said. "As usual. But I have. And I've told Polly all about it too. I'll thank you to let her go and stop subverting her. Come here, Polly."

Dad's arm clenched round Polly and he made a strange noise. It was a jeering groan, and a maddened shout, and the growl you make before hitting someone, and the sound you make trying not to cry, all in one. "Subverting!" he said. "Just what have you been making her think of me?"

And Polly was suddenly being pushed back and forth along the hall while her parents shouted at one another. The first push was Dad trying to use Polly like a shield or a hostage to get past Ivy into the living room. But Ivy stood barring his way to anywhere but the hall and put her arms round Polly protectively. Dad shouted that she was using Polly against him like she always did. Mum pushed Polly back to Dad. Back and forth Polly went, feeling so numb and stupid that she almost wanted to laugh, in spite of the way they were screaming.

In the midst of it the back door banged without anybody but Polly noticing. Granny was there, upright as the Queen Mother and stiff with anger, and taking everyone's attention, even though she was only a head taller than Polly.

"Polly's coming with me," Granny said, "until you've had your shout out. I'm not taking sides, and it doesn't matter to me what you settle, but Polly's not coming back until you have. Get your things, Polly."

Polly thought Dad seemed relieved. Ivy drew herself up angrily. "Reg, did you tell her to come here and poke her nose in?"

"I phoned to see how she was," Dad said defensively. "That's all."

"You—!" began Ivy.

"*Shut up!*" said Granny. Her voice banged like someone hitting a biscuit tin. "Reg is always glad for someone to do his dirty work for him—I'll give you that, Ivy—but he didn't ask me to come. I told you, I just came for Polly. When I've got her, I'll go. But not until."

Granny, naturally, won. Ten minutes later she and Polly went out of the front door with a duffel bag of Polly's clothes, Granny marching and Polly creeping rather.

"I know, I know," Granny said. "I'm not a saint, Polly. You'll have to learn that."

Saint or not, Polly thought there was a kind of holy calm about Granny's house, smelling of biscuits. She stayed there a week, and went to school from there. It meant a longer journey and not seeing so much of Nina, but it seemed worth it. Polly sat at Granny's kitchen table and painted Christmas cards for everyone she knew, including Mr. Lynn. Then she painted several big pictures of Tan Coul fighting a dragon and overcoming a wizard, with herself dressed as a boy, rather small, down at one side.

While she painted, Granny bustled quietly about and talked to Polly about things she had done as a girl. Granny had been what she called "a bold, bad girl." She had done a number of things Polly thought were really much more daring than gate-crashing a funeral. But she was surprised that Granny did not talk about Dad when he was a boy, the way she usually did.

"That would be taking sides," Granny said, "and I said I wouldn't.

Besides, I'm not sure I didn't spoil your father rotten. I'm not making the same mistake over you. Off to bed now, and no arguing."

Polly had the same bedroom she had shared with Nina. And there was her *Fire and Hemlock* picture hanging over her bed. She lay and looked at it, with Mintchoc curled up and purring on the pillow by her neck. Mintchoc had a smell too, but not of biscuits. It was a faint, clean scent, like talcum powder. Polly stroked her and looked at the shapes coming out of the smoke in the picture. They really were four men, rushing to put out the fire before the whole field caught. If Polly screwed her eyes up, she could sometimes see a fifth, smaller shape, a bit to one side, behind the flames. She liked to think it was herself as Hero. There was no doubt in her mind that the bigger shapes were Tan Coul and his three friends. If she went on staring with her eyes squinched, she found she could see the misty shape of the Chinese horse too, rearing amid the vapour that was rising all round the four men. The horse and the smaller shape disappeared when she knelt on her bed with her face right up against the picture, but the four men were always there.

Polly spent some time thinking what Tan Coul's friends might be like. When she was tired of painting, she wrote Mr. Lynn a letter about them. Some of the letter was about Awful Leslie and Dreadful Edna, and some of it was suggestions about how to fight dragons, but the friends were the important part.

Tan Coul has three frends who are heros too. They are Tan Audel who is sumone I don't know, and Tan Thare and Tan Hanivar. I know them. Tan

Thare is jolly, he can make music sound out of
nowhere to friten his enemies. Tan Hanivar is
rather a sad case becuse he keeps turning into
things and doesnt want peple to know. He can be
a wolf or even a dragon, it is very hard for his
frends not to kill him by mistake.

At the end of the week Granny took Polly home, with her paintings, cards, and letter in a new folder. Mum seemed glad to see her.
She hugged Polly and told Granny she was grateful. But Dad was
gone. His hi-fi had gone too, and an armchair, and a number of
smaller things from round the house. The divorce was definite.

"Definite," said Ivy, when Polly asked.

In a way, it made home as peaceful as Granny's house.

Polly got very busy then preparing for the Christmas play at
school. She remembered to send her Christmas cards, but she clean
forgot the letter. After all, hero-business was only a game and
school was real.

Mum and Dad both came to the school play, but they did not
look at one another and they sat on opposite sides of the hall. Polly
did not know Dad was there until she came on the stage as the
youngest of the Three Kings. Nina told her. Nina was King Herod.
She had turned out to be far better than any of the boys at ranting
and roaring and looking kingly. Miss Green said that none of the
boys could get on the stage without looking sheepish, and she
made them all shepherds, for obvious reasons, as she said. So Nina
was having the time of her life in a wriggly stuck-on moustache

and beard, shouting and strutting and having everybody executed. But her eyes kept moving from one side of the hall to the other, keeping tabs on whose parents were there.

"Your Dad's come," she said to Polly out of the side of her mouth.

"I know!" Polly whispered, with rather a jolt, because she had not known at all. And she got on with trying to offer King Herod some gold.

"Away with it!" cried Nina. "I am not your King of Kings!" [He's left your Mum, hasn't he?] And I know no more than you where he may be."

"It is not you but a child, Your Majesty [Yes]," said Polly. "[Shut up.] A star rising in the east told us that he was born."

"This is terrible news!" King Herod said to the audience. And to Polly, "[Are they going to get divorced?] And what else does that star tell you? [Is that what that boy Seb was talking about?] Do you know where the child is?"

Polly sighed and nodded to the first question. She shook her head to the second question, but it was one of the other Kings who had to explain that they were following the star, so she could not speak. This conversation, she thought, was exactly like the way the deeds of Tan Coul were mixed up with the real world. She wished she could have explained it to Mr. Lynn like this. She felt prickly anger with Nina for being so nosy, and it made her go cold and stony. She suddenly knew how Ivy felt.

"Then I tell you what," Nina was saying as she strutted round the stage. "I'll entrust the three of you with a very important mission." She strutted up behind Polly. "[Your Dad's girlfriend doesn't want him to see you, does she?] I wish to honour the King of Kings myself. I'd like you to tell me when you've found him. [It must feel ever so strange!]"

Polly pressed her lips together and refused to say more than the lines she had learned. The Three Kings left the stage. Nina had a good rant and then left too.

She pushed through the angels waiting to go on and found Polly. "Tell me what it's like not having your Dad at home. Was that boy a detective?"

"No," Polly said stonily.

"My Mum says divorce marks you for life," Nina persisted. "Do you feel very different?"

"I'm just the same as ever I was!" Polly said loudly. Miss Green looked round from arranging angels' wings and shushed. "Now go away," said Polly.

Dad left the hall before the play finished. "Why do you think he came?" Polly asked Mum as they walked home.

"Because I told him to," said Ivy. "I told him you had a right to have your own father take an interest in you."

"I wish you hadn't," Polly said. Not wanting to mention Nina, she explained, "He was bored. I saw him yawning."

"So was *I* bored!" Ivy retorted. "I didn't see why I should be the only one. That play has not changed one word since you started at that school. And before that I was the Angel Gabriel in it myself. I could almost scream by now."

This was one of the queer things about divorce which Polly could not have described to Nina—the way Mum said this kind of thing to her that she would normally have said to Dad instead. And the way Dad was not really gone. He was not there, but he hovered in the background all the time. Polly wished he would go right away and get it over with.

She went away with Mum for Christmas, to Aunty Maud. Aunty Maud's house was full of tiny cousins, staggering or crawling or lying in cots and bawling. Since they all thought Polly was marvellous, Polly barely had time to notice that Mum was out most of the day. "Ivy needs to relax," Aunty Maud told her. The only time Ivy was there during the day was Christmas morning, when they all opened their presents. Polly's big present was a dolls' house from Dad. He must have forgotten she had one already. Polly tried to be brave. She had wanted a fort, and some tanks and guns. She smiled.

"I told him that was what you needed," Ivy said, collecting wrappers. "I hope you like it."

Polly smiled until her face ached and slowly unwrapped the last parcel. She was lucky to get anything from Dad. Aunty Maud had told her so. She did not want to be ungrateful.

A shower of paperback books fell out of the parcel. With them was a badly typed note:

```
You've probabably read all these
already. If you have, throw them away.
They were the things they told me in
the book shop that nobody should grow
up without reading. Merry Christmas.
                              T. G. L.
```

They were from Mr. Lynn. The smile on Polly's face became real.

She sorted through the books. The only one she had even heard of was *The Wizard of Oz*. There were eleven others. Polly hovered a moment between *Five Children and It* and one most enticingly called *The Treasure Seekers*, and then picked up at random *The Wolves of Willoughby Chase*. She began to read it. She read for the rest of Christmas, mostly kneeling on the floor with her hair dangling round the book like a curtain, but sometimes, when a cousin crawled up and tried to grab the book, she took it away behind the sofa and crouched there in the shadows. She never heard the television. She only vaguely heard Ivy saying, "It's no good speaking to Polly when she's reading, Maud. She's deaf and blind. Reg used to stop her. You let her be."

Polly read greedily, picking up another book as soon as she had finished the first one. She felt like a drug addict. She had read *The Box of Delights* and *The Lion, the Witch and the Wardrobe* too before she went home, and was beginning *The Sword in the Stone*. She read the rest in the week before school. Then she surfaced, with a flushed face and a deep sigh. The feast was over.

"And I only sent him a Christmas card!" she wailed.

That was easily remedied. She had a whole letter waiting, forgotten, in her folder of paintings. But the letter, when Polly looked at it, seemed very thin and out of date. The twelve books she had read since made her realise how little she had really said in it. There was a lot more she wanted to say anyway. So she crouched on the floor with her hair dangling again and wrote three more whole pages, like a girl inspired. She told Mr. Lynn about the divorce—he had been divorced from Laurel, so she knew he would understand—and Nina and King Herod. Then she told him about

her disappointment over the dolls' house and how the books had
made up for it. She explained the best bits in all the books, and
ordered him to read *The Hundred and One Dalmatians* at once.

My v favrit thouhg is Henrietta's House,

she went on, forgetting the little she knew of spelling in her enthu-
siasm.

The peple in it do lik hero bisnis only they invent
a hous and in the end it is reely trew. They hav
aventeres in caves, Tan Coul must do that it is
esitin. I red til my eys look lik Ninas all fat
and pink. And thankyou, thankyou, thankyou.
                                              Lov Polly.

The letter was now vast. Polly had to steal one of Mum's big
envelopes for it, because there seemed no way she could fold it to
fit into one of her own. She posted the huge letter quite boldly, the
next time she went for fish and chips. By this time she was sure that
Seb had been fooled when she pretended to promise not to see Mr.
Lynn. She did not think he would bother her again. And she was
right in a way. It was a long time before she saw Seb or Mr. Leroy
again.

When school started, Polly began training seriously to be a hero.
It was not easy, and it caused a number of upheavals. The first
was with Nina. Nina might have been good at ranting and pretending, but she was not athletic. She ran out of puff after once round

the playground. When she found Polly had joined the Athletics Club, she was horrified. "What do you want to do *that* for?" she said.

Polly had not been so pleased with Nina since the Christmas play. "To train my muscles," she said coldly.

"Then stop," said Nina, "or I won't be your friend any more."

"All right. Don't be," said Polly.

It gave her a savage, free feeling to say it and then turn away, leaving Nina gaping. She made friends with two girls who were good at running instead. Nine years later Polly could not even remember their names. But she remembered very clearly how annoyed she was with her muscles. Polly tested them every night by trying to lift her bed in the air, all four legs at once, and the most she could ever get off the floor was three. Then Mum would shout to know what she was doing.

Besides, Polly said to herself, it's not just strength that heroes need. They need courage and good skills and timing. They need something to make the adrenaline really flow. These were all things she had gathered from watching sport on television. Ivy spent a lot of time around then sitting in front of the television, just sort of staring. Polly got to watch many things that Ivy would have turned off when Dad was there.

Polly did the logical thing and asked the boys who played football in the lunch hour to let her play too. They were surprised, but they agreed quite politely. And once Polly had got the rules straight—which took her a week, during which time she played on both sides together and scored fourteen own goals—she proved to be a fast runner and a ferocious tackler, and they let her go on. Her knees were perpetually skinned and grey, and the roots of her hair grew dark with mud from heading the ball. Her only worry was that she enjoyed it so much that she was not sure it counted as training.

But it was a peculiar thing to do. Mira Anderton, the huge girl who was the school bully, took to standing beside the game and jeering at Polly.

Polly was frightened at first. Then she straightened her shoulders and reminded herself that bravery was what training was all about. She was not going to be scared of Mira. She supposed she had better fight Mira at once and get it over. Then she had second thoughts. Heroes do not fight for themselves, but for other people. I'll wait until she does something to someone else, Polly thought. Then we'll see.

She caught Mira pulling the hair of a little kid on the way home that afternoon. "Right!" shouted Polly, and attacked.

It was a wild success. The truth was that Mira was so astonished that a peaceful girl like Polly should suddenly go for her that she gave up almost without a fight. The little kid ran away. Mira went over backwards into a puddle, and the only thing she managed to do to Polly was give her an accidental slap in the face as she fell. Polly's nose wept some drops of liquid. She wiped it off and looked at it as she walked away. It looked like blood to her, but it could have been adrenaline, and she was on the whole pleased at the way her training was coming on.

The trouble was, Mira had a position to keep up. She planned revenge. Two days later Polly was flying about the football part of the playground in the lunch hour as usual when she heard screams. Not just any screams either, but the yells of somebody being really hurt. She looked. She saw Mira had another girl down on the ground and was kneeling on her, banging her head on the asphalt. A fat leg in a grey sock waved feebly in time with the screams. Polly left the game and sped to the spot.

Mira got up and went for Polly as she came. Polly had just time to realise that the screaming girl was Nina, before battle was joined. It did not go on for long. A dinner lady noticed, in spite of everyone standing round to hide the fight, and the two were pulled apart after only a minute. But in that short time Polly had torn Mira's skirt off her and made Mira's nose bleed, and Mira had hit Polly in both eyes. Mira did some expert whining and said it was all Polly's fault. Polly and her two black eyes were marched to the Headmistress.

All the teachers had noticed the change in Polly this term. The Headmistress thought she knew the reason. So, after the usual telling-off—which Polly stood through as stony as Ivy—she said, "What's the matter with you at the moment, Polly? You used to be one of our nicest girls. Is there something wrong at home you'd like to tell me about?"

"No," said Polly. It was something like the way she had deceived Seb. She meant she did not want to tell the Headmistress.

"Then why are you doing it?" said the Headmistress.

This question seemed to call for the truth. Heroes have to be honourable. "I'm training to be a hero," Polly explained. "The adrenaline has to flow."

"Does it indeed?" said the Headmistress. "Well, I suppose Nina *is* your friend. You mustn't listen to all the silly ideas Nina has, Polly." And Polly had to listen, in silent indignation, to another lecture, this one about Nina leading her astray. At the end of it the Headmistress said, "I think I'd better talk to your mother, Polly. Will you please give her this letter as soon as you get home."

This was only the first embarrassment. Polly came away from the Headmistress to find that the rest of the school regarded her as a heroine. This is nothing like being a hero, which is inside you. This was public. People asked for her autograph and wanted to be her friend. She came out of school at the end of the afternoon surrounded by a mob of people all trying to talk to her at once. It made Polly's head ache. Each of her black eyes was going bump, bump, bump, and swelling in spite of the stuff Miss Green had put on them. And Nina was waiting at the gate. Nina's eyes looked odd too, because Mira had broken her glasses, but she was beaming with friendship and gratitude.

"Oh Polly, you were so brave! I was so thankful!"

Somehow Polly did not have the heart to explain. It was the first sign of an unheroic soft-heartedness in her which she later learned was part of her, and which no amount of reproaching herself seemed to get rid of. It caused her to go home with Nina, as she used to before, but she was really rather bored. Still, she stayed for tea, because it was rude not to, and came home quite late.

Ivy looked round from the television to see Polly with two black eyes, clutching a bent and dirty letter from school. "Oh, Polly! What have you been up to *now!*?"

It occurred to Polly, as she handed the letter over, that Mum always seemed to expect her to have been up to something. It annoyed her—not for now, but for all the other times in the past when she had been quite innocent. She was just going to protest about it, when her attention was caught by the programme Ivy was watching—or, rather, sitting in front of.

It was an orchestra, playing furiously, the way they do when the music is shortly going to end. The picture was sliding about, across banks of men in black coats and white bow ties, and one or two ladies in black dresses, picking up rows of stabbing violin bows, somebody's hands banging a big drum, and the face of a man blowing a pipe sideways. Polly's heart, and the rings round her eyes, banged like the big drum. She was suddenly absolutely sure that this was Mr. Lynn's orchestra. She held her hair back and leaned forward to see whether the camera would slide over him too.

"Oh Polly!" Ivy wailed, reading the letter. "What got into you?"

"Nothing," Polly said gruffly, staring at the television. The picture slid to the conductor waving both arms strenuously. Back to violins working like high-speed pistons. To rows of shiny trumpets. To fingers nimbly working keys on an oboe. And back to the drum. It was going to end any second, and they had not shown any cellos at all.

"But the Headmistress says here," said Ivy, "that she thinks you're not happy."

The picture slid sideways, broadening and retreating for the last chords, to show the full orchestra, banked up black and white and all hard at work, and just for an instant the screen was full of men sitting behind cellos. Mr. Lynn was there, quite near the front, sawing with the rest. Polly had a full glimpse of him, neat and colourless, the way he had been at the funeral, before he melted into the big view of the whole orchestra playing the last note.

"I'm perfectly happy," she said. "I'm training to be an assistant hero. I *have* to fight."

"Don't give me your nonsense," Ivy said wearily.

The screen was showing the audience now, clapping. It was obviously a big occasion. They were in evening dress too. The announcer was saying, "Tremendous applause here from this gala audience for this performance of Beethoven's Third Symphony, the Eroica, given by the British Philharmonic Orchestra . . ." The camera dwelt on rows of clapping people, and lingered across two that Polly knew. One was Laurel, wearing a green, gauzy dress. She was turning as she clapped to say something to the man beside her, and this man had bags of dark skin under his eyes, almost as black as Polly's were at the moment. Mr. Leroy.

"It's not nonsense," she said. "I think I may have to rescue someone."

"Oh for goodness' *sake*, Polly!" Ivy reached forward, in exasperation, to turn the television off.

"Don't turn it off yet!" Polly shrieked.

Ivy looked at her in surprise. "But it's nothing interesting."

She turned back and switched the set off. But Polly's interruption had delayed her just long enough for the titles to start rolling up over the audience. THE BRITISH PHILHARMONIC ORCHESTRA . . . EUROPEAN TOUR . . . ONE: HOLLAND . . . Polly had time to read this far before the picture zoomed away into nothing at the back of the screen. She did not mind. She had seen enough. Mr. Lynn was not in England. He had not got her letter. And Laurel and Mr. Leroy were not letting him out of their sight. She felt too miserable to care what Ivy said.

"Now, listen, my girl!" said Ivy. "I'm not having this from you. You're just like your father. He'll make up a lie and then he'll make himself believe it—I've watched him do it. And I'm not having you grow up that way. I want the *truth*. What was that fight about?"

Polly shrugged and said the thing Mum was most likely to believe. "Mira Anderton got Nina down and banged her head on the playground."

"Oh I see," Ivy said, mollified. "Why didn't you say so? Well, I'd better go and tell that to your Headmistress, then."

It made Polly feel an utter liar, but it served to get her out of trouble.

Term went on. Her black eyes got better. She decided she had perhaps been training a bit too hard, and she went at it more cautiously after that. She gave up trying to pick up her bed, but she still played football because she liked it so much. And she remained much more popular at school than she felt she deserved. She had troops of friends. One advantage of this was that she did not have time to go on being close friends with Nina. Another advantage was that Polly did not have time to be as miserable as she knew she felt underneath.

Ivy seemed to be trying to pull herself together. She surprised Polly by getting a job in the office of Middleton Hospital. Polly had to come in and get her own tea and do the shopping on Saturdays. Polly quite enjoyed that, though the house seemed very quiet.

Just before school broke up for Easter, a puffy brown bag of a parcel arrived for Polly. Ivy had left for work when the postman brought it. Polly nearly made herself late for school. It was from Mr. Lynn. Inside was a ball of cotton wool, and inside the cotton wool were five rather elderly-looking plastic soldiers. Polly did not mind their old look, because she saw at a glance they had been much loved. Each of them had been carefully painted in the correct colours for the uniforms. Since two of them were Highlanders with tiny plaid kilts, Polly could see the painting had been very difficult to do. Wrapped round them was one of Mr. Lynn's badly typed letters.

```
Dear Hero,
Yoru lettter was waiting for me when I
got back from Ureoep—sorry!—Preuoe—
sorry!—the Contintinent. Im glad you
liked the bokos so much, and very sorry
about your disaponitment over the
dollshouse. I had a front—sorry!—fort
once. Iv'e no idea where it went, but I
still seem to have these soldiers from
it. I hope you will like them. Sorry
there are'nt more.
     What with caves and other heroes,
there is a great deal for us to
dsicuss. Can you suggest a day when I
can call for you and take you out for
```

the day? I am free the first weeek of
April.

By the way, Tan Coul has mananaged to
change his horse into something else.
You will see what I mean when I see
you.

Yrs, T. G. L.

Polly was free the first week in April too. Holidays started then. She sat straight down to write and tell Mr. Lynn so. Then she looked at the clock and found she had to go to school instead. The day seemed endless. But she was home at last, and the letter was written and posted. The soldiers were put in a place of honour in Polly's room. And the day was endless again.

To have something to do, Polly got out her nice dress and tried it on. There was a grease stain in front where she had dripped butter and honey despite all her care, and a muddy patch on the back where she had crouched on the pavement, afraid of the horse.

The dress did not seem as big as it had been. It squeezed her round the chest and nipped her round her forearms, and the skirt came nowhere near her knees. But since it was the only nice dress Polly had, she went and looked at herself in Mum's big mirror, hoping it would do.

She saw a wild, gawky figure in a dress three sizes too small. Under the wrong-length frill of skirt were two thin legs with a scab on each knobbly knee. Round the scabs the knees were grey. The hands dangling out of the too-short sleeves were grey, too. The wild tails of her hair were not quite grey, but they were drab somehow and rather like snakes, and the face among the snakes had a sulky look, even though the sulky look was just breaking up into tears.

"Oh *no!*" wailed Polly, and completed bursting into tears as she fled downstairs to the telephone. Tears made white places on her hand as she dialled Granny's number. "Granny! *Granny!*"

"What is it, Polly?" Granny's voice said, sharp and comforting in the receiver.

"Mr. Lynn's asked me out and my nice dress is too *small!*"

There was a slight pause from the other end. Then Granny said, "Back from Europe, is he?" Polly was surprised and interested to find that Granny had been following Mr. Lynn's movements too. "Well, that's nothing to take on about," Granny said.

"But I've no good clothes at all!" Polly wailed.

"Polly!" Granny said, sharper still. "Stop howling and answer me one serious question."

"Yes," Polly gulped.

"Did Mr. Lynn ask *you* out, or did you ask *him*?" said Granny.

"He wrote and asked—I never said a word, promise," said Polly. "And he sent me a parcel with soldiers in—"

"All right," said Granny. "I'm not sure I like it, Polly, but if he's free to ask, I suppose he must want to see you. But be wary of what he gives you. Keep that to yourself, understand? Now, are you sure you want a dress? Wouldn't a pair of jeans and perhaps a nice jacket be better?"

"Well—" Polly remembered Mr. Lynn's old anorak. "Much better. But I haven't even got any jeans that fit, Granny."

"I thought that was what you were asking me for," Granny

retorted. "I'll buy you them for your birthday, Polly. I'm not made of money."

Polly's birthday was not till June, but it was worth having no present from Granny then, just to be properly dressed now. She thanked Granny gratefully.

"I don't do it to be thanked," Granny said, and rang off.

Polly went upstairs and carefully put the soldiers in her folder along with her paintings. When Ivy came home, she was waiting in the hall. "Mum, my hair needs washing."

"I suppose it does," Ivy agreed. Neither of them could remember when Polly's hair was last washed. They went up to the bathroom, where they both had rather a shock. Polly's hair hung in snakes because each piece was matted into itself, in a sort of rope, and Polly had head lice. Ivy had to go out for a special shampoo and a fine-tooth comb. But the comb would not go through Polly's hair. "Don't you ever brush your hair?" Ivy said, grimly dragging an ordinary comb through it.

The dragging made Polly's head sore. Her eyes watered. "Not often."

"Then you should!" said Ivy. "You're big enough now, in all conscience! I don't know, Polly—this is such a mess I think I'd better cut it all off. You'd look quite nice with it short, after all."

"*No!*" shrieked Polly. She jumped up and dragged her hair away. "Don't you dare touch it! I like it long!"

"After all I've done for you!" Ivy said, losing her temper too.

"You haven't done anything for me! You let me get lice!" Polly screamed back.

They shouted at one another for quite a while. At length Ivy gave in. "You always did have such a will, Polly. All right. But I thought you wanted it short."

"I don't any more," said Polly.

It took two hours to get Polly's hair combed, and another hour of washing after that. The water that came out of her hair was dark brown for the first two washes. Ivy washed it yet again, and combed it. Nits floated in the washbasin and had to be rinsed away.

"Let this be a lesson to you," Ivy said at last.

"Yes," Polly sighed. Her head ached worse than it had done with two black eyes. But she was rewarded by having a cloud of silver-fair, crackly hair, as clean as it was bright. She saw why Mr. Lynn had called it lovely now. She was rather careful about combing it after that.

6

O they rode on, and further on,
The steed went swifter than the wind,
Until they reached a desert wide
And living land was left behind.

THOMAS THE RHYMER

Mr. Lynn had a new anorak. It was the first thing Polly saw when she opened the door to him. He had an altogether more prosperous look somehow.

"Won't you come in?" she said politely.

"No thanks," Mr. Lynn said, smiling all over his face. "I want to show you my horse."

Polly locked the front door and hid the key for Ivy and went out into the street with Mr. Lynn. There was a small cream-yellow car nestling against the kerb, somewhat the shape of a teapot. He pointed to it proudly. "Like it?"

Polly laughed. The car's number plate was TC 123. "Oh yes! A modern horse. And TC for Tan Coul."

"Of course," agreed Mr. Lynn. "As soon as I saw the number

plate, I knew I had to buy it. Hop in." He opened the passenger door for her and Polly climbed in, feeling very grand and relaxed in her new jeans and jacket. "I don't know what I'd have done," Mr. Lynn said, climbing in the other side, "if I'd failed my driving test. I only took it last Thursday, you see. I'd have had to call for you in a taxi. Now. Let's see. Choke, ignition, handbrake, check mirror. Do you want to know where we're going?"

"Nowhere, of course," said Polly. They both laughed, Polly heartily and Mr. Lynn in his guilty, cut-off gulp.

Then they tried to set off. At first the car would do nothing but plunge up and down on the spot. Mr. Lynn managed to get it moving and they went down the street in a series of jumps, like a kangaroo with hiccups. "Horse very restive," Mr. Lynn apologised. "Feeling its oats." He was rather pink by this time. He tried moving the gear lever. There was a mighty crashing sound. The car gave another leap, backwards this time, and stopped completely. "Oh dear," said Mr. Lynn, pinker still. "Polly, I'm sorry. I'm very nervous. The car knows."

"Call it names," said Polly. "Like you did the horse."

"No, you call me names," said Mr. Lynn. "It's my fault."

"All right then," said Polly. "I'll call you Tan Coul, trainee-hero of the West, and ironmonger and Thomas Piper, axefighter and giant-killer, and horse-tamer and someone who's going to kill dragons soon."

This seemed to make Mr. Lynn feel better. The car snarled and started with a swoop, and they swept out into the centre of Middleton. There, after a number of interesting wobbles, they raced twice round the main square before Mr. Lynn could rein the car in enough to dive down the Gloucester Road. When he did, they howled swiftly out into the countryside, pausing only to miss a bus and skip the Miles Cross traffic lights.

"This car really is that horse, in a way," Mr. Lynn said as they flashed past the last limit sign at sixty miles an hour. "After you'd gone, I went back to that circus to see if it was all right. And apparently that wasn't the first time it had gone on the rampage. They were saying it would have to be put down."

"Oh no!" said Polly.

"Just how I felt," said Mr. Lynn. "So I had a rush of blood to the head and said I'd buy it. I couldn't bear to think of it dead. I knew I was going to get about enough money from the orchestra's European tour—but they wouldn't wait that long, however much I argued. In the end I had to sell one of those pictures—"

"Not the Chinese horse!" Polly exclaimed.

"No, no," Mr. Lynn said, as shocked as she was. "That's too beautiful. No, I sold that picnic picture, which was the one I liked least. Laurel had been more generous than I'd realized—it turns out to have been a genuine Impressionist, and it fetched quite an awesome price. So I could afford to feed the horse once I'd bought it."

"Where do you keep a horse in London?" Polly asked.

"I don't," said Mr. Lynn. "The circus people put me in touch with a woman who boards horses out in the country. And she discovered why I'd bought Lorenzo—I'm afraid the horse is called Lorenzo—and offered to buy him off me. That's how I got the car. I paid for it with the money Mary Fields gave me for the horse.

That's where I thought we'd go first. You'd like to see the horse again, wouldn't you?"

"Yes," Polly said dubiously. "Are we going anywhere else?"

Mr. Lynn gave his gulp of a laugh. "Stow-on-the-Water," he said rather triumphantly. "Did you know it's a real place? I thought, if you agree, we could go there and look for hardware shops. It's in the Cotswolds, not far from Mary Fields' farm."

Polly thought that was a marvellous idea.

"Good," said Mr. Lynn. "Though I know there really is no such shop, I almost believe it's real. I can see it, and even smell the beastly smell in Edna's kitchen if I close my eyes."

"Don't close your eyes," Polly said swiftly and firmly. She had realised by now that Mr. Lynn drove the way heroes drive. The little car seemed to have a surprisingly fast engine hidden under its rounded bonnet, and Mr. Lynn drove it with his foot hard down to the floor, turning to talk to Polly as he drove. He did not seem frightfully particular about which side of the road they were on, and he clearly had a passion for overtaking everything else going the same way. Polly was not at all frightened. After all, Mr. Lynn had driven all the way down from London without crashing. But it was clear to her that his heroic style of driving was not possible if he had his eyes shut.

"No, of course not," Mr. Lynn said with that slightly irritating meekness of his. And the car continued to nibble at hedges and swerve into the paths of oncoming lorries under a pale blue spring sky. Seagulls sat in ploughed fields on either side. Polly thought, We're driving away to Nowhere! and snuggled down in her seat.

She felt all easy and light, like you do when you stretch after sitting still, or get into your own clothes after playing dressing-up. Last term had been all wrong somehow. It was as if she had been pretending to be someone else.

"I saw you on television once," she said. "Just for a second."

"Oh. Did you?" Mr. Lynn hunched his high shoulders. "I wish you hadn't. I hoped I'd got away without being seen—they so rarely point the cameras at the cellos. I hate the way we look. Like a set of very neat carpenters."

"Only for an instant. I almost didn't," Polly assured him. And she felt so comfortable that she added, "And I saw your—Laurel, you know—in the audience with Mr. Leroy."

"Yes, they spent their honeymoon abroad," Mr. Lynn said. "I saw quite a bit of them."

It seemed comfortable still, but in some way it was not. Polly went on carefully, "And how's Seb? Have you seen him?"

"No, though I was wondering if you might have done," said Mr. Lynn. "He's at school in Middleton."

"What, at Wilton College?" Polly asked. Seb would obviously not go to one of the ordinary schools. She felt mixed awe and scorn, because Wilton College was a very posh school indeed.

"That's right. Now tell me about these three other heroes. Why don't you know Tan Audel?"

"I just don't." Polly saw Mr. Lynn was wanting to change the subject. She filed that away in her mind, along with the other things she knew about Mr. Lynn and Hunsdon House. She had a feeling they were beginning to add up into something she almost understood. She humoured Mr. Lynn and described the heroes. Tan Coul was the hero of the West, Tan Thare the South, and poor, shape-changing Tan Hanivar was the hero of the North.

"I like the idea of him," Mr. Lynn said. "Would you say he had a thin sort of face with a great, gloomy beak of a nose? What's Tan Thare like?"

They decided that Tan Thare was chubby, with curly hair. But Tan Audel remained a blank to both of them. They were still try-ing to discover what Tan Audel was like ten miles further on, when Mr. Lynn said, "Woops! Here's the turning!" and went screaming into a narrow lane on two left-hand wheels. A signpost flashed past, saying OLD ELMCOTT. The car lifted this way and that. Mr. Lynn had made some kind of mistake with the pedals, so that they were hurtling between black hedges, faster and faster.

Polly became almost nervous and cried out, "Oh, don't, Mr. Lynn, please!"

Mr. Lynn, sweating rather, succeeded in reining the car in. They stopped with a bounce only a foot from a five-barred gate. "Sorry," he said. "Bit between its teeth. We have to walk from here." They got out of the car, quivering a little, and went through the gate to a squishy lane beyond. "Do you have to call me Mr. Lynn all the time?" Mr. Lynn asked as they crowded onto the grass edge out of the mud. "How would you feel if I called you Miss Whittacker?"

"That's different," said Polly.

"How?"

"Because I'm not grown up," Polly said patiently.

"But people don't, do they, these days?" Mr. Lynn said rather pleadingly. "It felt very odd, that evening we met the horse, to hear you crouching on the pavement screaming, 'Mr. Lynn, Mr. Lynn! Help!'"

"Oh I didn't, did I?" Polly felt as embarrassed as Mr. Lynn was about being on television and turned her head away to look at the hedge. She had not known there had been words in her screams.

Mr. Lynn saw he had put his foot in it. "I did read *The Hundred and One Dalmatians*," he said encouragingly. "It was very good."

"I knew you would—you're so obedient," Polly said tartly. Then she made a great effort and said, "Would calling you Uncle Tom do?"

This time *she* seemed to have put her foot in it. Mr. Lynn swayed about on the grass, turning to look at her suspiciously. "Have you read *Uncle Tom's Cabin?*" he asked her.

"No," Polly said, wondering.

"Read it. And find out why that name won't do." Mr. Lynn turned and went on down the grass in long, hopping strides.

Polly leaped and scrambled after. "Another time I'll help, I promise," she called. "I've been training."

Mr. Lynn leaned into the hedge to let her catch up. She could tell he was embarrassed too. "But you *were* a help," he said. "I thought you saw. I was too scared to move until I realised you'd get trampled if I didn't."

After that, neither of them said anything until they came round a corner, beside a neat white fence like the kind you get in toy farmyards, and saw the horse himself in the field beyond.

"He really is just the same colour as the car!" Polly exclaimed. "I thought it was the streetlights."

"It was too good a coincidence to miss," agreed Mr. Lynn. He leaned his elbows on the fence and admired the horse. "I think it's one of the golden horses of the sun," he said.

"Oh," said Polly.

There were quite a lot of horses together in the next field, but the golden horse was alone. It knew they were there. Its head lifted, and it began to canter this way and that in the field, free and swinging. Polly was glad there was a fence. It shook the ground as it passed.

"Tell me how you train to be a hero," Mr. Lynn said. "I need to, far more than you do."

"I don't advise it," Polly said. She told him about the difficulties she had got into. Mr. Lynn gave several gulps of laughter, but when she got to the adrenaline, he suddenly burst out laughing just like other people did. Polly looked at him in surprise. She had not known he could laugh properly.

Mary Fields heard the laughing and came ducking out of the barn at the corner of the field. "Hello there, Tom!" she called. She was a small, angle-faced lady with a bush of short, light hair. The same colour hair as Laurel's, Polly thought. Mr. Lynn seemed partial to that sort of hair. He rubbed his hand over Mary's hair as he introduced Polly. Mary Fields shook hands with a grip that crunched Polly's knuckles, and they all went into her farmhouse for coffee. The house was yellowish stone, almost the colour of the horse, and smelled damp inside. Polly did not enjoy this part much. At that stage of her life, she did not like coffee, and Mr. Lynn and Mary seemed to have a lot to say that Polly could not join in, mostly about horses and music. Polly's one effort to join in was a disaster.

She politely asked Mary Fields if she went riding on the golden horse.

Mary gave a loud laugh. "Good Lord no! Anyone who tried would come off with a bloody sore arse, I can tell you! He was trained as a bucking bronco. I'm keeping him for stud."

Polly was shocked at Mary's language, too shocked to talk any more. She sat nursing her cold mug of coffee, feeling dejected. This is not Nowhere, she thought. This is horribly Here Now. I wish we could go.

At last Mary said, "Well, do you two want to stay for some lunch?"

Mr. Lynn looked meditatively at Polly. "No, thanks very much. We ought to be getting on."

They stood up to go. Among the moving chairs and Mr. Lynn's goodbyes, Polly distinctly heard Mary Fields say, "See you when you've got rid of Little Miss Prim there." Polly knew Mary meant her, and she knew Mary did not like her.

And I don't like *her*! she thought as she followed Mr. Lynn back along the muddy lane. She wondered why. Polly was not sure, but she knew the thing which had most upset her about Mary's shocking remark was not the words, but the way Mary had said it in order to shock her. Beyond that, she gave up. She was not used to grown-up ladies behaving like girls at school.

They got lost driving to Stow-on-the-Water. "The trouble is, I can't drive *and* look where I'm going," Mr. Lynn said helplessly over the map. "Can you read maps?"

Polly had never read a map in her life, but she tried. They had lunch at a pub by the river which served huge hamburgers and chips, but they had to eat outside because the dining room was full and Polly was too young to go in the bar. Polly did not mind at all. Mr. Lynn was describing Edna's kitchen to her, so that she could almost smell it too. And they both knew exactly the paraffin-and-dust-and-iron smell in the shop itself. Then Mr. Lynn went on to Awful Leslie, and his greasy black hair and hanging lower lip. He told her some of the rude things Leslie said. Polly wondered then if he was really thinking of Seb, but she did not say so. About that time she got cold in the wind from the river.

"We seem to have chosen a wintry sort of day," Mr. Lynn said, worried about her. "Would you like my anorak?"

"No. I'm an assistant, not a damsel in distress," Polly said. "Save it for them."

"As you please," Mr. Lynn said humbly. When Polly turned to him to tell him not to be so obedient, he added, "You can be very majestic sometimes, you know."

Polly got into the car, rather scrunched. That was when she realised that a lot of Mr. Lynn's humbleness was a joke, even if some of it was real. She never found it easy to sort out which was which.

Stow-on-the-Water, when they finally found it, was made of the same yellow horse-coloured stone as Mary Fields' farm. The main street opened up at one end into a market square, where there was a bridge over the river and a cross in the middle. After they had parked the car—with a jolt and a shriek of brakes that made everyone in the square whirl round to look—Mr. Lynn went over to the cross and leaned towards it studiously. He said he thought it was

Saxon. Polly tried to look as if she felt that was old and reverent. A War Memorial would have struck her as just as old and a lot more historic.

"Now," said Mr. Lynn, "to look for ironmongers."

They looked up. And there it was, facing them across the square. Thomas Piper Hardware. There were shiny folding ladders propped outside and stacks of new yellow wood labelled DO IT YOURSELF. The whole shop had a new, clean look, most definitely modern. But it was there. Thomas Piper Hardware. The discovery shook them both, more than they had bargained for. Polly looked up at Mr. Lynn, and Mr. Lynn looked down at Polly, and his eyes were as round and amazed behind his glasses as they had been when he first saw the horse.

"What do you make of that!" he said.

"I don't know," said Polly. "I don't—like it somehow."

They stood and stared at the shop. They stood until Polly began to shiver in the wind again.

"We're not being very brave, are we?" said Mr. Lynn. "We can do better than this. Come on."

They sauntered towards the shop. Polly wandered away to the left, pretending she was going somewhere else. Then Mr. Lynn wandered away to the right. But it was only a short distance. In no time they were standing beside the shiny ladders, looking at a display of bright orange jugs, bowls and lawnmowers in the window beyond.

"We ought to buy something," Mr. Lynn whispered. He sounded nearly panic-stricken. "Think of something we can ask for."

"Tools?" said Polly.

"Yes, people can always use more tools," Mr. Lynn said thankfully.

They went in. The shop was as bright and modern inside as it was outside. Everything was arranged on corridors of clean shelves, rather like Mr. Lynn had described the supermarket where the giant was. A clean, sharp smell of plastic and paint and detergent met their noses. Polly and Mr. Lynn went down the first corridor between teapots and kettles on one side, and hoses and brooms on the other. The place seemed empty except for them. They came up the second corridor, between paint and shiny hooks and rails for towels.

From here they saw there was a lady sitting at a desk near the door that said WAY OUT, an ordinary, smallish lady with a nice, nervous face and fluffy mouse-brown hair. She was busily doing sums on a scrap of paper. But she raised her head as they came up the corridor, without really looking at them, and said, "We'll have to reorder those electric kettles. They've not come."

Somehow it was clear she was saying it to Mr. Lynn. His eyes went round again and met Polly's almost desperately. Then he managed to say, "I—I beg your pardon?"

The lady's fluffy head shot round to look at them. Her face crumpled with dismay. "Oh, I'm sorry, sir! I quite thought you were Mr. Piper! You have just his walk." Her eyes remained on Mr. Lynn as if they found it impossible to move away. Amazement grew through the crumples in her face. "You really do look such a lot like him!" she said. "Were you looking for something particular?"

Under her eyes Mr. Lynn's face went pale and rather shiny. He swallowed—Polly saw a lump in his throat surge. "Just—just a screwdriver or so," he said rather stickily.

"Down at the end," said the lady. And suddenly she shouted. Her voice filled the silent shop and made Polly jump. "Leslie!" she yelled. "*Les!* Come and help this gentleman and young lady find a screwdriver!"

Rubber shoes squeaked at the back of the shop. Polly's head and Mr. Lynn's turned that way, fascinated, to see a boy of about Polly's age shoot cheerfully into sight. He was not dark. He had quite a mop of fairish hair. But he did wear an earring, and that earring was a little silver skull with glittering green stones for eyes. He grinned cheerfully at Polly, but the grin faded a bit as he looked up at Mr. Lynn, and he stared as hard as Polly was staring at him.

"Leslie," the lady called from the desk. "Am I going mad? Or does this gentleman remind you of your uncle too?"

"Yeah," Leslie said, staring wonderingly at Mr. Lynn. "They could be twins! Not being awful," he added to Mr. Lynn. It did not sound as if he liked his uncle much. "But you do look just like him."

"Oh not *that* like," the lady said hurriedly. "This gentleman's much younger than Tom is, Leslie." She smiled at Mr. Lynn. "That's kids for you. They think everyone over twenty is the same age, don't they?"

Mr. Lynn's face had gone from pale to a sort of muddy red. Leslie saw he had overdone things. "Said the wrong thing—as usual!" he remarked to Polly. "Opened my big mouth and put my foot in it. What did you want?"

"Screwdriver," Polly said faintly.

"Sure you don't want a left-handed hammer?" asked Leslie. "Or how about a pound of elbow grease?"

"Leslie!" Said the lady at the desk. She gave Polly a grin as cheeky as Leslie's. "He's a terror with his jokes," she said. "Take no notice."

"Down this end," said Leslie, and squeaked bouncily off to the end of the shop.

Polly followed him, scarcely able to see straight for confusion. She knew just how Mr. Lynn must be feeling. Leslie was nice. The discovery made her squiggle inside, in a way that could have been pleasant but was probably nasty. And she could see from the way the lady at the desk watched Leslie, not quite smiling, as he went, that she adored Leslie. She was obviously his mother, and clearly adored him because, not being stupid like Edna, she knew Leslie was worth it.

Utterly confused, Polly looked dimly at rows of screwdrivers, large, small, with wooden handles and transparent plastic handles, and picked up a packet of assorted small ones because they were nearest. Mr. Lynn, equally at random, seized a couple of large ones from higher up.

They followed Leslie back to the cash desk, where Mr. Lynn paid for all of them in a distracted rush. "Thank you, sir," said the lady. "I do wish Mr. Piper was here. I'd love to see the two of you side by side. I just can't get over how like him you are!"

"He is, you know," Leslie said to Polly. "See you."

"See you," Polly replied, looking to one side of Leslie's earring, and not meaning it at all.

When they got outside, Mr. Lynn's face was white again. "Ye gods and little fishes, Polly!" he gasped. "I don't believe this!" And he went away across the square in enormous strides. Polly sprinted after him, and together they threw themselves inside a door marked YE OLDE COTSWOLDE CAFÉ TEAS. Almost without seeing where they were, they collapsed at a table and Mr. Lynn ordered scones and cakes and Coke and milkshakes after one wild, random glance at the menu. The waitress looked wondering, and asked him if that was what he really wanted. "Yes, yes!" he said, and when she had gone he sat puffing as if he had run a race.

Polly sat sort of recovering too. Ordinary feelings began coming back like pins and needles. "It's all true," she said. "Except that it isn't."

"That's what's so unnerving," said Mr. Lynn. "Mr. Piper, the shop. Leslie—but none of it quite like we thought. Do you think the woman's name was Edna? I was dying to ask her, but I couldn't think of a way to ask that didn't seem rude."

"I bet it was," said Polly. "I can't get over Leslie being nice! And we got the name and the earring right, but he was fair-haired. I can't get used to him not being dark and sulky."

"Much the same with Edna—if that's her name. No dressing gown," said Mr. Lynn.

"And no curlers," said Polly. "But she *was* doing sums."

"We got her too old-fashioned," Mr. Lynn said glumly. "We got the whole thing about twenty years out of date."

"But it was there," said Polly. "It is still. I can see it out of the window."

"That's what's so appalling," said Mr. Lynn, hunching his shoulders in order not to look.

The waitress came back with a tray and a look which said, "Don't blame me. This is what you ordered." She set out two ice-cream cones, two cheese pancakes, two bright green milkshakes and an oatcake. Mr. Lynn stared at it rather, but he was too shaken to protest. He took the pancakes and let Polly have the rest, and they did seem to make him feel better. At length he interrupted the snoring noise Polly was making with the bottom of the second milkshake to ask in a rather hushed way, "Mr. Piper wasn't there—why not, Polly?"

Polly looked up, into his glasses, and found a hunted look staring out at her. "It's all right," she said. "He's not you. She said he was older. And she knew you weren't when she looked properly." All the same, she thought she would have been happier herself if Mr. Piper *had* been there and she could prove there definitely were two of them.

Mr. Lynn's shoulders sagged with slightly unhappy relief. "Then which of us," he said, "do you think is really Tan Coul?"

"You," Polly said. But she was not sure at all, and she knew Mr. Lynn knew.

Mr. Lynn summoned the waitress back then and, very slowly and plainly, asked for a pot of tea. Polly had some Coke to wash down the oatcake. After that, they felt like facing normal life again. They went out into the square, carefully not looking towards Thomas Piper Hardware, and explored the rest of the town. The most interesting thing they found was a small book shop, which Mr. Lynn dived into like a homing pigeon—no, more like a homing ostrich, Polly thought, with his long legs and the way he bent his head going in. Mr. Lynn bought a stack of books for himself, and one about dragons which he insisted on giving to Polly.

"I don't think Granny likes you giving me things," Polly said awkwardly.

"I don't think your Granny likes *me*," Mr. Lynn said. "But please take it. It keeps my mind off Edna—if her name *is* Edna."

They went back to the square with their parcels. The horse-car had a parking ticket stuck to its windscreen. The waitress from the café was standing beside it. Mr. Lynn looked from her to the ominous ticket. "Is this yours?"

"No, that's from Maisie Millet. She's traffic warden round here, not me," said the waitress. She held out another parcel, orange plastic, with PIPER on it in black. "Edna sent her Leslie over with this after you'd gone." Polly's head and Mr. Lynn's turned to look at Piper's shop. So the lady *was* called Edna. "You left it behind," the waitress explained. She had decided, right from the start, that Mr. Lynn was what she called "a bit in the head." She put the orange parcel in Polly's hand as the more trustworthy of the two. "Edna said to tell you she didn't notice straightaway—she and Leslie were talking about you," she said, and went back into the café.

"Polly," Mr. Lynn said in a slightly quaking voice, "what are we going to do with all these screwdrivers?"

"I don't know," said Polly. She gurgled. Mr. Lynn gulped. They both leaned over the car and screamed with laughter.

Mr. Lynn drove even more heroically on the way back. Polly could not blame him. He had a lot on his mind. But some of his

manoeuvres did bring a slight taste of green milkshake to the back
of her throat, and sometimes she could not prevent herself saying
things like "Aren't you supposed to drive on the other side of the
road?" or "I think that driver was hooting at us." And after he had
dropped her outside her house, she did wonder if he would reach
London without getting wrapped round a tree on the way.

He must have done. He wrote her a letter a week later.

> The thing I hadn't bargained for about
> hero business,

the important part said,

> is how terribly embarrassing it is. I
> wished the floor would open in Piper's
> shop. I squirmed. I realised in one
> blinding moment that when they speak of
> heroes having "iron nerve," they do not
> mean they can spring forward and seize
> the bridle of a wild horse. That is
> child's play—sorry, Polly, I mean quite
> easy by comparison really. No, what
> they mean by "iron nerve" is the same
> as "a thick skin." You have to learn
> not to notice how silly you feel.

Polly thought sadly that she understood.

You meen,

she wrote back,

that you want to stop plaing hero bisnis. I do not blame you. It is up to you, just say.

She got a letter back almost at once. It was on headed paper from a hotel in Edinburgh. Evidently the orchestra was off on its travels again. Mr. Lynn had written it by hand, but he had done his best to print it so that she could read it, though he had clearly been in a hurry.

Dear Hero,
I didn't mean that at all. I just meant that being a hero took a different kind of courage than I had thought. No, I am hooked on hero business. Now I have got over squirming, I want to know if everything we make up is going to come true the same way. Must stop. This concert is being broadcast.

Tom

The orchestra continued touring about for months. Polly did not see Mr. Lynn again for a long time. In fact, when she looked back over these memories, all coming alive and surging back into her head alongside the plain and normal memories she had thought she had, it surprised her to find how very few times she did see him. Just those three times in over a year. Of course, she saw him again after that, but it seemed odd, considering how well she knew she knew him. Meanwhile, he continued to write her letters and send her postcards of interesting places. Polly was the one who did not write so often. Sometimes she even forgot that hero business existed.

PART TWO

NOW HERE
andante cantibile

1

And fill your hands o' the holy water
And cast your compass round

TAM LIN

Granny did give Polly a birthday present after all. Polly was staying with Granny the week she was eleven, because Dad was coming back to settle up who was to have what. Ivy said, "You don't want to be in the middle of a row again, Polly," and Polly agreed.

And a row there must have been. Both Mum and Dad forgot Polly's birthday. The only present she had that year was the little heart-shaped pendant Granny gave her.

"I was going to wait a few years to give it you," Granny said, "but I think you could do with it now. Take care of it. It was my mother's."

Polly sat with Mintchoc draped purring across her knees and turned the heart shape back and forth in the light. From some angles it looked pearly white, but as she tipped it, colours rippled through it—pale crimson, blue and deep dragon green. "What is it made of?" she said.

"Opal," said Granny. "It's a pity it's opal, because opals mean tears, but you keep it and it'll keep you. My mother always said it was the luckiest thing she had."

"Should I wear it all the time?" Polly asked, trying to hook the thin silver chain round her neck. It got tangled in her hair and Granny had to help her fasten it.

"Not in your bath," Granny said. "Water spoils opal." And she told Polly that opals were really a thin slice out of a certain kind of rock, bent over a crystal to bring the colours out. If water got between the rock and the crystal, the colours went.

Polly pulled the opal heart up and managed to look at it again, squinting, with the chain cutting the back of her neck. "That's made me see it in two lights!" she complained.

"Quite right," said Granny. "Get out to the bus or you'll be late for school."

Polly spent a lot of that summer at Granny's too. "Not much of a holiday," Ivy said worriedly, "but the money's tight. I asked Maud to have you, but they're all off to France. Even Reg offered, but I'm not having you stay with *him*!"

It was a lonely, sleepy summer, with the warm winds blowing dust in Granny's garden and griming the rustling trees in the road outside. Some days Polly kept up her hero training by going jogging up and down the road. When she came to the end where Hunsdon House stood, she usually stopped and looked through the bars of the gate. You could see a curve of the drive from there, green and dark under the trees, and sometimes, when wind blew the branches aside, there was just a glimpse of the shuttered windows of the house.

"Yes, the place is all closed up and empty," Granny told her. "They're off on their travels again."

When she heard that, Polly seriously thought of getting into the house. She had a longing to go up round the joints of the stair-case and see the rest of the rooms up there. And there was a place beside the gate where she thought she just might be able to climb the wall. Next time she went for a run, she stopped a little short of the gate and looked at that place. It was not as easy as she had thought. Though there were two worn parts in the stones, they would only serve as footholds if she could jump high enough to hook her hands over the top of the wall first. Polly went back a step or so, gathering herself to jump her very highest.

Something made her look through the bars of the gate.

Someone was standing halfway up the drive, in the most shad-owy part. It was a tall, bulky shape, standing very still. The face, looking straight at Polly, was blurred by the shade and by the bars of the gate in the way. The eyes looked smudged and big. As Polly stood, looking guiltily back, caught in the act of measuring to jump, the face somehow crystallised into Mr. Morton Leroy's, watching her sardonically.

They stood and looked at one another. Polly twisted nervously at the opal pendant round her neck. Mr. Leroy just looked. It seemed to go on for an age. Polly was never sure what made her stop standing there, staring. Somehow it was suddenly over and Polly was walking soberly away down the road, knowing that Mr. Leroy had nearly caught her climbing in and that she would not dare to try again now.

She buried herself in books instead. She used Granny's ticket for the local library and got out *Black Beauty*, which made her cry outraged tears. She was glad Mr. Lynn had bought the yellow horse. Then, trying for something for cheerful, she got out Sherlock Holmes stories and found herself wanting to shake Sherlock Holmes for being so superior. Since he played the violin and obviously looked rather like Mr. Lynn, he should have behaved like Dr. Watson. She wanted to shake Watson too. Then she tried *Uncle Tom's Cabin* and understood why Mr. Lynn had not wanted her to call him Uncle Tom. Uncle Tom was a slave. Polly read to the place where the villainous Simon Legree came in, and suddenly realised she was reading "Leroy" every time the book said "Legree." She stopped, appalled, and took the book back to the library.

By this time she had got a reputation in the library for liking long, hard books. The librarian said to her, "Here's a book you might like. I used to love it. There is a shortened version, but I saved you the long one. Don't be put off if you find it difficult at first."

Polly looked at the book. *The Three Musketeers* by Alexandre Dumas. She wondered why Alexandre was spelled wrong, but she had seen the cartoon of *The Three Musketeers*. She thanked the librarian and took the book home to Granny's. It *was* difficult. Half the time she was not sure what was going on, or why everyone lived in hotels, and it was full of conversations where you could not tell which person was speaking. But Polly loved it even so. From the very beginning, when d'Artagnan appears on his yellow horse, she was utterly captivated. She loved huge Porthos and the elegant Aramis, but Athos was the one she liked best. Oddly enough, despite the yellow horse and the fact that d'Artagnan was long and thin, she knew Athos was the one who was most like Mr. Lynn. Athos had once been married to the beautiful, dreadful lady, and the lady was obviously Laurel.

Polly read it twice. Then she sat down and wrote a long and excited letter to Mr. Lynn.

Dear Tom,

she began. That looked wrong; it *was* wrong. She never could think of him as anything but Mr. Lynn, but she supposed she had better practise in order not to hurt his feelings. She told him all about *The Three Musketeers.* Then she told him all the latest ideas she had had about Tan Thare and Tan Hanivar, and the whole set of adventures for them all to have conquering the evil Cardinal ~~Leroy~~—sorry, Legris.

She got a postcard back from Cardiff:

Thank you, Hero. You have given me some ideas too.
                              More later, T. G. L.

Granny really did not go in for reading. Polly knew that now. She said too much reading would ruin Polly's eyes, and she taught Polly to cook to take her mind off books. Polly was not good at it. Her first sponge cake had a kind of soggy valley in the middle.

"Well, it's nothing a blind man on a galloping horse wouldn't see," said Granny, "but it doesn't look much like a sponge cake to me."

"It's a new kind," Polly said, "called volcano cake. That runny stuff in the middle is the lava."

"Oh is it?" said Granny. "Put it down for Mintchoc and let's try apple pie instead."

Someone had given Granny a basket of windfall apples. Granny was very good at peeling them in one entire long strip. "There," she would say, passing Polly a heavy green curl, "throw it over your left shoulder and it'll make the initials of the man you're going to marry."

Polly threw strip after strip of peeling, but they never did make anything except playthings for Mintchoc. Each one broke up and splattered about the kitchen floor into circles and lines that even Granny had to admit were meaningless. "You see? I'm not going to marry," Polly said, secure in the knowledge she would be a hero instead.

When Polly went home at the end of summer, she found everything had been moved out of her room into the tiny room at the back. Ivy, with a duster tied round her head, was briskly and cheerfully painting the room that had been Polly's.

"You're in there from now on," she told Polly, pointing to the tiny room with her paintbrush. "We're going to take in lodgers. They'll have to have this room because that one's too small."

Polly looked round the echoing empty square of her old room. The flowery paper was not quite hidden under white paint, and there were drips on the bare boards. "My folder!" she said. "With my soldiers in!"

"All through there," said Ivy. "I put everything on the floor. You can make yourself useful by sorting your junk out." She sat back on her heels and looked at the not quite white wall discontentedly. "It needs one other coat at least."

The folder was there when Polly raced through to look, with the soldiers safely in it. But a lot of her other things were not.

"No, I threw all the babyish things away," Ivy said when Polly raced back to ask. "You're a big girl now and you don't need them. Really, Polly, you do criticise! I'm trying so hard. I've just pulled myself together and taken a big step, and all I get is *Where's my dolls' house?*"

"But Dad only *gave* me the dolls' house at Christmas!" Polly protested.

"And the skirting board needs two more coats," said Ivy. "Yes, I know. Don't bother me now, Polly."

Later that day, when Polly had mournfully tidied what were left of her things—Mum had left the books and papers because they were grown up, and the sewing machine because that was almost real, but not much else—Ivy decided Polly needed an explanation.

"It's like this," she said, clutching a teacup with both painty hands. "Happiness is something you have to go out and get, Polly. It won't come to you, not in *this* world. I've suddenly seen that I've been so wrong all these months, looking back to my marriage and regretting it all. I was trying to put the clock back, Polly. Now I'm going forward again, and we're both going to have a new, happy life. We'll have a lodger for money, and you'll be at the new school—"

"When are we going to get my uniform?" Polly asked. "We start next week."

"Tomorrow," said Ivy. "Polly, I'm going to make that room so nice! I've got some lovely curtains and a matching bedspread. If I make it nice enough, I can charge a lot for it. It'll be good for us both, having someone else in the house to talk to."

In the end, it was Granny who took Polly to buy school clothes. Ivy was too busy painting. "Don't blame her, Polly," Granny said. "She's been very down, and she's trying to pull herself up. Ivy's got character—I'll give her that. Try and understand."

Polly did try to understand. She was positively saintly, she thought, not mentioning all the other things Ivy had thrown away. But she did regret her old room. The new little one was like a crowded box, and the water cistern chuckled loudly all night from a cupboard in the corner. Polly would have been very miserable in it, but for the excitement of starting at Manor Road School.

She loved it. The whole first term was like a long, long birthday party. There was a crowd of new friends, and a mass of new things to do, new ways of speaking, new ways of thinking. There was also Nina. Polly wondered how she could have forgotten how largely Nina figured in her life at Manor Road. Nina was the only other girl who came on from Junior School to Manor Road with Polly. The others had all gone to Miles End, which was said to be rough.

Nina set out to astound and shock and lead. After trying one or two other things, she came to school with a book she had found in her aunt's house. It was called *Popular Beliefs*. "I'm starting a Superstition Club," she said. "You join by having a superstition which isn't in this book."

Polly became a founder member of the club the same day. She had developed a habit of taking her opal pendant out from under her new school tie and twiddling it during lessons. She did it in French. The French master told her that jewellery was not allowed and she must either put it away or describe it to him in French.

"It's not jewellery! It's lucky!" Polly exclaimed indignantly. "It used to be Granny's mother's!"

Nina passed her a note enrolling her in the Superstition Club on the spot.

The club became all the rage in the course of a week. Everyone joined. The rules were to believe all the superstitions in Nina's book and to find as many more as you could. If you found ten new superstitions, you received the Order of the Black Cat, personally drawn by Nina on a page of her rough note pad. People's blazers soon became decorated with rusty pins they had picked up, their hands black with rescuing pieces of coal, and their shoulders sprinkled with spilled salt every lunch hour. Funerals and ambulances caused hands to leap to collars, and a number of people nearly got knocked down in the street, either by not walking under ladders or by going out of their way in order to be able to say a black cat had crossed their path. Two people were found crying in the cloakrooms because they had broken a mirror. Everyone's pockets became loaded with lucky charms, lucky bus tickets and lucky mascots. And as the club grew, a wave of superstition grew with it, mounted, and spread far beyond the club, right up to the senior end of the school, until it mixed with everything everyone did. Polly spared a little attention for music too. She had joined the choir, and enrolled for free violin lessons, because she knew next to nothing about music. She wanted to learn. Listening to Mr. Lynn talking about music to Mary Fields had made her feel really stupid.

But she did not think much about Mr. Lynn otherwise, even though he wrote her two quite long letters around then. One letter was a rewriting of the giant story, making Mr. Piper's shop much more like the real one they had found in Stow-on-the-Water. Polly preferred the second letter, which was about Tan Coul, Hero, and Tan Hanivar hunting for treasure in some caves. Here Tan Hanivar accidentally turned into a dragon, and the other two nearly killed him before they realised. Yes, but just a bit silly, Polly thought, and put the letters away in her folder without answering them. She was really far more interested in the Superstition Club.

The club gained a mighty boost from the approach of Hallowe'en. By then everyone in the school was a quivering mass of strange beliefs. Spirits were talked of, and auras, and astral bodies, and someone saw a ghost down near the Biology Lab. And on Hallowe'en itself a magpie landed on the windowsill during School Assembly. Assembly stopped short while everyone scuffled to cross fingers, touch wood, and intone, "Hello, Mr. Magpie, how's your wife?" The Headmaster said irritable, sensible things. The magpie flew away in a frightened whirl of black and white, and nothing much happened, either lucky or unlucky.

After that, Nina said she was tired of the club. She was possibly rather frightened by its success. But it is easier to start something than stop it. The superstition simply took a new turn and became a craze for fortune-telling. The day the craze started, Polly had her fortune told three times, once by paper top, once by palmistry, and once with a pack of cards. The next day she had it done by tea leaves and I Ching. Each one came out different. They varied between "Never marry for money" from the paper top to "To take a maiden to wife brings good fortune" from the Book of Changes. Then she tried the three bowls. One was full of water, one half full, and one empty. You asked a question, shut your eyes and dipped your hand. The full and empty bowls were Yes and No. The one half full was Maybe. It became a common sight to see girls squatting like witches around plastic cups of water, breathlessly watching someone's groping hand. Polly did it frequently. But no matter how often she tried, she always got her hand in half-full, lukewarm Maybe. She gave up and put her name down for the Prefects' mirror instead.

The Prefects were doing a roaring trade, charging ten pence a look, and the waiting list was long. You looked in the mirror in a nearly dark room—full of other people queuing for their turns, which perhaps accounted for it—and you saw the face of someone behind your reflection who was going to Influence Your Life. Unfortunately, by this time the teachers had had enough. The Staff Room contained stacks of confiscated cards, dice, dowsing twigs, bowls and even two crystal balls. Polly was queuing for her turn at the mirror when she distinctly saw the face of the Deputy Head appear in it behind the boy who was looking at that moment. It was clear he was real. He drew back the curtains, took down the mirror and turned everyone out of the room except the Prefects. Someone who kept their ear to the door after it was shut said they were glad they were not those Prefects. And the Headmaster said, "This must stop."

It didn't straightaway, of course. But the frenzy seemed to be over. Nina turned her attention to the Stamp Club. Polly turned hers to the violin—or she tried to. But it was a complete disaster. She was hopeless. As soon as she had the violin in her hands, she became slow, foolish and clumsy. Long after the other learners were playing proper tunes, Polly scraped and wailed and made noises like a sea lion in distress. Strings broke under her fumbling fingers. Hairs streamed from her bow and got mixed up with her own hair. She hated practising too. She had to do it at school because Ivy forbade it at home.

"I'm not having the lodger disturbed with that noise," she said. No lodger had yet appeared, but Ivy was always considering him as if he was there.

Soon after the affair of the Prefects' mirror, the violin teacher suggested Polly give up the violin. "I don't think it's your instrument," she said. "How about trying the flute class?"

But Ivy said, "Tootling away, disturbing the lodger! No way!"

So that was that. Polly could not bear to write to Mr. Lynn about her failure, so she joined the Indoor Athletics and did not write to him at all. She was therefore very ashamed, one morning in December, to find a postcard of Bristol Suspension Bridge lying on the doormat with the other post. She picked it up and turned it over, expecting it to be from Mr. Lynn. It was not. It was from Dad, addressed to Ivy and written in angry capital letters that Polly could not help reading.

WHAT'S ALL THIS, IVY?
I'VE TOLD YOU I WANT TO COME BACK!!!
REG

"I'll have that, Polly," Ivy said, coming up behind Polly on her way out to work. She took it from Polly's fingers with a snatch.

"I saw," said Polly. "Dad wants to come back."

"He meant you to see," Ivy said in her stoniest way. "And he's not coming." She opened the front door to go out.

Polly surprised herself by screaming at Ivy. "You're horrible! You're hard! You're unforgiving! He *wants* to come back and you won't let him!" Ivy looked round at her, holding the door open, and looked for a moment as if she was going to smack Polly. Then she simply slammed the door in Polly's face. "I hate you!" Polly screamed to the footsteps going away behind the front door. That surprised her too. She stood for a while and wondered if it were true. It did not seem to be, to her relief. Just something you shout, she thought. I'm glad.

2

She had not picked a rose, a rose,
A rose but barely one,
When up and started young Tam Lin

TAM LIN

The lodger came about a week later. He was a fattish, cheery man, full of energy, called David Bragge, who worked on the *Middleton Star*. He had been divorced too, Ivy said, and he knew how it felt. Polly was shy of him. David made jokes all the time and Polly never understood them.

She was shy of his pink, hairy arms—which she saw a lot of, because David sat watching television with his shirt-sleeves rolled up whenever he was in—and she was shy of his loud, cracking laugh. Ivy made her shyer still by making a great fuss of the lodger and cooking him huge meals.

"We shall be happy now, you'll see," Ivy said. Ivy did seem happy. David persuaded her to go down to the pub with him most evenings, and she seemed to like that. Polly was glad. She had a peaceful, empty house to do her homework in, which made it a good thing all round.

At school the fortune-telling craze was dying away at last. Everyone was rehearsing hard for the Carol Concert. Polly stayed late for choir practice two evenings a week. One evening she came latish out of the school gates with Nina, to find herself being waited for. A familiar figure was stamping its feet outside, looking rather withered with the cold but very glad to see her. Dad. Polly set out to run towards him, paused, and then walked up to him with both hands held out. She felt rather ridiculous, but that was the way it took her.

"Aren't you glad to see me?" Dad asked, taking her held-out hands.

"You know I am," Polly said. She was very conscious of Nina. Nina stood and stared a moment and then walked off with some other girls. When Nina had gone, Polly could smile. Dad smiled too, his well-known merry smile. He looked just the same, except that his eyes were more crinkled. "Have you come to meet me?" she asked.

He nodded. "Let's go home. You've got a key, haven't you?"

"Oh thank goodness!" Polly said. "It's been so strange!"

They walked home hand in hand. Dad was obviously glad to see her. He kept looking at her and smiling. "You have grown, Polly."

"Of course. What did you expect?" Polly said happily. "Why are you coming home? Has Joanna Renton gone off you?"

"Well you could say that," he said, sounding rather uncomfortable. "I didn't know you knew about her."

"Only a bit," Polly assured him, as if that made it all right. She was so happy that she had gone quiet all over. She felt like someone listening to great chords of music that were not to be interrupted by speaking. They walked most of the way home without saying a word, even though Polly's mind was crowded with things she wanted to tell Dad. She could tell him all that later. As they turned into their street, she said, out of the quiet, "Now you're back we don't need David Bragge, do we? Will you tell him to go?"

Dad half stopped walking. "David? Is *he* there?"

They went on more slowly, and Polly felt more thoughtful than quiet. It was the first sign she had had that David Bragge was rather more than just a lodger. Still, she thought, it was bound to be all right now. She unlocked the door and they went indoors. Dad, now she saw him in the hall light, looked rather thin and threadbare. She could see one or two grey hairs glinting on his head, mixed into the thick curls Mum used to call Dad's halo.

Mum was just coming downstairs. She stopped like a statue when she saw them. "Oh no!" she said. "Isn't that just like you, Reg! Sneaking in on Polly's coat-tails! What do you want this time?"

"What do you expect," Dad said, quite mildly for him, "when you won't answer any of my letters? Ivy, I told you I want to come back. Can't we talk about it at least?"

"No," Ivy said, and began to come downstairs like a statue walking.

Polly felt Dad move to back away and manage to stand still. "What's wrong with you, Ivy?" he said. "You've just shut down on me. You can't do that. You have to talk."

"All right," Ivy said stonily. "Talk if you must. Go in the living room and wait."

"Why?" Dad, and Polly too, glanced at the living room. The television was on in there, and they could see one of David's pink arms as he sat watching it.

"Because I'm going to phone your mother to come and take Polly away first," Ivy said implacably. "I'm not having her here for you to get round. Go on in."

Dad went into the living room, looking determined and a little nervous. He looked almost out of place there, Polly thought in some surprise. As Ivy went to the phone and dialled Granny's number, she heard David say, with one of his laughs, "An attack of the prodigals, eh, old son?"

"Something like that," Dad answered as he sat down. "None of your damn business, is it?"

"Oh, you knew?" Mum said to the phone. "You would! Yes, of course he's here. And yes, I do want you to fetch her now. She thinks he's the bee's knees, and I'm not having it!" She put the phone down and turned to Polly. There was an unusual look on Ivy's face, as if she pitied Polly. "You shouldn't let people play on your feelings, my love," she said. "In this world you get taken to the cleaners for having a soft heart. All he wanted was to get in this house, you know."

"Yes," Polly said dismally.

After what seemed an age, during which everyone simply waited, Granny arrived and took Polly away. Polly spent the rest of the month at Granny's and did not go home again till after Christmas. She also stopped being friends with Nina. Nina came up to her at school the next day and said, "You'll get into trouble. You're not supposed to go off with strange men."

"I didn't," Polly said. She could not think what Nina meant.

"Yes, you did," said Nina. "Twice. Once with the man at the funeral and then again last night."

"That was my Dad last night!" Polly said.

Nina was astonished. "It never was! He looks quite different!"

"He—does—*not!*" Polly shouted. She turned and walked away from Nina. But that was only annoyance, like the way she had shouted at Ivy. The real thing that made her stop speaking to Nina was the way people kept coming up to her all day, saying, "Is it true what Nina says—you come from a broken home?"

"Broken right in half," Polly replied to each one. "There's a hole in the middle where the garden is. You get rained on trying to go upstairs."

She walked home to Granny's trying not to cry. She lay in bed that night, staring at her *Fire and Hemlock* picture, and decided she would definitely climb the wall into Hunsdon House as soon as term was over. She was not quite sure what this had to do with anything, except that it did. She hoped Mr. Leroy would catch her doing it. She would have liked to go for him the way she had gone for Mira Anderton. She wanted to fight someone. But Granny remarked that the house was still shut up. "They can afford to go away to the sun," she said. "Pots of money—rolling in it."

The sun was shining the first day of the holidays, when Polly went down the road to the big gates of the house. It was a frosty sun, melting bleakly from streaks of hard grey cloud. The big leaves of the laurel bushes overhanging the drive of Hunsdon House were fringed round the edges with frost. Polly blew on her gloves to encourage herself, spat for luck, and ran at the wall where she had measured it in the summer. It was as easy as climbing wallbars. She was up in a second, unsticking her gloves from the frost at the top of the wall, and swinging over and down. Crunch. Into dead leaves under the trees. She crept crunching forward to the front of the house.

There it was, shuttered, sad and majestic. Even so, Polly at first did not dare come out from among the trees, in case there was someone inside it.

The Perry Leroys were clearly rich enough to have the garden looked after while they were not using the house. Someone had pruned the roses and cut back the lavender hedges beyond. It made the garden seem empty and much smaller. Unless, Polly thought as she tiptoed through, it was simply that she had grown. She looked back at the blind yellow pile of the house. That still seemed big, although the garden had shrunk. A mere few steps brought her to the empty concrete oblong that should have been a pond. Remembering that something had seemed to happen to that pond before, Polly stood for a while, watching it. But it remained a frosty oblong of concrete. She went past it, through further shrubs, until her way was blocked by the wire netting round a tennis court. Now she had a choice: to go back or to cross a slope of frozen lawn towards the house.

Polly hesitated. Crossing the lawn really would bring her out into the open. She stood in the bushes and watched the house carefully. And it was empty. Lived-in houses give you a sense of life, and Hunsdon House was dead, dead as the bare twigs of the pruned roses. The part facing her was a French window with three steps leading up to it. At the bottom of the steps were the two pillars, each holding a vase. And the window beyond was shuttered and dead like all the others.

"Come on," Polly said out loud. "Behave like a trainee-hero for once!"

She walked up the lawn towards the steps with the two vases as if she had a perfect right to be there. Under her feet the frozen grass made slow, wheezing munches, like somebody chewing ice cubes. Funny, Polly thought as her feet munched. She had remembered the steps with vases as leading up to a plain door, but they clearly led up to a shuttered window. The vases, when Polly reached them, still stood as she and Mr. Lynn had left them. NOW said one, glittering with frost. HERE said the other. By stretching her arms to their very widest, Polly could rest a glove on each one. She gave each an experimental push. Then a harder pull, the other way. It was no good. She could not budge them. Either they were frozen at the bottoms or Mr. Lynn was a good deal stronger than Polly. Frustrated by this, Polly went between the vases, past the hidden HERE on the left and the hidden NOW on the right, and up the steps to the shuttered window. She put her glove on the window's frosted handle and turned it with an angry push. It opened.

Polly recoiled. "I wonder they don't have vandals!" she said. "But I suppose they've locked the shutters inside." To see if this was true, she opened the window wider and shoved at the tall wooden shutter beyond it.

It moved under her hand, folding inward a foot or so. Polly

stood very still. The house felt dead, she was sure. There was nothing from the garden except a sparse twitter of birds—though when Polly looked round, she was dismayed to see her long line of footprints, green in the white grass, leading straight to the steps like a pointer. "So they'll know I was here anyway," she said, and slipped sideways inside, round the shutter. She left the window standing ajar. She did not want to be locked in the house.

She was in the room where the Will had been read. She knew it by the sharp, furry smell of the carpet. When her eyes got used to the dim crack of light from the window, she could see all the comfortable chairs she remembered, but not in lines now. They were arranged to make it a room for gracious living. The door to the hall was open. Polly tiptoed across to it. She felt rather silly tiptoeing, but she could not walk properly, although she could tell the house truly was empty by the smell and the feel. It was quite warm. That was what gave the carpet the sharp, unused smell. Clearly the riches which paid for the garden to be done could easily afford to keep the heating going all winter too.

The hall was a brighter dimness. Light lived in the shiny floor and in the white paint of the jointed flights of stairs going round the space and back again. And there were the Ali Baba vases, with their own faint fizz of light from the patterns on them. Polly avoided them rather—she knew they were empty, of course, but they were still big enough to hold a person—and tiptoed to the archway of the dining room. But it was too dark in there and, besides, what Polly wanted was to explore the rooms up the jointed stairs. She sped there, and up the stairs, in a light scudding of feet.

The room at the first landing was a dark hole. It felt bare. Polly could tell that the stacks of pictures had been taken away. She scudded on, up and round a joint, to the next landing, and gently opened the door there. A study of some kind, she thought. Books, leather chairs, a neat desk swam there in the twilight. But there was a bed too. And, as Polly's eyes adjusted, she picked out posters on the walls. The Who, Rolling Stones, David Bowie, and a spiky picture of an unreal landscape labelled *Michael Moorcock*. A boy's room. Polly realised it must be Seb's. She took her head out and closed the door, knowing she was spying.

Guiltily she went up and round to the next joint. The door there was slightly open. Polly slipped through to a short corridor with a blue-gleaming bathroom opening off one side, into a space of scents and silks. There was a real four-poster bed in here, on a white fluffy carpet. The faint shine of the bed's curtains, the frills at the top and the quilt across it suggested dark-pinkish satin. Polly took her glove off to touch it, and it *was* satin. She put the glove on again, because this room was cold. Or maybe it was the thievish way Polly was feeling. She knew this was Laurel's room. It was a big dimness, with rosebuds on the walls, a soft rosy carpet under the bed's white fluffy one, silken chairs. One whole wall was folding cupboards with clothes inside. A second wall had a lot of valuable-looking little pictures hung on it in a pattern. Near the window, instead of the lavish dressing table Polly had expected, there was a curious wooden chest, bent and carved, with silver hairbrushes and pearly-looking combs on it. Above the chest a luminous oval of mirror looked at Polly from the wall.

Polly stood in front of it and looked back at herself in the mirror, surrounded in a dim silver filigree of birds, leaves and animals. The cracks of light from the shutters made the mirror look dark and deep. Polly's hair blazed white in it, and her face looked shy and wondering, not at all like the face of the trespasser she was. Over her left shoulder, very clearly, she could see one of the photographs in the pattern of little pictures on the far wall. That made her snort with laughter and the face in the mirror grin, remembering the Prefects' mirror and the face of the Deputy Head.

She turned round to look for the real picture and was rather astonished to see that the wall was too far away for her to pick the little oval photograph out. The pictures seemed just a pattern of blobs from where she stood. She had to go right up to them and search, with her face close to the wall, before she found the right one, near the middle of the pattern. She could still not see it properly. She had to unhook it and carry it into the cracks of light from the window before she could. It was a slightly old-fashioned picture of a mischievously grinning fair-haired boy. Whoever he was, he looked older than Seb, and he was too fair anyway. He was nobody Polly knew. Yet there was a sense of familiarity about the photo, as if the mirror trick had worked and Polly was going to know this boy sometime.

Polly stood holding the little oval picture in both gloved hands, struggling between her superstition and her conscience. She was quite sure she was holding something that was going to be important to her and she was horribly tempted to keep it. On the other hand, it would be stealing if she did. And her conscience went on further and told her that she had already stolen one picture—no, six!—from this house. That jiggery-pokery with the pictures during the funeral, which she had conveniently told herself was a trick Laurel richly deserved, had caused Mr. Lynn to go off with six pictures that should have been Laurel's. Since just one of them had proved valuable enough to pay for a horse, then a car, this made it too serious to be a trick. And to steal another one now would be like victimising Laurel—wronger still.

No. Regretfully Polly crossed the room to hang the photo up again.

Halfway across the room, she heard voices down in the hall. After one moment when she seemed to be dead, Polly came twenty times more alive than normal. Her heart banged a little rapid stutter, like a row of dominoes falling over, and while it did she found she was speeding to the door in long, stealthy steps to look down between the white bars of the banisters. As she went, she heard one of the voices was Mr. Lynn's. It came echoing up quite clearly.

"If you like," she heard Mr. Lynn say. "Though I really don't see what business it is of yours."

The relief Polly felt at knowing his voice vanished when she heard the deep, chesty voice that answered. That was Mr. Leroy's. "Come off it, Tom," this voice said. "Laurel's interests are mine these days. You must have known Laurel would find out in the end. And you must have known she wouldn't like it when she did."

Polly clutched the photo guiltily to her chest and edged forward so that she could see them. They seemed to be standing in the middle of the hall below, side by side rather than face to face, as if they were about to walk into the dining room. The sun must have got round to the French window Polly had left open. A long shaft of light cut through the hall from the living room and fell across both men, so that Polly could see them from the knees up, as if they were floating. It gave both of them a pale, wintry look, particularly Mr. Lynn. He did not seem to be enjoying this meeting at all.

"I suggest you put it right by letting us finance you," said Mr. Leroy.

Spots of light from Mr. Lynn's glasses dazzled round the hall as he answered, "Thank you, Morton. But I've told you before that I prefer to pay my own way. I'm quite aware of the risk—"

"Risk!" Mr. Leroy's fatal laugh set up a faint, chiming buzz from the Ali Baba vases. "Tom, you haven't begun to see the risk you run! You've made Laurel furious."

"Can't Laurel tell me that for herself?" Mr. Lynn asked.

"Oh, she will if you want, believe me," Mr. Leroy said. "But I don't think you'd enjoy it. You'd better let me handle her. If you hadn't been so secretive about this venture of yours—"

"On purpose," Mr. Lynn said in his mildest way.

"*Of* course," Mr. Leroy agreed. "All right. I admit you've stolen a march on us and that I can't at the moment see how you did it. Now you'll have to pay the price of your low cunning. If you won't let us finance you, you'd better agree to come back into the fold. Laurel wants you where she can keep an eye on you after this."

"I am not," said Mr. Lynn in his most quietly obstinate way, "going to agree to live in Hunsdon House again, for you, or for Laurel, or for anyone else." He turned into the line of sunlight and walked away into the living room.

Mr. Leroy turned and went with him. "Some such arrangement's got to be made," he said. Polly watched their two backs moving away, one wide and upright, the other high-shouldered and thin. "We don't like to make threats," came from Mr. Leroy's broad back, "but we're going to keep tabs on you somehow, Tom, and you are going to let us do it. Or do you want trouble for your friends?"

Mr. Leroy's voice faded as they went into the living room. Mr. Lynn's voice came from in there. He sounded angry now, but what he said was drowned in a burst of Mr. Leroy's laughter, as if Mr. Lynn's anger was truly a joke. Then there was silence. And more silence. The house felt empty again.

But it *can't* be empty! Polly thought. They've gone in there, and Mr. Leroy will see the shutter and the window open, and then my footprints, and he'll know I'm still inside somewhere.

She felt cold to the very centre of her spine. Her hands shook as they held the oval photograph. When Mr. Leroy found her, she did not think Mr. Lynn would be able to do much to help her. From what she had heard, he seemed to be hard pressed to help himself. She backed away, very gently and quietly, through the open door and into Laurel's bedroom, back to the edge of the fluffy white carpet the bed stood on. If she hid under the bed, it would take a thorough search to find her.

But she stood there instead, listening and thinking. There really was not a sound from downstairs. Nothing but thick, dead stillness. She began almost to wonder if Mr. Leroy and Mr. Lynn had been there at all. There was only her banging heart to tell her that they had been. That, and her anger. Her anger seemed to have been growing all this time, underneath her fear, until it was large enough to hide the fear completely. She thought of Laurel and Mr. Leroy in the audience on television, watching Mr. Lynn. As if they owned him! Polly thought. They don't. They can't. Nobody owns anyone like that!

She laid the photograph carefully down on the satin quilt of the bed and went across to the pattern of little oval pictures hanging on the wall. Taking one out had left a rather obvious gap in the middle of the pattern. But there were, as Polly thought she had remembered, a number of spare hooks sticking out of the wall round the pictures. Evidently Laurel liked to spread the pictures about and arrange them into different patterns from time to time.

Quite carefully and calmly Polly unhooked pictures and rehung them in new places to make another, wider-spaced pattern so that it would not show that one was missing. I might as well do something useful while I'm waiting for Mr. Leroy to find me, she told herself. And I'm wearing gloves, like a good criminal should. It was lucky that all the pictures had the same kind of oval gold frame. Not all of them were photographs, by any means. Quite a number were tiny paintings of a face or a full-length person. Two were black shapes of people cut out of paper, and some were probably charcoal drawings. Polly arranged them with real artistry. There was one miniature painting of a young man in old-fashioned clothes, including a cloak thrown back across one shoulder, that Polly thought was much the nicest. He was leaning against a tree holding a sort of banjo, and his face looked nice. She would have liked to put him in the middle. But since the photograph of the fair boy had come from there, Polly sensibly replaced it with a photograph as like it as she could find, of another fair boy who was only slightly more old-fashioned. She left the paintings round the edges, where they had been before. It looked good when she had finished— almost the same. She went and picked up the stolen photo, zipped it carefully into her anorak pocket, and walked softly out of the room and down the stairs, telling herself she was going to her doom.

She did not quite believe she was, even as she went. The house felt so empty. Downstairs, she knew it was empty. The sun had left the open shutter, and the hall and the living room were dim, and as deserted as they were dim. Polly let herself out through the window and pulled the shutter closed. She pulled the window shut and heard the click as it latched itself. It would not open when she tried it. She walked down the steps, between NOW and HERE on the vases, and back across her line of footprints. They had spread wide and green in the sun, but they were the only set of footprints. Mr. Leroy and Mr. Lynn had not come or gone this way. The puzzling thing was that they did not seem to have used the front door or the side door either. When Polly peered at these doors from the bushes, she could not see any prints on the frosty gravel, nor any tire marks on the drive. She did not see another living creature until she met Mintchoc sitting on the wall in front of Granny's house.

3

O they rode on and further on,
They waded rivers above the knee,
And they saw neither sun nor moon,
But they heard the roaring of the sea.

THOMAS THE RHYMER

Feeling very guilty for a number of reasons, Polly bought Mr. Lynn a copy of *The Three Musketeers* for Christmas and got Granny to help her pack it up. Granny's parcels were works of art made of closely woven string and brown paper. "Well, it's bound to be late and I daresay he's a bit old for it, but they say it's the thought that counts," Granny said as they came back from posting it.

"Why are you always like that about Mr. Lynn?" said Polly.

"Like what?" said Granny.

"Sort of sarcastic," said Polly. "Why don't you like him?"

Granny shrugged. "Oh, I expect he's well enough, in himself. I just have my reservations about the company he keeps."

Since Polly knew exactly what Granny meant about the Leroy Perrys, she did not say any more. She just went quietly back to the paper chains she was making.

Dad stayed with them over Christmas, to Polly's delight. "Mind you," Granny said, "I said I wouldn't take sides and I'm not. But I think this is fair."

"Fair!" Dad said angrily. "I've a good mind to get a court order!" He told Polly rather grimly that Mum and David Bragge had gone away together for Christmas. But most of the time he was just as Polly remembered him from over a year ago, laughing and making silly jokes with Granny and Polly. Polly forgot the new wrinkles round his eyes and the grey threads in his curls and romped with him as if she were five years old. There was only one five-year-old thing she refused to do. "Play Let's Pretend now," Dad said pleadingly, several times.

"No," said Polly. "I've gone off it."

"Why?" asked Dad, but Polly did not know.

"Don't pester her, Reg," said Granny.

Polly did not dare show Dad or Granny—particularly Granny—her stolen photograph. She looked at it secretly when she went to bed each night, under her *Fire and Hemlock* picture. Looking back on that Christmas, Polly was rather surprised at the way she thought a great deal about both her pictures, and scarcely at all about that meeting she had overheard between Mr. Leroy and Mr. Lynn. That was so queer, somehow, that she had to push it to one side of her mind. Instead, she stared at the fire and the mysterious figures behind the hemlock.

Up to now Polly had assumed they were trying to put the fire out. But this Christmas it began to seem to her that the people might really be trying to keep the fire going, building it up furiously, racing against time. You could see from the clouds of smoke that the fire was very damp. Perhaps if they left off feeding it for an instant, it would fizzle out and leave them in the dark.

The stolen photograph had a much more ordinary look. It was slightly faded with age. Polly, from much looking at it, became certain that the bit of the house behind the grinning boy was Hunsdon House. But he was not Seb. From some angles his cheeky look reminded her of Leslie in Thomas Piper's shop. But he had the wrong hair to be either Leslie or Seb, too fair and long and untidy for Seb, and not curly enough for Leslie. Besides, he was older than both of them. Polly decided she simply had not met him yet. She hid the photo carefully inside her school bag before she went to sleep, because Dad was using the camp bed in her room.

The days passed. "Ah well," said Dad. "Back to Joanna again, I suppose." He kissed Polly and left. Polly went home to Ivy and David Bragge and took her photograph with her. But she hid it in her folder with the soldiers, and hid the folder in the cupboard where the cistern glopped. She did not trust Ivy not to throw it away.

"You forgot to give David a Christmas present," Ivy said, handing her a parcel from Mr. Lynn.

Polly had not meant to remember a present for David, so she pretended to be absorbed in opening the parcel. It contained a book about King Arthur and a book of fairy stories and one of Mr. Lynn's hastiest notes. Polly supposed King Arthur was all right, but fairy stories—! Still, she was sure—without wanting to think of Mr. Leroy—that Mr. Lynn had things on his mind, and she tried not to blame him.

School began next day, and rain with it. For weeks Polly arrived

at school soaking wet to find Games cancelled yet again and everyone depressed and coughing. The Superstition Club had vanished
as if it had never been. At home there was David Bragge and his
jokes to avoid, and Mum hanging lovingly over him, consulting
him about everything. "What do *you* think, David?" Ivy said this so
often that Polly took to imitating her secretly and jeeringly in front
of the mirror in her little box of a room. "What do *you* think,
David?" With it went a stupid, languishing smile. David did not
speak much to Polly. They both seemed to know they had nothing
in common.

Then, just before half-term, came a proper letter from Mr. Lynn,
thanking her for the book. It must have gone astray in the Christmas post, he said, because it had only just arrived. `Do you have`
`a hlaf trem?` he went on in his bad typing. `Or if not,`
`is oyur mother liekly to visit her lwayer`
`again? I have'ny seen yuo forages. If yuo`
`come up to London, I promise to meet yuo at`
`the statoin.`

Ivy did indeed go and see her lawyer quite often, but she saw no
reason to take Polly. "I've enough to buy without spending money
on unnecessary jaunts," she said. "You've grown out of all your
clothes again."

This was true. They spent a tiring Saturday shopping. "All
dressed up with nowhere to go!" Polly said bitterly, and she gave up
all hope of seeing Mr. Lynn.

Oddly enough, it was David Bragge who paid Polly's fare. Polly
did not understand quite why. It seemed to happen because she

met him by accident in the middle of town the day school broke up, when she was walking home with six friends. David was across the street, talking to a lady. Polly looked at them because the lady David was with seemed to be Mary Fields. She was not Mary Fields. Polly had lost interest and was turning away when David suddenly waved and came bounding through the puddles on his rather short legs—it was raining, of course.

"Hello, Polly!" he called. Polly had to stop and talk while her friends stood waiting impatiently and getting wet. "Polly," David said earnestly, "I've long felt you deserved rich rewards for sanctity and forbearance and all that jazz. Is there something you haven't got that you'd like to have? Speak up. Sky's the limit and so on."

Polly looked at his face carefully and saw he meant it. "I need a return fare to London," she said. "And some spending money for when I'm there," she added, since miracles seldom happen and it is best to get the most out of them when they do.

"Done!" cried David. "Money under plain cover this evening as ever is!" And he bounced off again, back to his lady.

He was as good as his word. He put an envelope full of pound notes into Polly's hand that night before she went to bed. Polly had a vague feeling he expected something in return, if only she could understand what it might be, but she did not let ignorance stop her taking the envelope. She wrote Mr. Lynn a hasty card and, on the day she had said, she mounted a fast train at Miles Cross Station and was rattled up to London on the morning of what proved to be the only fine day of the half-term holiday. She felt very brave and grown up, doing it, and she worried all the way in case

Mr. Lynn had not got her card or turned out to be doing something else that day.

To her relief, he was waiting for her on the platform, with the sun gleaming mildly on his glasses and a well-known large hand held out to shake hers. They were talking as if they had not met for five years—or only been away five minutes—before they had even got off the platform.

"Tan Coul must have some more adventures," Mr. Lynn greeted her.

Like a password, Polly replied, "And we *must* find out about Tan Audel soon. It's stupid not knowing him."

The horse-car, TC 123, was waiting outside, and they climbed into it, still talking. But there was a slight break in their talk as they set off and Polly discovered that Mr. Lynn still drove as heroes do. It seemed to be the way he was made. They shot into the traffic, squealing on two left wheels, cut in front of a bus, tipped a cyclist neatly into the gutter, and dived between two taxis through a gap that would have been small for the cyclist. But the taxi drivers knew a hero when they saw one and sheered off, honking their horns.

Those horns were drowned in a new outburst of honking as the horse-car shot across in front of the oncoming traffic and screamed into a side street on two right wheels. Two old ladies leaped for their lives.

"Missed them!" remarked Mr. Lynn. Polly was not sure if he said it with relief or regret. "The car's feeling its oats," he explained, realising Polly had gone quiet.

"Do—do you get killed often?" Polly said.

"Old heroes never die," said Mr. Lynn. "But I do rather surprisingly often drive the wrong way up one-way streets. I think I am now."

They were. Somehow they missed the van coming the other way. Polly tried to take her mind off this heroic driving by asking, very casually and carefully, "Were you in Middleton just before Christmas?"

"No," Mr. Lynn said, surprised. "I was stuck here with concerts. I'd have looked you up if I had been. Why?"

"I was staying at Granny's and I thought I saw you," Polly said carefully.

The little car leaped from the end of the side street and heroically dived among traffic going round a large roundabout. "You couldn't have done," Mr. Lynn said, whizzing across the front of a lorry and squealing into the next turning. "I really wasn't there."

"Did you see Mr. Leroy at all?" Polly asked. "I thought I saw him too."

With a jolt and scream of protest, the car stopped for a red light. "I did run into him just before Christmas. Yes," Mr. Lynn said, carefully and with just a touch of grimness. It reminded Polly of the way Dad talked about David Bragge. And he changed the subject by asking about her stay at Granny's.

The lights changed while Polly was in the middle of telling him about Dad and David Bragge. The horse-car set off with a bellowing roar before any of the other cars had moved. There were red lights at intervals all down that road. Mr. Lynn treated each one as if it were the starting block for the hundred-metre dash, screaming off ahead of all the other cars, only to rein in with a jerk as the next light turned red. It was fun. Polly began to enjoy the way heroes drove. She felt quite used to it by the time they roared into the street outside Mr. Lynn's flat and Mr. Lynn parked the car by the simple expedient of knocking the rear bumper off the car in front of the only space there. "I don't think my car likes other cars," he explained as he knelt in the road, putting the other car's bumper roughly back in place. "It does this rather often."

"Perhaps it would rather be a horse," Polly suggested.

"That must be it," agreed Mr. Lynn.

Mr. Lynn's landlady, Carla, opened the door for them before they got there. The baby from last time had grown into quite a large toddler, hanging on to Carla's hand and shouting, but otherwise Carla was just the same. "I thought it was you," she said cheerfully. "I heard the crash. Learn to drive, can't you!" As they went upstairs, she shouted after them through the toddler's yelling, "Get him to show you his collection of parking tickets. It may be a record!"

When they reached the privacy of Mr. Lynn's flat, Polly asked, feeling rather mature, "Is Carla a one-parent family?"

"Not quite," Mr. Lynn said. "I think there are several Mr. Carlas. It's rather confusing."

"Oh," said Polly, and felt childish after all.

Mr. Lynn gave her one of his considering looks. "People are strange," he said. "Usually they're much stranger than you think. Start from there and you'll never be unpleasantly surprised. Do you fancy doughnuts?"

They were excellent doughnuts, soft, sugary and fresh. Polly ate them absently, though, considering Mr. Lynn in return. He was behaving cheerfully enough, but he was not happy. She knew the signs, from Ivy. There was a sort of effort going into his cheerful remarks. She could feel the pushes. She decided not to say anything about it. She knew how useless it was with Ivy when she was in a mood. But Mr. Lynn was not Ivy. Without intending to, she said, "What's the matter? Are you very miserable?"

"Yes," Mr. Lynn said frankly. "But mostly I'm worried and undecided about something. I'll tell you about it, boring though it is, but there's something I'd like you to do first. I've got quite superstitious—"

"So have I!" Polly exclaimed. And they broke off for her to tell him about the Superstition Club. When she got to the Deputy Head in the mirror, Mr. Lynn gave a great yelp and began laughing properly. Polly stopped then, because she was getting unpleasantly close to telling him how she had stolen the photograph. "What did you want me to do?" she said.

"Cheer me up," confessed Mr. Lynn. "Selfish of me to drag you all the way to London for that, even though it seems to have worked. The other thing is—do you think you'd know the other heroes if you saw them? Tan Thare and Tan Hanivar anyway?"

Polly nodded. "I would. Positive." She could see them both as clearly in her mind as she could see Ivy or Nina or David Bragge.

"Then," said Mr. Lynn, "see if you can find either of them here. Or Tan Audel, if possible."

He plunged to his mantelpiece and brought down a roll of paper from it. After he had spread it out on the hearth rug and it had rolled up, and he had unrolled it and pinned it down with two books and a salt cellar, Polly saw it was a mass photograph of the British Philharmonic Orchestra. It was very posed. Everyone was in evening dress, facing the front, with their violins or clarinets or trumpets held out stiffly to the side.

"Yes, I know," Mr. Lynn said. "The BPO posing for Madame Tussaud's. Rows of stuffed penguins. The conductor comes along with a big key, probably A flat, and winds us all up. Can you see any of them?"

Polly saw Tan Thare almost at once. His face leaped out at her, in spite of an unexpected beard, chubby and carefree and possibly a little dishonest, from the front row of violins. She stabbed her finger on him, crying out with surprise. "Tan Thare! It really is! I don't like him in that beard, though."

"Neither did most of his friends," said Mr. Lynn. "He was held down and forcibly shaved on New Year's Eve. Anyone else?"

He sounded casual, but Polly could tell it meant a lot to him. She searched the photograph again. Mr. Lynn himself came to light among the cellos, although he was not so easy to find. He seemed to have faded away into the rest of the cellists, built into the orchestra like a brick. Tan Hanivar's long nose and gloomy face ought to be easier to find—and there he was! He was among the violins too, over to the right, behind Tan Thare. The gloomy face had a mop of dark hair above it, more than Polly had imagined, but it was definitely poor, shape-changing Tan Hanivar. Polly pointed. "Tan Hanivar. What's his real name?"

"Samuel Rensky. And Tan Thare is usually known as Edward Davies. Any luck with Tan Audel?" Mr. Lynn asked rather tensely.

But Polly still did not know what Tan Audel looked like. She searched and searched the mass of faces. "Sorry," she said at last. "I just don't know him."

"Him?" said Mr. Lynn. "Er—have you considered, as a female assistant hero yourself, that Tan Audel might be a woman?" He sounded really nervous about it.

As soon as he said it, Polly knew he was right. "Oh, good heavens!" she said. "I never thought!" Of course Tan Audel was a woman, now she thought. She even knew, dimly, some of the things Tan Audel was famous for. She went back to the photograph, scanning the ladies in dark dresses she had been ignoring up to then, very much ashamed of herself. And there was Tan Audel at last. She was in among the set of those big violins—violas, they were called. "Here," she said, with her finger under the strong, squarish face with strong, square, black hair. Tan Audel was not pretty. But she looked nice.

Mr. Lynn leaped up with a shout. "*Ann Abraham!* You've done it, Polly! You truly did it! I can hardly believe it!" He was so excited that Polly had to pull his sweater to get him to explain why. Then he seemed to think she might find the explanation boring. "It's like this," he said, folding himself down onto the hearth rug rather apologetically. "As soon as I joined the BPO, I found I wanted to leave it—not the orchestra's fault, just my habit of not fitting in very well—and play on my own. But I hadn't any money, and there's only a limited amount a lone cellist can do anyway. The best way to do it was to form a group, a quartet or a trio, because there are quite a lot of things four players can do. But of course they have to be known before they can make any money at it. You wouldn't believe how many good players in the orchestra wouldn't dream of taking the risk. They thought I was crazy. So did I, to tell the truth. Then you came along and told me about heroes. And then there was the horse, which made me sell a picture, and I thought: Damn it, I *can* do it! So I talked to some friends and, to cut a long story short, Ed Davies, Sam Rensky, Ann Abraham, and I got together and tried—"

"What went wrong?" Polly asked as Mr. Lynn trailed off.

"Nothing at all heroic." Mr. Lynn gave his gulping laugh. "Cold feet. If we want to form a proper quartet, we're going to have to leave the orchestra and try—but it's always possible we'll end up busking in the Underground a year from now. I thought I'd sell another picture." He pointed. Polly swivelled round to look at the pink-and-blue clown picture leaning against the wall. Her face went hot with guilt and she had to stay turned away when Mr. Lynn said, "I thought it *must* be a reproduction or at least a copy, but it turns out to be a real Picasso." He added, sounding unhappy, "It's not money, though. It's—well, are we good enough to foist ourselves on the public?"

That made Polly turn back. "Granny says the only way to find out is to try," she said. "I say that too," she added, thinking about it.

"I know," Mr. Lynn said in his humblest way. "And I hope you'll forgive me, Polly. Since it started with you in a way, I thought I'd let you decide. If you could find the right heroes in the photograph, I swore we'd go on. If you didn't, I'd superstitiously decided to scrap the whole idea."

"You took a risk!" said Polly. She was extremely glad she had not known how much depended on her finding Tan Thare and the others. "Suppose I hadn't found them? Or what if I did find them, but they weren't the ones you meant?"

Mr. Lynn bowed his head over his big hands and looked ashamed. "I think I'd have approached the ones you chose instead. You have a knack of telling me the right thing." And at that he sprang up. "Now you deserve a treat. Where would you like to go in London? What shall we do?"

The rest of the day was a great golden excitement to Polly. She had never been anywhere much in London, so it was all new and wonderful to her, whether she was in the horse-car screaming round and round the roundabout in front of Buckingham Palace because Mr. Lynn kept missing the road they wanted, or heroically belting along the Embankment, or looking at the Crown Jewels in the Tower, or eating kebab somewhere beyond that. Now Mr. Lynn was happy again, they talked and talked the whole time, but Polly only remembered snatches of what they said. She remembered being in front of the Houses of Parliament, eating a hot dog. She looked up at Big Ben and said suddenly, "Tan Coul and the others have to be on a quest for something."

"Do you insist?" said Mr. Lynn.

"Yes," said Polly. "All the best heroes are."

"Very well," said Mr. Lynn. "What are we looking for?"

Polly replied promptly, "An Obah Cypt." But when Mr. Lynn questioned her, she had not the least idea what an Obah Cypt could be.

Later they were standing looking at the Thames somewhere while Polly ate a choc-ice—she spent most of the day eating something—and Mr. Lynn asked her if she had liked the books he had sent for Christmas.

Polly did her best to be tactful. It was not easy, because the choc-ice had just fallen apart and she was trying to balance a sheet of chocolate on her tongue while she sucked at the dripping ice cream beneath. "King Arthur's all right," she said liquidly.

"You don't like fairy stories. Have you read them?" said Mr. Lynn. Polly was forced to shake her head. "Please read them," said Mr. Lynn. "Only thin, weak thinkers despise fairy stories. Each one has a true, strange fact hidden in it, you know, which you can find if you look."

"A' ri'," said Polly over a dissolving handful of white goo and brown flakes.

Later still the horse-car broke down in rush hour when they were racing to catch Polly's train. Mr. Lynn was quite used to this. Shouting that the brute always did it when he was in a hurry, he leaped out and pushed the car at a run onto the nearest pavement. There he first kicked it in the tyre, and then tore open the bonnet and prodded inside with the largest Stow-on-the-Water screwdriver while he called it a number of very insulting names. Then he kicked it again and it started. "The only language it understands," he said as they roared off again.

They arrived not quite too late for Polly's train and ran towards the platform among the thousands of other hurrying people. Polly shouted across the hammering of their many feet, "You know, the way you got the car to start is the only peculiar thing that's happened this time!"

"Beware famous last words!" panted Mr. Lynn. "Not true. Think of the way you spotted the heroes." As they came near the barrier, he stopped almost dead. Polly thought she heard him say, "Famous last words indeed!" She looked round to ask what he meant and saw Mr. Leroy coming through the crowds towards them with long, impatient steps.

Mr. Leroy was wearing a coat with a fur collar which made him look both rich and important, and he was holding a rolled umbrella out before him, slanted slightly downwards. "I don't want to hurt you with this, so get out of my way!" the umbrella said, and people obeyed it. With Mr. Leroy there was a smaller person in a sheepskin jacket. It took Polly an instant or so to realise that the second person was Seb—Seb about a foot taller than when she last saw him. In that instant Mr. Leroy's umbrella had cleared every other person out of the way and he was standing looking at Mr. Lynn. "I have you now!" said the look in the dark-pouched eyes, angry, triumphant, and accusing. The things Polly had overheard in Hunsdon House came out from hiding at the side of her mind when she saw that look, and she felt sick.

"Well, fancy meeting you here, Tom!" said Mr. Leroy. The friendly surprise did not go with his look at all.

"Hello, Morton," Mr. Lynn said. Polly wondered how he could take it so calmly. "Are you going down to Middleton?"

"No. I'm just putting Seb on the train after his half-term," Mr. Leroy said. "I assume you're doing the same with—" the dark pouches under his eyes moved as he looked at Polly "—this young lady."

Polly had an idea that Seb was looking at her too, rather consideringly, but when she tore her eyes away from Mr. Leroy to make sure, Seb was staring scornfully at a book stall.

"Yes I am," said Mr. Lynn. "And she's going to miss the train if she doesn't go now."

"Seb can look after her," said Mr. Leroy. "Got your ticket, Seb?"

"Yes," Seb said.

"Off you both run, then," said Mr. Leroy. "I can see the guard getting ready to signal. Hurry."

Mr. Lynn said, "Bye, Polly. Better run," and gave her a firm, friendly smile. Seb glanced at the air above Polly, jerked his head to say "Come on" and set off at a trot towards the ticket barrier. There was nothing Polly could do but call "Goodbye!" to Mr. Lynn over her shoulder as she ran after Seb. The train really was just about to go.

They caught the train by getting on the nearest end as it started to move. Then they had to walk down it to find seats. Polly expected Seb to lose her at this point, since he had done what his father wanted. But he stuck close behind her the whole way down the crowded train. Polly felt trapped. And she was horribly worried about Mr. Lynn. They found two seats facing one another. As Polly squeezed into one and watched Seb sit down opposite her, she was wondering if she would ever see Mr. Lynn again.

To her surprise, Seb said quite cheerfully, "Did you have a good time in London? I did."

Polly jumped rather. She had not expected him to speak. He had looked so fed up at being put in charge of her. But because he had spoken so cheerfully, she found herself replying, equally cheerfully,

"Yes. Lovely, thanks." Hearing herself, she went into a silent panic. Quite apart from the fact that Seb was guarding her, she had not the least idea what you talked about to boys of fifteen. At Manor Road no boy that age would be seen dead talking to a First Year girl. "I—er—I saw the Tower of London," she said lamely.

"I was there yesterday," said Seb. "Cigarette?"

"N-no thanks," Polly stammered, and watched with awe while Seb took out a packet of cigarettes and a silver lighter and lit himself a cigarette. It was all the more awesome because he was sitting beside a NO SMOKING sign on the train window. She could feel her eyes going wide and round.

"My father objects," Seb said, blowing lines of smoke like a dragon. "You don't, do you?"

"Oh no," said Polly.

"Good place, London," Seb said. "Better than school."

"Yes," said Polly.

That seemed to bring the conversation to an end. Polly thought she was relieved. But it seemed so awkward just to sit there that she began to feel compelled to say something else. But what? The only things she wanted to say were to ask about Mr. Lynn and why Mr. Leroy did not want him to see her. She was sure Seb knew why. But she did not dare. It was maddening. She seemed far more afraid of Seb now than she was when she was ten.

Perhaps if I could get him talking first about something else, she thought, I could lead round to it. But what *did* you say? She scrambled round inside her head, rooting in odd corners for something— anything!—she could say, and suddenly she came upon her secret visit to Hunsdon House. It dawned on her that she had a guilty inside view on Seb. "Which pop groups do you like?" she asked, in the greatest relief.

"Doors. Pity their singer's dead," said Seb. "Do you know the Doors?" Polly did not, but it did not matter. Seb told her. He talked all the rest of the way to Middleton, and all Polly was able to do was nod and listen. She never got a chance to ask anything. Before long she was glad she had put her question the way she did. The posters on Seb's walls were the groups he had liked last year, and he told her he was sick of them now. He still liked Michael Moorcock, he said, but this turned out to be a writer. "Great stuff," Seb told Polly. "You should read him."

By the end of the journey Polly was finding Seb almost agreeable. He looked much nicer when he smiled. His laugh was like Mr. Leroy's, but lower and more grating, which made it, to Polly's mind, much less fatal. A sort of elegant churring, really, she thought. And it was flattering that he did not seem to mind talking to her.

The train drew into Middleton. As they got up to get off, Seb said, "There's a disco at my school at the end of term. You could come, if you're interested."

Polly was so flustered at this that she said, "I'd love to!" and then wondered what had made her say it.

Seb said he would let her know when it was. They got off the train and walked out of the station together, into the dark and windy forecourt. Seb stopped near the fountain thing in the middle. "See here," he said quite kindly. "I warned you off a year and a half ago. You didn't take the blindest bit of notice, did you?"

This shook Polly exceedingly. By this time she had begun to believe that Seb had forgotten who she was. "No, I didn't," she said. "But you hadn't any right to, anyway!"

"You should have listened," said Seb. "You've got my father angry now, and he can be quite vile when he's angry. You'd better be careful from now on. Very careful. That's all. Want me to walk home with you?"

"No thanks," said Polly. "See you." It was a long way home from Miles Cross, but she ran all the way. It was a relief to find that Ivy and David were out when she got there. She did not feel like talking.

About a week later Mr. Lynn telephoned. Polly had got used to taking messages for David Bragge, and she answered the phone in the way she had invented to make it less boring.

"*Good* evening," she said in a silly squeak. Then, making her voice go deep and booming, "Whittacker residence here, and Bragge lodging."

"Good Lord!" said Mr. Lynn. "Is that what it is? Miss Jeeves, would you be so good as to tell Hero that Tan Coul wishes to speak to her?"

"Oh it's *you!*" shouted Polly, and found she was blushing at the telephone. "I thought it was—Are you all right? Really all right?"

"Very well, thank you," Mr. Lynn said in his polite way. But he was upset. Polly could hear he was. She clenched her teeth and half shut her eyes, thinking of all the things she had imagined Mr. Leroy doing to Mr. Lynn. "Polly, do you remember us discussing selling a picture?"

"Yes." Polly's conscience gave her a guilty jab somewhere in the middle of her chest.

"One of the ones you helped me choose," Mr. Lynn said, causing Polly another jab, "and I told you it turned out to be a Picasso. Well, it seems that we somehow got all the wrong ones. They've just found out. Laurel's been on to me, and Morton Leroy, and they're trying to trace the one I sold to buy the horse. Of course I've had to give the Picasso back—"

Oh no! thought Polly. This is Mr. Leroy's revenge. "Do they want my fire-and-cow-parsley one too?" she asked, with a further guilty jab because of the stolen photograph hidden upstairs in the cistern cupboard.

"They haven't mentioned that one yet," Mr. Lynn said. "It's a photograph, so maybe it isn't as valuable as the others. I won't say anything about it unless they ask."

"Thank you," said Polly. Then, because of her relief, her mind turned round to see Mr. Lynn's point of view. "Does that mean you won't have any money to start your quartet with?"

"I'm afraid not," Mr. Lynn said rather colourlessly.

"*All* the pictures?" said Polly. "The Chinese horse and the musicians too?"

"I can keep those two on condition I don't sell them. But I've had to give the carnival picture back with the clowns. It's fair enough. It was a mistake—"

But after all this *time!* Polly thought. She interrupted fiercely. "You're *not* going to stop doing your quartet! Not now you've decided! You mustn't!"

"Thank you for saying that," said Mr. Lynn. "That's why I rang really. I *am* going on with it. The others have said they'll risk it. But it means I'm going to be very occupied for quite some time, trying to get people to listen to us, and I'm not going to have time to see you, or think of hero business, or even write very much. I'm sorry."

"I see," Polly said miserably. "This is a goodbye call."

"Oh no, no, no!" said Mr. Lynn, but she could see it was, even though he added, "By the way, do you think an Obah Cypt is a sort of container of some kind? I see it as a small jewelled phial."

"A little vase with a lid," said Polly. "Carved out of one precious stone and worth a king's ransom. It may be. What's in it, though?"

"Something even more valuable, obviously. The water of life? The key to all knowledge?"

"Not quite. I'll work on it," said Polly. "Is Michael Moorcock any good?"

"We-ell," said Mr. Lynn. "You may prefer Asimov. I'll see you. For the moment you'll have to think of me as away on a quest for an audience."

Polly put the phone down, full of stony, Ivy-like anger. *Curses* upon Mr. Leroy! A very civilised revenge. He had stopped her seeing Mr. Lynn and punished Mr. Lynn for seeing her, all in one neat sweep. She knew she had broken the rules by seeing Mr. Lynn, which was what allowed Mr. Leroy his revenge. But it seemed so hard and horrible that her wrong-doing over the pictures should rebound on Mr. Lynn.

"I'll do something to Mr. Leroy one of these days," she said to herself. "Something quite legal this time, but quite awful." Then she went sadly upstairs and tried to read the book of fairy stories. "Cinderella! How stupid!" Polly turned to the next story, but instead of reading it, raised her head to look at the clown picture in her mind's eye. She could see it clearly. A man clown and a boy clown standing on a beach, rather dejectedly, so that they seemed gawky and lumpish in their pink-and-blue Harlequin clothes. Things had gone wrong for them. They could have been a hero and his assistant in disguise.

Resolutely Polly put her head down again and found herself looking at a story called "East of the Sun and West of the Moon." The title made her blink and think a bit. "It *could* be a way of saying Nowhere," she said aloud, doubtfully. She read it, but she could not find the one true fact Mr. Lynn had assured her would be there. The girl in the story was carried off by a man who was under a spell which made him a bear in the daytime. He warned her never to look at him when he was a man, but she did. Then of course he vanished to marry a princess, and she had a terrible job getting him back. Pointless, to Polly's mind. The girl had only herself to blame for her troubles. She was told not to do a thing and she did. And she cried so much. Polly despised her.

4

The truth I'll tell thee, Janet;
In no word will I lie

TAM LIN

Seb's disco haunted Polly. Of all the things which were coming to light in this second buried set of memories, Polly was most astonished to find how things to do with Seb had haunted her from then on. At that time it was the disco. Polly did not know how to dance and she was terrified. When school started again, she was forced to consult Nina, who had just developed a craze for disco dancing. Nina took her home and instructed her. And in this way she became friends with Nina again. Nina knew about Michael Moorcock as well. She gave Polly a paperback to read. Polly did not quite get on with it. She suspected she was too young. She thought she was probably too young for discos at Wilton College too, and she quaked.

But it all came to nothing. Seb must have forgotten he had asked her. At all events, the end of term came and he did not let her know. This made it rather difficult when she next saw Seb. And she kept seeing him from then on, here and there in Middleton, usually walking with tall, high-and-mighty-looking boys from Wilton College. Should she stick her nose in the air and look offended? Or smile as if nothing had happened?

In fact, Polly did both at once, in a confused way, the first time she passed Seb. Seb replied with a sort of wave and a sort of grin, at which the other boys looked round after her and murmured things. Polly's face went scarlet.

"That makes three strange men!" said Nina, who was with Polly at the time. She did not recognise Seb. Polly was so annoyed and embarrassed that she nearly stopped being friends with Nina again. Both of them were losing count of the times they had been friends and then not friends. This was another thing which astonished Polly. She had thought she had hardly spoken to Nina after Juniors, where in fact they dropped in and out of friendship so often that Nina went around explaining, "It's that kind of relationship, you know."

Whatever Nina thought that meant, Polly thought the real reason was that she and Nina were always getting out of step with one another, and only overlapped every so often. While Polly was catching up on discos, Nina had passed on to her tennis craze. When Polly took up tennis, Nina had moved on to ecology. And when Nina tried to interest Polly in that, Polly had discovered *The Lord of the Rings* and was reading it for the fourth time under her desk in Maths.

It was David Bragge, not Mr. Lynn, who put Polly on to Tolkien. By then Polly had got used to David's pink arms and his way of speaking. They had become quite friendly. It had started with the money for Polly's ill-fated visit to Mr. Lynn. It had gone on then because, after that, Polly had come in one day to find David roving round the kitchen like an irritated bear.

"The woman's a vampire!" he said angrily to Polly. "What does she want from life? I have to account for all my movements and every half p. these days, or she says I'm being secretive!"

"Dad let her down," Polly explained. "She wants to be happy."

David, at this, became uneasy and contrite. "Shouldn't say things to you about your mother, should I? Accept profound regrets and pretend it was never said. Right?"

"Yes, but Mum is difficult sometimes," Polly said. "When she closes down."

"Doesn't she just close down!" said David. "You're a sympathetic wench, Polly, you know. Understanding."

After that, because of her being so understanding, David took to handing Polly notes secretly, to be delivered to a certain Irishman on her way to school. Mr. O'Keefe was nearly always to be found leaning against the wall of the Rose and Crown. He always took the note with a huge wink and said, "Thank you, my darling."

"Fourth strange man!" Polly said the first time she met Mr. O'Keefe, since Nina was not there to say it for her.

David was rather anxious about this arrangement. To cover it up, he invented a game of elaborate compliments to Polly. "She's growing up so gorgeous!" he would say. "The silver-haired lovely of the eighties. What will she be like later if she's like this now? And I'm booked to be her father and give her away to some undeserving lout or other! Oh, Polly, I mourn!"

Polly supposed the compliments were meant to act like a smokescreen to distract Ivy from the notes, but they made her very uncomfortable and she wished he wouldn't. She could see they annoyed Ivy. She found she was not looking forward to the time when the divorce was at last settled and Mum and David would be able to get married.

Halfway through the summer term, a little before Polly's twelfth birthday, a packet came for her through the post. It was not a proper letter. It was something folded inside a typed wrap-round label.

"What's that?" Ivy asked as Polly tore the label off. Ivy was sitting in her dressing gown watching David eat his bacon and egg.

Polly was equally puzzled. She unfolded a medium-sized poster on rather cheap paper.

BATH FESTIVAL
Beethoven, Dvorak, Bartok
THE DUMAS QUARTET

"Junk post," said Ivy. "I'd like to know where they got your address. Throw it away, Polly."

David looked up from his dutiful eating. "It's a languishing letter from one of her numerous admirers. Eh, Polly?"

"No it isn't," Polly said, grinning. "It's from Mr. Lynn." Her eyes had found the bottom of the poster, where Mr. Lynn had scribbled,

Our first decent engagement. I know I can count on you to see
the joke in the name we chose. Is an Obah Cypt a kind of
talisman, perhaps?

T. G. L.

Joke? Polly's eyes leaped to the top of the poster again. Dumas?
What joke?

"David, that's not funny," said Ivy. "Who's Mr. Lynn?"

Polly sighed. "I went to see him in London—remember?" Of
course! *The Three Musketeers*, by Alexandre (spelled wrong) Dumas.
In the middle of the poster Mr. Lynn had helped her get the point
by scribbling things beside the printed names. *Edward Davies*, she
read, *alias Tan Thare, Porthos. Samuel Rensky, alias Tan Hanivar,*
d'Artagnan. Ann Abraham, alias Tan Audel, Aramis. Thomas Lynn,
alias Tan Coul. Polly smiled widely. It was a clever way to get round
Mr. Leroy. The poster must have gone out in a stack of others, so
that it did not look like something specially to Polly. And it was
interesting to see that Mr. Lynn thought of himself as Athos too,
even though he had not written it in.

"Oh, your musician friend," said Ivy. "School, or you'll be late."

Out of respect for the new quartet, Polly got *The Three Muske-*
teers out of the library and read it again. For a while too she kept
looking in *Radio Times* and the morning paper, in case there was
news of magnificent concerts by a brilliant new quartet now taking
the country by storm. But the Dumas Quartet never seemed to get
mentioned. Since Polly could think of no other way to find out
how Mr. Lynn was doing, she gave up looking. She took *The Three*
Musketeers back to the library and got out *The Lord of the Rings*

instead, which David said was much more her kind of thing.

After she had read it for the fourth time, Polly spent the last slack week of term and the beginning of the holidays busily writing an adventure of Tan Coul and Hero, and how they hunted the Obah Cypt in the Caves of Doom, with the help of Tan Thare, Tan Hanivar, and Tan Audel. After *The Lord of the Rings* it was clear to her that the Obah Cypt was really a ring which was very dangerous and had to be destroyed. Hero did this, with great courage.

When it was done, she put it in an envelope and addressed it to Mr. Lynn. Then, for two days, she did nothing with it. She was scared when it came to posting it. She thought of the way Mr. Leroy had come cleaving through the crowd at the station and looked at Mr. Lynn, when there was no way he could have known they were there, and she kept going cold all over. But at last she told herself it was silly to be scared. Mr. Leroy had turned up by accident to put Seb on the train. She went boldly out to the High Street Post Office and posted the story there.

She came out of the post office, with the deed done, and the first person she saw was Seb, walking along the other side of the street with a crowd of tall Wilton College boys. Seb, as he always did now, gave her his sort of wave and a grin, and the heads of the other boys turned as usual to see who he was waving at. Polly stood on the steps of the post office feeling like something caught in a searchlight beam. It can't be true! she thought. He must be here by accident! But she would have given a great deal to be able to reverse posting that letter, like playing a film backwards, and have it zoom up out of the letterbox into her hand.

For days she waiting for something awful to happen. She expected Mr. Leroy every time she ran down to the Rose and Crown with a note from David. But the trouble came from Mr. Lynn instead. A postcard came from Edinburgh. On the back of Edinburgh Castle it said,

> No, it's not a ring. You stole that from Tolkien. Use your own ideas.
>
> T. G. L.

It hurt Polly's feelings horribly. For a whole day she hoped Mr. Leroy would *get* Mr. Lynn for that. For another whole day she evolved nasty schemes for getting Mr. Lynn herself, by jumping on both his cellos. She could almost feel the satisfying splintering of precious wood under her shoes. On the third day she decided to have nothing more to do with Mr. Lynn. Ever. On the fourth day she got another postcard, of St. Andrews Golf Course this time.

> *Sorry,* it said. *I was v. tired in my last. Damaged my good cello. Forgive criticism, but you used to have much better ideas on your own.*
>
> T. G. L.

When she read about that damaged cello, Polly's mind jolted and flew to Seb passing in the street. She was appalled. I think that was my fault! she thought. But how *can* it be? She waited two days, to give Mr. Lynn time to get home to London, and then telephoned his flat. It was next to impossible, she thought as she dialled the number, for Seb to appear accidentally, or even on purpose, inside the hall of her own house.

Mr. Lynn's voice spoke. "This is a recorded message," it said like a robot. "Thomas Lynn is away on business with the Dumas Quartet. If you have a message, please give it after this recording stops. Speak on the tone." There followed a click, and a sharp beeping.

"Oh. Er," said Polly, totally disconcerted. "Um. Er. This is Polly. I just wanted to say sorry too. About the cello." Then she could simply think of no more to say. She put down the telephone, feeling cheated and incomplete. She stood. Then she turned round, threw open the front door, and looked up and down the street.

It was empty. There was no sign of Seb. She seemed to have got away with it.

Mr. Lynn did not reply. Instead, before Polly had time to get hurt again, a parcel of books arrived from Edinburgh. There was no letter, just a piece of paper from the book shop, saying in print: *Sent at the request of,* then a gap for the name, which someone had filled in as *Mr. T. Geeling.* It made Polly giggle, both for itself and because they were both thinking of ways to cheat Mr. Leroy. The books were all secondhand: Kipling's *Kim, The War of the Worlds* by H. G. Wells, *The Man Who Was Thursday* by G. K. Chesterton, and *Perilandra* by C. S. Lewis.

That was the first of any number of parcels, from all over the country, sent under all sorts of versions of Mr. Lynn's name. *The Napoleon of Notting Hill* from Hereford, from T. O. Massling. *The Thirty-nine Steps* from Oxford, from Mr. Tomlin, *Tom's Midnight*

Garden from Birmingham, from A. Namesake, and *The Oxford Book of Ballads* from Salisbury, apparently from a Chinese person called Lee Tin. And numbers more. All through those summer holidays and the autumn term that followed, parcels of books for Polly kept on coming. It seemed as if every time Mr. Lynn arrived in a new place, almost his first act was to find a book shop and get it to send Polly books under some idiotic new name.

The only trouble was that all Polly seemed to be able to do in return was to ring up the robot machine in London and tell it, "Um. Er. Polly. Um. Thanks." And to read the books, of course.

5

But aye she grips and holds him fast

TAM LIN

School started again in the autumn, with Polly and Nina both feeling very mature and Second Yearish. This was the term that Nina discovered The Doors—and made Polly look nervously over her shoulder for Seb every time Nina talked about them. Nina's parents did not care for The Doors either, or any of the other groups Nina listened to. They decided that Nina's tastes were getting corrupted and contrived somehow to push her into acting. Polly always wondered how they did it. Probably it was because they were friendly with Mr. Herring, who ran the school Drama Society. But Polly was fairly certain that Nina had only agreed to join the Drama Society on condition that she got a star part.

She was given the part of Pierrot, poor Pierrot, mournfully in love with Columbine who, of course, was thoroughly in love with

Harlequin. It did not seem to Polly to be quite Nina's thing. But when rehearsals first started, Nina harked back to her glorious career as King Herod in Juniors and decided she would be a great actress, after all.

"Mr. Herring's ideas are mag-ic!" she told everyone, Polly included, and so enthusiastic was she that Polly was persuaded to join the Drama Society too. She joined, and was made one of the chorus of clowns.

It soon became apparent to Polly, as she obediently did handstands and rolls with the other clowns, that Nina's ideas and Mr. Herring's were about as different as ideas could be. Nina wanted to rant and wave her arms about. Mr. Herring explained that he was wanting to put on a version of the old Italian pantomime in what he called "stylised semi-dance form." It was not easy to stylise Nina. If she had to be mournfully in love, she thought at least she should sing.

"No," said Mr. Herring. "The whole idea is to have dumb show to music. Think of it as a sort of ballet."

But Nina said she was sick of semi-dance. She made up a song—which owed quite a lot to the Doors—which she intended to sing during the performance when it was too late for Mr. Herring to stop her. Nobody thought she would dare. "Yes, I will!" Nina said. "This is it. Listen." She balanced a chair on a desk before Geography on Tuesday morning and stood on both and sang. The chair slipped and Nina went crashing down into the project on South America. She broke the project. She also broke her glasses and sprained her ankle.

Mr. Herring seized the opportunity to get rid of Nina. "The show must go on!" he said gleefully, and he made Polly Pierrot instead.

When Nina came back to school in her spare glasses, with her ankle strapped up, she took it quite calmly. "I've gone off acting," she said. "I'm heavily into guitar-playing instead." But, because of what her parents would say, she consented to join the chorus of clowns, where she annoyed Mr. Herring considerably by calling advice to Polly all the time.

Polly enjoyed being Pierrot. It was quite easy to pretend to be crossed in love, because Columbine was a very pretty Third Year girl called Kirstie Jefferson. Polly and Nina much admired Kirstie. On the other hand, neither of them liked the red-haired girl called Fiona Perks, who was Pierrette. Polly did not find it at all easy to pretend to love Fiona at the end. But that was the only difficulty. As rehearsals went on, Mr. Herring discovered that Polly could do flip-flops and cartwheels, and he made her do them, slowly and sadly. The part of Pierrot became strange and circus-like. Polly found she had become as enthusiastic about the pantomime as Nina had been, and she wanted to make sure Mum and David came to see it at the end of term.

"You *will* come and see it, won't you?" she said rather often.

Ivy said neither yes or no. She was in a bad mood. She and David did not seem to Polly to be getting on very well.

"You'll have to tell me soon," Polly said two weeks before the performance. "We'll be getting the tickets tomorrow."

"Will you shut up about that!" Ivy exploded. "I've told you before what I feel about your school shows. Solid boredom!"

"But this is different, Mum," Polly persuaded. "It's not a Nativity. It's supposed to be what pantos used to be before they started being Dick Whittington and things. It's more of a dance. My part's a sort of mourning acrobat."

"Oh it's arty, is it?" Ivy said disagreeably. "Then definitely no. I did my bit when you were in Juniors, and that's *it* as far as I'm concerned."

"Come on, Ivy. Where's the old esprit de corps?" David intervened. "It won't hurt to go."

"You keep out of this," said Ivy.

"I'd like to see Polly Gorgeous do her stuff," David said unwisely. "I bet she's terrific!"

Ivy rounded on him. "Gorgeous, is she? I've watched you, David. You've been making up to Polly on the sly for months now. You're always trying to get her on your side. Just leave off, will you!"

David began to be seriously alarmed. He gave Polly a look which warned her not to say anything about the notes to Mr. O'Keefe, and protested, "But that's nothing but good old togetherness, Ivy! I don't want Polly to hate me!"

"Hate you! She'd walk through fire for you these days, and you know it!" Ivy said. "Wouldn't you, Polly?"

"Oh, I wouldn't put it quite so high as that," David said. "Would you, Polly?"

Polly stood there, with Ivy looking at her angrily and David pleadingly, and did not know what to answer. If she said she hated David, Ivy would be angry. If she agreed with Ivy, David would be in trouble. "He's all right," she said. "But what about the pantomime, Mum?"

"Don't change the subject," said Ivy. "Hear that, David? 'All right,' she said. When Polly says a thing like that, she means it. I know Polly. You've got her eating out of your hand, and I'm not having it!"

Polly was annoyed at having her careful answer made to mean the wrong thing. "That's *not* what I meant!" she said. "You don't know what goes on in my mind. Nobody does."

"Yes I do," said Ivy.

"Better scarper, Poll," David said warningly.

"That's it! Advise my daughter what to do!" Ivy said.

Polly took David's advice and went upstairs to do her homework, where she sat against the glopping cistern instead and read *The Castle of Adventure*. It made a relief from the rather difficult books Mr. Lynn kept sending, and it almost distracted her from the sound of Ivy's voice downstairs. Eventually Ivy's voice stopped. Then Ivy came in and sat on Polly's bed.

"Sorry about that, Polly," she said. "Still, it's cleared the air and we know where we stand. Happiness depends on being honest. David's been quite honest with me now, and we've settled to go away for a bit together, to get to know one another again. I've rung Granny, and she says she'll have you till we get back. Would you mind terribly? We'll be back before Christmas—promise."

That meant they were not coming to the pantomime. Polly moved her shoulders against the cistern cupboard and sighed. "That'll be fine, Mum," she said nobly. "Have a good time."

"I knew you'd say that," Ivy said, which made Polly feel rather low. She would have liked Ivy to notice how noble she was being.

Still, it was good to go and live in Granny's biscuit-smelling house again, and to lie in Granny's spare bed staring up at her *Fire and Hemlock* picture. She was sure now that the picture was valuable. She was guiltily convinced it must be, since the other pictures she had chosen for Mr. Lynn had one and all turned out to be worth such a lot. She was still astonished that the Perry Leroys had not come and asked to have this one back too.

At school, rehearsals became frantic and Drama Society members were allowed to miss English in order to rehearse. Nina's Mum was helping with the costumes. She came to school almost as often as Nina in order to sew clown suits. Everyone in the pantomime and the other two plays was given a book of five tickets to sell to their relatives. Granny bought one of Polly's.

"Of course I'll come," she said. "I wouldn't miss it for worlds. I wish I could sell the rest for you, but all my friends are such old ladies you'd never get them to stir." Granny's main friends were Mrs. Gold and Mrs. Ormond, and they were indeed old. Granny always said, "I call one Aches and the other Pains. The rest of the people I know are just Grumbles and Moans."

Polly, left with four useless tickets, was struck with a very daring idea. She had been longing to write to Mr. Lynn. She wanted to tell him about the pantomime, and also of a new idea she had about the Obah Cypt. And here was a way of doing it without Seb getting to know.

She went to school with her tickets and a clean new envelope with a stamp on. At the end of the morning she went to where Nina was sitting on the teacher's desk waving a book of tickets and bawling, "Two more tickets for Saturday! Two more tickets only for the greatest show on earth!"

"I'll swop you those two tickets for my four," Polly said. "If you'll do me a favour."

"Done!" Nina said. She loved selling tickets. "What's the favour?"

"Write something on them and address the envelope for me," said Polly.

"OK," said Nina. She lay full length along the teacher's desk and poised her pen expectantly over the tickets. "What do you want written?"

It felt a bit silly now Polly came to it. Polly went pink as she dictated, "I am in this. Call me Pierrot. The O.C. is an egg-shaped locket with T.C.'s hair in it."

"Wow!" said Nina. "Mysteries! Is that all?"

"Yes, Now address the envelope," Polly said, and dictated Mr. Lynn's address.

"Hey!" exclaimed Nina. "Isn't that the strange man your Granny—?"

"Maybe," said Polly, and firmly removed the envelope. She put the tickets in it and stuck it down. Leaving Nina waving her book of four tickets and bawling, "Four tickets for Friday now! Four whole tickets! Bargain of the century!" Polly took the addressed envelope away to the school hall. She peeped in and found, as she had hoped, Nina's Mum was in there with four other Mums, sewing diamonds of colour on to Harlequin's suit.

Polly went up to Nina's Mum. "Mrs. Carrington, do you think you could post this letter for me?" She was not going to trust Nina with anything so vital. Nina's Mum was a good deal more reliable.

"Yes of course, dear," said Mrs. Carrington, and put the letter in her rush basket, with one corner sticking out so that she would remember it, Polly thanked her gratefully, and even went on being grateful when Mrs. Carrington turned to the other Mums while Polly was going away, and said in a loud whisper, "Poor kiddy! Broken home, you know. I always try to help her." But Polly had long known where Nina got her tendency to gossip from, and it did not bother her much. Her main feeling was triumph at the cunning way nothing of that letter now had anything to do with her.

The costumes were finished and tried on. Polly had to practise in hers because the sleeves were so long and drooping—after which Nina's Mum had to take the costume away and wash it before the Friday performance. It was white, with enormous black bobbles down the front. When she was dressed in it for the show on the Friday, with her hair pushed away inside a black cap kept firmly in place with sixteen hairgrips, Polly spent some time in front of the mirror in the back room, admiring herself. The Art mistress had given her a white face with purple lips and had spent a long time carefully painting an enormous black teardrop just under Polly's right eye. In the mirror Polly was rodlike and droopy at once. She could have been a bleached version of the smaller, disconsolate clown in Mr. Lynn's stolen Picasso.

She was swept away from the mirror by the two other sets of actors. The show was in three separate bits so that everyone in the Drama Society could do something. The Sixth Form were doing a one-act play about a delinquent boy in prison. The Fourth and Fifth Years were doing extracts from *The Importance of Being Earnest*, and the pantomime came last. There had been arguments

about how late this made it for the Second and Third Years, but Mr.
Herring had insisted. He said it was traditional. But it was perhaps
unfortunate that none of the three groups, or the orchestra, had
really rehearsed together before that night.

Polly went to part the curtains just a tiny crack, to make sure
Granny was in the audience. She was. In the middle, near the front,
looking small but royal in her old fur coat. The mutter of talk from
all the parents out there made Polly's stomach squiggle.

The orchestra played the overture they had not rehearsed quite
enough. A number of people behind the scenes said it was a pity
someone had chosen such modern music. Somebody else pointed
out that it was, in fact, tunes from *Oklahoma!* The curtains were
drawn. And everything proceeded to go wrong. In the first play
the delinquent boy turned out not to have bothered to learn his
lines. He made them up as he went along, with such freedom and
eloquence that the people acting with him just did not know what
to do and simply went to pieces. Everyone would have been glad
of the interval, except that no sooner were the curtains drawn
than the lights failed and left the audience in darkness. In the dark,
Mr. Herring tried to make a speech explaining this, but the delinquent boy had so unnerved him that he said, "We'll have you in
darkness again any minute now." The audience clapped him for
that.

The lights came on again for *The Importance of Being Earnest*,
but disaster is a very catching thing. The two boys playing Algy and
Ernest forgot their lines. They were supposed to be strolling round
a table eating cucumber sandwiches as they talked. When their

minds went blank, all they could think of to do was to go on walking round and round the table, eating sandwiches. Nobody realised
that anything was wrong. *"Help!"* Algy said hoarsely at last over his
shoulder. The stage manager promptly put all the lights out. He
said afterward it was the most helpful thing he could think of, but
it caused utter confusion, because the prompter could not see to
tell Ernest and Algy what to say.

The pantomime players went on, thoroughly undermined but
determined to do better. Harlequin and Columbine met among the
clowns. Harlequin, as he fell in love, trod on Columbine's dress,
which at once came in two pieces with a mighty ripping sound.
Kirstie Jefferson, luckily, was wearing tights underneath and she
managed to carry on as if this was meant to happen. Nina was so
impressed by Kirstie's coolness that she stood staring at her admiringly and forgot to go off the stage with the rest of the clowns. She
was forced to loiter miserably at the back of the stage, getting in
everyone's way, until she noticed Mr. Herring fiercely beckoning
from the wings. Whereupon she sprinted for the wings and cann-
oned heavily into Polly as Polly came on. Polly reeled on to the
stage like a drunk and was further put off by hearing an extraordinary noise from the orchestra, where the girl playing her melancholy tune on a violin had made a terrible mistake. It was so unlike
the taped tune Polly had practised to that she fell over doing her
first cartwheel. She tried to get up, but her foot was on one of her
trailing sleeves and she fell flat on her back. The audience thought
this was meant to happen and laughed heartily. This drowned the
noise of the violinist bursting into tears.

"Never mind," whispered Fiona Perks as Polly lay miserably at her feet. "Nothing's broken."

Polly gazed up at Fiona's made-up face and thought that this was exactly the irritating sort of thing Fiona Perks *would* say. "Nothing! Only my spirit!" she retorted as she struggled to her feet.

"Wasn't it *awful!*" she wailed to Granny afterward.

"So-so," said Granny. "I enjoyed most of it. And it's no more than you'd expect on a Friday."

Granny, Polly thought, was probably the most superstitious person in the world. Even the Superstition Club at its height had not been a patch on Granny. She tried to smile. "I wish you'd come tomorrow instead. I bet we get it perfect tomorrow."

And of course they did. Everyone was ashamed of Friday. The delinquent boy spent all Saturday learning his part. Algy and Ernest came early in order to rehearse their sandwich scene. The Science master worked on the lighting for hours, and Mrs. Jefferson put Kirstie's dress back together with tape to make sure it stayed. Even the orchestra tried to pull itself together.

The show went like a house on fire, as Nina kept saying. Nina's parents were there that night, to her great glee. She kept going to the curtains and looking out at them, and getting in the way of all the people waiting in the wings. Polly was rather nervous. She was meanly glad when, just after the first interval, Mr. Herring took Nina by the scruff of her clown suit and threw her into the girls' dressing room.

"I was only looking!" Nina grumbled at Polly. "It's interesting seeing everyone. Your strange man is sitting near the back. Did you know?"

Cold fear hurt Polly's throat for a moment. "Seb? Or Mr. Leroy?" Then she had a feeling that all this had happened before. "You mean my Dad?"

"No, stupid, the one you sent the tickets to," said Nina.

"*What!*" Polly exclaimed. She shoved Nina aside and sped to the stage. The audience was rows of dim pink blobs, but she saw Mr. Lynn's glasses glinting near the back. There was no mistaking the angle of them as they sat on his nose. "*Good* heavens!" she heard herself say.

"What do you expect—if you go and send him tickets?" Nina said behind her.

Polly turned round to tell Nina to keep her mouth shut about that and found Mr. Herring bearing down on them. Both of them fled back to the dressing room, Polly laughing like an idiot. She could not remember ever having been so pleased, or so flattered, or so nervous about anything in her life before. And she was sure she was going to make a worse mess of the pantomime even than Friday.

But when the time came and the orchestra started the clown music, a sort of steely goodness came upon Polly. She suddenly knew she was going to be excellent. She came drooping on to the stage exactly right, and this time the girl playing the melancholy tune on the violin got it exactly right too. Polly turned slowly through Pierrot's first cartwheel, with her legs drooping just as they should, and she had a sudden sense, as she turned, that she was part of a transparent charmed pattern in which everything had to go in the one right way because that was the only way it *could* go. She came out of the cartwheel and went on her knees to Kirstie

Jefferson, with her drooping sleeves imploringly raised. The violin sang along. And the audience began going "O-oh!" half jeering at Pierrot, but half on his side too. They went on doing it, and that was right as well. The pattern had been there always, even though they were all making it just at that moment.

Polly went through her part in it with a sort of wondering, alert stillness inside. It was right. It was even right when Kirstie laughed at her and went off with Harlequin. Polly mourned, and the clowns whirled round her, making another part of the pattern. And the audience cheered so much when Fiona Perks came and offered her pink paper heart to Pierrot that Polly felt a real gush of liking for Fiona. She swapped pink paper hearts with her, both of them laughing lovingly, like people enormously relieved about something.

As soon as the curtains closed on their last bow, Polly burst off the stage and struggled through crowds of people getting changed, out into the cold, stinging dark of the car park, to catch Mr. Lynn. He was unlocking the door of the horse-car, about to get in. Mary Fields was with him. Polly slowed down and approached rather hesitantly. But they were clearly expecting her. They both turned round.

"Hello, Polly!" they both said.

"Did you like it?" Polly asked.

Mr. Lynn nodded. Mary Fields said, "Oh, enormously! You were terrific, Polly. You ought to take up gymnastics seriously—or acting, for that matter. Shouldn't she?" she asked Mr. Lynn.

"Quite possibly," he said. Polly knew he did not really agree. She thought it was because he knew there were other things she could do better than those, but she wanted to make sure.

"Frankly," Mary said to Polly, "I wasn't too keen when Tom insisted on coming all this way. You know the way he drives. But it was worth the sacrifice. Really."

"Thanks," Polly said. She did not like Mary Fields, and she could tell Mary still did not like her, but she could tell Mary was truly meaning to be generous. She smiled warmly at her, and felt the white make-up on her face crinkle. "What was wrong?" she asked Mr. Lynn.

"Nothing," he said. "It was sheer magic, mostly because of you. But do you really want to be called Pierrot?"

"A joke," Polly explained, embarrassed because Mary Fields was standing there with her hands in her pockets, shivering. "A mixture between Polly and Hero."

"Yes I got that," Mr. Lynn said. He laughed, and put out a hand and rubbed Polly on the top of her little black cap. "Good night, Pierrot. You were splendid. But we have to go. See you."

Polly stood back while the horse-car started with a snarl. She watched its headlights come on like angry eyes and watched it leap into motion as if someone had kicked it in the rear. She waved a drooping sleeve after it and went in to change.

Changing took quite a while. Polly's clothes had got scattered by numbers of people all too excited by success to be careful. By the time she had found them, everyone else had gone. Polly came out with her hair down, but still with a chalk-white face, to find the last people distantly banging car doors and shouting "Good night!" She felt dejected. She did not feel like walking all the way to Granny's alone. Some of the roads were quite dark. But it was too late to cadge a lift now. She set off, turning left out of the school gate, under the streetlight.

Immediately there was a tall person walking beside her. Polly could see him, sideways from behind her hair, and hear his feet heavily hitting the pavement. But she could not bring herself to look properly. She knew it would be Seb. The trick with the tickets had not worked and Seb knew. Her heart banged and she walked faster.

The heavy walker beside her kept up with her. Polly could feel him waiting for her to be scared enough to look round. She put off looking, and put it off, until she came to the next streetlight, and then she could not bear not looking any longer. Her made-up face with its black teardrop turned almost helplessly towards the left. Her black-rimmed eyes met the heavy face and black-pouched eyes of Mr. Leroy.

Polly rather thought she stared at him like a rabbit. Mr. Leroy stared back sarcastically. His expensive coat made him look big as a bear. He smelled of fine cloth and expensive living. Instead of an umbrella this time, he was carrying one of those shooting-sticks with big rings for a handle that unfold into a seat. He swung it while they stared, gently and unpleasantly.

"You keep ignoring warnings, don't you, little girl?" he said. "Why?"

"And *why* to you too!" Polly retorted. She was so frightened that she seemed to have gone right out the other side, into bravery again. "Why? *You* tell *me!*"

"Laurel," said Mr. Leroy, gently swinging his stick, "my wife, is rather a special person. What's hers is hers for keeps. So, to put it bluntly, keep your thieving hands off, little girl. This is the last warning you'll get."

"What about Mary Fields?" Polly asked angrily. "Do you give *her* warnings too?"

"Mary Fields," said Mr. Leroy, "hasn't been inside Hunsdon House. Or," he added, with a specially hard and sarcastic look, straight into Polly's face, "taken anything away from there."

Polly knew then that Mr. Leroy knew all about the *Fire and Hemlock* picture hanging in Granny's house above her bed, and maybe about the stolen photograph too. The jolt of guilt that gave her, and the jolt of yet more fear, seemed to shock a lot more courage into her. "You've no right to keep warning me," she said. Her voice sounded so firm it surprised her. "It's none of your business what I do. You don't own people—you or Laurel."

Mr. Leroy's stick stopped swinging and poised, raised. Polly flinched, thinking he was going to hit her with it, but she managed not to cower away. "Do you think you're safe or something?" Mr. Leroy said. He sounded almost astonished. "Do you truly think that pendant you wear is going to keep you safe?" Polly's hand dived to make sure of the opal pendant. It was still there, a well-known little lump under her sweater. "It won't," said Mr. Leroy. "I got its measure a while back. Now will you heed my warning?"

"No," said Polly. She meant it. But one part of her mind suddenly stood away from the rest and wondered. Is this me saying that? What's so worth getting in a fight with Mr. Leroy about?

Mr. Leroy's stick swung and stopped, pointing at Polly, "In that case," he said, "prepare to regret it, little girl. Believe me, you'll regret it. You haven't even begun to see what can happen to you yet." The pointing stick poised, not quite hesitating. "You're very young," Mr. Leroy said. "You've got angry and decided to be defiant. Change your mind."

Polly found she was shaking her head. Why? asked the other part that found her doing it. He's right.

"Or perhaps you don't understand?" suggested Mr. Leroy.

The part of Polly which seemed to be questioning everything at once agreed. No, you don't understand, do you? You could have got it all wrong. He's probably only accusing you of stealing pictures. So you'll give them back before he goes to the police. But the main part of Polly had no doubt at all. She said challengingly, "Then you make me understand. You say what it's about."

"All right," said Mr. Leroy. "We are talking about Thomas Lynn. Now, for the third time, will you do as you have been told?"

"No!" Polly almost shouted. The two parts of her came together into a pillar of white anger. "I told you no, and I *mean* no!"

"You silly little girl!" said Mr. Leroy. The stick swung a little further, to point properly at Polly, and then swept contemptuously away. Mr. Leroy turned as the stick swung and walked off down the street, a triple rhythm of two heavy feet and the sharp *tweet* of the stick hitting the pavement.

Polly hurried home to Granny's, expecting horrors to jump out at her at every corner. She made herself walk, though, and not run, because she did not want Mr. Leroy to know how terrified she was. She was sure he knew everything she did.

"What's up, love?" Granny asked while she was helping Polly take the white off her face. "Didn't it go well again?"

Polly did not dare talk about Mr. Leroy in case he knew and did something to Granny.

"It was magic!" she said. "And I was superb!"

"That sounds like your friend Nina, not you," Granny said. "Didn't Mr. Lynn come after all, then?" Polly stared at her. Granny chuckled. "No. I'm not a mind-reader. He rang up and asked if you'd really like him to come. I told him about yesterday, and about Ivy being away, so he said he would."

So was this how Mr. Leroy knew? Polly wondered. Or was it through Nina somehow?

"Didn't you see him there?" Granny asked.

"Yes," Polly said grumpily. "Mary Fields came too."

"Who's Mary Fields?" asked Granny.

"Mr. Lynn's girlfriend, of course!" Polly snapped.

"I'm glad to hear he's got one," Granny said. "And you look worn out. Go straight to bed and I'll bring you up some cocoa."

6

And pleasant is the fairy land
For those that in it dwell,
But at the end of seven years
They pay a tax to hell.

TAM LIN

For a long time Polly waited in real terror for Mr. Leroy to carry out his threats. But nothing seemed to happen. Ivy and David came back, and Polly went home. Mr. Lynn did not send her a Christmas present, but that was the only unusual thing.

School started, with its usual feeling of this term being the dead end of the year. After a fortnight of it, when nothing still had happened, Polly decided that Mr. Leroy was either bluffing or trying to play on her nerves. She gave up worrying. If something happened, well, it did. If not, how silly she would be worrying about nothing.

So, as a way of defying Mr. Leroy, Polly began compiling a book called *Tales of Nowhere*. First, she made a list of all the things she and Mr. Lynn had made up about Tan Coul and Hero. Then she drew a map of Nowhere. She did a tracing of a real map of the Cotswolds and gave the places different names, except for Stow-on-the-Water. This seemed right for the way Nowhere was supposed to mix with real life. It rather pleased her to write DRAGON over the farm where Mary Fields lived. Then, rather thoughtfully, and a little frightened, she put Hunsdon House in too, right in the middle. That seemed right also. The next stage was to paint illustrations for the book she was going to write. Then she settled down to write it. This part of the plan went very slowly.

Nina meanwhile had given up acting and the guitar for boys. She and Polly were out of step again. Nina had come back to school with a figure. It seemed to have grown overnight—or, at least, over Christmas. All the plumpness which had hitherto been all over Nina had somehow settled into new and more appropriate places, and then dwindled, to make a most attractive shape. Nina looked good, and knew it. She spent perhaps half her time with other girls who were in the same happy state, comparing bosoms, talking of diets and discussing clothes. The rest of the time Nina pursued boys. The boys in her own year were considered quite uninteresting. Nina and her friends mostly went after boys in the Third and Fourth Years, but enough of the hunt spilled over into the Second Year for the boys there to start diving under desks whenever Nina appeared, shouting, "Help! Here comes Nympho Nina!"

"It's a shame she's started so early," Fiona Perks remarked to Polly. "What will she have left to do when she's an old woman of fifteen?"

Polly liked that remark. It was the kind of thing Granny said. "Nina has to be where the action is," she explained. "She always did." And she looked upon Fiona with a great deal more friendship after that. She and Fiona were rather thrown together that term anyway. They were both put in the Under Fourteen athletics team, and they both seemed to remain skinny and rodlike while the other girls burst out into hips and bosoms.

"We may be late developers," Fiona said, "but when it happens, everyone watch out!"

Polly took to Fiona more and more. They were not quite at the stage of sitting together in class, but Polly went once, timidly, to have tea in Fiona's house. Fiona's house was quite grand—not as grand as Hunsdon House, but a little on the same lines. Polly wished she dared ask Fiona round to her house in return. But things had become really difficult there.

Ivy had decided David was deceiving her. Their Christmas holiday seemed to have done very little good. Sacrifice in vain! Polly thought bitterly. They could have come to the pantomime for all the good it did! Now, whenever David was out, Ivy telephoned all the people she knew and asked them where David was. One day Polly came in from school to find the kitchen a white fog from the kettle, and Ivy, red in the wet heat, busy steaming David's letters open.

"I know. I'm insecure," Ivy said defensively to Polly. "But he's so secretive. How can I trust a man who doesn't tell me anything?"

This made things awkward for Polly, because she was still taking notes from David to Mr. O'Keefe. She had thought David would stop asking her to take them after the row before the pantomime. She was astonished when he stopped her, the first day of school, and handed her another note.

"Be an obliging wench," David said pleadingly. "Don't stop up my only outlet, there's a gorgeous. I'll do the same for you one day."

He seemed to mean it so much that Polly's annoying tender-heartedness was aroused. Besides, she liked Mr. O'Keefe and the way he called her his darling. She agreed to take the note, and a good many others after that. All that term, even after the kettle incident, Polly was taking notes for David.

Then, towards the end of term, she came in from a cycle ride with Fiona to find Ivy opening a parcel. Polly could see the address, because it was on a label and very black, first the name of a book shop in Exeter and then *MISS POLLY WHITTACKER* . . . "Hey!" said Polly. "That's mine! It's from Mr. Lynn."

Ivy's answer was to thrust the half-opened parcel across the kitchen table at Polly. "Is it?" she said. "Then show me. Open it right out. Go on."

Under Ivy's suddenly ominous stare, Polly rather resentfully finished undoing the brown paper. In it was a fat book called *The Golden Bough*. The typed slip of paper with it said it was from Mr. Tea-Gell. Polly grinned. But her pleasure was a good deal spoiled by Ivy taking the book by its covers and shaking it, and then spreading the brown wrapping out to make sure there was no other message.

"It's all right, Mum," she said. "I know it's from Mr. Lynn. That's the way he always does it now."

"Yes, but I don't, do I?" Ivy said. "Where does it say it's from him?"

"The name he gave the book shop," Polly explained. "It's a joke. His initials are T.G.L."

"It makes a good story," said Ivy.

"What do you mean?" said Polly.

"Mr. Lynn, Mr. Lynn!" said Ivy. "You may be always on about this Mr. Lynn of yours, but I don't believe he exists. *I've* never set eyes on him!"

"Yes you have!" Polly cried out. "In London—the first time you went to the lawyer."

"No I did not," said Ivy. "You went by yourself in a taxi, as you well remember! You always were a sly little devil, even in those days. I can see now that you went to meet Reg behind my back. Oh, I have been a fool!"

Polly felt horrible. For a moment she wondered if Ivy had gone mad. But she felt so hurt and bewildered that she thought Ivy must be quite normal. If a person is mad, they cannot say things that hurt you. "Granny's met him," she said. "Ask her."

"She'd only stick up for you. It's no use asking her," said Ivy. "She spoils you rotten, just like she did your father. And I reap the reward!" The front door clicked quietly. Ivy heard it. "David!" she shouted. "Come in here a moment!"

David came in slowly, sensing trouble. "The old homestead feels a bit stirred," he said. "What's the earthquake about?"

Ivy held the book and the typed note out towards him. "David, did you do this?"

David looked, wincing a little. "Not guilty. I couldn't write a book like that to save my life. All that research—" He stopped, seeing the way Ivy was looking. "I didn't give it her, if that's what you mean. It's that admirer fellow again. Whatsisface."

"I know it was *supposed* to be," Ivy said grimly. "My lady here has it all set up for you, doesn't she? She makes herself up this story about this man who doesn't exist. No doubt she believes it. She doesn't know truth from lies, just like her father! Then you step in and start sending her presents, pretending they come from her Mr. Nobody!"

"That's not true!" Polly shouted. And David said at the same time, "Be reasonable, Ivy. Why would I send Polly presents?"

"Why indeed?" Ivy said. There was a sort of miserable triumph to her. "Because she's been running your errands for you, hasn't she? *I saw you look!*" she shouted as David's eyes met Polly's without either of them being able to help it. "Don't deny it. She's been taking your love letters for that Irishman to hand on, in spite of all you *swore* to me before Christmas—!"

"Just the odd pound on the dogs, Ivy," David said.

He would have done better to have denied everything. The resulting row seemed to shake the house. David got as angry as Ivy and roared that he was not going to stand for being spied on. Ivy screamed that he had reduced her to it by ganging up with Polly. David yelled that he did not care two hoots about Polly. Ivy accused both him and Polly of lying. Polly, in tears by now, tried to make at least David believe that Mr. Lynn had sent her the book. That made Ivy angrier than ever, and she sent Polly away upstairs. Polly defiantly grabbed *The Golden Bough* off the kitchen table as she went, at which Ivy screamed, "Yes, take your ill-gotten gains! Much good may they do you!"

Polly closed the door on David yelling that he did not send Polly that book. She went upstairs and tried to read it. But she was too upset. The book shook in her hands and she could not focus on the pages. The only thing she could seem to do was to get out all Mr. Lynn's longer letters and go through them again, first to assure herself that Mr. Lynn indeed existed, and then to lay them all out as proof to Ivy. She knew Ivy would come up and talk to her. She was dreading it.

She was right. Ivy came in about two hours later. She had been crying and was carrying a letter.

"Polly," she said, "how could you do this to me?"

"I didn't do anything," Polly said sulkily. "Mum, look at these letters. Mr. Lynn sent them. He *is* real."

Ivy picked a letter up and glanced at it. "Typed," she said. "Anyone can type a letter, and it was you that typed them by the look of all those mistakes." Before Polly could protest that there was no one she knew with a typewriter, Ivy dropped the letter back on Polly's bed. "Tell all the lies you like in your own mind," she said. "It's when you tell them to me that it matters. You've been secretive with me. You've destroyed my happiness with David. You've made him secretive too. I can't have it, Polly. You'll have to leave."

"Leave?" said Polly. She did not understand.

"Leave," said Ivy. "It's my only chance of mending things with David. I had this letter from your father a while ago. Read it. He wants you to live with him and Joanna in Bristol. So there you'll go as soon as school ends. You and Reg should see eye to eye. He believes what he wants to believe too."

Polly took the letter Ivy held out. At first she could focus on it no more than she had been able to focus on *The Golden Bough*. It swam about behind blinding, rebellious thoughts. The same thing was happening to her now that had happened to Dad two years ago. She was not secretive. Neither was Dad. But Mum was not the kind of person who listened when you told her things. So you ended up not telling her, and when Mum realised, she was hurt. And when Ivy was hurt, she shut you out completely.

While Polly was thinking these things, some parts of the letter steadied enough for her to pick out phrases: *a right to see my own daughter . . . very welcome in Bristol . . . try living with us at least . . .* Well, Dad seemed to want her anyway.

It was settled that Polly should go to Bristol the first day of the Easter holidays. Polly packed her clothes and books in boxes for Ivy to send after her. She seemed to be packing all the rest of term, living in a house she no longer really lived in, going to a school she no longer really belonged to.

She kept looking at things and thinking, This is the last time I'll listen to Nina discussing bras, or This is the last time I'll have a French lesson here, or This is my last Indoor Athletic practice. She felt empty with waiting for her new life to start. But every so often, bitter thoughts spurted up into the emptiness. Everyone seemed to have hurt her, including Mr. Lynn. He just thinks of me as a sort of mascot, she found herself thinking. I don't know why I bothered to have a row with Mr. Leroy about him. She was glad to be leaving. Almost the only thing she was sorry about was not going on with her new friendship with Fiona Perks.

PART THREE

WHERE NOW?
allegro con fuoco

1

It was mirk, mirk night, there was no starlight;
They waded through red blood to the knee,
For all the blood that's shed on earth
Runs through the springs of that country.

THOMAS THE RHYMER

Ivy, stony and distracted, hurried Polly to the station on her way to work. Polly was carrying the things she would need for the first week in her old duffel bag. Among those things were her stolen photograph and the folder with the five soldiers and Mr. Lynn's letters in it. She was not sure any longer that they were valuable, or quite why she wanted them, but she did not want to leave them in case Ivy threw them away.

The train went early, and Ivy had forgotten to go to the bank the day before. She had to buy Polly's single ticket to Bristol with her credit card. "Have you got any money?" she asked Polly irritably.

"Not much," Polly said.

"Well, you won't need much, except on the train," Ivy said. "Your father will be paying for you after this."

Polly cried out, in a sudden spurt of anxiety, "But, Mum! Suppose he doesn't want me!"

"Then you can both make the best of it," said Ivy. "You're not coming back *here*." She put Polly on the train and went away without waiting to see if Polly found a seat.

It was a long journey. Polly had to change trains at Swindon. By that time she was so hungry that she bought a roll in the station buffet there. It cost nearly all the money she had. Polly had not realised food was that expensive. She ate the roll and went on reading *The Golden Bough*. She read *The Golden Bough* the whole way. At first, as the train drew out of Middleton, she had thought she felt too nervous to concentrate on it. But as soon as she read the beginning, with its strange story of the man pacing round the sacred grove waiting for the man who would kill him and take his place, she was gripped. From here the book went on a voyage of discovery through beliefs and stories Polly had never imagined before. She read as absorbedly as she had read Mr. Lynn's first parcel of books: through "Artemis and Hippolytus," "Sympathetic Magic," "The Magical Control of the Sun," "Magicians as Kings," "Incarnate Human Gods," "The Sacred Marriage," and it was Swindon. Then to "The Worship of the Oak," "The Perils of the Soul," "Tabooed Things," "Kings Killed at the End of a Fixed Term." Polly was about to begin on "Temporary Kings" when she looked up to find she was in Bristol Temple Meads.

Dad was waiting for her outside the ticket barrier. Polly had a moment of shock when she realised his hair had gone white, nearly as white as Granny's. Dad must have felt some of the same shock too, because he stared at Polly as if he was not quite sure it was her. But almost at once he smiled his well-known crinkled grin and wrapped her in a sinewy hug. He had gone thinner, Polly could feel.

"Ye gods!" he said. "You look almost grown up! Did you have a good journey?"

"I read," Polly said, and showed him the book.

Dad made a face. "Heavy stuff," he said. "Come on. We have to get a bus. Joanna uses the car to go to work in."

On the bus Polly expected Dad to ask her about the row with Mum, or at least to want her to tell him about school. But he asked nothing at all. Instead he chatted, very amusingly, telling her things about Bristol. They had a strange accent there, he said, and the oddest thing about it was the way they put an "l" on the end of any word that ended in a vowel. And he told her a joke about the Bristol woman who called her three daughters Eva, Ida, and Norma—only, because of her accent, they came out as Evil, Idle, and Normal.

Polly laughed. All the things Dad said made her laugh, but the effect of Dad's talk was to make Polly feel unfamiliar and shy, as if she was a visiting stranger whom Dad was politely entertaining. Well, he hasn't seen me for years, she kept telling herself. And there was no doubt Dad was glad to see her. "It's marvellous to have you here at last!" he said every so often. "Joanna's going to love it."

They got off the bus at a place where there were big, square-built houses, made of blocks of pinkish stone, all rather rich and elegant looking, where they walked about for a while. Polly thought at first that they were walking to the house where Dad lived, but after they had been along the same road twice, she realised they were just walking about. Dad talked happily, and they walked until it got dark and Polly started to shiver. At length Dad looked at his watch.

"I think Joanna should have recovered from work now," he said. He took Polly to one of the square stone houses further up the street.

Dad and Joanna had a flat that was the top floor of the big stone house. Dad unlocked the door and showed Polly into a high-ceilinged hallway with clean, clean painted walls and a carpet like very clean porridge stretching away into the distance. Ornaments—painted spoons, marble eggs, shells—were placed in careful clusters on white tables along the hall, or hung in patterns on the walls.

"Oh. By the way. Take your shoes off," said Dad. "The carpet."

He took his own shoes off. Polly did the same and padded after Dad in her socks along the porridge carpet, feeling as strange as you did going to the house of a new friend at school. At the end of the corridor there was a white-floored kitchen which had green enamel lights, trailing green indoor plants and a white, white scrubbed table in the middle. Joanna was standing at the table, pouring hot water out of a bright red kettle onto tea in a Chinese pot. She raised her smooth, dark head to look at them, and Polly at once felt completely untidy. Everything about Joanna was beautifully neat.

"Joanna," said Dad. "This is Polly."

"How nice to meet you at last, Polly," Joanna said. She said it in a cool, social sort of way, as if Polly had only dropped in for a cup of tea. But then, Polly reminded herself, she and Joanna *had* never met before. She thought at first that Joanna was actually surprised to see her—maybe she had expected a smaller girl—but after a minute or so Polly decided that the look of surprise was to do with the way Joanna's eyes were wider open than most people's. Joanna's dark, pretty eyes almost strained open most of the time, as if Joanna was perpetually trying not to raise her eyebrows at something. "You'll need the bathroom," Joanna said to Polly. "Reg, the tea hasn't infused. Don't pour it till we get back."

She showed Polly the bathroom. It was a wonderful, palatial room of gold and grey, lined with mirrors, with a grey carpet on the floor, grey-and-gold bath, grey towels, gold soap. Even the toilet paper was grey, stamped with golden flower patterns.

"What a beautiful flat this is," Polly said awkwardly.

"Yes I like to keep things nice," Joanna said. "Reg wants a cat, but I've told him we can't. Cats make almost as much mess as children do."

Polly started to assure Joanna that she would try very hard not to make a mess, but Joanna was gone by then. Polly used the beautiful grey loo and hoped she had used the right one. There was another thing that looked like a loo, which Polly thought was really a duvet—no, bidet, that was the word. She looked anxiously round in case she had messed anything, and went back along the porridge carpet to the kitchen, where Dad and Joanna were making polite, public sort of conversation over scented tea. Polly did not like the tea, but she politely did not say so.

Everything in the flat was neat and beautiful except the spare room. That had brooms in it, cardboard boxes, the ironing board and an old red couch that had to do as Polly's bed. This seemed to trouble Joanna terribly. "I hope you won't be too uncomfortable. We haven't organised in here yet," she said. "We don't go in for visitors much." And she raced around, laying out three mauve towels of different sizes, and making up the couch with lilac-striped sheets and matching blankets, while Polly hung uselessly about asking if she could help. "Oh no," Joanna said. "This is a thing your hostess should do."

She kept saying the same thing when Polly asked if she could help get supper. Joanna did it all, with neat, precise movements and much careful folding of tinfoil over things. Polly hung round, watching, not knowing what else to do. "We're vegetarians," said Joanna. "I hope you don't mind."

Polly did not mind what she ate. She started to say so, then thought it sounded greedy and turned it into a mumble instead. And when supper was ready, she could not help thinking, No wonder Dad's gone so much thinner! But of course she did not say so. Dad seemed happy enough, smiling and laughing from Joanna to Polly, but after a while Polly could not help wondering at the way Joanna and Dad never said anything personal to one another. It was all polite talk, as if they were entertaining Polly. Perhaps they did not like to say anything that mattered in front of her until they were used to her.

There turned out to be a dishwasher, so Polly could not help with the washing-up either. They went into the beautiful living room, where the carpet was like thicker, hairy porridge and the chairs were white leather, and sat listening to tinkling music. Polly did not remember Dad liking this kind of music before.

"Are we going to show Polly Bristol?" Joanna asked. "Shall I take the day off work tomorrow?"

"No, no," Dad said hastily. "I know what a brute your boss is. I'll take the day off and show her."

Polly did not sleep well that night. The visitor's couch was not comfortable. And she felt strange, agitated, and peculiarly uneasy. Something was odd somewhere, something was not quite right. From the way Joanna behaved, it seemed almost as if she thought Polly was only here on a short visit. But surely that couldn't be true? Dad *must* have told her that Polly was living here now. Or had Mum not explained to Dad properly? That could be it. Ivy had written to Dad, but in her stony mood she did not always say things completely. And Dad was not behaving as if he thought Polly was here for good either. In which case, how awkward it was going to be when Polly had to explain.

These thoughts made Polly feel so strange in the end that she unpacked the stolen photograph from her bag in the dark. She did not like to turn on the light, in case she fell over a broom or the ironing board and disturbed Dad and Joanna, but she gripped the little oval frame in her hand as she wriggled back among the lumps in the couch, and it was somehow comforting. She fell asleep clutching it.

Next morning she tried to ask Dad and Joanna straight out if they knew she was living with them now. She tried several times, but she never seemed to get further than "Do you know—?" Joanna was hurrying through her routine of getting off to work and was far too busy getting Polly's breakfast as well to listen or talk. She still would not let Polly help. Polly gave up for the time being and decided to ask Dad during the day.

After breakfast she and Dad walked to Clifton Suspension Bridge. While Polly admired it, Dad told her the famous story of the Victorian lady who had tried to commit suicide by jumping off the bridge. But it was such a long way down to the Avon in the gorge beneath that the lady's crinoline had acted like a parachute and saved her life. Then he told her the equally famous story of the students who had jumped off the bridge one April Fools' Day on the end of elastic ropes. They had stayed there, bobbing up and down like yo-yos, until the police had hauled them all up and arrested them for disturbing the peace. Polly laughed. But it seemed to get more and more difficult to ask Dad if he knew this was not just a visit.

They walked to the Zoo then. Polly found she could not ask straight out. But in front of the polar bears she said bravely, "I seem to be an awful trouble to you and Joanna—"

"That's just because Joanna hasn't settled down and got to know you yet," Dad interrupted quickly. "Give her time." He sounded so confident that Polly thought, with great relief, He does know! That's all right, then.

They looked at sea lions and elephants, and then went to the Tropical Bird House. That was quite magical to Polly, because the birds were all loose inside, darting past their heads to perch on the trees, which were also growing there, indoors, under the glass roof. The moist, warm air was full of twittering and flashing wings.

"It's like when I dream I'm inside my own brain!" Polly exclaimed. "Oh, I'm going to come here often and often!"

"I hope so," Dad said, rather soberly and devoutly.

The way he said it made Polly anxious again. "Do you know which school I'll be going to in Bristol?" she asked, trying to sound casual.

Dad laughed. "That's a knotty problem in this town," he said. "Let's not worry about that for the moment. Plenty of time when we've all settled down."

Polly's uneasiness came back at that, and grew. It went on growing all through the day, interesting though the day was. They had a snack at the Zoo and then went to see one of the first ever iron ships. Polly could hardly take it in for her uneasiness. And once again, when they went back to where the flat was, they stayed outside, walking about, until Joanna had time to recover from work. Polly looked back to the old days and knew that Dad was very nervous about something. As soon as she knew that, her uneasiness flooded everything else, blotting through all her other feelings like spilled bleach. Her throat felt like a sore white tunnel of shame. Dad hasn't told Joanna! she thought. He didn't tell her I was coming, and he hasn't told her I'm here for good! But it did not seem possible. Dad was not like that. It was only Mum who said he was secretive.

She was so bleached through by her uneasiness that she found it hard to eat even the small nut cutlet Joanna cooked for supper. Dad was now talking feverishly. Neither Polly nor Joanna laughed at his jokes. Joanna simply got up and went to fetch the sweet.

She came back and set a glass of yoghurt in front of Polly. "Polly," she said, "without wanting to pry, is there any chance of your telling us how long this visit of yours is going to go on? Reg and I do have to go out tomorrow night, as it happens."

Shame bleached Polly right through. She knew for certain that Dad had not told Joanna. He had simply hoped, or made himself believe, that Joanna would take to Polly. And Joanna hadn't. "Oh, that's all right," she said brightly, without even having to think. "I'm going tomorrow morning."

"What time train?" Joanna asked, almost eagerly.

Polly glanced through her hair at her father. There was profound and utter relief on his face. "Ten o'clock," she invented. She was drowning in bleach. That look on Dad's face. Mum had been right about him after all.

"Then we can all leave here together," Joanna said. "If we go really early, I'll have time to drive you to the station."

A bleached kind of pride rose through Polly's shame. "That's perfectly all right," she said. "I can easily find my own way."

"Then it's all settled," Reg said heartily. "What shall we do this last evening?"

Polly nearly said, "Play Let's Pretend," but she bit it back in time. They watched television and Polly went to bed early, where, to her surprise, she slept a heavy sleep, as if she had been drugged. She still felt drugged when she got up next morning and packed, putting her nightclothes and the photograph back in her bag on top of the other things that she had never even taken out of it. In the same heavy, half-awake state, she went into the kitchen, where Joanna was racing through her routine as before.

"I'm afraid I haven't time to pack sandwiches," she said to Polly. "But you can get something to eat on the train, can't you?"

"Of course she can," said Reg. "Hurry up, Poll. We have to get to work."

Polly nibbled some nutty brown toast she did not want, and then the other two were racing her out of the flat. Outside in the road, Reg waved goodbye to her as he and Joanna hurried to where the car was parked. "Shall I drive today?" Polly heard him say, "Or is it better if I guide you out?"

Polly was left standing on the pavement with her duffel bag hooked on one shoulder. She turned and walked the other way. Her pride would not let her stand and watch the car drive away. She heard it drive off as she reached the end of the road. Then, when it was too late, she remembered that she had no money and no ticket back to Middleton. And he never even asked me if I had! she thought. She knew it was her own fault too. She had been too bleached with pride to remember. But she also knew that Dad had not asked her about money because that was part of the pretence that she was only here for a short visit. Naturally, she would have a return ticket, and spending money for her stay.

Polly went on walking away. She walked among strong stone houses, then she walked among rows of older, airier houses joined together into yellow terraces. She walked through a stretch of green park with bushes. It rained a little. The sky was full of rolling, thick clouds, black as bruises and fat and wet. It did not surprise Polly that rain kept falling out of them. And yet, in a queer way, she was surprised at everything. She kept on walking. She crossed a road and walked on more green, under bare trees swaying and clawing against the clouds. Through the black branches she saw two lofty grey towers holding an upside-down arch of white metal. There's the Suspension Bridge, she thought, and aimed towards it.

You had to pay to go on the bridge. Polly felt in her pocket and found her last two p. She handed it over and walked out to the middle of the bridge, under the great upside-down arch of the suspension cables. The bridge was a flat double strip under the cables, hung high, high up between two cliffs. Polly walked out to the middle and stopped. The wind took her hair there and hurled it about. She leaned both arms on the chubby metal fence at the edge and looked down, dizzyingly far, to the sinewy brown water of the Bristol Avon racing between thick mud banks below. The wind hurled seagulls about in the air like wastepaper. The bridge swayed, and rumbled under cars passing behind Polly. March, she thought. Wind. The trees on the opposite cliff were the same bruise colour as the clouds, only pinker. There were no leaves yet. She thought of the parachute-crinoline lady, and wondered if something like this had happened to her too.

A long time later, when she was nearly frozen, the wind flapped Polly's hair in her face so hard that she had to turn her head to shake it away. Among the flying light strands of hair, she caught sight of someone standing at the far end of the bridge, leaning on a stick and looking at her. Only a glimpse, of a tall, bulky figure with the wind flapping its coat. Polly kept her head turned towards the river. She counted a hundred. Then she looked. Mr. Leroy had gone by then, but she knew it had been him. Now she knew whom she had to thank for the situation she was in.

She turned and walked back across the bridge. Mr. Leroy was not going to be able to stand and gloat over her. But what was she to *do*? There was a notice pasted up at the end of the bridge. SAMARITANS, it said, and a telephone number. But Polly had no money to telephone, and if she begged money off someone and rang them up, the first thing they would do would be to get hold of Dad. It would be the same if she explained at the railway station, or went to the police. They would get Dad, and he would be exposed, and so would Polly's shame. And Joanna would open both eyes so wide. Anyway, it was all Mr. Leroy's doing really. But she still had to do *something*.

Polly thought, If I see a policeman, I'll say I've lost my memory. And set off walking again. This time she went steeply downhill and walked and walked. Terrace after terrace of elegant houses, but she never saw a single policeman. Then I'll go to the railway station and tell them I've lost my memory there instead, she thought. Somewhere near a big church she met a traffic warden and asked him the way to the station. He was kind. He directed Polly just as if she was a car.

"After the Centre, you drive over three roundabouts, see."

"I see," said Polly. "Three roundabouts."

"That's the ideal," he said.

They really do say it! Polly thought. Evil, Idle and Normal. She knew she was going to get lost, not being a car, and she did.

She found herself in a part with tall office blocks, narrow towers of office, each with a thousand windows. Like stripes of graph paper, she thought. The wind hurled seagulls round the graph paper and old peanut packets round her feet. She turned a corner, and instead of offices, she found a narrow street. Here the houses were suddenly old, dark, and a little bulging. Like stepping from Here to Nowhere, Polly thought.

She went up the winding, lane-like street and there, like part of Nowhere coming when she called, she passed a small car crouching against the kerb with a parking ticket flapping from its wiper. It was cream yellow and kettle-shaped, and Polly only had to flick her eyes to its number plate to make sure. TC 123. She passed it without even slowing down. Mr. Leroy was not going to realise that she had recognised that car. But inside, she was saying, Oh, thank heaven! over and over again. Oh, thank heaven!

2

They'll turn me in your arms, lady,
Into a serpent or a snake

TAM LIN

Polly went on walking, but now she had somewhere to go. She was following a tugging in her head. It was like an instinct, the way migrating birds go, or salmon swim, sure and unhesitating, to the right place in the end. It took her round in a devious U-turn, back through the small streets, under the graph-paper buildings, across two very busy roads and up a slanting street to one side, to the elderly-looking front of a concert hall. Notices were stuck on it, one for wrestling—THE WESTON WHIRLWIND V CLAPHAM PETE—and one for a concert—THE DUMAS QUARTET TONIGHT 7:30. The part that said DUMAS QUARTET was an oblong strip of paper stuck on top of some other name and flapping loose in the wind. But it was there. Thank heaven!

The doors of the hall were shut. Polly knew at a glance that she could not get in that way. She only turned her eyes sideways to make sure, and to read the notice, and walked on without pausing, so that Mr. Leroy would not know, uphill and round the side, a way she could not have found without her instinct, and arrived at a side door, which was not quite shut.

She went straight in. Nobody seemed to be about, but now she had something to guide her beyond instinct. There was music. Overhead somewhere there were thumps and shuffling. Maybe it was the wrestling. The music was coming from below. Polly went down bleak stone steps, and down more, with the music getting louder all the time. She opened a door.

Inside was a dingy green-painted cloakroom sort of place, fairly brightly lit. In the middle of it, four musicians were sitting on tubular metal chairs in front of music stands, playing. They seemed so wrapped up in what they were playing that Polly simply stood by the door, not liking to interrupt. It did not matter anyway. Her instinct had brought her to the right place.

Mr. Lynn said, "Just a minute," and stopped playing. The rest of the music broke off while he was leaning his cello on its spike against the chair and carefully laying his bow across the seat. The first violin said, "But I *swear* I got that right this t—" to Mr. Lynn's back as he went over to Polly.

"What is it, Polly?" he said, without fuss or exclamation, quite quietly. "What's wrong?"

Now that Mr. Lynn was really there, standing in front of her in shabby old jeans, with his chin covered in unshaven golden hairs and a faint, familiar scent coming off him, Polly found it hard to speak without crying. She blurted out what had happened with Dad and Joanna, and then bit her lips together hard.

"Jesus wept!" said Mr. Lynn. "Lucky we happened to be here."

Polly breathed in, then out. "And even if I *had* any money, I can't go home." Her voice started to jiggle about. "Mum thinks—thinks— Anyway she says I ganged up with David against her."

"I see. Pig in the middle again," said Mr. Lynn. "Can you go to your grandmother?"

Polly nodded. Tears were pushing to get out of her eyes.

"Then don't worry about a ticket," Mr. Lynn said. "I'll get you one. Wait till you feel better and then we'll see what we can do."

Polly waited, breathing fiercely in and out. When her tears had stopped pushing and retired a little, she nodded. Mr. Lynn put his large hand in the middle of her back and guided her over to the other three. They had been talking together, tactfully, in small murmurs, but they looked up with interest as Polly arrived.

"Polly Whittacker," said Mr. Lynn. "Ann Abraham, Sam Rensky, Ed Davies." He gave one of his gulps of laughter. "I told you we were all heroes, didn't I?"

The three faces broke into friendly, recognising smiles. They know all about me! Polly thought in amazement, looking from Ann's frank friendliness to Ed's twinkle, and on to Sam's great, gloomy grin. She almost felt as if she knew them too.

"Polly finds herself stranded," said Mr. Lynn. He looked up at the ceiling. "Now, who might happen to have the times of trains to Middleton?"

There was a groan and a laugh from the other two as Ann bent down to a bag on the floor beside her.

"We wonder why Ann doesn't trust motor transport," Sam Rensky said.

Ann turned her face to Polly while she dug in the bag. The dark hair dangling across it was almost the same colour as Joanna's, but nothing like so neat, and Ann's brown eyes looked out among the strands, direct and amused, with friendly creases underneath. "I never ride with Tom if I can help it," she explained. "It's far too frightening."

"Tom's what I call a creative driver," said Sam. "And the cello's always allowed the best seat."

"I was told you were his very first passenger," Ed Davies said to Polly. "What horrible bad luck!"

Funny to think of Mr. Lynn telling them all about her, Polly thought. She felt better already. Sam got up and fetched her another tubular chair from the stack by the wall. Ed took the timetable from Ann and propped it on a music stand, where he held it down with his violin bow so that they could all see it. There was a through train at six-thirty.

"That's the one," said Mr. Lynn. "I can put you on that and still have time to get ready for the concert. I'll phone your grandmother and ask her to meet the train."

He went away to look for a telephone. Ann said, "Would you like some coffee?" Polly still did not like coffee, but she nodded shyly. Whereupon Ann pulled a thermos flask out of her bag and poured Polly a cupful. It was warm and dark and sweet, and Polly found it surprisingly nice.

Ed Davies said, "What *isn't* in that bag, Ann?"

"Would you like a sandwich?" Sam Rensky said to Polly. When Polly nodded, he fished in his trouser pocket and produced a bent cheese sandwich wrapped in plastic film. Ann and Ed laughed.

"Sam always has food somewhere," said Ann.

Sam smoothed the sandwich out and passed it to Polly. "I'm not like other people," he said mournfully. "I have hollow legs. It's a great trial."

The sandwich was warm as well as bent, but it made Polly feel almost good again. Ann poured her another cup of coffee to go with it, and by this time Polly felt she knew them all well enough to explain, a bit shyly, to Sam that he was Tan Hanivar the shape-shifter and that shifting shape took a lot of energy. "I expect that's why you're always hungry," she was saying when Mr. Lynn came briskly back.

"Your grandmother says you're not to worry. She'll be at the station to meet you," he told Polly.

"Thank you," Polly said gratefully.

"Tom, you never told me I was a shape-shifter!" said Sam. "What's Ed?"

"He calls music out of the air," said Polly.

"I do! I do!" Ed said enthusiastically.

Mr. Lynn gave Polly one of his blandest joke-sharing looks. "Sometimes," he said, "it can be quite deadly."

"Hey!" cried Ed, as everyone laughed.

"And what am I?" Ann asked Polly.

Polly saw Mr. Lynn looking at her with interest. They had never yet decided what Tan Audel did. But now she saw Ann, with her square, quiet face and her deep, friendly brown eyes, Polly knew exactly what Tan Audel did. "You never give up," she said. "But your main gift is the gift of memory. You remember everything—"

Ed and Sam exclaimed, and looked at one another in astonishment. "How did she know?"

"Knowing things is Polly's heroic gift," said Mr. Lynn. Polly had not realised before that she had a gift herself. It was a surprising discovery. She and Ann looked at one another and laughed, Ann, with her head flung back, obviously very pleased.

After that, everyone became more sober. Ann said doubtfully to Polly, "Would you mind *very* much if we got on with our practice?"

"We agreed to give the same programme as the Hertzog Quartet," Sam explained, "because they'd already printed all the stuff."

"Which means doing one thing we've only done about twice before," Ed said. "We're having devilish problems with our ensemble in that one."

"Oh yes. I didn't mean to be a nuisance," Polly said.

"You're not a nuisance," said Ann.

Everyone waited while Mr. Lynn considered Polly, tipping his face until Polly looked at him, just as he had done at the funeral, to judge whether she would be all right.

"I think I will be," said Polly. "I've got your book to read."

Mr. Lynn nodded. That seemed to reassure the others, and they got down to playing music again. While they were making strange

whinings and plunks, tuning strings, Polly moved her chair back
and got out *The Golden Bough*. But she hardly got halfway through
"Temporary Kings" and nowhere near "The Sacrifice of the King's
Son." The practice was too fascinating. She laid the book down on
the floor and leaned forward to listen and look.

The music halted as she did so. "What did I do now?" said Ed.

"Nothing," said Mr. Lynn. "Polly, for the love of the strange gods
of the heroes, don't do that to that *book*!"

Polly looked down at the book, bemused.

Ann said, "Tom, I really do think you have eyes in the back of
your head now!"

"You've got it open, lying on its face," Mr. Lynn said. "The poor
thing's in torment."

"One of his obsessions," Sam said to Polly.

"Humour him," said Ed. "So that we can get on."

"Or I shall never send you another," said Mr. Lynn. But he
looked round at Polly as he said it, to make sure she knew it was
one of his half-jokes. Polly hastily shut the book and laid it down
again, and the practice went on.

Of all the things Polly found she had forgotten, some six years
later, this was the one she was most hurt and astonished not to have
remembered. At the time, she had kept telling herself that she
would never forget this afternoon. How could she have forgotten
how kind they all were, without the least fuss? Even more, how
could she have forgotten watching and listening while they practised, as if it was a special private performance just for her? They
made it seem like that, by turning and looking at her apologetically

when things went wrong, or smiling at her in triumph when the music went right.

Ed seemed the one everyone blamed when it went wrong. Polly was rather indignant about that at first. Ed was small and round and only just as tall as Ann, and she thought they picked on him because of his size. But after a while she began to realise that it was Ed himself who took it on himself to be in the wrong nearly every time one of the others made a mistake. She was pretty sure Ed was pretending, because the others all got ashamed at admitting they were wrong. Polly began to suspect Ed was really a superb violinist, despite the daft, dismayed look he kept on his face while he played.

Beside Ed, Sam Rensky's face went through incredible contortions. It was a rubbery, long-nosed face—his nose was nearly as long as Granny's—with a long chin like a rubber boot toe. He was as tall as Mr. Lynn, but a good deal skinnier, and the violin looked like a little toy under his long chin. Above it, his face grinned, glared, pursed its lips and ran down to new shapes in ripples. You might have thought he was mad if you had not known he was living the lovely sounds he and Ed were making. Bright, sharp streaks of sound, Polly thought. If you were able to hear lime juice, it would sound like violins.

It took Polly some time before she could hear Ann's viola at all. The composer never seemed to give it a bit on its own, and Ann did not help by keeping her face plain and straight as she played, with her jaw sort of ground downwards to hold the big viola in place. But at length Ann did have a piece on her own—Polly heard it several times, because Sam kept coming in at the wrong place—

and the sound was vibrant and full, not as low as Polly expected. Ann played as precise and sweet as Ed, and there was a sort of excitement behind her playing quite at odds with the plain look on her face.

Polly probably watched Mr. Lynn most—Tom, that was. She began to think of him as Tom a bit, now there were three other people all calling him Tom. Apart from that glimpse on television, she had never seen him play his cello. He sat wrapped round it in a way that amused her, with his head bent to dwell in the cello's sound. One huge hand deftly planted itself on the strings, firmly trembled there—the trembling was something all four did—and then moved elsewhere while the bow carved sounds that thoroughly surprised Polly.

Up to then Polly had thought of a cello as an accompanying sort of instrument, deep but a little dull. Certainly Mr. Lynn made it chuff and rumble at times, but that was only one of the things he made it do. He seemed to be able to make every sound, from a melodious groan to high song right up in the same range as Ann's viola, either in a tactful undertone, or a smooth shout, or a stringy rasp. But it was the bell-like song in the middle which surprised and delighted Polly most. She liked that even better almost than the moments when Sam or Ed would gasp, "Put your back in it, Tom!" and the music suddenly widened until it seemed amazing that only four of them were making it.

I am lucky! Polly thought. Dad and Joanna seemed to be something that had happened last month, instead of only that morning. Just how lucky she was Polly gathered from their talk during the times they were all leaning forward, pointing at the music on the stands with their bows.

A lot of these times they were saying things like "Sam should be watching Ann when Ann comes in off the beat here," or "Tom, how about starting that forte here, instead?" or "OK. Let's take it again from D." But they said enough round the edges of these things for Polly to gather that they had been asked to do this concert at very short notice, late last night, because the Hertzog Quartet, who should have been doing it, had all gone down with flu. They were pleased to get the chance to play, but they were all rather nervous. And but for this chance, they would have gone back to London today.

Finally they all put down their instruments and stretched. Ed said, "That'll have to do," and Sam said, "I'm starving."

"Polly and I had better go," Mr. Lynn said. "Will someone look after my cello?"

Polly stood up, rather regretful. She would have liked to hear the proper concert now.

"Wait a moment," Ann said. "Money."

"Oh, yes. A whip-round for Polly," Ed said. "She'll need to eat on the train, won't she?"

Each of them gave Polly a pound. She was so grateful, she almost cried again.

"It's nothing," Ann said. "We happen to have it. You don't. I'll see to the cello, Tom."

Polly and Tom left the peeling green cloakroom with Ed and Sam, who were going to look for food. "And we have to look for my car," said Mr. Lynn. "I know I left it somewhere quite near." It was dark outside by then. He took Polly's bag off her, and they set off the opposite way to Ed and Sam.

"I saw it," said Polly. "That's how I knew you were in Bristol. It had a parking ticket."

"It's used to them," said Tom. "Where was it?"

"I'm not sure," Polly said.

"Lucky we left time to look, then," he said.

They crossed the two busy roads, which were now busier than ever. As they arrived safely on the other side, Polly asked hopefully, "Do you think you might marry Ann?"

"Not a hope," Mr. Lynn said cheerfully. "Ann has her own ideas about such things."

They turned into a narrow street with old houses, which Polly was sure was the street where she had seen the horse-car, but it was empty, all blue twilight and orange streetlight. The wind met them here. It whipped Polly's hair in front of her, set Tom's anorak rattling and the rubbish in the gutter rolling and pattering as they walked up the street.

Polly thought of herself walking in the wind all morning. She found she was able to talk about Dad and Joanna now without threatening to cry, and she began telling Tom, shouting against the wind at first, and then talking normally, as they turned into another narrow street, where the wind was less. There was no car there either. Paper and old leaves tumbled gently along behind them.

Mr. Lynn yelped with laughter over the grey-and-gold toilet

paper. "I wish I'd known you were here, having that kind of time," he said.

"It makes me think," said Polly. "What happens to all the people who don't have someone like you they know?"

"God knows," he said very soberly. And they walked the rest of the way down that street without speaking. The rubbish pounced and pattered behind them in the wind. Almost like little creatures running after us, Polly thought in a dreamlike way.

At the end of the street they were among the graph-paper towers and the wind was fierce. "This is wrong," Polly said. "It was in an old street."

"I know. This is the most confusing town I've ever been in." Mr. Lynn turned round to go back up the old street. Polly felt him go stiff. "I think we'll keep on the way we were going," he said carefully.

Polly turned too, against the wind, and looked back up the street. Her dreamlike feeling at once became the feeling of pure nightmare. For a moment, as you do in nightmares, she could not move. In the middle of the dark little street, the pattering rubbish was slowly piling upon itself, floating slowly and deliberately into a nightmare shape. It could have been a trick of the wind, but it was not. It was too deliberate. Plastic cups, peanut packets, leaves, and old wrappers were winding upwards, putting themselves in place as parts of a huge, bearlike shape. As Polly watched, a piece of newspaper rose like a slow ghost to make the creature a staring face. Tom seized her wrist while she stared and pulled her away, among the tower buildings. They did not exactly run, but they went in long strides as fast as they could walk. Both of them kept looking back. The creature of rubbish was following, billowing on pattering, manlike legs.

"What can we do?" said Polly. "Throw a lighted match at it?" Her head was turned over her shoulder. It was coming rustling after them against the wind.

"I thought about that, and I don't think so," Mr. Lynn said. "There's a risk it will just come after us burning. Let's find somewhere where there are a lot of people."

Beyond the towers, they came to some kind of shopping precinct. It was wide and paved and quite well-lit, with lighted shops all round. A lot of people were there, heads down against the wind, hurrying, so that the place was full of banging feet.

The creature of rubbish came after them faster here, travelling in swoops, changing shape as it travelled. Polly could see the thing more clearly every time she looked. She could see the spaces between the writhing newspapers and the peanut packets riding in it alongside dead leaves.

It was collecting more as it came. Every time Polly looked, it was larger, with more legs, but it never fell apart and it always had that staring newspaper face.

"It's mostly made of air," she said. "It may not be able to hurt us."

"Do you want to bet on that?" said Mr. Lynn.

As he said it, the thing was near enough to put out a pattering piece of itself and search towards their heels, so near that they could hear the hundred papery parts of it scuttling along the pavement. They both ran. They ran sideways across the precinct, behind a kiosk and some concrete seats. But the thing streamed sideways too, round the kiosk and rattling across the seats, and kept on coming after them. Quite a few people looked up curiously as Tom and Polly pelted past them.

"No one else can see it!" gasped Polly.

"I know. Proper clowns we must look!" Mr. Lynn panted. "If only we could find my damn *car*!"

They raced along beside lighted shops and whirled round a corner into another open stretch of precinct. They could tell by the rustling and rattling that the thing was close behind. Both of them were sure that the car was somewhere over to the left of this space. Tom took Polly's wrist and dragged her over that way. And then retreated hurriedly as the newspaper face and a storm of small rubbish rose billowing and reaching for them. As they backed round the corner again, Polly caught a glimpse, between the spaces of it, of a dark, bulky figure standing watching against a lighted shop window.

"Mr. Leroy—"

"Yes," Mr. Lynn said. "I know." It was that quiet manner of his that ran you up against silence. Since Polly was not ten years old any longer, she knew better than to say any more. She simply sprinted back the way they had come, with Tom's hand lugging at her wrist and the creature scuttling close after, wondering if this nightmare would ever end. They missed the way they had come into the precinct and simply plunged up the first street that seemed to lead away.

And there, up a short hill, was the horse-car crouched against the kerb at last. Tom let go of Polly's wrist to get out his keys as they dashed towards it. He got there before Polly. When she pelted up, he had the doors open and was throwing her bag into the back seat.

"Get in," he said. "Fasten the seat belt."

Polly dived into the passenger seat. While she was fumbling with the belt, the car started with its usual whinny and jerk. She looked up to see its headlights glaring two bright spots on a solid, writhing mound of rubbish. The great newspaper face leered. It was entirely blocking the end of the narrow street.

"Hold on. I'm going to drive through it," Tom said. It was one of those times when heroic driving might pay off, Polly thought dizzily. The car clunked into gear and leaped from the kerb, roaring. They hurtled at the thing of paper and leaves. Blue, orange and red paper whirled in the lights, a solid thickness, and the great white paper face seemed to stoop at them, so real that Polly almost saw eyes in the crumpled eyeholes. It was too real.

"Tom!" she screamed. "*Ian Hanivar!*"

Mr. Lynn swore and dragged the steering wheel round. Polly had an instant's slow-motion glimpse of Sam Rensky sliding sideways off the car bonnet along with a cloud of little glass cubes from the windscreen. On the other side there was Ed Davies, with his mouth open, yelling. "Tom, what the hell—!" Polly heard faintly through the hole in the windscreen. They nearly hit Ed too. The tyres shrieked as Tom missed Ed by bouncing up on the kerb on the other side of the street. They jolted down again. He was still driving flat out. Polly supposed she must have turned round then, because she had another glimpse of Sam Rensky rolling over in the road, trying to get up and looking utterly astonished, before they screamed round a corner and she could see nothing but white cobweb shapes from the broken windscreen.

"Stop!" she shouted. "You ran him over!"

Mr. Lynn found a handkerchief somehow and punched at the smashed windscreen with it over his fist as he drove. The car wagged. "Sam was all right," he said. "I think. Ed was there. I'm getting you to the station before anything else happens."

Polly helped smash the rest of the glass out of the front window. The wind howled in. They were both shaking. Polly wanted to scream out that this was the meanest trick yet of Mr. Leroy's. It was meaner even than all the things he had done to Polly herself. He had nearly made Tom kill Sam. Sam had probably been badly hurt anyway. But she knew Tom would not talk about Mr. Leroy.

"Was it Sam and Ed all along?" she said as they roared along a huge, orange-lit road. "Not paper at all?"

"I don't know," Tom said. "I just don't know." Polly thought he was going to run into silence then, but he went on, "What is it about us?" and roared through some traffic lights just as they turned red. Cold air whistled in Polly's hair. "We make things up, and then they go and happen. I wrote you a letter something very like this."

Mr. Leroy uses them, Polly wanted to say. But there was more to it than that. She thought of Mr. Piper's shop in Stow-on-the-Water, which seemed to have nothing to do with Mr. Leroy. "I don't know," she said wearily.

The car bucketed round a corner and screamed up the slope to the station. A big, lighted clock said twenty-five past six. In a dreamlike way Polly noticed birds roosting in a row along the hand of the clock. "Just time!" said Tom. They jumped out of the car and left it standing while they ran inside through the glass doors. Tom used a credit card, like Ivy, to get Polly a ticket. It seemed to take hours. Polly snatched up the ticket and they pelted to the platform to find the train already there, standing waiting. There were still two minutes to go.

Tom handed Polly her bag, panting. They were both still shaking. "Will you really be all right?" he said.

"I will now," Polly said. "But what about you? You won't be able to give your concert if Sam's hurt, will you?"

"That I shall have to go and find out," he said. "Don't worry about us. Better get on the train." He reached out and undid the handle of a door and swung it open for Polly. The other hand he put behind Polly's head and squashed her face against his old anorak for a second. "Take care of yourself."

The burr of his voice coming through the anorak almost drowned the sound of footsteps coming up beside them, but not quite. Out of one squashed eye Polly saw polished black shoes stop and stand just beyond Tom's. "This is becoming more than just a joke, Tom," said Mr. Leroy's chesty voice.

Mr. Lynn's hand changed direction. It was now pushing Polly hard towards the open door of the train. "Get on it, Polly," he said quietly. "Quick. It's just going."

The whistle blew as he spoke. Polly scrambled up the steps and the door slammed behind her. The train moved before she could

turn round, and she was moving further away when she did turn
and look. Mr. Leroy and Tom were standing face to face on the
platform, leaning towards one another, in fact, both talking angrily
at once. She was fairly sure Tom was shouting at Mr. Leroy. She did
not blame him, considering that Mr. Leroy had probably just
ruined the Dumas Quartet.

3

But, Thomas, you shall hold your tongue

THOMAS THE RHYMER

P olly did not seem to be able to read on the train. She felt odder and odder, and the things which had happened in Bristol began to seem more and more phantasmagoric. Long before the train reached Middleton, the only parts that were real to Polly were Sam Rensky sliding off the car bonnet and terrible worry because of the way Mr. Lynn had shouted at Mr. Leroy.

Granny met her at Miles Cross with a taxi, which was just as well because Polly had a high temperature by then. "Mr. Leroy made Sam Rensky look like a monster!" she told Granny indignantly.

Granny felt her forehead. "I'm not surprised," she said.

She put Polly straight to bed and called the doctor the next morning. Polly had flu. It was the season for it, the doctor said. Stay in bed.

Polly lay in bed and worried about Sam and Mr. Lynn. The flu got into her head, the way flu does. By the time her temperature came down she was really not clear what had happened in Bristol. Sometimes she doubted her clear memory of Mr. Lynn's large hand squashing her face against his old anorak.

But the time in the green cloakroom watching the quartet play never seemed to be touched by doubt. It stood out, quiet and real, from all the rest.

Granny said very little about what had happened. Polly only remembered one thing Granny said, in the taxi. "I'm ashamed, Polly," Granny said. "Your Mr. Lynn behaved better than my Reg." And that was all she said. Granny seemed to take it for granted that Polly was living with her now. When Polly began to get up, she found that Granny had been round in a taxi and fetched her things from Ivy.

For quite a while after that, Polly lay around fretfully reading *The Golden Bough* and annoying Granny considerably by insisting on having a proper bookmark so that she would not need to lay the book down on its face. She had to mark her page in some way or she kept losing her place, and she could not find where she had left off in Bristol for days. "The Hallowe'en Fires" was it, or "The Magic Spring" or "The Ritual of Death and Resurrection"? Or was it "Kings Killed When Their Strength Fails" or "Kings Killed at the End of a Fixed Term"? It took her ages to discover that she had been in the middle of "Temporary Kings."

She worried about Sam Rensky. But she did not dare tell Granny, or write to Mr. Lynn, or even phone, because Mr. Leroy had proved he really did know all she did. She had to wait until nearly the end of the holidays, when a postcard of Bath Abbey arrived for her. It was written in clear, bold writing that she did not know.

Don't worry. Sam is made of rubber and the show went on even though he was black and blue.

Love from us all, Ann

Polly was glad, but quiet. She did not see how she would ever manage to see Mr. Lynn again.

She still felt quiet when she went back to Manor Road. It was rather embarrassing at first, because everyone had thought she was leaving and was very surprised to see her. Fiona was the only person Polly explained to, and she did not tell even Fiona very much. Fiona was delighted to see Polly. "I'm glad you didn't leave," she said. "You'd have missed a right joke if you had. Look at Nina!"

Nina was into clothes and hairstyles as well as boys that term. She came to school in a shiny golden hat and purple spangled tights. She got herself new glamorous glasses. She experimented with false eyelashes.

"I shall die!" said Fiona the day Nina's eyelashes slithered down inside her new glasses during Biology and fell off onto a dissected frog. "I'm getting a figure now, by the way. If I breathe in, I almost have a waist. How about you?"

"Sort of," said Polly. As Granny remarked when Polly introduced her to Fiona, both their figures were a pinch of faith, a spoonful of charity, and the rest entirely hope. But she admired Fiona's red hair and told them both not to wish their lives away.

Polly and Fiona took Granny's advice, on the whole, and turned their attention to other things. They invented a sport called *slodging*. You pretended you were urban guerrillas who were planning to blow up the Town Hall or some other target. You sneaked into the place and spied out the best place to plant your bombs. In this way Polly gatecrashed a number of places at least as imposing as Hunsdon House and was once caught red-handed lurking in the yard at the back of Woolworth's. Polly could not think what to say and had to leave it to Fiona. Fiona said a boy had thrown her purse over the wall and she and Polly were looking for it. "It had my dinner money in it," she explained, with an artistic sniff.

Oddly enough, Polly remembered *slodging*. It seemed to be in both parts of her memory. So why was it she had not remembered her thirteenth birthday party? Granny said invite some friends. She knew Polly needed cheering up. Polly invited a number of people, including Fiona and Nina. And it turned out that Nina, as well as Granny, admired Fiona's red hair. With Polly's party as her excuse, Nina bought a packet of red hair dye and tried to dye her hair. But she forgot to read the instructions on the packet.

The result was spectacular. For one whole day Nina blazed through the school like someone's prize dahlia, red and sort of blonde and near-black in streaks, with her hair in an enormous shock. Her Mum met her at the school gates and marched her to a hairdresser. Nina arrived at Polly's party with almost no hair at all. That was, Polly knew, about the last time Nina's Mum had any say in what Nina did. What made her forget that?

And here was another thing Polly had all but forgotten. About a week later, right at the end of term, when Nina's hair was already beginning to grow back in little wriggles, they all went on a school outing to the Cotswolds. It was a scorchingly hot day and Mr. Partridge, who was in charge, began to look martyred long before they even reached the Cotswolds.

Polly envied Nina her cool hairstyle. Sweat ran out under Polly's hair, wetting her neck and dripping past her ears. She drank five cans of fizz while they were seeing round the Roman Villa. Laughing and shouting, they were herded back on the coach again, getting hotter and hotter. Fiona's freckly face went a pale mauve which clashed with her hair. Polly was in a hot, fizzy daze by the time the bus stopped in the market square at Stow-on-the-Water.

Out they all got again. Mr. Partridge gathered them all round the cross in the middle and told them it was a very old Saxon cross. The sun beat down. Polly stayed at the back where it was cooler. People round her filtered quietly away, over to the supermarket to buy more fizz.

"Oh boredom!" said Fiona. "What's the first sign of sun-stroke?"

Polly looked round, over her shoulder. It was there. It was still there. Thomas Piper Hardware. There was a display of garden seats outside this time. It would be cool in there. "Let's pretend we want to buy a lawnmower," she said.

The idea made Fiona giggle. They were edging quietly away when Nina came plunging after them, asking in a loud whisper where they were off to.

"Nowhere that would interest you, Nina," said Fiona. Since Fiona did not like Nina much, that, Polly thought irritably, was a stupid thing to say. Naturally, Nina crossed the square with them, and they all went into the clean, cool shop together.

School holidays must have already started in Stow-on-the-Water. The only person in the shop was Leslie. He was sitting at the cash desk in a brown overall some sizes too big for him, minding the shop. These days he had a lot of fair, curly hair. Polly could only just see the skull earring glittering through the curls. Leslie's face lit up cheekily at the sight of them.

"Ay, ay!" he said. "What can I do for you today?"

This was invitation enough for Nina. She leaned her elbows on the cash desk and stuck out her much-discussed bosom at Leslie. "A lawnmower," she said.

Leslie pretended to back away. "My doctor told me to give those up," he said. "Lawnmowers are bad for you. Where are you from?"

"That's telling," said Nina.

"We're three mystery women," said Polly.

"What have you got besides lawnmowers?" said Fiona.

"Wouldn't you like to know!" said Leslie. "Come on, tell us where you're from."

"Wouldn't *you* like to know!" said Nina.

Everyone seemed to understand everyone else so well that the flirtation went with a swing for some time. Then Leslie pointed to Polly. "I know you," he said. "You came in once with that fellow who looks like my Uncle Tom." When Polly had finished being astonished that he remembered, Leslie said, "And you're all from Middleton, aren't you?"

"How do you know that?" exclaimed Nina.

The questioning turned the other way round for a while, with Leslie playing mysterious, until he laughed and said, "Saw you getting out of that coach. Tweedle Brothers, Middleton. I'm coming to Middleton myself soon. That's why I asked." All three of them clamoured to know why. Leslie winked at Fiona and said, "Heard of Wilton College?"

"You're never going *there*!" said Nina. "It's a Public School!"

"I am so!" said Leslie. "Won a music scholarship. I start next term. Tell me your names and I'll look you all up when I come."

None of them really believed him. Nina said pull the other one. "Other what?" asked Leslie. Fiona said Leslie would be a fish out of water there. Polly said college boys were not allowed to meet girls from the town.

"*I* will. I'm different. I'll be out and about," Leslie promised. "I swear I'll meet you. What's the date today?"

"July the twenty-fourth," said Polly.

"Then September the twenty-fourth," said Leslie. "Let's make a date. Come on, tell me a good place to meet."

"Town Hall steps?" Fiona said dubiously.

"What time?" said Nina.

"Yes, if we *are* going to make fools of ourselves, we don't want to stand on the steps all day," Polly said. "When?"

"Nor do I want to," said Leslie. "I tell you what—Oops!"

A tall man in a brown overall like Leslie's came and leaned both knotty hands on the cash desk. His glasses glinted ominously at Leslie. Leslie edged away, looking thoroughly subdued. "Are you girls wanting to buy anything?" Mr. Piper asked unpleasantly.

None of them could think of anything they could even pretend to buy. Nina gulped. Fiona looked at the floor. Polly stared. Mr. Piper was in some ways quite startlingly like Mr. Lynn. He was the same height, with the same sort of high shoulders and the same forward thrust of the head. His face was a very similar shape. But there, to Polly's relief, the likeness stopped. Mr. Piper's mouth was pinched with self-righteous bad temper. His face was lined with peevishness and his eyes were dark. The hair above it was grey, cropped as short as Nina's.

"I see," he said. "Then get out, all of you! I know your kind. I'm not having girls like you in my shop!"

Fiona blushed bright, unhappy mauve. Nina sullenly unhitched herself from the cash desk. Polly said, "We were only talking. There's no need to be so rude."

"There's talk and talk, isn't there?" Mr. Piper said nastily. "Out!"

They began to move sluggishly towards the door. Nina, with great presence of mind, said loudly, "Half past twelve—lunchtime!" and looked ostentatiously at her watch, which in fact said twenty minutes to three. Leslie, looking demurely down at the desk, nodded slightly.

"Get out!" snarled Mr. Piper.

They hurried outside into the heat. "What a horrible man!" said Fiona. Polly nodded. She hated to think that she had, in some back-to-front way, half made Mr. Piper up. The likeness to Mr. Lynn made her feel sick.

"I was clever, wasn't I?" said Nina. "Over the time. Do you think he'll—"

But at that stage they were interrupted by Mr. Partridge, in a mood which made him at least as unpleasant as Mr. Piper, striding across the square and shouting to know where the three of them had been.

4

They'll turn me in your arms, lady,
Into a deer so wild,
But hold me fast, don't let me go

TAM LIN

David Bragge left Ivy soon after Polly was thirteen. Polly knew because Ivy came round to Granny's house at the start of the holidays and told her about it. "I'm not saying it was all your fault," she said to Polly. "But it was partly through your slyness and meddling. I couldn't trust him after that. I was only trying to get a little happiness for us both and now it's gone."

Polly squirmed. Her time in Bristol had left her raw and embarrassed. Ivy did not seem to her to be telling the truth any more than Dad did.

"Is that all you have to say?" Granny said to Ivy, after an hour or so.

"Well she can come back now," said Ivy.

"She's not coming," said Granny.

"She's my daughter," said Ivy.

"And you sent her off without making sure she had anywhere to go to," Granny said. "But not once—not *once!*—have you mentioned that this afternoon. You haven't even asked how she got back here to me. She stays here, Ivy. That's my final word."

Granny was altogether warlike that summer. She was determined that Polly should be legally allowed to live with her, and that there should be money for her keep from both Reg and Ivy. She sailed out, like a small upright army of one, to do battle with offices and banks and solicitors. She got her way too. When Polly went to be interviewed with Granny at one of the offices, she heard a man in a side room say, "Oh my God, it's Mrs. Whittacker! I don't care what she wants—just give it her!"

After that interview they went to a tea shop for a treat. Granny loved treats. They had coffee and cakes, and Polly had ice cream as well. She had taken to coffee after the coffee from Ann Abraham's flask. It had seemed like the perfect drink then, and it still did. She still thought ice cream was the perfect food. The difficulty of drinking one while eating the other fascinated Polly.

"You *are* being generous," she said to Granny, out of her new embarrassed rawness. "Arranging to keep me, I mean."

"No, I'm not," Granny retorted. "Being generous is giving something that's hard to give. After I gave up teaching, I'd next to nothing to do and I began to feel no one in the world needed me. Now you need me. It's a pleasure, Polly."

"Thanks." Polly contracted her throat with ice cream, expanded it again with coffee, and asked, "What made the man in that office say 'Give it her!' like that?"

Granny chuckled. "Remember that day I was so late home? I had him that day. Refusing this, denying that, saying maybe to the other. And I lost patience, I said, 'Young man', I said, 'if you don't give me what I want—and I made you a perfectly reasonable request—I shall just sit here until you do give it me.' And I did," said Granny. "I sat in front of him and I looked at him. They couldn't close the office at closing time."

Polly laughed. She could just see Granny sitting there, unbeaten, small, a lot smaller than Polly was herself now, filling the office with her personality and her bright, unnerving stare. "How long did he last?"

"Two and a half hours," said Granny. "He was a tough one. Most of them only last twenty minutes."

Polly laughed again and looked up in the middle of laughing because the table got dark from the shadow of someone standing beside it. It was Seb. He was standing staring at her in a confused sort of way, awkwardly clutching a camera. "I saw you through the café window," he said. He seemed as tall as the ceiling. Polly didn't know what to say, except that she really had not done anything this time. Her hand rattled her coffee.

"And I'm her grandmother," said Granny. "Are you going to sit down, or have you put out roots in the floor?"

At this, Seb evidently remembered the very polite manners he had been taught. He apologised to Granny and, to Polly's surprise, slid into a chair at the table. But once he was there, he refused cake and ice cream and coffee, and just sat. What does Mr. Leroy think I've *done?* Polly wondered, near to panic.

"Talk about photographs," Granny advised Seb, at which Polly jumped guiltily. "I see you're carrying a camera."

Seb took her advice. He talked of shutter speeds and lenses, types of camera and kinds of film. Of lighting, developing, and printing. It was his latest passion. Polly was bored stiff, even through her alarm. At length Seb turned to her and said, "I really came to ask if I could photograph you. Would you mind posing for me outside? It won't take a minute."

"And it won't hurt a bit," said Granny. "Well, we've finished here. Better go outside and get it over, Polly."

Seb photographed Polly beside the tea-shop railings. Then he photographed Granny too because, he said, she had an interesting face. Granny snorted. "I'll bring you the prints when I've done them," he said. "You live just up the road from us these days, don't you?"

Then, at last, he went. Polly realised that Mr. Leroy still kept a very close watch on her and turned shakily to Granny. "What did he want?"

"Goose!" said Granny. "You, of course. The poor boy's smitten pink over you."

"I don't believe it," said Polly.

But it seemed to be true. Seb arrived at Granny's two days later with the photographs, and stayed all afternoon explaining the exact method he had used to develop and print them. This time he was much less awkward. He told them he preferred not to be called Seb these days, but Sebastian, and that he was doing A Levels next year. After that he intended to be a barrister. He looked at Polly most of the time he talked. Polly tried not to be awkward either, but it was not easy when someone so tall and old and well dressed seemed to admire her so much.

She did not like the photographs as all. Seb had done things with strong light and dark shadows that made Polly and Granny look like two white-haired witches. "Well, you see," Seb explained to Polly, "you're not beautiful, or pretty, but your face is interesting, and I've brought out the interest."

"*What* a thing to say!" Granny exclaimed when he had gone. "He'll go far with the girls, that one, on those kind of compliments! My pretty granddaughter *interesting!* I never heard such stuff!"

"You don't like him, do you?" Polly said, in great relief.

"When he's noticed there are other people in the world besides himself," Granny said, "there might be no harm in Master Sebastian. But I'm prejudiced. He comes from That House." Granny always called Hunsdon House That House.

Seb came round rather often after that. He lived so near. It was, Polly felt, almost the only drawback that summer to living with Granny. Granny was marvellous. She had only two faults, as far as Polly knew. The first one was surprising—Granny was scared of small animals. Mintchoc, who adored Granny as much as Polly did, was always bringing her mice or frogs or voles and laying them lovingly at Granny's feet. Whenever she did, Granny climbed on a chair and screamed for Polly. It always amazed Polly, and irritated her too, to see someone as dauntless as Granny standing on a chair clutching her skirt and screaming at a mouse.

"Don't hurt it!" Granny shouted. "Don't kill it! It's somebody's dead soul!"

Polly was amused and exasperated. "How *can* I kill it if it's dead anyway?" she said, carrying the mouse or frog to the window.

"You can and it is," Granny said, quite impervious to reason. "Is it gone?"

"Yes," said Polly.

That was Granny's other fault, of course—superstition. It was because of Granny's superstition that Polly went on wearing the little opal pendant, although she knew Mr. Leroy had found a way to get round it. Granny became so alarmed the one time Polly took it off that Polly humoured her and put it on again. There was no arguing with Granny about such things. She had superstition written all through her like the words in seaside rock.

The pendant did not even seem to be able to keep Seb away. He called most afternoons. By the end of the summer Polly was not scared of him any longer, but she was quite bored. One afternoon they were in the garden, where Seb was telling her about the agonies of withdrawal he had suffered when he gave up cigarettes, when he suddenly broke off talking and grabbed Polly and kissed her.

It was the first time anyone had done that to Polly. She should have asked Nina about it, she thought wryly, as Seb's face met hers and their noses seemed to get tangled up. It was not much fun. She wondered whether to wriggle loose, but Seb was breathing heavily and passionately and seemed to be enjoying it so much that it brought Polly's annoying soft-heartedness out. She stood there and let him lay his mouth against hers, and tried to decide if you kept your eyes open or shut them, and in the end she settled for one of each. What a funny thing to invent to do! she thought. What *do* people see in it?

"I'll send him packing if you like," Granny said when Polly came in pretending nothing had happened. "I didn't before because I thought he might cheer you up."

"I'm quite cheerful!" Polly protested. She was ashamed that Granny should offer to manage Seb for her. But Granny was right about her not being cheerful. The time in Bristol seemed to have bitten deep and it took her a long time to get over it. She found it hard to concentrate on anything, even when she was back at school that autumn.

Nina was still into boys. It was, as Fiona said, a lifetime's obsession with Nina, but Nina was still quite up to running various other crazes side by side with boys.

That term Nina's craze was protesting. Women's Rights, Vivisection, Oppressed Ethnic Minorities—Nina went on a march for each one and found a new boyfriend on every march. She was always trying to make Fiona or Polly march too. Consequently, they both thought it was a demo of some kind when Nina came rushing up to them one morning calling, "Are you two coming to the Town Hall or not?"

"What are we protesting?" asked Fiona.

"Moron!" said Nina. "Where's your memory? We said we'd meet that boy from Stow-on-the-Water there!"

Polly and Fiona had clean forgotten Leslie. Fiona said Leslie had just been having them on. Polly thought it might have been a joke too, but she was suddenly seized with pleasure at the thought of seeing Leslie again. She pointed out to Fiona that three people waiting an hour on the steps of the Town Hall didn't look nearly as silly as one, or even two. So in the end they all three went.

They approached the Town Hall expecting to feel foolish. But, to their astonishment, Leslie was there. He was standing waiting on the step—a surprising sight in every way, for he was dressed in a spruce grey suit like other Wilton College boys, with a Wilton tie, and his mass of curly fair hair was smooth and short and neat. His skull earring had been replaced by a small gold sleeper.

He was quite as surprised to see them as they were to see him. "There! And I made sure you'd forget!" he said.

After that, they all stared at one another awkwardly, until Fiona, who also had pierced ears, remarked on his sleeper. "Doesn't Wilton allow earrings?" she asked.

"No way!" said Leslie. "Rules about everything. But I wanted to keep my options open, as you might say. No one's made me take it out yet. Where is there to go in this town?"

The ice was broken and they went to the Blue Lagoon for chips, talking busily. The girls wanted to know what Wilton College was like inside. Leslie told them it was all made of concrete, got up like a church, with pointed arches, and cold as the grave. "Except Hall— that's pink marble and done Roman," he said. Lessons were easy, though all the teachers were mad. The most difficult part was getting on with the other boys.

"Half the time they make me feel like an old man," he said. "Maybe you grow up quicker being brought up common, the way I am, but it gets me down, the way they all laugh at me." Seeing how concerned Polly was looking, he said, "It's OK—nothing I can't handle—just stupid. Because of me playing the flute. Joke of the century, because my name's Piper."

"But I thought—" Polly began. Fiona at once kicked Polly's ankle and leaned forward to change the subject.

Leslie, however, smoothly changed the subject himself. "Did you know you were famous in our school?" he said to Polly. "Everyone says our Head Boy's in love with you. Leroy—know him? He's got a photo of you up in his study. I've seen it. It's awful, but it's you, definite. Can I say I know you? It'll do me no end of good with the crowd."

Polly found Fiona and Nina staring at her, awed. "Oh, Seb," she said gruffly. "Yes, I suppose I do know him. And so do you know me, so you might as well say."

"Thanks," Leslie said. He was obviously grateful. "Now I've got a real touch of class!" he said.

Fiona and Polly got up to go soon after that. Nina said, "I'll be along. I need the Ladies'. You lot go."

"Why did you kick me?" Polly asked as they walked back to school.

"Broken home of some kind," Fiona said. "I saw the look come on his face. I know it from you. Sometimes I can see you think, 'God! Someone's going to *ask!*' Nice, isn't he—Leslie? Do you really know the Head Boy of Wilton?"

"I know Seb Leroy," said Polly. "I didn't know he was Head Boy."

Nina did not come back to school that afternoon. Neither, Polly suspected, did Leslie. The next day it was all over Manor Road School that the Head Boy of Wilton College was in love with Polly Whittacker. People kept coming and asking Polly if it was true.

Polly got very gruff about it. But it did make her feel more kindly towards Seb.

The day after that, a parcel came for Polly, addressed in strange writing. In it were several cassette tapes—Bach, Beethoven, Brahms—and a note in small, fat writing:

> *Tom thought you might like these. He says throw them away*
> *if you don't. We gather he didn't kill you that eventful night,*
> *or someone would have tried to sue him by now. Our show is*
> *still on the road—just about. Ann and Sam send love.*
>
> > *Yours, Tan Thare (alias Ed)*

Almost on tiptoe, in case Mr. Leroy found out, Polly borrowed Fiona's radio-cassette player and listened to the tapes. She got so addicted to them that Granny promised her a cassette player for Christmas. And Mr. Leroy did nothing. Polly relaxed, and then relaxed further, from a tension she had not known she had. Suddenly she could concentrate again. A week after the tapes arrived, she got out her map and the story called *Tales of Nowhere* for the first time in months, and began to compose a long, careful narrative.

It turned out a bit different from the way she had planned it. Remembering how scornful Mr. Lynn had been at her borrowing from Tolkien, Polly decided to let her imagination take her where it would. All she knew at the start was that it was an account of how Hero came to be Tan Coul's assistant, and then their quest together for the Obah Cypt. The result was that the story got huge. Small extra stories sprouted off it everywhere, giving detailed histories of every character who appeared. Hero herself became a king's daughter who had to run away from home because of the machinations of her beautiful but evil girl-cousin. Tan Coul found her wandering in disguise and made her his assistant, thinking she was a boy. From there it became an epic. Polly was writing at it most of that school year, almost until her fourteenth birthday, on and off, with numerous interruptions from real life.

Seb was one of the interruptions. Polly was continually trying to get rid of Seb, or at least evade his grabbing and kissing her. She was ashamed to ask Granny to help. But each time she tried, Seb got so upset, so humble and miserable, that Polly got soft-hearted and did not send Seb packing after all.

"I don't know how Nina does it!" she sighed more than once to Fiona. Nina was always sending people packing, except, perhaps, Leslie.

Leslie kissed Polly too, at Fiona's Christmas party, a soft, moist kiss which Polly preferred to Seb's grabbing and hard-breathing kind, even if it was not so valuable. Leslie was turning out to be a great kisser of people. It was around then that Fiona took to calling him Georgie-Porgie. And he seemed to be surviving Wilton rather well. Polly asked Seb how Leslie was doing, and Seb rather loftily admitted that Piper was a popular little beast.

More tapes arrived for Polly at Christmas, *With love from the Dumas Quartet*, in Ann's writing—Britten, Chopin, Elgar. Ann had put her address at the top, which Polly carefully kept. She was going to need that. There was another parcel of tapes a month later, this time from Sam—Fauré, Handel, Haydn.

"Going through the alphabet, isn't he?" Granny remarked. "What does he do when he gets round to Webern? Go back to Bach?" She, like Polly, had no doubt who the tapes were really from.

Polly finished her huge narrative during the summer term. The day after she had finished it, she went round with the oddest mixture of feelings, pride at having got it done, sick of the sight of it and glad it was over, and completely lost without it. By the evening, lost-without-it came out on top, and she began to make a careful copy in her best writing.

That too suffered interruptions. Polly was put in the athletics team again, and she was also a courtier in the school summer play. This was Shakespeare's *Twelfth Night*. Polly was much struck by the similarity of its plot to her own story of Hero and Tan Coul. She would have given a great deal to act the part of Viola, but that went to Kirstie Jefferson, and Polly consoled herself by going on copying her story.

Shakespeare, she discovered, borrowed plots for his plays from all over the place—so there, Mr. Lynn! Her story was all her own. The longer she spent copying, the more she admired it. Some parts were really good. The part, in particular, where Tan Coul is wounded in the shoulder and Hero has to dress the wound. She strips off Tan Coul's armour and sees "the smooth, powerful muscles rippling under the silken skin of his back." Wonderful! Polly went round whispering it admiringly to herself. "The silken skin of his back!"

She was still wonderfully pleased with that bit when she finished copying it at last. Oh, well done! Polly packed it in a vast envelope addressed to Ann, with a note asking her to give it to Tom. *I seem to have lost his address*, she wrote, to fool Mr. Leroy. For the same reason, she got Fiona to write Ann's address and post it for her. Then she waited for signs of applause and admiration from Mr. Lynn.

Nothing happened for quite a while. And when it did, it was clear Mr. Lynn felt strongly on the matter. He had risked writing himself. Maybe this was because he was far away. Or maybe not. The postcard was from New York. It had two words written on it.

Sentimental Drivel. T. G. L.

Polly stared at it in outrage. She could barely believe it.

"What's up, love?" asked Granny.

"Oh nothing. Only one of the famous Lynn postcards," Polly said bitterly. "I hope he treads on his cello."

She went to school, furious. That day she went without lunch so that she could put the money in Granny's telephone jar. Granny worried a lot about the size of her phone bill, Polly walked home in the afternoon, still furious. He *can't* have gone off hero business! she kept thinking. What's the *matter* with him? He used to *like* it! He told me he was hooked on it. What's wrong?

Seb crossed the road and tried to walk beside Polly.

"Oh stop bothering me!" Polly snapped.

"Polly! That's not like you!" Seb said in a huffy, pleading way.

At this, Polly was angry enough—and hungry enough—to turn round and say, "Yes, it *is* like me! You just don't know what I'm like. I told you to stop bothering me. Go away and don't come back for a year. I'm too *young!*"

Seb stood and stared at her. He was even angrier than Polly was, and fighting so hard to control it that for just a moment he almost looked like Mr. Leroy. Like Mr. Leroy, he said, "You're going to regret that." Then he walked away.

Polly went home without another thought for Seb except a mild relief that he seemed to have been sent packing at last. She put her lunch money in the telephone jar and dialled Mr. Lynn's number.

She was answered by the robot, sounding a bit old and scratched these days, but she had been expecting that. "Polly," she said crisply. "What the hell do you mean—sentimental drivel?" And slammed the phone down again.

Again it was some time before anything happened. During that time Polly had been taken out of the Hurdles and put in the Relay and the 400 Metres, and asked to be a sailor as well as a courtier in the play. Also during this time Ivy kept telephoning to tell Polly all about her new lodger, Kenneth Curtis. She had had a couple of girls before that and had not got on with them. Kenneth, she wanted Polly to know, was different. "It's quite platonic," she said, "but I feel so peaceful now. I think I may have got my hands on a little happiness at last." She wanted Polly to come round at least for a visit.

"Don't you," said Granny.

At last, the Saturday before Polly was fourteen, a letter arrived from London. It was in the spiky, flowing writing of Sam Rensky.

Dear Polly,
Tom wishes you, for some reason I can't understand, to

consider the human back. He says there are many other matters
you should consider too, but that was a particularly glaring
example. He invites you, he says, to walk along a beach this
summer and watch the male citizens there sunning themselves.
There you will see backs—backs stringy, backs bulging, and
backs with ingrained dirt. You will find, he says, yellow skin,
blackheads, pimples, enlarged pores and tufts of hair.

This is making me ill, but Tom says go on. Peeling
sunburn, warts, boils, moles and midge bites and floppy rolls
of skin. Even a back without these blemishes, he claims,
seldom or never ripples, unless with gooseflesh. In fact, he
defies you to find an inch of silk or a single powerful muscle in
any hundred yards of average sunbathers. I hope you know
what all this is about, because I don't. I think you should stay
away from the seaside if you can.

Yours ever, Sam

This, if possible, made Polly angrier still. She hurled the letter in
the bin and stormed off for a walk. And, having walked some way
in that direction, she decided angrily that she would, in spite of
Granny's advice, go and visit Mum. Poor Ivy. She did so deserve a
little happiness.

"Good heavens!" Ivy said, opening the door to her. "I never expected your grandmother to let you near here. Well, come in, now
you've come."

It was not very welcoming, but Polly went in and followed Ivy
to the kitchen. The new lodger was sitting at the table over the same

sort of substantial breakfast that Ivy used to give David. He was a stringy, quiet little man, with not very much hair brushed over to make it look more.

When he saw Polly, he jumped up with such violent politeness that his chair fell over.

"Sit down, Ken," Ivy said soothingly. "She's only Polly."

Ken sat down guiltily. He had, Polly noticed, a mole on the side of his nose with a tuft of hair growing out of it. A vision came to her of how Ken would look on a beach. But Ivy seemed to like him well enough. She and Polly sat and chatted until Ken had finished eating. Then Ivy sent him to the living room to look for the newspaper Polly could see on the other chair.

When Ken had shuffled off, Ivy said, "You haven't quarrelled with *her* too now, have you?"

"No," said Polly. "Of course not!"

"You do quarrel with people," said Ivy. "It's your besetting sin, Polly." Polly opened her mouth to protest, then shut it, almost with a snap, like Granny. She let Ivy go on, "But don't think you're going to come back here. It wouldn't do at all. I can't have Ken upset."

When Ken came shuffling back to say there was no paper in there, Polly got up to leave. He looked puzzled. Polly said goodbye to Ken politely, because it was not Ken's fault, and left. As she walked back to Granny's house, it began to seem to her that she knew what Tom meant. She had Ivy's example to show her that there were ways of thought that were quite unreal, and the same ways went on being unreal even in hero business. Her first act on getting in was to rescue Sam's letter and shake the tea leaves off it. Her second act was to get out her own first copy of the huge narrative and look at it carefully.

She found she knew exactly what Tom meant. She writhed. Oddly enough, it was all the bits she had been most pleased with that now made her writhe hardest. She would have torn it up—except that it had taken such months to write. She wondered what she could do to show Tom she understood now. The book of tickets she was supposed to be selling for *Twelfth Night* caught her eye, piled on a heap of other notices from school.

She hesitated. Was it worth risking more reprisals from Mr. Leroy? "Why not?" she said. "He probably won't come."

Without giving herself time to regret it, she wrapped the tickets in all the other stuff—notices about uniform, the price of dinners, Sports Day, the Swimming Bath Appeal and choir practice—and stuffed the lot in an envelope. Perhaps Mr. Leroy would think it was a bundle of waste paper. She addressed the bulging envelope to Old Pimply Back at Sam Rensky's address and went daringly out and posted in herself.

No one except Granny came to *Twelfth Night*. Polly looked carefully on all three nights, but it was so. She just had to accept it. Granny enjoyed the play anyway, although sitting in the draughty hall gave her sciatica. She could scarcely move the next day. But she vowed she would all the same, even on crutches, come to Sports Day later that week.

"You don't have to come to everything, Granny!" Polly protested.

"I'm the only family you've got who cares enough to come, and I'm coming!" Granny said.

She was so firm about it that Polly did not argue any more then. But when Sports Day turned out to be cold and drizzling, Polly had another try at persuading Granny to stay at home. Granny turned warlike on her. She gave Polly the stare which unnerved men in offices and she said, "I know my duty, Polly. Don't argue. I shall wear my fur coat and carry my umbrella and I shall be there to watch you win. Let's say no more about it."

So very fierce was she that Polly was seriously alarmed when Granny did not turn up that afternoon. There was, in spite of the rain, quite a large crowd of parents, teachers, and brothers and sisters of competitors spread round the field. Polly kept hoping she had missed Granny among the rest. But Granny and her fur coat were very recognisable, particularly together, and the umbrella was even more so, since it was very large and made in green and white triangles. Look as she would, Polly could not see that umbrella.

"Should I go home?" Polly asked Fiona while Fiona was helping her put her hair into a tail with an elastic band.

"Perhaps the bus she was on broke down," said Fiona. "Or she may be behind some big people. Let's go round the field and look."

They toured the field with Fiona's plastic mac across them both to keep their track suits dry, but no fur coat or green and white umbrella could they find. Polly was grateful she had a friend like Fiona. Fiona was entirely sensible and soothing, Polly's stomach felt queer, and she kept saying to herself, If Mr. Leroy's done something to her now, I shall go to Hunsdon House and *kill* him! I really shall!

"Go home after the Four Hundred, if you must," Fiona said as they stood in the drizzle, jumping from leg to leg to keep warm. "You ought to win the Four Hundred first."

Polly took off her track suit and went heavily to the start with the rest of the runners. She knelt, knees and knuckles wet, with the rain feeling like pins and needles falling on her arms and legs, and took a last worried look round the field. And the umbrella was there at last, in the distance near the gate. Granny was under it, but she was not holding it. Mr. Lynn was holding it over both of them.

The gun went and Polly got left at the start. She thought that, in the circumstances, it was pretty speedy of her to come third. But her speed in the race was nothing to the speed with which she covered the distance from the finish to the gate, frantically tearing the elastic band off her hair as she ran. It wound itself up in her hair and she only got it off just as she arrived at the umbrella.

Granny was holding it alone now. Mr. Lynn had gone.

"Tom was here—surely he was!" Polly cried out.

"Put something on, Polly. You'll catch your death," said Granny. "Yes, he was here, but he had to go. The quartet's just off to Australia. He left you this." She held out a paper.

Polly dropped the elastic band all trammelled in fine silvery hair and slowly took the paper. Rain pattered on it. The drawing on the paper bulged and blurred from tears Polly was determined not to let go of. "How's your sciatica?" she said while she waited for her eyes to clear.

"Not too bad, thank you for asking," Granny said.

Polly could see now. It was a drawing of a kangaroo wearing

glasses, and he had made it look really quite like him. And Mr. Leroy had won—hands down. "He thinks I'm just a child!" Polly said angrily.

"Well you are," said Granny.

5

"Harp and carp, Thomas," she said,
"Harp and carp along with me,
And if you dare to kiss my lips,
Sure of your body I will be."

THOMAS THE RHYMER

Polly stirred and shifted her shoes around on Granny's bed-spread, remembering the desolation of that Sports Day. After that, Polly had seriously set herself to grow up. She had worked at it all that next year. Granny had been quite sympathetic, but just a little sharp about it, rather like she was over Sports Day.

"Don't wish your life away," she said. It became almost a motto of Granny's. Don't wish your life away. Polly stirred uneasily again. Because, it seemed to her, she might have done precisely that. Wished her life away. She had only a year left of those second, hidden memories. After that, her memory ran single again, and disturbingly blank and different.

For instance, the memory she had thought was her real one told her that she had met Seb for the first time at that party of Fiona's two years ago. The hidden memory insisted that was nonsense. She had known Seb since she was ten. And he had turned up again the summer after that Sports Day, quite soon after she had told him to leave her alone.

"I don't think you were angry with me. I think it was about something else," Seb said, standing on Granny's doorstep with a box of chocolates.

There was enough truth in that to make Polly soft-hearted again.

And the single memories did not contain Leslie at all. Polly was astonished that she could have forgotten someone like Leslie. Leslie was a well-known figure all over Middleton. Wilton College did not seem to be able to contain him like it contained its other boys. Leslie was always out and about, as furiously in pursuit of girls as Nina was of boys. Naturally, he and Nina came on a collision course fairly often, but Polly saw a fair amount of Leslie too. So did Fiona, although she got tired of him quite soon. She said she had other fish to fry and a lot of leeway to make up on Nina—which was fair enough, since Fiona was now rather better-looking than Kirstie Jefferson—and she said Leslie was flimsy. She called him Sexy Leslie and Georgie-Porgie, and she said it was a wonder Wilton didn't expel him. Polly thought it was a wonder too. He was almost never in the place. Granny said it must be because Leslie was so good at playing the flute. She said the school would want to keep him for that—that or he had the devil's own luck and cunning.

Polly thought the second part was the true bit. But then she heard Leslie play the flute. It was at a Christmas concert in Wilton

College. Leslie bet Polly and Nina they would not dare go. So they dressed finely and went. In Nina's case this meant green hair—Nina's Mum had long ago given up trying to control the way Nina looked—and an arrangement of shiny orange-and-black fishnet which made most of the heads in the pink marble Hall whip round to look.

Leslie stood forward on the platform, with the lighting glinting charmingly on his hair and his demurest look, and he played the flute. The music soared among the pretend Roman pillars, teasing, trilling, coaxing. Polly was entranced. She had not known Leslie had it in him. He seemed to have the gift of keeping your attention on him too. Until Leslie had finished, Polly did not look at anyone else.

Then, during the much duller violin-player, she saw Seb in the audience. Seb was around all that year, Polly's hidden memories told her, doing Oxford and Cambridge entrance first, and then plunging round Middleton on a motor bike, bored. Both memories lost sight of him then, for nearly two years, until he turned up at Fiona's in his last year at London University.

Seb was sitting across the Hall from Polly. Laurel was with him. It gave Polly quite a jolt to see Laurel, She hung her head and looked across at them through her hair, and hoped and hoped that Nina's finery would not cause Seb to turn like everybody else and notice her. She somehow could not bear the thought of going near Laurel, or talking to her, and yet she felt a good deal of squeamish curiosity about her. She let her hair dangle and stared.

Laurel was beautiful. Polly saw that now, where she had not seen it when she was ten. With her pearly-pale face, big eyes and dark eyebrows in the clouded pale hair, she was quite staggering. She looked young and slender too. She could have been the same age as Nina. Seb was leaning over Laurel, being very attentive.

Laurel was obviously the kind of person who needed attentiveness. Polly was glad Seb was too busy to see her, and irrationally annoyed about it at the same time. She seemed to hover between the two feelings all the rest of the concert.

Afterwards, Laurel went up to talk to someone near the platform, taking Seb with her. Polly and Nina left without Seb seeing them.

"Hideous place," said Nina. "Stuffy old people. But wasn't Leslie fabulous! I'd no idea Mozart was such sexy stuff!"

Inevitably after that, Nina got a craze for Mozart and borrowed all Polly's tapes.

Next time Polly saw Seb, she meant to say casually that she had seen him with his stepmother at the concert. But she forgot, because Seb started to talk about Thomas Lynn. "Old Tom's doing quite well in Australia," he said. "Funny, because no one thought he would make anything of that quartet. He was always supposed to be such a fool."

From then on, every time Polly saw him, Seb seemed to make some remark or other about Mr. Lynn. He always referred to him as "old Tom" in a disparaging way, and made it clear that he himself thought Mr. Lynn was not up to much, but he did let fall, all the same, continuous little drops of information. Polly was thirsty for them. No letter had ever come to her from Australia. Seb was her only source of information and she drank the drops up greedily.

"Of course he was always hanging around the house when I came to stay as a kid," Seb said, "and he was quite nice to me—I suppose he was bored—so I mustn't get at him. He gave me quite a good camera once."

Another time Seb told Polly, "I remember the row there was when old Tom decided to take the cello up professionally. Laurel and he split up over it. Of course everyone agreed with Laurel. 'Thundering away on that stupid great fiddle for money,' everyone said. 'You don't need the money.' And he said in that daft way of his, 'It's not for money,' and stuck to it. My father says old Tom always was as obstinate as six mules tied head to tail."

Most of the things Seb told Polly, however, were more recent than this. Polly vividly remembered the fine spring day when Seb remarked to Polly that old Tom had been flat broke at the time of the funeral and heavily in debt when he had to give the pictures back. "Trust him to make a mistake like that!" said Seb. "There can't be many people who'd walk off with a Picasso by accident!"

Polly flinched at Seb's churring laugh and said she did not feel well. She went home to Granny's to sit in her room and stare at her *Fire and Hemlock* picture. Stolen too. And Mr. Lynn flat broke and still sending her books from all over the country. Then she got out her stolen photograph and looked at that. Now she knew Leslie, the boy in it was less like him. When it was taken he was—or had been—the same age Leslie was now. And of course I never met him, she thought. I was as superstitious as Granny in those days!

That seemed to make keeping the photograph much less of a

crime. She decided to hang it on her wall opposite the *Fire and Hemlock* picture. I might as well have all my crimes on view, she thought as she hammered in the nail. But holding the photograph, ready to hang it on the nail, brought back to her suddenly that odd scene she had overheard while she was stealing it. Mr. Leroy talking bullyingly to Mr. Lynn, and her feeling that Mr. Leroy seemed to own Mr. Lynn. And they had not been in the house, Polly was sure of that now. They had been in London or somewhere, and she had somehow got tuned in to their talk. And why would Mr. Lynn himself never talk about the Leroys? Not that he ever talked about himself much.

Thoughtfully, Polly hooked the little oval frame on the nail. Mr. Lynn would not stay in Australia for good, she knew. The Leroys would want him. For good or ill, that was nevertheless a cheering thought.

Granny noticed the photograph the next time she came into Polly's room. "That's a new one," she said. She went up to it and looked. "Hm," she said. "He looks to have been a nice lad. I'll give him that at least."

"Give who that?" said Polly.

"Your Mr. Lynn, of course," said Granny. "I thought that's why you had it."

"No. I had it from superstition," Polly said. She could not believe Granny was right. People changed as they grew old, that was true, but the difference between Mr. Lynn and the boy in the photograph was more than that. Polly thought of photos she knew—Granny as a girl, Dad as a boy. Granny as a girl had a recognisable bright snap to her face, and Dad, now Polly knew what he was like, had, even in those days, the gleaming, shifty smile she had seen in Bristol. The boy in the photograph did not have the same look as Mr. Lynn at all. It was as if he was going to grow up in a different direction, a careless, light-hearted direction, into someone more like Leslie Piper.

Polly thought for a while. Then she carefully drew and cut out a tiny pair of paper glasses. She unhooked the photo and laid the glasses on the boy's face. They were too big. Still, Polly pushed them into place with her fingernail and then, with a nailfile, gently tipped them to the right familiar angle. Then there was no doubt.

"Perhaps it's Mr. Piper," said Polly. But it was not. The boy was definitely Thomas Lynn. "Oh, heavens!" Polly cried out. "However young did they get him?" She clapped her hand over her mouth. She had not meant to say that, not out loud, not even in her head, and Mr. Leroy could well have overheard. She added carelessly, "Anyway, he's gone to live in Australia now, so why bother?"

But she did bother. Now she thought, she realised that Seb, whenever he gave her news of old Tom, had seemed to know exactly whereabouts in Australia he was. Next time she saw Seb, she asked innocently, "Does Mr. Lynn write to your parents a lot, then?"

Seb laughed, "Old Tom? Laurel says he'd rather do anything than write a letter!"

That, Polly knew, was not true, but she guessed that Seb was telling the truth as he saw it. In that case—She was left with a strong feeling about Mr. Lynn that seemed to be foreboding. It was something she had known almost from the moment she had met him, but it seemed only now to have come up to the surface. Once it had, it would not go. It ran through everything, the way superstition ran through Granny. It seemed to get worse through the rest of that year, like a thunderstorm gathering, through the summer term, through exams and Sports Day, even through Polly's fifteenth birthday, gathering like a cloud.

Soon after her birthday she got a letter from Ann.

Dear Polly,

We're back! And there's something we want to show you. Tom says there's a pub called the Mile and a Half out on the London Road, where we could have lunch and then perhaps go on an outing of some kind. Next Saturday would suit us, about twelve thirty. Don't bother to let us know, unless you can't make it. If you can't, we'll try again.

Best wishes, Ann

P.S. Ed says bring a friend of yours for him. He loves blind dates.

Needless to say, this letter threw Polly into a near-frenzy of excitement. Yet it was an odd kind of excitement, more like the kind you feel when you get what you expected for your birthday. Polly knew that, somehow, all through the gathering cloud of foreboding, she had been expecting this, saying to herself, It's getting to be nearly time they were back, without quite knowing she had been. When she first opened the letter, she felt *Ah, yes!* like a relief.

All the same, the frenzy was real too. It was all she could do not to let the excitement flow over into her invitation to Fiona. But she managed to say, in the right casual way, "I've got rather a good date for us next Saturday. Are you interested at all?" It was not that Fiona would have minded, but Polly would have. The pride that had risen up in Bristol rose up now, and she could not bear anyone except Granny to know how important this was to her.

She was determined to look her best. She washed her hair twice that week. She tried on outfits, earrings, and shoes, and rejected them, and then tried them on again, until Granny said, "Lord, Polly! I'd rather share a house with Nina! What's wrong with blue denim? Better that than overdressed any day."

Granny was right. Polly put on her newest jeans and realised it at once. Hero's clothes. She looked at herself anxiously in the mirror, rejected the green top on superstitious grounds and decided on the plain white. Leslie had once said she looked almost Swedish with her hair. Did she? She was quite tall, but not willowy, not any longer. She had become rather plump lately. And even if she went without food from now to Saturday, there was not time for it to show. She would have to settle for being plump and pretty—she was pretty, she knew that. But she would have given her ears—and then hidden the blank spaces under lots of hair—to look as beautiful as Laurel.

Then on Saturday morning Fiona rang up to say she had gone down with chicken pox. "But that's something only children get!" Polly cried out in her dismay.

"If it is, it missed me," Fiona said snappishly. "And you might show a little sympathy. I itch all over and I feel lousy. My face looks *awful!* I'm sorry about the date, but he'd take one look and pass out. Ask Nina."

Polly could not endure the thought of Nina making a pass at Ed, or gushing about the sexiness of Mozart. She told herself that Nina was bound to be busy anyway and went alone.

6

They'll shape me in your arms, lady,
A hot iron at the fire,
But hold me fast, don't let me go,
To be your heart's desire.

TAM LIN

The Mile-and-a-Half was right on the edge of Middleton, almost out in the country. It sat at the back of a forecourt that was overshadowed by a mighty old tree.

The quartet were sitting at a table in the shade under the tree. Tactful of them, Polly thought. She had been all prepared to pretend to be eighteen.

Before she reached the table, she realised there were six people sitting round it. While she took that in, she was noticing that the quartet were all very brown and healthy-looking after Australia. Tom, lounging back in his chair, had new glasses and his hair was bleached quite fair from the sun. His green shirt made him look particularly brown. The fifth person, sitting beside him, was Mary Fields. The sixth, sitting with his back to Polly, was, astonishingly, Leslie.

"Leslie!" Polly said, coming up behind him. "Is there *anywhere* you don't turn up?"

Leslie turned and grinned. There were welcoming cries of "Hello, Polly!" Ed sprang up, very trim and curly, and found her a chair. Sam unfolded upwards, beaming, like a long brown streak. Ann jumped up and hugged Polly. Ann's eyes were very clear and bright, and she had a dark pink dress on that showed she was the brownest of the four. Leslie advised Polly to try a pork pie. Mary Fields smiled and said, "Hello, there!" By the time Polly was settled with a glass of fruit juice, two pork pies, a cheese roll, crisps, pickled onions, and a cherry on a stick, she was feeling really happy. Really she was, she told herself. Tom had done nothing but smile briefly from beside Mary Fields.

"Drink the juice up quick," Ed told her. "That's nothing but a disguise for an illegal act. We're celebrating."

"We've got two things to celebrate," said Ann. "Here's the first." She opened her handbag and passed Polly a paperback book from it.

"And the other thing is that we've been asked to make a record!" Sam said. He was too pleased with the news to wait any longer.

I'm glad it wasn't worse, Polly found herself thinking.

"Fame at last!" said Ed. "Or a bit, anyway. And some money."

"That's marvellous. I *am* glad," Polly said, and meant it. She looked at the book. "Good heavens!"

It was called *Tales from Nowhere* by Ann Abraham, Edward Davies, Thomas Lynn and Samuel Rensky. The cover was a smoky bluish green, with pink hints of fire to it, and across the front was the gaunt tree shape of a dead hemlock. "Who chose this cover?"

"The publisher did that," said Ann. "We just made up the stories."

Sam and Ed interrupted one another to tell her how they had done it. "We had to spend such hours travelling, or sitting about waiting, you see, that we got into the way of telling one another stories to pass the time. Tom started it. No, wasn't it Ann? Anyway, it *was* Tom who said we should write them down. So we wrote them down, and read them aloud, and told one another where they stank, and rewrote them, and Tom typed them. Then Ann went behind our backs while we were in New York and sent them to a publisher. We all nearly dropped when they said they'd print them!"

They smiled at Polly proudly while she flipped through the book. "I'd love to read it," she said. "Can I borrow it?"

"That one's your copy," said Tom. It may have been the first time he spoke to Polly. "We saved it for you."

"On condition I don't put it face down on the floor—I know!" Polly said, and managed to meet his eyes for the first time. "Thanks. Thank you all so much." They had written their names in it, she found, now she looked properly. She was touched. It was an honour.

"Now the celebration," said Ed. "Everyone's glass empty? Good."

He and Sam fetched a couple of bottles of champagne out from the shade under the table. Leslie's eyes met Polly's, awed. Neither of them had ever had champagne. The most Polly had ever had was a couple of glasses of red wine at a Christmas party. In fact, four years later, as she brought this up from her memory, she thought it was a marvel she behaved later on as well as she did. She remembered Ed bending over one cork and Sam's long, curving thumbs forcing at the other. There were two swift, loud pops. Corks soared up into the tree. Sam and Ed secretively foamed champagne into Polly's and Leslie's empty glasses, and then turned and filled everyone else's openly. The other people on the forecourt stared rather.

They drank toasts—to the record, the book and to Australia. By that time Polly's head had gone a little muzzy. Probably Leslie's had too, because he remarked that champagne seemed to act quickly. Polly remembered Ann passing round snapshots of Australia. Some of them were quite hard to focus on.

"The blurred sideways ones without heads are all Tom's," somebody said.

"I used to do a lot of photography," Tom said ruefully. "I seem to have lost the knack."

Mary Fields, who no doubt felt a little left out, Polly thought, blurrily charitable, took over the conversation then. She had been to Australia as a nurse, a few years back. She had tried to buy a horse there and someone had cheated her. Leslie and Polly were left to one another. For a while they simply smiled and lay back in their chairs. Polly remembered looking up at the big leaves of the tree and tracing the heavy skeleton of branches among them. Soaring, she thought. Like music made solid.

"How *did* you come to be here?" she asked Leslie.

"Tom asked me," said Leslie. "To look after you."

"I don't need looking after," Polly said, stabbed with annoyance. "Besides, you hardly know Tom."

"Know him quite well," said Leslie. "Used to come into the shop a lot—him and Mary. That's how I got sent to Wilton. Mum asked him about schools once. He said Seb Leroy seemed happy at Wilton—what's the tie-up between him and Seb?" But before Polly could get round to deciding how you described the stepson of an ex-wife, Leslie gave a great champagne-filled grin. "Leroy's step-mother, now—she's quite something!" he said, staring happily up into the tree.

"Don't tell me you know *Laurel*!" Polly exclaimed. It rang out rather. She saw Tom glance over at them.

"Laurel asked me to tea," Leslie said, swirling the last of his champagne smugly.

Polly's champagne had turned into warm, thin wine. She drank it away in one long pull. "Yuk!"

And suddenly everyone wanted to leave. They were getting up, arguing where to go next. That part was very fuzzy to Polly, but she knew that the group headed by Ed and Leslie won. "It's only just round the corner!" they insisted. Polly was preoccupied with aiming *Tales from Nowhere* at her bag. She kept missing, and only got it put away safely as they all rushed off and swept her away with them. After that, somehow, they were in a fairground.

"Of course! Middleton Fair!" Polly remembered saying. She was somewhat restored by the sharp scent of petrol and squashed grass, and bewildered again by the music battering through the sound of heavy engines. It all seemed bright and peculiar in the hot sunlight.

She found Tom beside her. "Polly," he said. "Do you think a fair-ground is the best place for the two of us to be? In the light of past events?"

"Past events? Paper monsters and so on?" Polly said. A little mistily, she saw Tom nod. She had meant to behave with great dignity, but that nod assured her that they had, after all, shared a number of experiences in the past, and he knew it as well as she did. "I don't mind," she said. She seized his arm with both hands and hugged it. "I don't care. I'm just so glad to see you again!"

"All the same—" he began.

Mary Fields was suddenly standing in front of them, laughing heartily. "Tom! You should see yourself! You look like father and daughter!"

Tom took hold of Polly's hands and unwrapped them. Polly did not exactly resist, but she did not help either. "All right. We're coming, Mary." Mary moved off, lingering sideways, waiting for Tom. "In that case," Tom said, pushing Polly's hands away, "we'd better stay clear of things like the Big Wheel and the Octopus." He moved off after Mary.

Polly followed him, not quite stopping herself making movements to take hold of him again. "Why, why, why? Tom, tell me why at least!"

Tom answered over his shoulder. "You know if you think about it."

It was his way of running you up against silence. Polly stood where she was. Vaguely, she knew there were lines of light bulbs, red things and gold things turning, engines grinding, rifles cracking, assembled round her to the music of a brass band no one was playing. Such was her misery that she herself seemed nowhere among it all. She was no more important than the little ping-pong ball bouncing on top of a jet of water in the stall beside her.

Leslie came scouring back to find her. Tom had sent him. Polly let him seize her hand and tow her into the festivity. Pride came to her, as it had over Joanna, and she made herself violently happy, fiercely enjoying herself. It was like pushing your hand on the jet of water to hold it down. Ann went on the Big Wheel with Sam. Leslie and Ed rode the Octopus, yelling. Polly came off a roundabout and met Seb. The sky was wheeling round the dark figure, but she knew it was Seb. I think he follows me around, she thought.

"Oh hello, Seb!" she cried out, violently glad to see him.

"Hello, Seb," Tom said from somewhere near. "Come and join us on the Dodgems."

Someone paid huge sums of money for them all to have several turns on the Dodgems. Seb dropped out after the first go. It did not suit his dignity to be doubled up in a small red car. The rest of them drove like idiots, yelling and whooping, until the money ran out. Polly had a violent duel with Leslie. She chased him round and round the rink, with her hair flying and both of them screaming, until Leslie turned and knocked her neatly into Sam. She pursued Sam then, took time off to give Mary a hearty thump, and then went after Ann, whereupon she ended up stuck, spinning round on the spot and howling for help. Ed came and knocked her loose and she went after him like a fury. She did not go near Tom.

"Polly's a regular Amazon!" she heard someone saying as the cars coasted to a grating silence for the last time. "I'd rather have Tom's driving any day!"

Polly got down from the rink, a little weak at the knees, to find herself joining a laughing line, hurrying to find further enjoyments. As they streamed in and out among the stalls, Leslie shouted, "How about the Tunnel of Love?"

"No," said Tom.

Leslie, clearly, had not been run up against Tom's silence before. It made him blink and grunt slightly, and then turn away looking as if he did not quite know what had happened. Not that it worried him for long. Almost at once he was leading the rush towards a tall plywood fort at the end of an alley of stalls. The fort had slit windows and battlements and was painted in splashes of red and grey. A plywood Dracula stood at the entrance.

"The Castle of Horrors!" Leslie shouted. "Let's go!"

The others, inspired by Dodgems and champagne, raced after him. Ed was shouting, as loudly as Leslie, "It's Tan Coul's castle! This I must see!" which made Ann double up with laughter.

Polly was behind the rest, going slower. The effort of holding down the jet of misery inside her made her chest ache. Seb caught her up from behind and put his arm round her. "There you are, Pol. Where are those fools going now?"

"To interview Dracula," said Polly. "You come too."

"Let's not," said Seb. "Let's just you and me go in the Tunnel of Love. Come on."

"No thanks." Polly slithered out from under his arm. "I'm going with them. It would be rude." Which was true, although it was just an excuse. "You come to the Castle of Horrors with me." But Seb refused. Polly left him standing irritably in the lane of trodden grass and ran to join the others at the plywood castle.

They were just going in. Someone had already paid for her. Polly dodged after them under a plywood portcullis and fought round a sacking curtain into lurid red light. A skeleton loomed at her, yattering its teeth. Polly swerved round it, pretending to laugh, though it was not very convincing. The others had got ahead of her, thanks to Seb, and she was all on her own. She could hear their exclamations in the distance, and their feet treading hollow boards. She pushed through string cobwebs, past a barred window with mechanical groans coming from behind it and Dracula towered at a corner. His fangs gleamed. He was almost convincing. Polly hurried, feeling deserted, into clanks, groans and rattles, to a part where the light was dim and blue. She drew back with a gasp from a ghost.

"Oh thank goodness!" Tom said beside her, amused but relieved. "I thought I'd lost everyone."

It was quite dark, but Polly could see the blue light glinting on his glasses and pick out the stoop of his head as he looked at her. The jet of misery tried to force itself up past her hand. She crammed it down. "Not very convincing, is it?" she said, and hated her voice. It sounded bright and social.

"No, but I suppose they can't have people going mad with terror," he said. "Your hair looks pale blue."

"All the better to drive you mad with terror with," said Polly. "They put me in here as a hallucination."

Tom gave his yelp of laughter. "Not very convincing, are you?"

"Spit!" said Polly. "Round one to you."

They walked along the hollow boards under the clutching arms of two more ghosts. Polly thought Tom had run her into silence again. But the jet of misery seemed to be dying down. Then he said, "Leslie seems quite happy. How's he really doing at Wilton?"

Hint, Polly thought. Leslies are for Pollys. "All right," she said, "when he's not skiving off. Seb said he was a popular little beast. But he had a bit of trouble at first, not being the same as the other boys."

"I was afraid he might," Tom said. "I feel responsible. I told Edna how good the music was there, but I didn't dream she'd take me seriously. I hated the place when Laurel sent me there."

"Laurel sent you?" Polly said.

More string cobwebs surrounded them. It was quite a fight to get through. Polly thought silence had descended for certain this time, but Tom said, dim and blue, and breathless from being tangled in string, "My parents had died and we'd nothing. I was in Council care when Laurel almost adopted me. I know how Leslie felt."

Telling me things, Polly thought. A farewell gift. She came loose from the string and turned to watch Tom fight through. Something clanked beside her. A suit of armour with an axe raised in its metal first was seemingly bearing down on her. Knowing it would stop before it reached her, Polly ignored it. "Leslie's tougher than—"

Tom shouted, "Watch *out!*" and tore loose from the string.

Polly snapped round to see the suit of armour, really coming for her, and another clanking up from the other side. After that, things happened so fast that her memory had it simply as a clanking, blue-lit whirl. She remembered aiming a great kick at the nearest suit of armour and seeing it sway away backwards. The whistling

wind from its axe as it just missed her face was one of the things
that stood out. So was the gong-like ringing from her other kicks.
But her chief memory was a dim blue sight of Tom wrestling to
hold up the arm of the second suit of armour, which kept going
mechanically up and down, up and down, with the axe just missing
his hair. With that went a rumbling of some sort from overhead.

Polly came at a run to kick that suit of armour too. Tom said,
"No, don't be a fool!" and kicked her instead, hard, on the thigh.
Polly staggered sideways and fell over, in a whirl of frantic blue
metallic sights—something was falling out of the roof, and the first
suit of armour was raising its axe again. Polly rolled desperately
away, deafened by crashing metal. Next thing she knew, an iron
portcullis had dropped out of the roof, trapping Tom underneath
it. That held him in place while the first suit of armour brought its
axe down. Polly knew, because she felt him jerk while she struggled
to heave the spiked metal grille up off his back. She did not remember getting up. She was just there, heaving at the bars.

"Get this *off* me!" he said.

"I'm *trying*!" Polly snapped. Lucky I've got muscles, she thought
as she somehow rescued his glasses and rammed them in her pocket.
The portcullis was mechanically forcing itself down and down. Polly
trembled with the effort of heaving it. Tom fell on his face under her
feet, and that just enabled her to hold it clear of him while he rolled
out from underneath. It dropped with a clang then, and the metal
spikes ran into the floorboards. "Jesus wept!" said Polly. Tom was
simply lying there with his face in his arms. In the blue light the back
of his shirt seemed to be oozing black, shiny stuff.

"Get us out," he said, "before anything else comes for us."

Polly looked round rather wildly. Quite near her face a white crack of light threaded the blue dimness. She put out her hand and felt plywood. "Here's a way," she remembered saying, and after that a fury of kicking and tearing until she had managed to loosen a panel of plywood and let sunlight come blinding in. She went on bashing and made a bigger hole. Tom climbed to his feet and she somehow helped him drop several feet down into the white, white daylight, to trampled grass smelling of petrol, into a roar of heavy engines.

Tom went on his knees there, bent over, muttering things. The stuff oozing from his shirt was red by daylight.

"You're bleeding," Polly said, shouting above the engines. "A lot."

"That's what it feels like," he said. "It hurts like hell. Can you get my shirt off and look?"

"Yes." Not at all wanting to, Polly helped him get one arm out of its sleeve and then gingerly took hold of the green shirt by its collar. She had to peel it off. It made her teeth ache and her spine fizz with horror. More blood kept coming, and she was terrified that he was only being held together by the shirt.

While she peeled, Tom said in a tight, grating sort of way, "You are now about to see a human back."

"Oh shut up," she said. "You would say that! I've seen backs every time I go swimming." And, having by then pulled the shirt down and seen the mess the portcullis and the axe had made between them, Polly could think of nothing else. She dithered, holding the shirt wadded up, not knowing whether to press it to the big oozing cuts or not. Her teeth felt about to fall out. There were maroon-coloured dents too that must have been really painful. "Tom, this looks awful!"

"But how about the bit round the edges?" Tom said almost jeeringly.

"Brown—and you've got muscles," Polly said. "I don't know what to *do*!"

People's feet appeared, trampling round them in the grass. Ed said, "Hell's bells! That's what the noise was!" Ann threw herself down on her knees beside Polly, demanding to know what had happened. Sam took hold of Polly's elbow and pulled her to her feet. "Are *you* all right? What happened?"

"It was—" Polly began, but Tom interrupted her. "From playing the cello in Australia," he said. "That's all."

"What's he on about?" said Ed.

"Nothing," Polly said. "There was a portcullis and it fell on him."

"Leroy again," said Ann. "Polly, can you run and find Mary? She used to be a nurse. I don't know enough to touch this."

"We'd better find a doctor or an ambulance," said Sam.

He and Ed and Polly hurried away in different directions. Tom called after them in that scratchily painful voice, "*And* Leslie! Find Leslie! I *must* talk to Leslie!"

As Polly ran, she could hear Ann trying to say soothing things to Tom. They were in a back lane of the fair, among engines on huge wheels, blue oil fumes, and the canvas rears of stalls. The sensible place to look for Mary would be the proper exit to the Castle of Horrors. Polly dived through the nearest gap that seemed to lead to the main fairground and cut in past a deafening lorry engine. Mr. Leroy and Seb were just beyond the gap. Polly saw them both in profile, yelling at one another, and backed hastily out of sight.

"—do it this way! There's a much better way!" Seb almost screamed. His voice cracked as badly as Tom's.

And Mr. Leroy bellowed, "To save our skins! That's why!"

Polly fled, found another gap, and sped through. There was a throng of people outside the Castle of Horrors, most of them angry and frightened. The man in charge was waving his arms and shouting, "It's all quite safe, I tell you!" He seemed panic-stricken. "It's quite safe!"

Mary turned away from the back of the crowd and saw Polly. Her face changed from annoyance to horror. "Polly! What's all that blood?"

Polly looked down and saw that the front of her white shirt and some of her hair were stained with bright red blotches. "It's Tom's," she said. "Come quickly. A piece of the castle fell on him."

Mary put a firm arm round her. "Easy now," she said. "Show me where. It'll be all right." That was the thing about Mary. She was nice, even though she and Polly did not like one another.

They were slower getting there than Polly wanted to be. Her leg and side quite suddenly began to hurt appallingly where Tom had kicked her. Mary helped her limp through into the back part of the fair again, where they arrived too late to be of use. An ambulance, with its blue light flashing on top, was already backed up into the grassy lane. Two ambulance men were just finishing putting some kind of dressing on Tom's back. Everyone else was standing watching, including Leslie, who looked as sick as Ann did. Polly gathered that Leslie was the one who had called the ambulance.

Tom was now swearing steadily. His face looked odd. Polly remembered she had his glasses in her pocket, and she limped over and gave them to him. He put them on, as he was, still crouched over the grass, and went on swearing. His face looked just as odd with his glasses on. It had gone a strange colour, which was not white, as Polly might have expected—muddier than that—and it went stranger as the ambulance men helped him to his feet.

"Up you come now, sir! Can you manage to walk up the ramp?"

Polly heard Sam mutter to Ed, "Curse this. What about that recording session on Tuesday?"

"I know," said Ed. "We'll have to cancel. He can't possibly play in that state."

Tom contrived to hear this somehow, through his own swearing and the cajoling of the ambulance men, in spite of the noise of the fair and the grinding of heavy engines. He turned and called over his shoulder, "Don't you dare cancel it! Either I'll play or you'll get Dowsett or someone. Ann, do you hear? You're not to cancel that recording. And Leslie," he added, turning the other way, "don't you forget what I said either!"

"Gives his orders, doesn't he?" Leslie said to Polly as the doors of the ambulance closed.

"He was in pain, you little fool!" Mary snapped. Mary, Polly remembered, vented her feelings in anger. She raged at Ann and Ed and Sam and wanted them to sue the fair for negligence. The three of them just shrugged, which made Mary angrier than ever.

"We'll try if you like," Ann said at last, in an effort to pacify her, "but I'm willing to bet you there'll be no evidence to go on."

Polly understood what Ann meant when she looked round to find the place where she had forced a way out of the Castle of Horrors and saw only a smooth painted plywood wall, with no sign even of a loose panel.

7

Out then spoke her brother dear—
He meant to do her harm—
"There grows a herb in Carterhaugh . . ."

Tam Lin

Ed drove Leslie and Polly back to Granny's, while the other three went in Tom's horse-car to the hospital. Ann promised to ring up as soon as there was news.

Granny was upstairs resting. Polly and Leslie sat on the sofa with the telly on, waiting for Ann to telephone. They both felt so strange that they wrapped their arms round one another and leaned head to head, unseeingly watching cricket. Polly kept reliving the wild blue clanking scene, over and over, and her desperate effort to hold the iron portcullis up as it forced itself down.

Leslie was a comfort against that, but nothing seemed to plug the jet of misery inside her. That seemed to be a separate thing, and stronger than ever.

"I hate that Mary Fields," Leslie remarked. "First female I've ever hated."

"So do I," Polly confessed. "Leslie, those suits of armour—"

"I saw," Leslie said. "I was coming along behind those cobwebs, but you were talking about me, so I didn't call out. That's how I got the ambulance so quick. I went back out the front way. To tell you the truth, I thought he might have been even worse hurt than he was."

"He—he—" Polly began again.

"Needn't have got hurt at all," Leslie said, "if he'd stayed put. They were both after *you*, weren't they? Must have been programmed like robots."

"Yes," said Polly. She had been trying to tell herself that Mr. Leroy had done his usual thing of injuring both Polly and the quartet in one go, but she had not convinced herself this time. She knew Leslie was quite right.

They stared at cricket a while. "Something's going on," Leslie said at length, in an injured way. "I don't understand about Tom. He kept coming into our shop, Mum said. And she said each time he came, my Uncle Tom hid out the back until he'd gone. Now, why would he do that? Don't get me wrong. I've nothing against Tom. I like him—even though he had no business warning me off Mrs. Leroy like he did just now. Really angry he was, about that."

Polly sighed. "He used to be married to Laurel. Leslie, he does know."

"Ah," said Leslie. "Then in that case he's bound to think she's bad news, isn't he? I thought there was something."

Granny came down then, and they had tea. Ann did not ring until two hours later, around the time Leslie was uneasily saying he would have to get back for Roll Call. "Tom's all right," she said.

"They stitched the cuts and seemed to think it looked worse than it was. So they gave him injections and things and let him go—he refused to stay in overnight anyway. They told him he'd have to stop playing for at least a week, but he won't hear of that either. He says if Sam could play after he ran him over, then he can record on Tuesday. We'll have to see how he is then, I suppose. Anyway, not to worry. We're all at Mary Fields' place at the moment—she's being really good with him, considering. I don't think Tom's stopped swearing once since we got here."

"Well that's that, then," said Leslie as he got up to go.

Which was just how Polly felt too. There was a sort of flatness and finality to everything. Her jet of misery burst through the flatness like a drowning flood. She floated in it like a corpse for nearly a week. She could not even talk to Fiona because Fiona was too ill to be disturbed.

Seb came round the next Saturday while Granny was resting. Polly did not feel like seeing him, but it was not easy to tell him that. She suggested they go out for a walk, or round to Nina's—anything not to be alone with Seb. All Seb did was to throw himself on the sofa and grin languidly at her. That meant he wanted her to go over there and be kissed, and she did not want to. "Oh, come on!" he said.

It made Polly feel she was being mean. "I'm not in the mood," she explained, trying to sound kind.

Seb sighed and looked at the ceiling. "I hear old Tom copped it," he said.

"*What!*" Polly said.

"Didn't a piece of the scenery fall on him at Middleton Fair?" said Seb.

"Oh yes," said Polly. "But—isn't he all right, then?"

"Fit as a fiddle—cello, I should say," Seb said cheerfully. "Last heard of making a recording in London, so my informant tells me."

Polly felt empty—stupid—with relief. "What informant? Who tells you about Tom all the time?"

"My father does," said Seb.

Polly took herself by surprise by suddenly, violently, needing to know everything now, at once, at last. "Yes, your father keeps tabs on Tom the whole time, doesn't he? Why, Seb? *Why?*"

Seb shrugged. "How should I know? Jealousy maybe."

"It can't be!" said Polly. "I know it can't be, or he wouldn't do something to me every time I so much as see Tom. And he does, Seb—you know he does. That can't be out of jealousy. So why *is* it?"

"No idea," said Seb, yawning a little. "I expect it must go back to something I was too young to know about."

Polly cried out in frustration, "Well, can't you guess even?"

Seb turned to look at her in astonishment. "You *do* want to know, don't you? I'm afraid I haven't a clue. If you really want to know, why don't you ask old Tom? I should think he knows all right."

"*He* won't say," Polly said resentfully.

"I told you he was obstinate," said Seb. "But you must know how to get round that. There are ways and ways of asking, aren't there? If you really want to know, you have to ask him the right way— make it impossible for him *not* to answer somehow."

At this, Polly felt such blinding relief and gratitude that she was almost willing to go over to Seb and be kissed. But Seb swung himself up, saying he was not in the mood now, and they went for a walk instead.

And she did ask Tom, Polly knew, about a month after that—a month of hesitating and guilt and misery such as she had never known. It was an awful time all round. Fiona was still ill. The chicken pox had given her shingles and she was ill most of that summer.

Polly was thrown back on Nina's company, and she no longer enjoyed being with Nina very much. Granny caught a bad cold. And Ivy telephoned to say that Ken was acting very secretively and she thought he was deceiving her.

"Oh, not *again*, Mum!" Polly said angrily, out of her misery.

"Yes—again," said Ivy. "It must be destiny or something. I didn't realise at first, because Ken's so quiet, but do you know—"

"I didn't mean that," Polly said. "This is the *third time*, Mum!"

"I know," said Ivy. "I did think third time lucky and I was bound to get a little happiness this time, but—"

"*Mum!*" Polly nearly shouted. "Have you thought? Maybe it isn't poor old Ken who's wrong. Have you thought it may be *you*?"

Ivy made an incredulous, angry noise and put the phone down.

"And it *is* you," Polly said into the whirring afterwards, before she hung up too.

The jet of misery, from being a flood, became a waterfall that month. Inch by inch, the strong rapids pushed Polly down. She fought the whole way, clinging, struggling, grasping at slippery thoughts, hooking her fingers desperately into ideas. She tried to stop her slide by consulting Nina.

"There's something I ought not to do," she said to Nina. "But if I don't do it, I won't understand something enough to be any good to someone. Do you think I shouldn't do it?"

"Wow!" said Nina. She gave the rich chuckle she had cultivated to replace her giggle. "If you mean anything like I think you mean, why not? Where's the harm? What's wrong with finding out things?"

That was nearly enough for Polly. Not quite. She had a feeling Nina was probably talking about something else. As the last desperate ledge to cling to, she read the quartet's book, *Tales from Nowhere*. She had not read it before, because her misery made her unable to concentrate on anything else.

But there was not the least thing in the book anywhere to help Polly. She enjoyed it, but that did not help. Sam's stories were grotesque and far-fetched and pathetic, about some sad, twisty monsters. Ann's were direct and spine-chilling, two ghost stories. One of them had been called "Fire and Hemlock," Polly was sure of it now. Ed's two were both SF. The first was about Martians and the other was the one called "Two-timer," about the man who altered his past and ended up with double memories. Polly thought that was less good than any of the others.

Tom's were both about the Obah Cypt. He seemed to have got obsessed with that, Polly thought. The first was a funny story which reminded Polly of the giant in the supermarket. The Obah Cypt, in this, was a thing like a coat hanger with the owner's name on it, which kept turning up in unlikely places and getting the owner into trouble, in spite of his attempts to get rid of it, until it eventually interrupted a Royal Occasion and the Queen ordered it burned. In his second story the Obah Cypt was much more sinister. It was an evil thing, but nobody knew what it was, and it was never seen. Polly could hear Tom's voice as she read it and kept thinking of his badly typed letters. That story pushed her finally off her ledge. She made up her mind to take Seb's advice. And she did.

But what on earth had she done?

PART FOUR

NOWHERE
presto molto agitato

1

Had I the wit yestreen, yestreen,
That I have got today,
I'd pay my tax seven times to hell
Ere you were won away!

TAM LIN

Four years later Polly sat on the edge of her bed and took a bewildered look at the book as it now seemed to be. Only the cover design seemed to be the same. The title was different, the stories were different, and the writers were six people Polly had never heard of. She turned to the blank pages at the front, and there were no signatures written there. The only story which seemed to have been in both sets of memories was that one—She turned to the list of contents. "Two-timer" she read, by Ann Abraham.

Ann Abraham!

"But that one was Ed's!" she cried out. "I remember—or do I?"

Slowly she turned to look over her shoulder at the opposite wall, where she had, she thought, once knocked in a nail to hang her stolen photograph on. The nail was there, all right. It held a dangle

of things she had won for Athletics at school. There was no photograph. She went up close and looked, and there was not even a
mark that a small oval frame might have made.

She dived for her old wooden box where her papers were kept
and began pulling them out feverishly. The photo might be in there.
There ought to be a folder too, containing five painted soldiers and
some childish paintings of bulging monsters. There should be two
more photographs, of herself and Granny looking like witches and
squinting in the sun. There ought to be a map of Nowhere, lots of
half-finished stories of Hero and Tan Coul, one fat finished one,
and letters, postcards, letters. There ought to be a badly typed letter
about a giant in a supermarket.

None of those things were there. Polly scrabbled through wad
after pile of paper, flinging each to the floor around her as it proved
to be wrong. Stories there were, and letters from Fiona, Dad, Aunty
Maud. A whole bundle of letters from Seb. *My Pol*, said the top one,
*You are being unreasonable. I only said you were bound to meet other
men when you go to Oxford, and I want to be sure of you. Why not
let's get engaged? . . .*

Polly threw these aside with an impatient noise and scrabbled
on downwards. A Level certificate, O Levels, babyish stories, quite
good drawings, quite bad ones, a photograph of the school doing
Twelfth Night, school reports, her birth certificate. And she was
down at the bottom, gathering grit under her fingernails. Nothing.

She sat back on her heels among the heaps of paper. "I *know*
they were there! What happened?" But when had she last looked?
Not for some time before her hidden memories stopped. The last

time must have been when she thought she had dug out the stolen photograph and hung it on the nail. Nearly five years ago. To
make sure, she ran back through the plain, single memories of
the last four years. Fiona's astonishing escapade came first, then O
Levels, A Levels, and herself and Fiona doing Oxbridge entrance
together. Meeting Seb. Her first year at college. She had simply
thrown papers in on top and never looked. Now there seemed no
sign that Thomas Lynn had ever existed. Yet even in this plain,
single time there were things she could only have learned from
him, like her dread of being sentimental, or hating to lay a book
open face downwards. She had thought she had learned these
things from Granny, and she had been wrong for four whole years.
What had happened? What had she done to make him vanish so
completely?

Granny came in, yawning a little from her afternoon rest. "Polly
dear, have you seen Mintchoc? It's time—" She looked from the
spread heaps of paper to the empty suitcases. "I thought you were
going to pack."

"I got sidetracked. Mintchoc was in here a while back," said
Polly.

Mintchoc heard her name and emerged from under Polly's bed
as Polly spoke, portlier these days. She picked her way through the
papers towards Granny with the dignity of a lioness. A small black-
and-white lioness. Granny, whiter and more withered, had much the
same dignity. A small white countess or something, Polly thought,
watching Granny stoop lovingly and stiffly to gather up Mintchoc.
"Here, my precious. Feeding time."

"Granny, do you remember Mr. Lynn?"

"Who's that? No, I don't think so."

"Oh, you *must*, Granny! Thomas Lynn. He was a cellist."

"I don't recall anyone of that name playing the cello. Here, Mint-choc." Mintchoc, with a bit of an effort on both their parts, arrived in Granny's arms. Granny stood up with her, murmuring about nice fish for supper.

She really doesn't remember! Polly thought. Neither did I. What's wrong? "Thomas Lynn, Granny. I met him by gatecrashing a funeral at Hunsdon House."

"That House?" Granny's head darted round at Polly. A strange look which, in anyone else but Granny, Polly would have thought slightly mad came into her sharp old face. "What about That House? I don't know about That House."

"Hunsdon House, Granny," Polly said. "You do. Seb comes from there. So did Mr. Lynn."

"I don't know about it," Granny repeated, still with the same look. Is she going crazy? Polly wondered. What shall I do if she is? "I've lived here for thirty years now," Granny said, "and there's only one thing I do know, Polly. Every nine years, at Hallowe'en, a funeral comes down this road from That House. Old Mrs Oaks told me that it's a woman every eighty-one years, and she comes down on Hallowe'en. Every other time it's a man, and he comes down the day after."

Cold all through, with her hair pricking at the back of her neck, Polly knelt and stared at Granny. Mintchoc, aware that something peculiar was delaying her supper, began squirming indignantly.

And Granny, who normally indulged Mintchoc's every whim, seemed not to notice. "Mrs. Oaks?" Polly asked, trying to make things seem normal again. "Is she the one you call Aches? Or is she Pains?"

"I'm talking about their mother," Granny said. "And if I were to tell you what they were in That House, you'd laugh and not believe me. Nowadays they lay it on the men not to tell, you know."

Here, to Polly's relief, Mintchoc distracted Granny by wriggling free and jumping to the floor. Granny's face took on its usual look of sharp intelligence. "She needs her supper, that cat," she said, and followed Mintchoc downstairs.

Polly got up and followed them both. Granny was in the kitchen at the sink, cutting up expensive plaice with a pair of scissors, and Mintchoc was on the draining board beside her, tail up and complaining loudly. Mintchoc had the best of everything and was very strict about the time she had it.

"I did something terrible to Mr. Lynn," said Polly, "and he went."

Granny said, while her scissors went crake-crake-crake, "Don't come to me for sympathy, then. I never did like your Seb."

"I'm not talking about Seb," Polly said. "Thomas Lynn, Granny."

"Then it's no one I know." Crake, went the scissors.

"I'm telling you," said Polly. "I did something awful, and I can't remember what I did."

"Then you'd better think, hadn't you?" crake-crake, said Granny.

"I can't—"

"Can't is won't, most like, if it's that bad," Granny replied. "Here we are, Mintchoc. Nice fish." She pushed the plate of cut fish across the draining board. Mintchoc's head went down into it ravenously, snatch, snatch, tossing strips of fish into her gullet.

"You're hopeless when you talk in proverbs," Polly said. "You don't listen."

"I heard you," Granny said. "If you've something buried in your head, then you'll have to fetch it out before I can help you, won't you?"

Polly sighed. Mintchoc crouched, crunching sideways at the fish. "I think I'll go and ask Mum if she remembers."

"Do that. You owe her a visit before you go off again." These days Granny was very particular about Polly paying Ivy regular visits. "But be back to pack," she called after Polly. "It's not right to keep Mr. Perks waiting while you do it tomorrow."

Polly went out under the tingeing trees and turned right rather more quickly than usual. Hunsdon House, hidden down at the end of the street behind the yellowing leaves, seemed remarkably close at her back. It was a feeling she had not had for years now.

She walked, knowing the way too well to notice it, feeling like a thin skin bag in the shape of a person, crammed full of memories. The pictures, the appalling horse, Stow-on-the-Water, the quartet rehearsing in the green basement, the jet of pure misery at Middleton Fair. It was like yesterday, that misery. In a way, it was yesterday, because of the blank in between. It seemed to have burst up again, just as strong, as if those four years had not been there—but altered, because of whatever she had done a month after Middleton

Fair, into something urgent and angry. It hurt Polly so that she moved her eyes away from a pair of happy lovers galumphing towards her down the pavement.

She saw them, even with her eyes on the fence. They had their arms round one another, pulling one another from side to side, laughing. The girl shone out in glistening purple and green. Her hair was crimson. Polly did not look at her pulling the boy almost over into the road. Nina Carrington, she thought, as she had thought many times, with yet another boyfriend. This boy was good-looking, with curly fair hair.

Then she looked. The boy was Leslie. "Hello, Nina!" she said.

Nina paused, clinging to Leslie's arm with both her own shiny green ones, and gave Polly a puzzled, unfriendly look. "Oh, hello," she said, and tried to pull Leslie on again.

Leslie, however, was true to Polly's hidden memories of him. He hung back and peered at Polly round Nina's crimson head. He grinned at her. "Who's your friend?" he asked Nina. It was clear to Polly that he had not the least idea who she was.

"Polly Whittacker," said Nina. "And she's not my friend. She's an intellectual."

"Oh come off it, Nina!" said Polly. "We've known each other forever."

Nina heaved at Leslie to make him walk on again. "We have?" she said coldly. "You've not spoken one word to me since we were in Junior School. So why the sudden interest?"

This was true, according to Polly's plain, single memories. And Polly herself had believed it enough almost to walk straight past without speaking. Nina obviously resented it, and resented even more the way Leslie was grinning at Polly.

"My name's Leslie," he said. "Live in Middleton, do you, Polly?"

Polly nodded. "I live quite near Hunsdon House," she said deliberately. "Do you know the Leroys?"

"The Leroys." Leslie's face suddenly looked as if a pink light was shining on it. And, Polly thought, it took quite a lot to make Leslie blush. "Sort of," he admitted. But he was obviously too uncomfortable to go on talking, and he let Nina pull him on past Polly.

Hell! Polly thought. That worked a bit too well! "Leslie," she called after him. "If you know the Leroys, you must know Tom too!"

Leslie's too-pink face turned to look back at her. "I don't think so. What name?"

"Thomas Lynn," said Polly.

Nina turned round too. "Eff off," she said.

Leslie was shaking his head and clearly not faking it. Polly could see he did not know Thomas Lynn any more than he had known her. "It doesn't matter," she called, and let them go on, wrestling and pushing and laughing, down the street.

She walked the other way, in an empty kind of horror. Real life, which yesterday had seemed safe and dullish and ordinary, was not real at all. It was a sham. Nina should have known her. So should Leslie. And what, in heaven's name, did the sham hide?

She reached the road where she had once lived. The bushy tree across the road, where she remembered Seb once lurking, had been cut down. She wondered when. Ivy's house needed painting, badly. She had not noticed that either, till now. Inside, it was even shab-

bier, with most of the pretty floral wallpaper from Polly's childhood still there, but stained and faded. Polly went in through the
small, untidy kitchen and found Ivy in the front room, aimlessly
watching television. Ivy's face sagged these days and she had put
on weight. She had obviously not been to work that day, for she was
wearing a greasy old padded dressing gown, and her these-days
bulging feet were shoved into man's slippers. But she had made a
bit of an effort with her hair, enough to put it in curlers.

Polly, who had still been seeing her as the young, pretty Ivy
of her childhood, stood and stared. My God! she thought. She's
turned into the way I used to imagine Edna! "Mum! You're not ill,
are you?"

Ivy turned, nursing a mug of tea in both frayed-looking hands.

"Oh it's you. There's some tea if you want to get yourself a cup."
She nodded to the teapot on the floor beside her. "I'm all right.
Don't worry about me. It's only my nerves again."

Polly, as she went to find a cup, told herself that this was not the
real Ivy. The real Ivy was the one she remembered, bustling about,
keeping the house pretty, keeping herself pretty, making strenuous
efforts to keep things together after the divorce. Ivy and she were
quite fond of one another these days. Life had not been kind to Ivy.

"I'm off to college tomorrow," she said, coming back and pouring herself some tea. She had to shout a little because Ivy had the
television turned up very loud.

"That's right. Go and waste your time reading useless books,"
Ivy said in her usual gloomy, matter-of-fact way. "Run through the
taxpayers' money. See your stuck-up boyfriend and never think

about me. Never care that I'm sitting here a bundle of nerves, with the new lodger starting deceiving me already, and not a soul to turn to in my trouble."

She always talks this way, Polly told herself. She steeled herself to listen sympathetically as usual.

"I only asked for a little happiness," Ivy began again. "You have to go out and take it in this world. Happiness won't come to you. I thought I'd found it this time, but he's being so secretive, Polly."

Polly found herself attending properly to this. And it was such nonsense. It always had been. "Oh, honestly, Mum! You and your search for happiness!" she said. She tried to say it in a light and kindly way, but it took such an effort that her hands shook round her teacup. "Happiness isn't a *thing*. You can't go out and get it like a cup of tea. It's the way you feel about things."

"But things have to go right if you're to feel happy," Ivy retorted. "And it's only my own little share of happiness that I want. Everyone's due that. I'm only asking for what should be mine."

"Who says it should be yours?" Polly said irritably. "What law is it that says that?"

"*I* do," said Ivy. "It's because there's no law that I have to go out and collect it. But you've always been against me," she added, as if it were an accepted fact. "You never come here unless you're after something. What do you want this time?"

It's not her fault, Polly told herself. Still trying to speak lightly, she clenched her hands round her cup and said, "You know your trouble, Mum? You're a miser—a happiness miser. And I'm not always after something. This is the first time I've ever asked you for anything, and even now it's only information. Do you remember Mr. Lynn at all?"

"Mr. Lynn? And who might he be?" said Ivy.

"A man I used to know when I was small. He played the cello and used to send me books."

"One of those," said Ivy. "Your Mr. Nobodies. You were always making things up. The way you used to believe in them used to make me fear for your reason, Polly. I'll never forget the time you made yourself believe poor David Bragge was sending you presents, when it was your father all the time. I've forgiven you now, of course. But you knocked the happiness clean out of my hands over that."

"It was not Dad," Polly said, "who sent me those books."

"Then it *was* David," Ivy said broodingly. "Ah, well."

"No," said Polly. "It was Mr. Lynn."

"Go on!" Ivy said, chuckling a little. "You made him up!"

Polly stood up and put her cup on a chair arm, balancing it carefully. Mr. Leroy had got at Ivy through Mr. Lynn sending *The Golden Bough*. Had Mr. Leroy made Ivy like this? It was a horrible thought, because, if so, it was indirectly Polly's fault.

"Look at you," Ivy said, brooding still. "You've rotted your mind with reading books. You can't take a realistic view of life like I do. You can't see the world as it is any longer."

"Thank you for that," Polly said, gasping a little. "You make it hard for anyone to be sorry for you, Mum. Goodbye."

"You're not going already?" Ivy protested. "What have I done to deserve this? Where are you off to so fast?"

"Nowhere," Polly said, without thinking. Hearing herself say it, she gave a cackle of laughter as she hurried out of the house. Behind her, Ivy called out, "This is what you get for wasting good money on a college education!"

Polly ran, in order not to hear any more. No. No! she thought, as she shut the back door. I didn't make Mr. Lynn up—surely—did I? And yet, if you thought of it, what more likely thing for a lonely child to do? Particularly if that child was not happy and knew her parents were going to get divorced.

If so, it was a pretty odd set of things to make up, she thought.

But not impossible, she had to admit.

Without calculating, she walked towards the Rose and Crown, the way she had so often gone once with David Bragge's secret notes. And there was the Rose and Crown, and there was Mr. O'Keefe leaning against the wall, just as he always used to do. Does he ever go away at all? Polly wondered. Mr. O'Keefe seemed just the same as ever, just as shabby, just as skinny, wearing the same disgraceful dirty hat—though there seemed to be a few more teeth missing from the wide smile with which he welcomed her.

"Hello my darling! It's a long time since you were here carrying me your notes. You've had time to grow up a lovely young woman since you came this way last. Look at the hair on you still! Such lovely hair. I used to dream of it at nights!"

"Oh—thank you—I suppose it *is* a long time," Polly said, rather taken by surprise at this welcome. "How are you, Mr. O'Keefe?" He was well, he told her. Couldn't complain. And Polly? Polly explained she lived with Granny these days, and then asked what she realised she must have come to ask. "Tell me, Mr. O'Keefe—are you still in touch with David Bragge?"

Mr. O'Keefe's eyes slid into the unshaven corners of his face and he looked at her narrowly. "I am. But take advice from me. He's not the man to go to in your trouble, my darling."

"I—Oh. I only wanted to ask him something," Polly said. "Why not?"

Mr. O'Keefe tipped a skinny hand to his mouth, acting someone drinking. He winked, a slow, sad wink. "Far worse than I am," he said. "Don't see him, my darling. It wouldn't be fair to the both of you."

"Then—could you give me his telephone number instead?" Polly asked.

Mr. O'Keefe tried to dissuade her, but he did not pretend not to know it. At length he gave her an old betting slip and lent her a pen, and Polly wrote the number against the wall of the Rose and Crown as Mr. O'Keefe dictated it. She gave the pen back and thanked him fervently. "Hey now! Don't go doing that!" he said. Polly turned back, not sure what he meant. "Smiling like that at the men," Mr. O'Keefe said. "You've a soft heart someone will take advantage of, if you go tempting us poor lads that way."

Polly laughed, hoping that was the right way to respond, and ran to the nearest phone booth. It was no wonder, she thought, seeing her face in its mirror as she dialled the number, that Mr. O'Keefe thought she was in trouble. She looked white and strained and desperate.

David's voice, when he answered, sounded thick with drink.

"This is Polly Whit—"

"*Polly!*" David shouted. "Long time no see! Must be years since I last clapped oculars on—" His voice thickened and stammered as he remembered the circumstances in which he last saw Polly. "Live with your grandmother still? Nice old lady."

"Yes, that's right," Polly said. "Listen, David, this may strike you as an odd thing to ask, but do you remember the time someone kept sending me books—?"

"And Ivy thought it was me. Wasn't me," David interrupted earnestly. "Remember it well. Always had a soft spot for you. Lovely, warm-hearted kid you were, Polly. How old are you now? Fifteen, sixteen?"

"Nineteen," said Polly, and cut through his amazement at how time flies by asking, "Who did you think those books were from?"

"Seem to remember Ivy said it was your father," David said. "Muddled sort of business. You said not, didn't you? Always inclined to believe you rather than Ivy, Polly. Soul of honour you were to me. Come round and see me. Tomorrow. Make an effort, be sober tomorrow. Say you'll come."

"I'm leaving for college tomorrow," Polly said. "I'll come round when I'm back at Christmas, if you like. Didn't I say the books were from Mr. Lynn?"

"Can't say I remember you mentioned any name. But if the books weren't from your father and they weren't from me, it stands to reason they had to be from someone else. Clever thought, that," David said, pleased with himself. "Polly, I'm longing to see you again. I know I'm nothing but a lonely old soak these days, but you'd gladden my heart, Polly. Do come round."

"I'll come at Christmas," Polly promised, and rang off rather wishing she had not said that. He sounded as if he cherished a sentimental affection for her a little warmer than she had bargained for—maybe all those compliments that used to annoy Ivy so had not been a game after all—and this was what Mr. O'Keefe had been warning her about. Oh, well.

Polly squeezed out of the phone booth and let the heavy door shut behind her. David had provided the one hint so far that Thomas Lynn might indeed have existed. If only for that, she would have to go and see him at Christmas. As he said, someone must have sent her those books. It was not much, but it was something. She remembered reading those books, all of them, vividly, and, what was more, she had gone on remembering them even through the plain four years when her memories ran single again.

So, who else could she ask?

The obvious answer was Seb. But if there was any truth at all in those hidden memories, Seb was the one person she could *not* ask. She might as well go straight to Mr. Leroy and Laurel. Oh, that was rich! Polly gave an unhappy laugh as she strode unseeingly home to Granny's. She had indeed gone to see Mr. Leroy and Laurel, earlier this summer. And Laurel had then been to her simply Seb's stepmother, a beautiful Mrs. Leroy she had never met before.

Fancy forgetting Laurel! she thought as she strode. Or Mr. Leroy, for that matter!

It had been when Seb had at last cajoled, bullied and pleaded with her to get engaged to him. And then he said she must meet his parents. The Leroys had not been at Hunsdon House. Polly had gone up to London, to their large and exquisitely furnished flat. She had been awed by the statues and pictures and antique furniture in it. A great contrast—she realised now—to the flat where she had gone to visit Mr. Lynn. And she wondered if Mr. Lynn could have lived in this magnificent flat at one time, when he was married to Laurel. There had even been, she remembered now, a picture in the hall with a little light over it—an Impressionist painting of a picnic party—which could have been the very one she had caused Mr. Lynn to steal nearly nine years before.

At the time, this had meant nothing to Polly. She had thought about nothing but not letting Seb down, and she had been quite startled by how very pleased Seb's father had been to see her. "Well now, this is clever of you, Sebastian!" he had said, more than once. Polly had not wholly cared for Seb's father, his ragged grey hair, his yellowing teeth and the loose, dark pouches under his eyes. "Clever, Sebastian, clever!" he said, and his loud, chesty laugh dissolved into the cough it reminded her of. Laurel had almost glared when Mr. Leroy said this. She had smiled, and she had talked softly and charmingly to Polly, but Polly could tell Laurel was not pleased, not pleased at all.

It had been obvious enough for Polly innocently to ask Seb about it in the street afterwards.

"Yes, I knew she'd object," Seb said, "so I didn't tell her."

"Why? Did she want you to marry someone else?" Polly asked.

"I suppose you're her heir, aren't you? She must have had other plans for you."

Seb gave a loud, hacking laugh, quite unlike his usual well-controlled churring. "Plans!" he said. "Inherit from Laurel! I'll be lucky! I'm only a half Leroy anyway. My mother was as ordinary as you are." Then he became serious and put his arm round Polly, which was a thing he very seldom did in the street. "The fact is, Pol, I'm in a fairly tense situation with Laurel. Laurel and my father used to be married before, you see, before my father met my mother."

"And Laurel doesn't get on with your mother?" Polly guessed.

This made Seb laugh again. He churred this time, long and amused. "My mother's dead. She died nearly nine years ago."

"Oh," Polly said, stricken and embarrassed. She had been thinking of the way Ivy hated Joanna, and she wanted to kick herself for being so self-centred. She could tell Seb was upset. He was almost grinding her against him. Yet she could tell he was laughing at her too. She was too confused to ask any more.

That was puzzling, Polly thought now, marching home to Granny's, and it was even more puzzling how pleased Mr. Leroy had been to see her. She shuddered. If there was one thing she was sure of now, it was that Mr. Leroy had it in for her. So what *was* going on? She ran through her memories, across the jolt where she had done God alone knew what, and on into the plain, single four years beyond. Back and forth. There was always that jolt, then such a difference: Mr. Leroy glad to see her, and Seb behaving as if he had never met her before that party of Fiona's.

Polly well remembered first seeing Seb at that party. Fiona said Seb had gatecrashed it. She had seemed rather surprised that Polly had not come across Seb before. Seb had made straight for Polly. Polly had looked at him, tall, smooth-haired, with his air of self-possessed slight scorn for other people, and Seb had seemed immediately familiar, although Polly had never, as far as she knew, set eyes on him before. They had fallen easily into conversation. Which was, Polly had thought then, just how she had always thought it should be. It had surprised her later that something so much as it should be should turn out to be so unexciting.

This made Polly laugh now, a short jolt of laughter. Unless, she thought, Seb and Mr. Leroy had forgotten too. So many people had—Granny, Ivy, Nina, Leslie. But she could not believe that Mr. Leroy had forgotten. Seb, on the other hand—Seb had always been on her side in a way. Perhaps Seb had forgotten too, in which case there was no point in asking Seb anything.

So who else was there to ask?

Polly turned into her own road, where Hunsdon House stood blocking one end, facing the fact that there was almost no one else to ask. Thomas Lynn, if he had ever existed, had been so separate from her everyday life that it had been an easy thing to slice him out of it—as easy as Granny filleting plaice for Mintchoc. Except that he had not been separate at all. Almost everything Polly did in those five years went back to Mr. Lynn somehow. The four years after that had been formless and humdrum years. Polly had done things, true, but it had all been without shape, as if she had been filleted away from her own motives and the things which gave her shape.

Granny looked at Polly when she came in. "Have you fetched it out yet?"

"No," said Polly.

She spent the whole night packing, and going round and round in those memories. And she did not understand. Quite apart from the truly strange things she now remembered—which she thought she *must* partly have imagined—Mr. Leroy had been so determined to stop her seeing Thomas Lynn that she knew it had been important to go on seeing him. Yet it was equally clear that Tom himself had been trying to freeze Polly off. Which put a stop to everything rather, didn't it?

It did not stop Polly trying at least to remember Ann Abraham's address, or Sam Rensky's. And she could not. They were not left out of her mind with a jolt, like the space between her double and single memories. They had simply faded, as things do that you have not paid much attention to. She wrote letters to them both, all the same, in the course of the night, and addressed them after a fashion, hoping that the post office might just manage to deliver them. But she was not going to post them in a box at the end of a road which also held Hunsdon House. She packed them to take to Oxford too.

Granny looked at her again in the morning. "What set you off?"

"A book," said Polly.

Mr. Perks and Fiona arrived in Mr. Perks' car, and Fiona helped Polly load her things into a boot and back seat already crammed with Fiona's things. Though Fiona and Polly were at different colleges, they were sharing a tiny flat this year. Fiona was in great excitement about it. She did not seem to notice anything wrong with Polly.

Granny plainly did. She looked at Polly again as she reached up to kiss Polly goodbye. "Take care," she said. "And if a book set you off, a book may help again when you've fetched it out of you. Try it. Goodbye. And don't forget to write."

2

O first let pass the black, lady,
Then let pass the brown,
But quickly run to the milk white steed—
Pull you his rider down.

TAM LIN

Polly posted her sketchily addressed letters in the first box she came to in Oxford. Then there seemed nothing she could do but hope for a reply.

A week passed, during which she and Fiona arranged their flat. One tiny room was Fiona's and also the dining room. The other was Polly's and doubled as the living room. There was a kitchen like a cupboard and a bathroom they shared with tenants upstairs. They saw tutors, went to lectures and libraries, worked, read. Friends of both of them poured in and out. The flat's main luxury was a telephone in the dining-Fiona's room. It rang constantly, mixing with the sound of Polly's tapes and Fiona's records. And all of it passed Polly like a show of shadows on the wall. The only things which were real were the people and events going round in her head.

Round and round. Thomas Lynn had befriended a little girl at a funeral. I wonder if I embarrassed him even then, Polly thought, trotting round holding his hand, obviously adoring him. No. She knew she had amused him. But later she had become less amusing and, in the end, plain embarrassing. He had shown her she was. And she had replied by doing something . . .

Unless I simply made him up, she thought. Ivy could be right. It seemed so much the sanest explanation. But would you make up the smell of an old anorak, or the feel of a large hand squashing your face against it? Would you make up resistance against you in the muscles of an arm you were hugging? Polly squirmed at that. It was so much the way Nina had hugged Leslie's arm, with Polly standing there like Mary Fields had done. Double purpose. You showed him you had a nice bosom, and you showed the onlooker the arm was yours to hug. Small wonder Mary had made a catty remark!

Oh! Polly thought. Why aren't all girls locked up by law the year they turn fifteen? They do such *stupid* things! It was that same year that Fiona had run away to Germany after a German businessman her father happened to bring home one evening. If only, Polly thought, she had done something so pointless herself! But she had done something so harmful that it had expunged Thomas Lynn from her own mind and from the rest of the world as well.

The second week brought no letter from Ann or Sam, but a letter came from Seb. It was long and quite amusing. Seb had written it—or the half of it that Polly read—in stages during a court case he was working on. He said that he was beginning to regret choosing to be a barrister, and he still wanted Polly to marry him at

Christmas. Polly had barely patience to read this far. "I ought to send you packing," she said, holding the letter but not reading it any more, "considering the way I feel." But that seemed mean and unreasonable. Nothing had really changed. Seb had done nothing except—Polly now knew—become devoted to her from the time she was thirteen. Or maybe even from the moment she had asked him about pop groups nearly two years before that. Polly had not the heart to break with Seb, but she had not the heart to reply to his letter either.

Instead, she recollected that Oxford was not so far from the Cotswolds, and looked up Mary Fields in the telephone directory. And there she was. Old Elmcott Farm, Elmcott.

Polly put the directory down and shrank away. She could not face Mary. She thought of Mr. Leroy as she had last seen him, grey, with dark hanging skin under his muddy eyes, and she knew she did not dare do anything which might alert Mr. Leroy. Then, at the beginning of the third week, she said to herself, "Was this the creature that once called itself an assistant hero? And why should Mr. Leroy bother? Aren't you safely engaged to his son?" She waited till Fiona went out, then dialled Mary Fields' number.

She was taken aback, all the same, when Mary answered. She had not realised that Mary's voice was so clipped and horse-personish. Or that she would remember it so well.

"I'm interested in a horse I believe you have," Polly said cautiously and found, on listening, that her own voice had got clipped to match Mary's. "A horse called Lorenzo that once belonged to a circus." And now she'll tell me he's dead long ago, she thought.

To her surprise, Mary said, with more than a trace of eagerness, "Do you want to buy Lorenzo? He *is* for sale, as it happens."

Lorenzo was unridable, of course. Polly grinned, thinking of the amount of her student grant, dwindling fast in the bank. "I was wondering about it," she lied. "But I'd heard he was rather wild."

"Oh no. He's quite a sedate old thing these days," Mary said, also lying, Polly was ready to bet. "Who told you he wasn't?"

"The previous owner," said Polly. "Mr.—er—Mr.—What *was* the name?"

"Sebastian Leroy," said Mary.

"*Who?*" said Polly.

"Sebastian Leroy," Mary repeated, "used to own Lorenzo."

He did? Like my left thumb! Polly thought. "Oh—er—" She heard her voice falter and picked herself up. "Now, that's very odd. The person who told me about Lorenzo was called something else. What was it now? Lynn. That's it. Thomas Lynn."

"I'm afraid I don't know who he can be," Mary said coldly. "Do you want to buy the horse, or are you simply pumping me about my boyfriends?"

"I—" said Polly.

"In that case, get off the line," said Mary, "I'm expecting the vet to ring any moment."

Polly put the receiver down quick, hoping Mary would not ask to have the call traced. I don't believe this! she thought. Seb! As a child, she had gone about expecting to meet giants and dragons round every corner, and they had disappointingly never seemed to be there. But they were there all the time, in the person of Seb. Had she been afraid of the wrong Mr. Leroy all these years? Oh, no, she thought. I can't think that ill of Seb. But, from what Mary said, it did seem as if Seb had not only bought Lorenzo, but had also taken the obvious steps to get Mary on his side and make her keep her mouth shut. But Mary had not denied knowing Thomas Lynn—quite. Boyfriends, she had said, in the plural.

"So what *am* I to think?" Polly said aloud.

The answer seemed to be: think of any other line of inquiry which might just be separate from the Leroys. Polly thought, for the next few days, in libraries, among friends, with a pen in her hand trying to write an essay on Keats. "As though of hemlock I had drunk," wrote Keats. Me too! Polly thought, and could not go on with the essay. She went for a walk instead by the river, in a mild, windy drizzle, thinking, thinking, and the result of the thinking was that she went on walking through the drizzle until she came to the bus station, where she got on a bus to Stow-on-the-Water.

This is a mad thing to do! she thought, staring out of the bus window. There was brown ploughed earth on either side, soaking in the drizzle, and a few sad seagulls trying to feed off the earth. Not so different from the first time she had come that way, hero-ically swooping from hedge to hedge in the horse-car, and yet there was all the world of difference. The bus passed the end of Mary Fields' lane, billowing the hedges in a cloud of spray. Autumn was late this year. Trees that were still green, or dingy brown, wept leaves into the air soberly. Stow-on-the-Water, when the bus rum-bled into it, was a bleak yellow colour, and the tarmac of the market square was black with wet.

Polly got off the bus and walked straight into the shop of Thomas Piper Hardware. It was clean and quiet and smelled of paraffin. The striplights were on against the dark of the day. The only person there was Edna, doing sums at the cash desk.

Polly went round the shelves and found some light bulbs, which the flat seemed to need all the time, and a shiny red colander. She found a garlic-crusher too and took that, because Fiona kept saying she wished they had one. Then, with these things, she approached the cash desk.

Edna looked up and smiled, friendly to the tips of her fluffy hair. "Awful weather," she said.

"Terrible," Polly agreed. "They're saying it's the wettest October on record, aren't they?"

"Oh, it is," said Edna. She laid an orange plastic bag on the desk and took Polly's purchases, ready to pack them in it. She began to ring the prices up on the till, but slowly, obviously ready to chat. "We've been warned about flooding," she said, "and what to do if the river bursts its banks. We're right down near the river here, you know."

Polly looked at her, liking her, and resolved to go about this carefully and reasonably. "It must be frightening," she said. "I've never lived near a river. Where I come from—Middleton—we never get any floods."

"Do you come from Middleton?" Edna exclaimed. Her face lit up. "My son used to be at school in Middelton. Leslie Piper. But I don't suppose you'd know him, would you?"

"You're never Leslie's mother!" Polly exclaimed in return.

That was enough to open Edna up. She could hardly talk fast enough, about Leslie and Leslie's good looks and his amazing talent as a flute-player. She told Polly how good Leslie was to her, and how clever, and how much she had worried and inquired to find the right school to send Leslie to. And then, just as Polly was preparing to ask if Thomas Lynn was one of the people she had asked about schools, Edna's eagerness was pushed aside by desperate worry. The worry had been there all along, Polly realised, seeing how easily it took its place in the lines on Edna's face.

"And then what does he do but take up with this rich married woman!" Edna said. "It's her I blame. She must be twice his age. *She* should know better, even if Leslie doesn't. And he's always there, always dancing about after her, and can't seem to think of anything else. I swear he didn't pick up his flute once all summer. And that's not right. He's at music college and he should be studying, if he's to earn a living from his playing, not chasing about after that rich Mrs. Leroy—Oh, hello, Tom! I didn't see you come in."

Polly turned round to find Mr. Piper looming over her under the striplights. The white light caught his glasses, turning them to a blank glare. The lines round his mouth were more bitter than ever. He had on a wet anorak which seemed to enlarge his height, high shoulders, and huge hands, and underline everything about him that was so like Mr. Lynn. Polly backed away from him. Her mouth dried, and her heart battered so that she could barely hear him when he spoke.

"What do *you* want?" he said to her. "Spying, aren't you?"

"Oh now, Tom!" Edna protested. "We were just chatting."

Mr. Piper's huge hands worked, drawing Polly's eyes. Like a crab's claws, she thought, horrified.

"I heard her," he said. "She was pumping you." And he barked at Polly, "What are you after?"

Polly held herself steady against a shelf of crockery. There seemed nothing to gain by denying things. "I'm only trying to trace a friend," she said. "A Mr. Thomas Lynn. Do you know him, by any chance?"

She had a feeling that Edna might have reacted to the name, but she forgot to look, because Mr. Piper took a threatening step towards her. His hands looked ready to throttle. "I do not," he said. "Get out of here, young woman!"

"In a second," said Polly. "I haven't paid for what I bought yet." Biting down her fear, she slipped round Mr. Piper to the cash desk. She fetched out her purse, feeling him towering beside her. "Do *you* know Mr. Lynn?" she asked Edna as she handed her the money.

But Edna was, of course, on Mr. Piper's side. "I'm afraid not, dear," she said, and held out the orange plastic bag full of hardware to Polly.

Then fear and failure seemed to break through a barrier in Polly. Because of Mr. Piper's uncivilised behaviour, she asked something which it would never have occurred to her to ask otherwise. She reached out for the bag, but kept her hands an inch or so from taking it. "Was there ever a giant in the supermarket here?" she asked.

"Funny you should say—" Edna began. Mr. Piper interrupted with a noise of irritation. "Oh, but it's got nothing to do—" Edna began again. Mr. Piper made a threatening little move. Edna said hurriedly and placatingly, "But you were ever so brave, you and Leslie—the year we first came here. That huge lunatic over in Robinson's, throwing tins about—"

"That," Mr. Piper said scornfully, "has got nothing to do with anything! I said out, young woman!"

Polly moved back from the orange bag. "How long have you been here?" she asked Edna.

"Nine years," said Edna. "Here's your bag, dear."

"That's enough!" Mr. Piper barked as Polly drew breath to ask more. "If you don't get out this instant, young woman, I shall call the police!"

"Why?" Polly asked bravely.

Mr. Piper, clearly too angry to think, said, "For pestering my wife. Sister, I mean. Now get out before I throw you in the street!"

He meant what he said, and advanced on Polly so angrily that she snatched the orange bag from Edna and went.

3

But the night is Hallowe'en, Janet,
The morn is Hallowday

TAM LIN

The bus had turned round in the square and was waiting to go back to Oxford. Polly climbed back on it and rode away through the darkening drizzle, feeling she had now come to a dead end.

Everything I try seems to go nowhere, she thought. But there *was* a giant in the supermarket—sort of. How odd. She tried not to think of Mr. Piper. His likeness to Thomas Lynn was too appalling. And they've been there nine years, which puts it just about the time we invented Tan Coul. But they're real people. We didn't invent them. And *why* won't anyone talk about Mr. Lynn? People *can't* just disappear off the face of the earth and everyone conspire to keep it dark. Not in this day and age.

She got off the bus, walked to the flat, dumped the orange bag in the tiny kitchen and threw herself down on the twanging old sofa. She was exhausted, but she hardly noticed. She was too busy thinking. Round and round again. And did she dare risk ringing Seb up and demanding to know? That would be blowing the gaff completely—letting Seb know she was remembering things she was not supposed to remember. Or was that a ridiculous thing to think? Seb couldn't really be that kind of villain. Could he? Besides, she was still sure, certain, that whatever was wrong was her fault, not Seb's.

"Polly." Fiona came in and switched on the light. "Polly, your tutor rang to know why you missed your tutorial today."

"What? Oh, my God!" Polly leaped up, blinking. Fiona stood there, severe in a blaze of red hair, staring accusingly. "I thought my tutorial was tomorrow," Polly confessed.

"Good," said Fiona. "You heard me for once. And it *is* tomorrow, and he *didn't* ring, but I had to get through somehow. What's the matter? You're not eating, you're not listening, you walk about half the night, and I don't think you're doing a scrap of work. Come clean. Are you in some kind of trouble over Marmaduke?" Marmaduke was what Fiona always called Seb. She did not like him at all.

"No," said Polly. "Or not exactly."

Fiona looked meaningly to where the pages of Seb's letter still lay on the floor where Polly had dropped them a week ago. "Then what is it?"

"I don't know," said Polly. "I may be going mad. It's something that can't possibly happen in this day and age."

"I've often noticed," Fiona said, "that when people say, 'This can't happen in this day and age,' they say it because it *is* happening. So what is?"

"Thomas Lynn," Polly said, "seems to have vanished out of everyone's mind. Sometimes I'm not even sure he existed myself. And don't say," she went on hurriedly as Fiona's mouth opened, "Who is Thomas Lynn?' or I shall scream. *Everyone* asks that. And I *know* you don't know him, because the only time you could have met him was when you got chicken pox. That was almost the last time I saw him myself."

"I wasn't going to ask that," Fiona said. "You used to talk about him. And I think I *have* seen him. Didn't he come to that panto when we were Pierrot and Pierrette?"

Polly stared at Fiona and clung to the sofa, unable to believe this sudden, amazing stroke of luck. "How could you have seen him?"

"I was wanting to get to know you then," Fiona said. "I was interested in everything you did. And on the second night of that panto you suddenly went different, as if you were inspired, and the whole panto took off with you. And I wanted to know why. So when you went racing outside afterwards, I tiptoed nosily after you and kept out of sight by the cycle sheds. He was just getting into his car with a horsey-looking girl. I was quite far away, of course, but there was enough light for me to see he was good-looking—"

"Good-looking?" said Polly. It would never have occurred to her to think of Thomas Lynn as that.

"I thought he was," Fiona said apologetically. "And I was awed. But I think I was even more awed by the marvelling sort of way he looked at you—as if you were some kind of miracle. The girl with him looked really fed up, and I didn't wonder!"

Polly sprang up and threw her arms round Fiona. "Oh, thank God! Fiona, you life-saver! I was going mad!" She was near laughing at the sheer little chance which had caused the Leroys to miss Fiona. They had not known one another then. Fiona's memories would not have seemed important. But how nearly she had missed asking Fiona herself.

"Any time," Fiona said. "After all, I wept on your shoulder enough over Hans. You were the only person who seemed to understand. It's the least I can do. Have you written to him?"

"No," said Polly.

"Why *not*?" said Fiona.

Polly did not feel equal to explaining about Mr. Leroy, or her suspicions of Seb. She gave what was, after all, the main reason. "I think it would be just like you and Hans. You know—patting you on the head and sending you kindly back to England."

"Well, I was fifteen and didn't speak a word of German, and Hans didn't speak English," Fiona said. "It *is* exactly the same, isn't it? Even so, if Hans had looked at me once that way, I'd have taken handcuffs with me to Germany to make sure he couldn't send me home without coming as well. I'd have swallowed the key, quite cheerfully. Sit down and write at once."

"It's my turn to cook," said Polly.

"I'll do it," said Fiona. "I'm sick of burned food every other night. You, my girl, are going to write that letter. After that, you are going to write your essay, which I know you have not even started—"

"I did three sentences," Polly protested.

"Then you've nearly finished it, haven't you?" Fiona retorted over her shoulder as she went into the kitchen.

Polly sat down, eased, relieved, and, she thought, almost cheerful, until she tried to write the letter. It was not that this was difficult. It had always been easy to write to Mr. Lynn. It was not that. It was that she knew it would be no use. The letter would simply be written into a void. The Leroys would have thought of that.

She sat chewing her pen while scents of fried onions filled the air. She was still chewing it a while later when Fiona called, "Come and eat your nice spaghetti!"

Polly got up and went into the dining-Fiona's room, where food was on the table.

"You're to *eat* it," Fiona said. "You're beginning to look ill. Haven't written, have you?"

"No," confessed Polly. "You see, there's something else—something that I did—"

"Bound to have been," said Fiona. "Think of me. I wonder if Hans still walks with a limp. *Eat!*"

She said nothing more until Polly had managed half a small pile of spaghetti. Then, "You know," she said, "when you said the name like you did—Thomas Lynn—it rang some other bell. What did he do for a living?"

"Played the cello," Polly said. "He was with the B.P.O. first, but he left to form a quartet. They were trying to make good most of the time I knew him."

"Tough business," Fiona said. "I wonder if he did make good, since I really do seem to have heard of him." Seeing Polly was not going to eat any more, she scraped Polly's spaghetti onto her own plate and began to eat it, sighing. "This makes me realise that I have truly got over Hans," she said. "I'm hungry all the time. You know, it might be worth going and looking in a record shop, on the off chance they did a recording."

Here was another gift from Fiona's untrammelled memory. "Why didn't I *think?*" Polly said, leaping up to do it at once.

"Sit down. The shops are shut," Fiona said. "You do nothing until you produce an essay, even if I have to lock you up. Or why don't you ring him up?" Polly blenched. "If you've got an address, you can get the number through Enquiries," Fiona continued remorselessly. "Want me to try for you?"

Polly nodded. The phone number was in her head, printed on her brain, but it was useless to her. Mr. Leroy would know the moment she dialled it. She started to give Fiona the address instead, and, as she did so, found her hand leaping to clutch the opal pendant round her neck. She stopped, realising she had caught herself in the middle of something so habitual that she had never noticed till this moment. Is *this* how they did it?

"Hang on," she said to Fiona. "I'm not sure I've remembered it right." Pretending to think, she leaned over with her elbows on the table and undid the catch of the silver chain. The little opal heart slid softly among her hair and chinked onto her empty plate.

"Yes, I think this is it," Polly said, and she gave Fiona the address, right down to the postcode.

While Fiona went to the phone, Polly sprang up, busily and briskly, and piled the plates together. She carried them to the kitchen and scraped the remains of the food, and the pendant among them, into the bin. It seemed a wildly extravagant act, she thought as the lid clapped down, throwing away her one good piece of jewellery, and on mere suspicion too, but it seemed the only thing to do. Her neck felt naked without it as she went back to the dining room.

Fiona turned and held out the receiver. "Here you are. It's ringing."

Polly took it, and it rang and rang. Into a void, she thought. "He must have moved, Fiona. He used to have an answering machine."

She had her hand stretched out to put the receiver back on the rest, when she heard it answered by a breathless female voice.

"Hello?"

Polly snatched the receiver back. "Hello?"

"Oh, you're still there!" panted the voice. It was Carla's. Polly knew it from the buoyant shrillness, and even more from the loud yelling of a child nearby. "I'm sorry," Carla said, still breathless. "I keep forgetting his damn machine's not working. I'm supposed to take any messages for the Dumas Quartet or Lynn Musicians. Is that who you want?"

Confirmed! Polly thought. He really exists! "Could you take a message for Thomas Lynn?" she asked, wondering if Carla could hear her through the noise. It was not just one child yelling. There were at least three. It sounded as if there was a fight going on in the background. "This is Polly—"

"Just a second," said Carla. Her voice receded, and rose to a scream. "Shut up, will you! Stop that, or *I'll* thump you as well!" It came close again and spoke normally. "Sorry about that. Poly Tours, did you say?"

The children, Polly realised, had saved her from doing something very foolish. "How many children have you?" she asked, fascinated.

"Five," Carla said despairingly. "Can I have the name again?"

Across the room, Polly caught sight of Fiona staring with open-mouthed sympathy, and nearly laughed. "This is Polyphonic Assistants," she said. "Will Mr. Lynn be away long?"

"Mr. Lynn is on tour with the quartet at the moment," Carla said. She had gone all formal, thinking she was speaking to a firm of some kind. She recited the rest of the message she had evidently learned. "Mr. Lynn asked me to inform all business callers that he is sorry that he will not be available after October the thirty-first."

"Oh," said Polly. "Thank you."

"What is it?" Fiona asked impatiently as Polly slowly put the receiver back. "Married with six children, is he?"

"No," Polly said, frowning with another, much stronger uneasiness. "At least, she didn't say. No, it was the landlady. She said she had five children. I seem to remember Tom once telling me she had three husbands."

"Should keep her busy," Fiona said. "I wonder how that feels—three sets of slippers to warm, and so on. Now what?"

"I'm going to write an essay," Polly said. "First things first. Now I've spoken to two people who know Thomas Lynn exists, I may actually be able to think about Keats instead."

The essay got written, though it took Polly most of the rest of that night. After her tutorial, which went better than Polly felt she deserved, she went straight to a record shop, walking in a daze, thick-mouthed and light-headed from lack of sleep.

Two little girls, crouching on the pavement outside the shop, cut through her daze. "Penny for the Guy!" they shouted.

Polly glanced at the terrible thing they called a Guy. Heavens! she thought. The year *is* getting on. It must be nearly Guy Fawkes already!

She gave the girls five p. and went into the shop, a hushed temple of music where, under the clear light in the centre, she fumbled through a catalogue of records. Who wrote string quartets? Haydn, Mozart, Beethoven—loads of people. Try Beethoven. Ah! *Here they are!* Beethoven, the Late Quartets, a whole list of performers and, among them, the Dumas Quartet. Would it have been this one they recorded after Middleton Fair? They *did* do it, because Seb had known of it. Polly's teeth and spine felt the same queer pain she had felt at the Fair, as she remembered the mess Thomas Lynn had been in when they did that recording. She could have prevented that, by going with Seb when he asked her to. Seb had known what was likely to happen, definitely. He had tried to stop her going into the plywood castle.

Polly looked down to find that some pages of the catalogue had flopped over. The name leaped out at her. Cello sonatas, a well-known pianist and Thomas Lynn, cello. She was at the counter instantly, waving the catalogue at an assistant.

"Can I have this record, please?" And I bet it's not in stock, she thought as the assistant went away to look for it.

But he came back with it. Polly paid for it, numbly, a great deal more than she could afford. He put it in a bag and gave it her. She took it out again the moment he turned away and stared at the picture on the sleeve.

There sat Thomas Lynn, doubled round his cello in the way which had amused her in Bristol, with his head bent to listen out his music, just as she remembered. The large hand on the strings was the one she had hung on to at the funeral. His face had that look you could not argue with. It made Polly smile briefly and wonder what the photographer had tried to make him do. Take off his glasses, probably, in order to look better. Well, there was no need of that.

It gave her a huge shock to see it, even though she had expected just such a photograph, unreal lighting, black background, and all. For one thing, Fiona had been right to call Thomas Lynn good-looking. Polly, who had been thinking of him in terms of his likeness to the gaunt and unpleasant Mr. Piper, now saw that they resembled one another only in the way a caricature looks like a real person. Laurel, after all, liked them good-looking—witness Leslie.

But the thing which gave Polly the greatest shock was to see that Thomas Lynn was nothing like as old as she had thought.

She turned the record over and took a bewildered look at the notes. It was a new record, out that year, so the photograph had to be fairly recent. *Thomas Lynn*, she read, *these days recognised as Britain's leading cellist* . . . Yes, she thought, he had made himself that, by sheer hard work and determination, shaking himself loose from Laurel's disastrous clutches by fierce, dogged stages, dragging the rest of the quartet up with him. When Polly first met him, she suspected he must have been so bleached and drained from the struggle to get divorced from Laurel that she had taken him for an old man, as children do. But he was not, she thought, turning the record the other way again. He simply had that kind of colourless fair hair, darker than hers, which she had vaguely taken for grey. Instead of which, he was young, with a career in the making.

Until, of course, Polly had stepped in and destroyed him.

Polly put the record back in its bag and went out of the shop, stepping over the two little girls with the Guy on the way. They had the cheek to ask her for another five p.

"Get lost!" Polly told them, and marched unseeing back to the flat. There, with absent-minded industry, she dragged Fiona's turntable and speakers through to her own room and put the record on.

It took only a few bars to assure her that Thomas Lynn was a very good cellist indeed. His playing had that drive to it which gave you the sense of the shape of the music opening out before him as he played. And he kept that drive and shape, whether the cello was grumbling against the piano, crisply duetting, or out on its own, coaxed into hollow golden song. That feeling of a pattern being made, Polly thought, that I had in the panto. Except that this was so expert and so varied that it was hard to believe that it was being done with a musical instrument in somebody's hands.

Halfway through, Polly could hardly bear to listen to more and nearly took the record off. She knew what she had done now. But she kept it on, and turned it over, then back again to the first side, several times, while she recalled that time a month after Middleton Fair.

4

That is the path of Wickedness,
Though some call it the Road to Heaven.

THOMAS THE RHYMER

As soon as she had made her decision to ask Tom, Polly's misery gave way to a gleeful, furtive excitement. She stopped worrying about right and wrong. She did not even have to consider how to do it.

It had been obvious to her, from the moment Seb first suggested it, that simply asking Tom in the normal way was no good at all. Something quite other was called for. She set about it as methodically and secretly as someone planning a crime. In the morning she went for a walk, as far into the outskirts of Middleton as she could get, where the houses began to give way to the country. There she searched the sides of the road for dead hemlock. Since the hemlock was high and flowering in the hedgerows just then, she was unlucky and had to make do with a handsome living green stalk of it.

But she was lucky enough to find a large wad of greying old straw near the riding school. She took a number of hawthorn sprigs from the hedges too. These she brought home and hid from Granny as if they were things she had stolen.

Granny had a bad cold and was not very observant. She went away to lie down in the afternoon. As soon as she had, Polly gleefully grabbed up the large silver ashtray from the front room and hurried upstairs with it. There she made sure of privacy by wedging a chair under the doorknob and set about her final preparations. Remembering it four years later, Polly was amazed at the amount she had worked out and the things she knew, almost by instinct.

She took down the *Fire and Hemlock* picture and propped it against the wall at the back of her low table. She put the ashtray in front of that, so that she could stick the twigs of hedge in the crack between it and the picture. Carefully, between the twigs, she balanced the five painted soldiers Tom had once sent her. She had to use all five, because she had never been sure which two stood for Tan Coul and Hero. In front of the ashtray she stood the hemlock head, upright in a milk bottle. She put the straw in the ashtray itself, heaped as far as possible into the same shape as the burning straw in the picture, and mixed it with a few strands of her own hair. She knew it was important to mix herself and Tom together in the elements of the picture. She had it all worked out, as blindly and instinctively as a flea jumps to suck blood. She was rather annoyed that she had nothing to stand for the horse that sometimes appeared in the smoke, and she wished she could have used Tom's blood, but her white top had been washed. Instead, she used the postcard which said *Sentimental drivel*. She did not mind losing that.

When everything was ready, Polly unhooked the stolen oval photograph and knelt down in front of the table, facing the picture, in the greatest excitement. She remembered seeing her own face, vivid, almost laughing, reflected in the glass of the *Fire and Hemlock* picture while she struck a match and lit one corner of the postcard. When that was burning, she carefully poked it among the straw and hair in the ashtray. She knelt, holding the stolen photograph, while chaffy smoke began to wreathe upwards. The photograph, she was sure, had power to bring Tom to her. Both pictures together would surely make him tell. She told herself that she did not really think it would work. But she knew it would.

Smoke poured upwards in a sudden cloud that made Polly cough, suffusing the hemlock in the milk bottle and hiding the picture entirely. There was an instant when Polly was terrified, unable to see anything but smoke. But then, with a sort of flick, she seemed to be somewhere else where she could see perfectly well. It was a room she did not know. She knew she was not really in it, because she could feel her knees pressing into the mat in her own room all through, but when Tom got up from the large sofa in the strange room and came hurriedly towards her, she knew he could see her as if she were standing there.

"Polly!" he said, quiet and horrified. "What are you doing?"

Now it had worked, Polly's glee returned. She chuckled with it. When Tom got up, she thought she had seen a woman on the sofa too, probably asleep. She leaned cheerfully and cheekily round him to see if it was Mary Fields, and answered rather triumphantly, "I've come to ask you some questions at last." The woman was not Mary. She was Laurel, Laurel asleep and looking staggeringly, heart-rendingly beautiful. Polly said indignantly, "What are *you* doing, come to that? How often do you get together with Laurel?"

"As little as I can help—hardly at all, these days," Tom answered, whispering in order not to wake Laurel. "Polly, go away! It may still be all right if you stop now."

"But I want to know!" Polly said. "Does Laurel own you, or something?"

"You could say that." Tom turned to make sure Laurel was still asleep.

Polly knew he was completely miserable, but she felt no sympathy at all, only a hard kind of triumph. "Well, you should have told me!" she said. "I can't help you if you don't tell me anything, can I?"

"I sent you enough books about it!" Tom said angrily.

"That's not the sa—" Polly was saying when Tom moved sharply aside.

Behind him, Laurel was awake, sitting up on the sofa. "Tom?" she said like a little icy needle.

"The undying Laurel is awake," Tom said to Polly. He said it fiercely and meaningly and she noticed that he had put one hand up to his face almost as if he was trying to shield his eyes.

Polly did not understand. Laurel said, "Tom!" again, warningly. Polly looked at her and met Laurel's eyes. After that, Polly was only aware of Laurel and the empty tunnels of Laurel's eyes . . .

Everything went a little muzzy then. Polly knew she cleared up the charred stuff in the ashtray and hung both pictures up again. Probably she tidied everything away. She must have taken the ashtray back to the living room, she supposed, because it was certainly there afterwards. She knew she was downstairs with the kettle on to make Granny some tea, when the doorbell rang. Unless that was a day later. If it was the same day, Laurel had worked awfully fast.

Anyway, the kettle was on and the doorbell rang. Polly went to answer it. It was Seb. Smiling.

"Polly, come round to the house and meet my folks. Everyone's there. Even old Tom's come down for the weekend."

That, of course, fetched Polly along at once. She combed her hair, took the kettle off—like the rhyme, she remembered thinking—and went along with Seb.

There were a lot of people gathered in the room in Hunsdon House where the Will had been read. Most of them were people Polly dimly remembered from the funeral. They were having a moving-about kind of tea, sometimes sitting down with teacups, sometimes getting up and helping themselves to sandwiches or cakes from a couple of trolleys and then sitting down somewhere else. It was the kind of event you dread when you are fifteen. You know you are going to tread on a sandwich or sit on your cake. Polly would have felt quite crushed in the ordinary way, even, but this was worse. Here was Mr. Leroy confusingly coming and shaking hands as if Polly was an old friend, Laurel turning round to give a nod and a gracious smile, and Tom in the distance not coming near her at all. Uneasiness grew in Polly, the way it had over Joanna in Bristol. She was not muzzy any more. Everything was quite sharp, but the uneasiness grew. Tom, typically, was sitting hunched up on the arm of a sofa, with one foot on the cushions, bending forward to talk to a Leroy Perry lady. He did not seem to know Polly was there. Polly tried to tell herself that he could have looked at her sideways, with the look almost hidden by his glasses, but she knew she was deceiving herself.

She was forced politely into an armchair by Mr. Leroy. He fetched her a cup of tea and Seb gave her a plate with a sandwich on it. Polly was by then so uneasy that she wanted to scream and run away, but everything was so polite that she did not dare.

Before long, Laurel came to sit leaning sideways towards her from another armchair. Scents from her wafted across Polly's tea-cup. "Polly, dear. I've been wanting to have a little talk with you for quite a while now. Seb tells me you may have some very strange ideas in your head about poor Tom."

Polly tried to pull herself together. "I don't think so," she said bluntly.

"No, dear, but they may be, for all that," Laurel said kindly. She smiled affectionately across the room to where Tom was hunched up, talking. "I suspect that you may have mistaken the situation quite appallingly. We're all very fond of Tom, you know, and so sad about him." She turned back to Polly, and Polly was aghast to see tears twinkle and brim in Laurel's eyes. "Poor Tom," Laurel said. "He's going to die. In about four years now. The doctors can't do a thing." Her voice caught throatily and she put up a knuckle to catch the tear making its way down her face. "Terrible, isn't it?"

Oh God! Polly thought. Is this why Tom would never talk about himself? I may have been an awful fool! In her shame and horror, she could only stammer, "Wh-what of?"

"One of those cancer things," Laurel said sadly. "That's why I said I'd speak to you when Tom asked me to."

"He *asked* you to?" Polly said.

"Of course." Laurel put a knuckle to her other eye. "Or I'd never have dreamed of saying a word. I still adore Tom. We only got divorced because he insisted on it when he heard the news."

Oh my heaven! Polly thought. What an idiot I've been! Of course Laurel and Mr. Leroy would want to keep an eye on Tom if they knew he was ill. It was quite possible that she had gone blundering in, mistaking the whole thing entirely. She had thought there was something supernatural—but how stupid and babyish! There was no such thing.

"He's the soul of consideration—poor Tom," Laurel said. "And loving him as I do, I quite understand how you feel, Polly. Let me see, you first met Tom at Seb's mother's funeral, didn't you?"

"I—thought that was *your* mother's—" Polly managed to say.

"No, dear. It was poor Seb's," said Laurel. "And then of course you were quite a *little* girl. Children always adore poor Tom. But I do think nowadays you might show him the kind of consideration he always shows you. You're embarrassing him, dear. You've got what's called a crush on him, haven't you?"

Polly could not say anything. Shame rose up in her and scoured through her, bleaching everything. This was far worse than she had ever felt in Bristol. She could only look across at Tom's hunched shape, bleached faint and wavering like a mirage. Oh, what a fool she had been!

"I'm asking you to leave poor Tom in peace for the little time he has left," Laurel said kindly, gently. "I know it's hard. But couldn't you agree to forget him?"

"I—" Polly tried to say. Everyone in the room must know what a fool she had been. She could see faces turning to her, dimly, smiling kindly and pityingly.

"He's only *got* four years, and you've got the rest of your life," Laurel said gently. "Think what it means to him, when he had to ask me to ask you—"

Polly could take no more. She put her teacup down on the small table near her chair and then backed away from it with her hands stretched out to push it from her, as if the teacup were her stupidity. And that was a silly way to behave too. The people who had been looking at her were all turning away, embarrassed to look.

"Think," said Laurel, "if someone was hanging round *you*, pestering and sighing, for all the life you had—"

"Oh all right! Don't go on!" Polly cried out. "I didn't mean—Of course I'll forget him! Just leave me alone!"

Things began to go dim again after that. Polly remembered sitting for a while, bolt upright and staring at nothing, wishing she could leave, or that she could crawl into a hole and die of shame. She remembered her relief when Seb came and said it was time to go now. Polly got up and went with him into the hall with the jointed staircase and the Ali Baba jars, where things were already fading, fading—bleached away by her shame, she thought then—

when she heard Seb say, "Hey! Now, look here, Tom, you're not supposed—Oh, well—"

Polly looked round to find that Tom had come out into the hall too. "Goodbye, Polly," he said and bent down to give her a kiss on her forehead. Since Polly turned and looked up as he did it, the kiss landed, briefly and awkwardly, on her mouth. Brief, awkward, and sideways, Polly remembered, which caused Tom to take hold of her shoulder to pull her into a better position. But Seb gave a meaning cough and he let go. And that was really all she remembered. As soon as she left the house, her memories started to run single.

And plain, and dull, she thought. And she had done it to herself. And deserved it all, even being engaged to Seb, for not having the sense to remember something Tom had said himself: that being a hero means ignoring how silly you feel. She had let Laurel embarrass her into a state in which she could not even think straight. Laurel's persuasions, she could see blazingly clearly now, had all been aimed at making her say she would forget Tom. Without that, they could not have done a thing to her. And not, it seemed to follow, to Tom either. But they would have kept on at me, Polly thought. They would have got me to say it in the end. That was bound to follow, once she had opened the way by doing her peculiar piece of prying on Tom.

And that had been an awful thing to do. She knew that now. It had not been knowledge she was after. She had been just like Ivy—a miser who thought her hoard was being taken away—and she had been after revenge, because Tom had hurt her. So she had let Seb egg her on. But, she had to admit, she might have done it anyway, without any suggestion from Seb.

"And the most awful thing is the way I got it right!" Polly said aloud.

At some time, as she sat hunched over, thinking, Polly had been aware that Fiona had come in, hearing music playing. She had seen her look meaningly at the borrowed turntable, pick up the sleeve of the record to look at the picture, then nod and go out again.

"I must cook tonight," Polly said. Instead, she hunted out the paperback book which had jogged her memory awake. *Times out of Mind*, edited by L. Perry. Laurel evidently had quite a sense of humour, didn't she? But there seemed no more to be got out of this book, except the odd fact that Ed's story was printed as being by Ann. Polly smiled slightly. Ann had known too, perhaps in the same instinctive way Polly had—though, looking back on it, she thought that all three of the others in the quartet must have had some idea of what was going on. And Ann seemed to have done what she could. Tan Audel, famous for memory. She must have thought Polly could still do something. But what, what, what?"

Granny had said a book might help.

"All right," Polly said. "Let's try picking a book at random off my shelf." She swung back in her chair and, without looking, hooked her fingers round the first book she touched. "Probably *The Golden Bough*, if I'm anything like right now," Polly murmured. But it was not. She seemed to get hold of two books initially. One flopped to the floor. The other, which was much smaller, slipped easily into her hand. Polly stooped to the fallen one first. It was the book of fairy stories Tom had sent her once for Christmas that she had been too old to read. Naturally, it lay open face downwards in the way he hated books to be.

Polly scooped it up and looked to see where it had opened. It was the story called "East of the Sun and West of the Moon." Oh, that one! The one where the girl gets too curious, and the man vanishes to Nowhere to marry someone else, and she has an awful job to get him back. Yes, Polly thought, they may have laid it on him not to tell, but he made sure that I knew. And I did know, really.

Then she looked at the other, smaller book in her hand. *The Oxford Book of Ballads.* For four years she had seemed always to have had this book, with no idea where it came from. Now she knew it had arrived when she was twelve, under the name of Lee Tin, from a cathedral city somewhere. And this was the one. Polly's fingers shook as she opened it to the list of contents. The first two ballads were "Thomas the Rhymer" and "Tam Lin." Of course, when she was twelve, she had not known that Tam was simply a North Country form of the name Tom.

"Oh my God!" Polly said, and whipped over the pages to a certain part of the second ballad. She threw the book down and went dashing into the other room. *"Fiona!"* she screamed. "What *date* is it?"

Fiona looked up over the glasses she wore for reading. "Go away," she said unconvincingly. "I have an astute and beautiful essay to write myself now. The date is October the thirtieth."

Polly screamed, "Then it's tomorrow! I shall be too late! I must go home to Granny's at *once!*"

"The last bus went at six. You have to get permission. And there are two frozen platters heating in the kitchen at this moment,"

Fiona said. "Apart from that, you're free to go instantly. A taxi? Or do you prefer to hire a helicopter? Myself, I'd recommend the first bus tomorrow, and dear Fiona to see to all the rest. What's happened?"

"Nothing yet—I hope," said Polly. "But I'm going to interrupt you by ringing Seb." She seized the phone and dialled, with Fiona watching interestedly.

"Sebastian Leroy," said Seb's voice. He always answered the phone like that.

"It's me—Polly," said Polly. Her hand was so wet that the receiver nearly slipped out of it.

"Pol!" said Seb, and Polly winced at how glad he sounded to hear her. "I wrote you a letter. Did I get the address wrong?"

"No, but I've been awfully busy," Polly said, "so I thought I'd phone instead of writing, because things have slacked off now. Seb, can I come to London and see you tomorrow night?" She crossed her fingers and pressed them against the wood of the table, hard. Her hand jerked and slid with apprehension. If Seb agreed—

"Oh, bother! I wish you could," Seb said. "Pol, any other weekend but this! I'll be out of town from tomorrow till Monday. There's a tedious family gathering."

"In Middleton?" Polly asked brightly. "Can I come to Hunsdon House and see you there, then?"

"No, precious," Seb said, with his most indulgent churring laugh. "For tedious, my love, read private conclave. Strictly family. Anyone less than half-blood definitely not admitted. Make it next weekend. Please."

"I'm not free then," Polly said. But she dared not refuse outright, for fear he would realise the real reason for her phone call. "How about the weekend after that?"

"Fine. I'll ring you up about it the moment I get back," Seb promised.

Polly rang off. So it was true. Carla had said Thomas Lynn was not going to be available after October the thirty-first. Seb was at his so-called tedious family gathering tomorrow. The same day, And she had to stop it. Somehow.

"Our phone bill," said Fiona, "will jump up and hit the gong at this rate. Polly, I'm disappointed. From the look on your face, I made sure you were going to give Marmaduke the push."

"That was collecting evidence for the push," said Polly. "Don't worry, he's got it. Now find me the bus timetable and I won't bother you again."

5

About the dead hour of the night
She heard the bridles ring,
And Janet was as glad of that
As any earthly thing.

TAM LIN

On the bus to Middleton the following day, Polly sat clutching the book of ballads. She did not need to read those first two. She had them more or less by heart by then. But she thought about them the whole way.

They were both about young men Laurel had owned, but their fates had been rather different. Thomas the Rhymer was a harpist, and a man of considerable spirit. When Laurel proposed rewarding him for his services by giving him the gift of always speaking the truth, Thomas objected very strongly indeed. He said his tongue was his own. But Laurel went ahead and gave it him. And what an awkward gift, Polly thought, one which could be downright embarrassing if Laurel happened to be annoyed when she gave it him. True Thomas, she called him, and turned him back into the ordinary world with his awkward gift after seven years. In the book, the story stopped there. But Polly knew she had read a longer version, perhaps in another book Tom had sent her, which made it clear that Thomas the Rhymer was still Laurel's property even after he got home. Years later she came and fetched him away and he did not come back.

The second Thomas had been taken as a boy, and he had escaped. He was rescued by a splendid girl called Janet, who was forever hitching her skirt up and racing off to battle against the odds. When the time came, Janet had simply hung on to her Tam. Laurel, or whatever she was calling herself then, had been furious.

Polly could only hope she might manage to do what Janet had done, but she was very much afraid it would not be quite like that. Despite the similarity of the names, it was not Tam Lin but Thomas the Rhymer whom Thomas Lynn most resembled. He had been turned out too, also with a gift. And Laurel had been furious with Thomas Lynn at the time. She was still furious at the funeral. So the gift had been given with a twist. Anything he made up would prove to be true, and then come back and hit him. Which must, Polly thought, have made things so much easier for Mr. Leroy.

But this was where Polly herself had come in. She had become connected to the gift because she had helped Mr. Lynn make up Tan Coul. And she rather thought that the gift had been intended to be conveyed through the pictures Tom had been allowed to take—shoddy, second-rate pictures, until Polly had stepped in there too and mixed the pictures up.

So I did some good, Polly thought as she got off the bus and hurried with long, anxious strides to Granny's house. Even if I cancelled it out later. Cancel it she had. Neither ballad more than hinted at what Laurel really needed young men for.

Granny opened the door blinking, roused in the middle of her rest. "My heavens!" she said delightedly. Then sharply, "You fetched it out."

"Yes," said Polly. "Come and sit down, Granny. I want to read you two things."

"Then just let me get the big pot full of tea," Granny said. "I can see this is going to be a session."

They went into the kitchen, where Granny made the tea and fetched out a tinful of her best biscuits. Then she sat opposite Polly, with Mintchoc draped across her knees, very upright and looking curiously obedient.

Polly read both ballads aloud to her, slowly and emphatically, pausing to explain the difficult words. "Well?" she said when she had finished.

"Read them again," said Granny.

Polly did so. "Does that mean anything to you, Granny?"

Granny nodded. "It's laid on them not to say, nor me to remember, but I keep what I can in my head by living where I do. She likes them young, she likes them handsome, and musical if she can get them. She seems to have a fancy for the name Tom too, doesn't she? But those rhymes have got one thing wrong, Polly. It's every *nine* years that the funeral comes down."

"And last time was a woman," said Polly. "Seb's mother— supposedly Laurel's mother, who is of course the same person as

Laurel. Laurel takes a new life every eighty-one years, and I suppose she has to pretend the dead woman is her mother so that she can inherit from herself. I think Thomas Lynn was lucky he didn't have to go then. Do you remember him now, Granny?"

"Oh yes," said Granny. Her hand smoothed Mintchoc. "The young man with the pictures. I should have been kinder to him for bringing you away from That House. But I was scared. I was going by Mintchoc, you see. She ran away from him on sight. And I thought He's one of Hers, that one. He'll be lucky if he can call his soul his own. And I was right, wasn't I?"

"You may have been then," Polly said. "But he was getting free somehow—I know he was—until I stopped him."

"I know it," Granny said. "Mintchoc sat on his knee the second time he came. That was a rainy day, and he was just off to Australia. I'd terrible sciatica that day."

Eh? thought Polly. Granny never rambled on about weather or sciatica unless she was trying to distract attention from something else. And of course she was. Mr. Leroy had got at Granny that Sports Day, just as Polly had feared he would. She leaned back in her chair and looked at her. "Granny, come clean. What did you do?"

"Told him off," said Granny. "You can look at me how you like, Polly, but I did right, and you know it! You were barely fourteen, and you worshipped the ground he walked on, and it was not right of him to let you. You'd your own life to live, Polly. It wouldn't have been right even if he was what he seemed and not one of Hers. And so I told him. He took it well too. I don't think he'd quite seen it before."

Polly sighed. "I suppose you were right—but, oh, I do wish you hadn't. That accounts for—It led to what I did—Never mind. What did he say?"

"Looked stricken, and then said he wouldn't forgive himself for using you," Granny replied.

"*Using* me?"

That was an odd thing to say, Polly thought. Chilling.

"So that was what I did," said Granny. "And what did *you* do, my lady?"

"I used that *Fire and Hemlock* picture," Polly said, bleaching with shame to admit, it even to Granny. She described what she had done that day. But she had barely got to the part where it had worked, and she had seen Tom with Laurel, when Granny arose, creaking a little, and gathered up Mintchoc.

"See what they do to your mind from That House," she said. "I'd wondered about that picture often, but I never thought to look. We'd best look at it at once, Polly." She marched up the stairs to Polly's room, and Polly marched after her, both of them so determined that Polly felt they needed military music playing to express it. "Take it down," Granny said, with her arms full of Mintchoc, nodding at the picture.

Polly carefully unhooked it and laid it on her bed. While she did it, she found she was watching Mintchoc as carefully as Granny was, but Mintchoc sat serenely against Granny's chest and did not seem perturbed. There seemed nothing to perturb anyone about the picture. It was a big, enlarged colour photograph, exciting enough, but still empty of the mystery Polly had seen in it as a child. "I've often wondered," she said, "why they never tried to take it back."

"My guess is they couldn't," Granny said. "It must have been his to give, and he gave it you. It looks to me as if the back unclips. Take it up, but carefully."

Polly turned the picture over to show the typewritten label that said simply *Fire and Hemlock*, and loosened the big clamps that held glass to picture and picture to the board behind. She pulled the board up. "Oh." There was a hank of hair inside, between the board and back of the photograph, pale hair, a little wavy. The sort of hair the boy in the stolen photograph had had. "The Obah Cypt," she said. "He never could think what it was. And I had it all the time." She put out a cautious fingertip and touched the hair. The wavy end she touched dissolved to dust as her finger met it. She snatched her finger back.

"Don't do that!" Granny said sharply. "Let it lie. You may have voided the charm, but there's no need to kill him. Put the back on again and let's have some more tea."

Down in the biscuit-scented kitchen again, where the clock seemed to tick louder as the room darkened, Polly sipped the new brew of tea and asked, "But have you any idea what I can *do*?"

"Maybe," said Granny. "Read me the charm out of the second song again."

"Charm?" said Polly.

"Goose," said Granny. "The bit that sticks out from the rest. Give it here. I'll know it. It talks generally." She took the book and leaned back so that her long-sighted eyes could see the print. "Here we are—and I wish I'd known of it when I was your age—

The night it is good Hallowe'en,
The fairy folk do ride,
And they that would their true-love win
At Miles Cross they must bide.

There's what you do. Plain as a pikestaff."

"What? Go to the station?" Polly said.

"Where else?" said Granny. "Between twelve and one o'clock, it says. But I should be there by eleven, if I were you. We don't know what clock they're keeping."

She seemed so certain that Polly took the book back and looked at the rest. The instructions, once you began to see them as that, were very clear and detailed.

"And there'll be three companies, it says, and he'll be in the last. And not the brown or the black, but the white. Are you sure?"

"Well, you'll have to look sharp about you. It may not seem the same in these modern days."

"And then just hang on to him, I suppose, whatever they do to stop me," Polly said. "That's what Janet did. But I've a feeling that won't seem the same either."

"If *she* could, *you* can," Granny said. She chuckled. "I must say I like that Janet, even though she was no better than she should be." She was quiet for a moment, sitting very upright, with the clock ticking loudly in the near-dark of the kitchen. Polly could see the white outlines of Granny's face and no more. It struck her suddenly that she now knew what Granny looked like when she was young, knew it properly, not just from a photograph. "And I envy her too," Granny added.

"What do you mean?" Polly asked.

"Your grandfather," said Granny. "He was called Tom too. She does like that name. You should have heard him play the violin, Polly. But she took him when the nine years were up. I didn't know any charm to help. I was left alone, with Reg ready to be born."

"Oh." There seemed nothing Polly could say. This explained so much about Granny, and probably a great deal about Reg too. She sat in the dark, thinking of Granny, all these years doing what she could not to forget, and a memory came to her. Her own hands with woolly gloves on, carefully hanging a little oval photograph up in the place of the one she had decided to steal. She wondered if the old-fashioned boy in it had been her grandfather.

From there she passed to wondering about the way Hunsdon House had opened that time to let her in to take the photograph. It must have been hers to take, then. Did that mean there was some hope now, or not?

Here Granny sprang up, saying, "This won't do!" and turned on the light. "I must get some food into you if you're to walk to Miles Cross before eleven." She looked closely at Polly. "You're not wearing your pendant."

"No," said Polly.

"Better be safe than sorry," Granny said.

"But think of being both at once," said Polly. "I've passed the point where I care about being safe. Besides, they've been able to get round it for years."

Granny sighed, but accepted it. Apart from insisting as strongly as Fiona that Polly eat something, she said very little else. When

Polly got up to leave, Granny kissed her goodbye without comment and went to the door with her. It proved to be pouring with rain outside. Granny picked the famous green-and-white umbrella out of the hall stand and put it in Polly's hand. "Any other time I'd say make sure to bring it back," she said. "But don't put it up inside the house, all the same."

Granny, Polly thought as she trudged off into the rain, was not really expecting to see her back.

The rain had slacked to a drizzle by the time Polly reached the station. The forecourt was black and shiny, and unreal with orange wriggles of light. A little hesitantly Polly crossed it and approached the thing in the middle that she had always thought was a fountain. She now saw it was a cross, old and weather-bitten and eroded, like the one in Stow-on-the-Water. She climbed the steps to it and stood leaning against the upright. And waited. The entire place seemed deserted, although there was dim light in the station building. There were no people about, and nothing to do but watch the rain run in little orange-lit shivers across the black forecourt.

I'm on a wild-goose chase, she thought some time after eleven had struck in the distance. The railway station was a silly place to be. It had to be wrong. She should have gone to Hunsdon House. But the book had been so clear, and she had no other guide. She went on waiting. She knew she would still be standing here at two o'clock, just on the wild chance it was true. It was not because of the things Fiona had said, or Granny, or because she was determined not to be embarrassed off this time. It was not even because Tom had given her an awkward, sideways goodbye kiss. It was because this really was the only way she knew to prevent certain murder.

The drizzle kept gusting in under Granny's umbrella. Polly was soaked through and her feet were numb by the time she heard midnight striking. And still nothing had happened. She put her wrist close to her eyes and tried to see her watch in the murky orange light. I'll give it five minutes, she thought. If nothing's happened by then, I'll have to go, and run like crazy to Hunsdon House. This *has* to be wrong! It was stupid to trust an old rhyme like that. Her hand shook drops from the spikes of the umbrella from the effort she had to make not to start running to Hunsdon House that instant. She put her watch to her eyes again. It was ticking, but the hands did not seem to have moved.

But there were some people coming. Polly heard them crossing the court in the distance, in an irregular splashing of feet, a lot of them, with whistles, catcalls, and loud, drunken-sounding laughter. She moved the umbrella to look and saw a riotous crowd of dark shapes stampeding towards the station entrance. Only a crowd of drunken youths, after all. Polly subsided against the cross, feeling rather exposed and more certain than ever that she had foolishly come to the wrong place. The boys did not notice her. They went straight to the station building, laughing and whooping and pushing one another about, where, in the doorway, their progress was interrupted by the inevitable drunken quarrel. The group milled about, and loud, young voices barked like dogs for a second or so. After that, they seemed to sort it out, and all went piling into the booking hall. But just for that second enough dim light fell on the struggling bodies for Polly to see that one of them was Leslie.

I think this really is it! she thought.

Shortly after that, several big cars drove into the forecourt. Each raced past Polly, slashing rain across her, gleaming under the light so that they looked almost unreal, and stopped in a group near the station entrance. The doors opened. The headlights blazed ample, freckled light.

Laurel got out of one car with a number of other women, all beautifully dressed. Mr. Leroy and Seb, in smart suits, got out of another. And a crowd of other people, equally well dressed, whom Polly vaguely knew as Hunsdon House folk, climbed out of the other cars. All held their hats or put up umbrellas and hurried into the station.

There was no longer any doubt. Polly leaned on the knobby stone of the cross, knowing she only had to wait. And behind the umbrella she heard more cars. One stopped. Another. Handbrakes croaked. A third stopped, with a wild squeal of wet tires. Doors slammed. Feet barked on the tarmac. Two dark figures hurried by, one short, one tall, carrying violin cases. Ed seemed to be in black, Sam in dark brown. Neither of them saw Polly. Tom came next, wearing a light-coloured padded parka, carrying his cello case, and turning his light-coloured head to say something to Ann, who was a little behind.

6

And see you not yon bonny road
That winds across the ferny lea?
That is the road to fair Elfland
Where you and I this night must be.

THOMAS THE RHYMER

Polly found herself smiling because of the well-known way Tom's head turned. It was an utter delight just to see it again. Now watch it! Watch it, she told herself. She was reminded of the glee she had felt while she set up that piece of witchcraft with the picture. It was not to be like that this time. This was not what it was about. All the same, she was so glad! She was still smiling as she slipped round the cross and down the steps, tottering a bit on her numb feet, and seized hold of Tom's arm. She felt it tense and jerk. "Hello," she said.

It did not surprise her particularly when Tom turned and peered at her blankly through his rain-speckled glasses. "I think you've made a mistake of some kind," he said.

"No I haven't," Polly said. It was bound to be like this. "And I'm hanging on to you from now on."

By this time Ann had passed them and joined Ed and Sam. Tom hurried after them, shaking his arm to free it from Polly, and Polly went with him, hanging on. "Will you please let go," he said.

"My good woman," Polly prompted him. "No, I won't."

"What's the matter with you? Do you want money or something?"

"You know perfectly well I don't!"

"I don't know anything about you. Let go!"

They passed the car Laurel's party had come in, practically fighting. Polly saw Ann, Ed and Sam pause in the station doorway and look round for Tom. Seeing the struggle, they turned away, obviously embarrassed, and went inside. "I'm not going to let—!" Polly was panting, when another person pushed past them and hurried into the station too. Tom tore himself loose from Polly with almost no trouble at all and plunged after. Polly saved herself from falling by catching hold of the wing mirror of Laurel's car, but her numb feet let her down. She could hear the thumping of feet from inside the booking hall, and raised voices, but by the time she made her feet take her through the doorway, the quarrel seemed to have died down.

Ed was standing with Ann and Sam, blocking the way through to the platform. All of them looked angry and Ed was rubbing his arm. Mr. Piper was looming in front of them, like something at bay. Tom was buying a ticket, with his back to everyone.

"Let me through," Mr. Piper said peremptorily. When none of the three moved, he turned and shouted, "Tom! For pity's sake! I'm in a hurry. She's got Leslie now!"

Tom turned round and gave his yelp of laughter. "So much for your hiding and pretending!" he said. "If you'd told the truth, you could have warned him. Don't worry. The train will wait for me."

Ann and Sam moved slowly aside. Ed moved even more reluctantly, and as Mr. Piper dived past him, out onto the platform beyond, he shouted after him, "And be careful who you're shoving another time!" While Ed was shouting, Tom picked up his cello. All four hurried after Mr. Piper, so quickly that Polly nearly got left behind. She ran to the ticket window, fumbling out her student card and a five-pound note, which was all the money she had.

"The same, please," she said. She supposed the clerk behind the window knew. A ticket came back, and quite a lot of change. A short journey, then. Polly snatched it up and ran. The train might wait for Tom, but it would not wait for her, which Tom of course knew. But, thanks to Mr. Piper, Polly also knew that Tom had not been trying to shake her off as hard as he had pretended. She ignored her lifeless feet and sprinted.

The train was at the platform, beginning to move. Polly was in time to see Tom's white parka through the glass of one of the doors. She put on a spurt and managed to claw hold of that door. Then, hopping on one foot as the train gathered speed, she got it open and threw herself inside the train. The door crashed shut behind her.

Inside, it was a perfectly normal train, with a gangway down the middle and rows of foursome tables on either side. Ann, Sam and Ed had already taken three seats at a table some way along. It was obvious that Tom would join them in the fourth seat as soon as he had finished stowing his cello. Polly darted up the gangway and stood in front of the fourth seat, stopping him. Ed and Ann looked at her, and looked away. Sam's face twisted with embarrassment as Tom turned round and saw Polly. He stood waiting.

"Get out of my way, please."

"No. And you do know me," Polly said.

"I've never seen you before in my life," said Tom.

"Nonsense. I haven't changed that much," Polly said. She leaned one hand on the table to look at Ed. "Ed, do *you* know me?" Ed shook his head and tried to avoid her eyes. It was the way anyone behaves when a stranger tries to pester him on a train. Sam was already looking away when Polly turned to him. They really did not know her, any more than Leslie had done. Still, I'm *not* going to be embarrassed out of it this time! Polly thought. That was something of a clue, really. Laurel thought she would be. Laurel worked by admissions, one way or another. Polly looked on to Ann. "Do *you* know me, Ann?"

Ann was clearly very tired. She was leaning sideways with her head on Sam's shoulder. She looked up at Polly, direct and penetrating and dark, and frowned. "I think I do, somehow. But I'm afraid I don't know your name."

"Bless you, Tan Audel!" Polly said. She turned to Tom in triumph, but he simply walked up the gangway to another seat and sat there. Polly followed, and sat down facing him. Tom behaved as it she was not there.

He took his wet glasses off and cleaned them with a handkerchief. Without them, Polly could see how white and hollow-cheeked and strained his face was. Water dripped from her hair, and her elbows left damp smudges on the table while she sat there studying him. The train clattered round them, hurrying away into the night.

He did know her, Polly was sure. What he felt about her turning up again like this was another matter, but it did look as if Laurel had forced some kind of prohibition on him not to know her. So it followed that it must be important to get him to admit that he did. Or was this simply Polly's own feelings making her think this? She had been prepared to be cool and alert and collected, and it was all overthrown by her utter delight at seeing him again. She wanted to burst into wild, joyful laughter.

"I know I must be one more damn thing to you," she said, "but I have come to help if I can. I want to make amends for what I did to you—or apologise at least." Tom held his glasses up towards the light overhead to see if they were clean, and did not answer. "Do you know," Polly said, "the Obah Cypt turned out to be the *Fire and Hemlock* picture? I had it all along. There was a lock of your hair in the back of it—I found it today."

Tom put his glasses back on and unzipped his wet parka. He sat back, staring beyond Polly. "I seem to be shut in a train with a raving female," he said. "There is no such thing as an Obah Cypt."

"Well, it's the only name I know for it," Polly said. "Who *is* Mr. Piper? He seems to have been Tan Coul as much as you were. There *was* a giant in the supermarket. Edna told me."

"What institution did you escape from?" said Tom.

Some of the wild laughter did break loose from Polly. "St. Margaret's College, Oxford. I share a padded cell with Fiona Perks."

"Go back there," said Tom.

"How ungrateful!" said Polly. "Don't forget you started it by hauling me out of that funeral."

Tom did not answer.

Polly bit her own tongue angrily. Polly, you fool! Keep off funerals. Of all the things to remind him of! "I think," she said, "I've gone and left Granny's famous umbrella on the steps of Miles Cross. You know the one? The big green and white umbrella you held over her that Sports Day before you went to Australia." Tom did not reply. Polly tried again. "I don't exactly blame Granny for telling you off then. She was right, according to her own lights, even though I suspect Morton Leroy had got to her. After all, Granny wasn't to know you'd already made it quite plain at the panto that I was nothing but a complete nuisance to—"

"Come off that, P—!" Tom began violently. And stopped. "Did you happen to remark what your name was?" he asked carefully.

The laughter tore loose from Polly again. "No." she said. "I didn't, and you know it. And, of course, my name isn't Polly, as you also know. It's Hero."

She had done it, Polly realised. She had got it right. Tom took his glasses off again and attended to what was probably an imaginary smear, and he was smiling as he wiped them, all over his strained face, in the same way that Polly was, as if he could not help it. He put the glasses on again, leaned his elbows on the table, and did at last look at Polly. "Polyphonic Assistants," he said. "You shouldn't have done that. You never did understand the risk."

"Yes I did," said Polly. "I had a talk with Morton Leroy after that pantomime. Had you known all along?"

Tom shook his head. Around them, the train rushed and rattled into darkness. The noise and the pressure suggested they were going through a tunnel. Tom had to shout against the clatter. "Not a notion, to begin with—it was too unbelievable—just like Tan Coul in the supermarket—slowly realising it could only be a giant—"

"That's the gift she gave you," Polly shouted back. "Things you make up to come true and then turn round and hit you."

"Not till you wrote Leroy by mistake for Legris," Tom shouted. "Then I saw. But you still think 'This can't happen to me!' I still do."

The things Polly wanted to shout in reply to this were lost, because the train rushed out of the tunnel again, into bright daylight. It burst across them so that they both had to shield their eyes from the brightness. When Polly managed to blink out of the window, she found they were travelling along beside the sea. White surf was folding and smashing almost beside the rails, and a myriad dazzles flickered off the grey water stretching towards the sun.

"Is it always like this?" she said.

"I think it varies," said Tom. "I've only ridden in Laurel's train once before. It was hills and deserts then. Whatever suits her sense of humour, I think."

"I could do without her sense of humour," Polly said bitterly. "True Thomas. You haven't got cancer, have you?"

"Is that what she told you?" Tom pushed his hands wearily over his face, lifting his glasses to rub his eyes. The train was slowing down now, noticeably. Tom's face looked as if his rubbing hands were wiping the colour out of it with every rub.

"If I'd been thinking of you at *all*," Polly said, angry and remorseful, "I could have seen through that. She only lied when I asked. You taught me about sentimental drivel, but I didn't think of that *once*!"

The brakes of the train were shrieking. A station of some kind was sliding into view. Tom stood up. "Well, I'd had years of Laurel, and you hadn't."

Polly stood up too. Down the carriage, Sam, Ed and Ann were collecting their instrument cases and moving to the door. When they got there, they stood looking back doubtfully, waiting for Tom.

"You go on," Tom called to them. "There's only one way to go. You can't miss it. I'll catch you up in a minute." Ann nodded and got off the train. Sam and Ed looked at one another before they followed her, clearly wondering whether to come back and rescue Tom from Polly, and then deciding that it would be too embarrassing. They got off too, and Tom turned to collect his cello.

"Can't you just not go?" Polly said.

"I don't really want them coming to fetch me," Tom said. "Off you get."

Polly and he climbed off the train onto an empty, sunlit platform. The place seemed deserted. They walked across the platform, and their feet boomed on the hollow wooden floor of the booking hall. Outside was a long street, lined on each side with chestnut trees, from which big orange leaves, like hands, drifted down across Ann, Ed and Sam, walking ahead in the distance. Above the trees stood the moon, flat and white in the blue sky.

"You shouldn't have come," Tom said as they set off down the street. "I'd suggest you don't come any further, except that I think the only way out now is to go on."

"I know you won't want me looking on—" Polly said.

"I don't," he said. "But it's not that. You don't understand—there's nothing you can do now."

"Yes there is," said Polly. "I have to hang on to you."

Tom sighed. "I knew you didn't understand. You were doing that for about five years, but you stopped. I can't say I blame you." A hand-like leaf felt on the case of the cello, and slid off again. Polly shuddered. "Anyhow," Tom said, "I'm quite glad of a chance to apologise."

"Apologise!" said Polly. "I'd have thought it was the other way round."

"Both ways round then," said Tom.

"Mary Fields?" asked Polly.

He shrugged. "That too, I suppose. Some of it was an attempt to keep the heat off you. Poor Mary. I haven't seen her for over a year now."

They walked on, with leaves pattering to the street around them. Polly cheerlessly considered. At least she was not being troubled with that pointless gladness any more. Allowing for the fact that Tom was bound to be in a strange state of mind, things seemed no different from the way they always had been. "Then why are you still trying to choke me off?" she said. "You are. You have been ever since I knew you."

"What else could I do?" Tom demanded. "I had to keep getting in touch, and sending you things, because you were my only chance, but I didn't have to like what I was doing, particularly after Morton found out. And I drove a bargain with Laurel after that, not to harm you—"

"Don't tell me!" Polly said. "And I've just made you break that one too. I told you not to protect me. Years ago."

"But you also told me not to be obedient," Tom pointed out.

At this, Polly rounded on him in exasperation, and found they had come to the end of the street. It ended in two stone pillars supporting an open gate. The name Hunsdon House was engraved deep into each pillar. "We seem to have got Nowhere," she said dryly.

"What did you expect?" Tom put down his cello in the gateway and leaned against the left-hand pillar. Polly did not blame him for being reluctant to go in. "Let's not wrangle any more," he said. "I'm almost out of time." He held out a hand towards Polly.

Polly stumbled over the cello in her hurry to get near and nearly fell against Tom's chest. They wrapped their arms around one another. Tom was more solid and limber than Polly had expected, and warmer, and just a little gawky. He threaded both hands into Polly's damp hair and kissed her eyes as well as her mouth. "I've always loved your hair," he said.

"I know," Polly said.

They stayed clenched together in the gateway until Polly became aware of Laurel's sweet, tinkling voice. "Tom!" it said from somewhere in the distance, more and more insistently. "Tom!" It became impossible to ignore. They sighed and let go of one another. Tom picked up the cello again and they walked side by side up the shaded drive and round towards the garden where Laurel's voice was coming from. Polly was light-headed with strange, miserable joy. In a way it was worth it, she thought, except that it was such a total waste.

At first sight it seemed to be autumn in the garden. The trees there were an unmoving glory of rust, copper-green, olive-silver and strong yellow, fading to purple and deep rose red. But it was hot as summer. Polly's hair and Tom's parka steamed in the heat. Swallows flickered in the blue sky overhead, and bees filled the crowding roses to one side—not white roses as Polly remembered, but heavy red and bronze and glaring pink. The shape of the garden had changed too. The lawn now sloped clear down from the house to the place with the empty concrete pool, which was in full view, flanked by six-foot growths of hemlock. The pool was not precisely empty any longer. It was shimmering, all over a surface that did not seem to be there. Strong, colourless ripples bled upwards from it, like water or heated air, wavering the hemlocks and the trees where they passed. Polly could not look at it.

The people were all gathered in the upper part of the lawn, holding wine glasses. It could have been a harmless, charming picnic. They were in elegant clothes, the women in long dresses and picture hats, the men in white or in morning dress. There was a murmur of talk and laughter. Laurel, wearing a long green gown, was reclining in a swinging garden seat under a little tree whose leaves were the same orange-brown as the drink she was sipping. Leslie was lolling beside her on the seat. He did not seem to be able to take his eyes off Laurel. The look on his face was dreamy, besotted, adoring, but spiced with wickedness, as if at least half his feelings were guilty ones.

Seeing Leslie, Tom muttered something and turned rather sharply away to one side of the garden seat, where four chairs and four music stands were set out. Ann and Sam and Ed were there, unpacking music and getting out their viola and violins. They looked round as Tom and Polly came up, with relieved recognition.

"So you got here!" Sam said to Polly. "That makes me feel better."

"Let's hope we can do something," Ed added.

Ann just smiled at Polly, tensely and meaningly. So they know me, Polly thought. Which means that Laurel has no need to bother any more. She watched Tom shed his parka to show a sober, ordinary suit like Sam's and Ed's. The four of them sat down and began tuning strings, as if they had been hired to entertain the picnic party. And the elegant, chatting people took no more notice of them than they did of the various servitors going round with drinks. Nobody offered the quartet a drink. They were just hired servants too. Which, Polly thought, was what Tom had been all along to these people.

Here she looked up to see Seb and Mr. Leroy staring at her. They were standing together lower down the lawn, and Polly had seldom seen two people look more aghast. The identical horror on their faces brought out the likeness between them, although Seb was tall and trim and elegant in white, and Mr. Leroy was elderly and yellowing and ill, sagging inside his grey morning coat. As Polly looked, Seb said something to his father—it was clearly, "Let me handle her!"—and hurried up the slope to Polly.

He's even getting dark places under his eyes, Polly thought as Seb came up to her.

"My Pol!" said Seb. "What are you doing here?"

"I remembered," said Polly. "I've come for Tom."

Seb sagged, so that he looked even more like Mr. Leroy, and fixed her with a sort of desperate glare. "Polly! Think of *me*!"

"I am," said Polly, "and I don't like what I'm thinking. I don't like what you did."

Seb, to do him justice, made no attempt to bluster or pretend. "But it was between me and him," he said. "It always was. And Tom used you too. Surely you understand, Polly! If they don't take him, they'll take me instead."

Polly turned her eyes from his desperately glaring face. Beside her, Tom was bending over the strings of his cello, not looking at her, pretending he could not hear every word Seb said. She thought of the way Seb had gripped her that time, outside the Leroys' London flat, and she did see that Seb had been afraid for most of his life. Beyond Seb, Mr. Leroy saggingly propped himself on a stick, and down beyond him the transparent living current bled upwards from the pool, shimmering the hemlocks. Seb had managed her, Polly thought, just as he always did, and brought her to a complete dead end. Her eyes moved on to Leslie. He was gently swinging the seat, smiling languorously at Laurel. And I didn't even do anything about him! she thought. I should have rung up Nina and *made* her understand. That's one thing I should have done.

Seb saw her looking at Leslie. "Laurel's not through with him," he said. "She won't let him go yet. Besides, he's not much of a life. Polly—please!"

"Oh shut up, Seb," Polly said. "I wasn't—"

"One of us has got to go," Seb insisted. "My father's on his last

legs. He's been waiting eighteen years now. And Tom's ten years
older than I am, He's had some time at least!"

Oh God! Polly thought. What am I to do?

Beside her, the strings were tuned. The quartet started to play.
When Tom began it, gently rolling sullen, swelling notes out of the
cello, she assumed it would be designed to show him as the superb
cellist he was. But when Ann's viola came mourning in, she wondered if it might be intended as a dirge. Beyond Ann, Sam's violin
sang, and Ed's sang and soared, and the music became something
else again, nearly light-hearted. Showing how much the quartet
needed Tom? Polly wondered. There was no question they were a
good quartet these days. They had improved almost out of mind
from the afternoon Polly had spent hearing them practise in the
green basement. Everyone was attending. The strolling people
gathered round and sat on the grass to listen. Laurel turned round
in her seat. Even Leslie forgot Laurel sufficiently to sit up and lean
forward raptly. Only Seb, standing close to Polly, was tense and
inattentive.

The music broadened and deepened, put on majesty and passion, and moved onward in some way, fuller and fuller. All four
players were putting their entire selves into it. Polly knew they were
not trying to prove anything—or not really. She let the music take
her, with relief, because while it lasted she would not have to make a
decision or come to a dead end. She found her mind dwelling on
Nowhere, as she and Tom used to imagine it. You slipped between
Here and Now to the hidden Now and Here—as Laurel had once
told another Tom, there was that bonny path in the middle—but
you did not necessarily leave the world. Here was a place where the

quartet was grinding out dissonances. There was a lovely tune beginning to emerge from it. Two sides to Nowhere, Polly thought. One really was a dead end. The other was the void that lay before you when you were making up something new out of ideas no one else had quite had before. That's a discovery I must do something about, Polly thought, as the lovely tune sang out fully once and then fell away to end, as the piece had begun, in a long, sullen cello note. And her mind was made up.

There was a polite patter of applause. "Isn't it odd," Polly heard someone behind her say, "how they always do something like this? It seems to bring out the best in them."

And if I hadn't decided, I would after that! Polly thought. Everyone was looking at Laurel now. Laurel was sitting up straight, smiling at Tom. "You mustn't think I don't understand," she said. "But it's time now, Tom."

Tom got up and propped his cello carefully against the chair. Polly felt Seb begin to relax beside her. Ann turned round and, rather grimly, stowed her viola in its case. Ed and Sam sat where they were, looking urgently at Polly. My move, Polly thought. Mr. Leroy was coming heavily up the slope towards Laurel's seat. The King, Polly thought. The King who takes the lives of other men to make himself immortal.

But before Polly could move, Mr. Piper burst out from among the rose bushes and pushed his way through the elegant crowd until he was in front of Laurel's seat. "Leslie!" he shouted. Leslie blinked up at him from beside Laurel, and then looked over at Tom in a puzzled way and seemed to wonder what was going on.

Laurel sat up very straight. There was suddenly not the least doubt that this was a Court, and Laurel was its Queen. "Charles Lynn," she said coldly. "What are you doing here?"

Mr. Piper loomed in front of her, grasping at the air with his huge hands, which looked queerly useless to him, as if he had been born with lobster's claws. "Let Leslie go," he said. "You cow!" Laurel simply looked at him. He put up a lobster hand to guard his eyes. "All right," he said. "You can take me instead if you want. Just let Leslie go."

"No," said Laurel. "I never make more than one bargain, Charles, and I made mine with you sixteen years ago when I let you go in exchange for your brother."

"Well, I knew what I was in for, didn't I? And you didn't like that," Mr. Piper said. "Besides, he was the one you really wanted anyway, wasn't he?"

"Oh, go away, Charles," said Laurel.

"Just a moment," Tom put in. Mr. Piper turned round awkwardly and backed away when he found Tom right beside him. "Didn't I have any say in this bargain at all? Who took that photograph?"

"You did—you were always pinching my camera. I only made the enlargement," said Mr. Piper. "Leave me alone, can't you! Why do you keep trying to hunt me down?"

"Because I knew it was you," Tom said. "It had to be, from the way you kept out of sight when I came. It was a pretty poor trick, making Edna pretend to be your sister, and it didn't fool me for long anyway. And I needed to know how that bargain was made."

"And you helped her get Leslie!" Mr. Piper said. "I'm glad I made it!"

"Be quiet, both of you," Laurel said. "I'm obliged to you, Charles. Tom's life is one of the most valuable we've had—even his infuriating habit of fighting everything I do. Morton needs a strong life just now. But the obligation has nothing to do with Leslie."

At this, Mr. Piper lost his uneasy temper and shouted, "You unfeeling bitch!"

Laurel raised her face and looked at him. "Go away," she said. Caught in the tunnel of her eyes, Charles Lynn put his arm across his glasses and staggered. Two servitors came up and took hold of him, and looked at Laurel for instructions. "Take him home," said Laurel. "His wife will be worrying." As Mr. Piper disappeared backwards among the crowd, still faintly trying to shout insults, Laurel turned, gently and sweetly, to Tom. "I'm sorry, Tom, but you will find the bargain holds. The picture *was* yours."

But it isn't! Polly thought. He gave it to me! Mr. Piper was still to be heard in the background as she pushed her way forward. Seb made an effort to hang on to her, but she shook him off, hardly noticing.

"I never agreed to it," Tom said. "Don't look her in the eyes, Polly."

Laurel smiled at him indulgently. "Oh no, Polly," she said. "Didn't you hear me tell Charles that I never make more than one bargain?"

"Yes," said Polly. "And I agreed to forget Tom, though I never said for how long, and that isn't the same as giving him up. But I haven't come to quibble." She looked carefully between Laurel and Leslie, two fair heads. "I claim that Morton Leroy has forfeited his right to Tom's life. And he'll have to find someone else or go himself."

"We second that," said Ed. He and Sam and Ann were standing beside Polly, all looking very determined.

Mr. Leroy propped himself on his stick opposite. His eyes were bloodshot. He looked so much on the point of disintegration that Polly could hardly bear to see him. He could have been a walking corpse. "Laurel," he said, "I don't think these people have any right to be here."

"Yes we have," said Ann. "My mother was a Leroy, and she told me we had a right to invite three friends."

Laurel looked at Ann carefully. "Very well," she said. "In that case, I'll investigate. Polly dear, I hope you're not just wasting our time."

"I'm not," said Polly. "It is right, isn't it, that Tom's life is sacrosanct up to this? I mean that, no matter how crazily he drives or whatever other dangerous thing he does, he wasn't supposed to get hurt."

"Of course," said Laurel.

"But Mr. Leroy made two attempts to kill me when I was with Tom," Polly said. "Sam and Ed were there the first time, and Leslie was there the second time, when Tom got quite badly hurt—"

"I can vouch for that," Sam said. "We all can."

"And you must know it's true yourself," Polly said, "because I saw you with Tom only a month after—"

"Tom dear," said Laurel. "You told me—"

"It doesn't matter what he told you," Ann interrupted. "Only

Morton Leroy *could* have hurt him, and you know that even better than I do!"

There was silence. In it Polly heard for the first time a faint rippling whisper from the current bleeding from the pool. Laurel seemed to be considering. "Very logical, Polly dear," she said, "but please tell your friends not to presume." Then she looked up, behind Polly and Ann. "Seb dear," she said, and when Seb had grudgingly moved up near the seat, "Seb dear, I don't think you were quite honest with me. When we made our plan, you never said a word of your father." She looked the other way, at Mr. Leroy. "Morton, my dear, I think you may have been rather foolish."

Mr. Leroy was shaking. His red-rimmed eyes rolled vengefully to Polly. "It was my life she was stealing," he said chokily. "But she was the one who stole the portrait from your room. You can get her for that."

"I'll take that into consideration. Thank you," Laurel said. "But I shall have to support Polly's claim, Morton, you see that. Come here, Seb dear."

Tom reached out and seized Polly's hand.

"Who, me? Why?" said Seb.

"Silly." Laurel smiled and beckoned. "I shall need you if Morton loses."

Seb walked slowly over to the swinging seat. There was a look of such utter horror on his face that Polly realised that this was what Seb had been afraid of all these years. She would have felt sorry for him if he had not said to her as he passed her, "Laurel's not the only unfeeling bitch around here."

"It won't kill you," Polly said. "Literally."

Laurel meanwhile gave Leslie a gentle push. "Up you get, dear. Seb's young. I may not need you."

Leslie sprang up, hurt, guilty, and puzzled, and stared at Seb settling into his place. "What's going on?"

"Hush, dear," said Laurel. "Now, Morton, this is what I say. I shall give both of you a chance. Tom can use anything which is truly his. You can use the exact equivalent. The one who enters the pool first is the one who goes. Don't you think that's fair, Polly?"

"No," said Ann, and Mr. Leroy cried out, "Laurel! I've no strength!" and Ann added, "But Tom has. That's the catch, isn't it?"

"Maybe," said Laurel. "But that's what I've said, dear."

Polly looked down at the grass, trying to work out what this meant. Laurel had taken steps to show Tom he could win. But why? Around her, everyone's feet were crowding as if people were trying to see something, and Seb, for some reason, was churring with laughter. She looked up. Seb was laughing at her, and Tom was no longer beside her. Seeing Seb's jeering face, it came to her that Seb had always loved her the way most people bear a grudge. He knew what Laurel meant.

Tom and Mr. Leroy were standing halfway down the lawn. The sound from the near-invisible current had changed to hoarse rasping. The ripples had reversed and were now bleeding back into the pool. The pool itself was—wrong somehow. It lay above, or beyond, or perhaps below the two standing on the lawn, like an open trench in a different dimension. Polly's mind kept trying to tell her it was not really there, in spite of the funnel of ripples sucking back into it. Those ripples only showed because they rippled everything they passed in front of. As Polly was turning to look, they spread

and ponded like a sea tide to shimmer across the green lawn and
cover Tom and Mr. Leroy from the knees down. Or had the ripples
risen? Neither Tom nor Mr. Leroy had moved, yet the funnel of
transparent ripples was now somehow up to their waists.

Mr. Leroy had his stick grimly planted, undulating like a snake
in the current. Tom put out a bleached, shimmering hand. It was a
habitual sort of gesture, though it had doubt and experiment in it.
His cello swam into being, still propped on its chair, on the rippling
green slope above him, and its bow was somehow in his hand. And
it seemed as if the ponding funnel of ripples tipped about without
moving. Mr. Leroy was out of it from the knees upwards, but Tom
was under up to his shoulders. Polly saw him realise and stand back
from the cello with his arms folded and the bow dangling, rippling
under one elbow.

There was polite pattering applause from the elegant people
round Polly. A voice cheered Mr. Leroy. Several others called jeeringly to Tom to use the cello, since he had made such a point of
having it. Without thinking, Polly plunged forward to fetch that
cello away.

"No!" shouted Ann. Sam and Ed seized Polly by her arms and
held her back. Polly stopped resisting in a hurry. Even this—her
attempt to help and the others' to stop her—had tipped the cone
of ripples about again. Mr. Leroy's bent grey figure stood clear
against the green grass. Only his feet and the tip of his stick rippled.
Tom was right underneath, blanched and wavering, and, in the
odd, wrong perspective down there, he was in some way a lot nearer
to that coffin-shaped trench into which the current was bleeding.

The bright garden and the elegantly excited people smeared round Polly as she understood. Tom on his own could not send Mr. Leroy to the pool. Any help sent Tom there instead. Out of the smear, the one clear thing was Laurel, sitting upright in her seat, watching Tom with a small, grave smile. Laurel, with chilly, malicious logic, had made sure that there was only one way Tom could win.

All right, Polly thought. So the only way to win is to lose. I'll have to lose.

There was a sort of conference going on among the other three, mainly in mutters and jerks of the head, in case this would be construed as help to Tom. "Try it," said Ann. "It's all I can think of."

Ed picked up his violin off the grass where he had dropped it in order to grab Polly, put it under his chin, and played, not his usual sweet notes, but a rapid downwards squalling. A whinny. Below, the bleached, shimmering shape of Tom tilted his head. He said something. Polly knew he was asking her what she thought, but his voice belled into a thousand echoes in the ripples and all she could hear was, "Think-ink-ink?"

She could see the way the others were thinking. Tom had changed the horse for a car, but since Tom was Laurel's man with Laurel's gift, that horse was still truly his. It was all the wild strength he had summoned up to get loose from Laurel. They were asking him to summon it again to defeat Mr. Leroy, hoping to use Laurel's unlucky gift against her. But Polly knew it would only turn against Tom.

"Don't expect any help from me!" she shouted. It was all the hint she dared give.

But a voice did not cut through the current like Ed's violin. Tom must have thought she agreed. He nodded. The ripples sped over him faster and faster as he leaned forward and tried to get his bow to the strings of the cello. It seemed to have drifted upwards from him and he could barely reach it.

Polly set off down the lawn again before he could do it. She was sure the others would not dare try to stop her a second time. She passed the elegant people crowding and clapping like spectators at a contest. They laughed and called out at her. She came to Mr. Leroy. He was leaning on his stick watching Tom sarcastically over his shoulder. He broke into his loud, fatal laugh as he saw Polly. But the laugh stopped as she walked past him into the miasmic ripples, and he looked at her uneasily.

Polly kept her eyes on the greyed, uncertain shape of Tom below. He was definitely below now, in the wrong perspective of that current, deep beneath her. Around her, everything became grey-green ripples, but she did not feel the ripples, or anything else particularly. She had meant to harden her mind and be as stony as Ivy, but she seemed stony already. Kind feeling seemed to bleed away from her as she went downwards. Love, companionship, even Nowhere meant less and less. All she felt was a numb kind of sadness. The truth between two people always cuts two ways, she thought. And she had to go on.

As you do in water, she saw Mr. Leroy floating above her, and the blurred soles of his shoes. Tom was floating below, fighting the current to get near his cello. Neither had gone up or down. By which Polly knew she had to go on and lose.

She was quite near to Tom when he succeeded in drawing the bow across the cello. It made a thundering rasp, which was taken up by the echoes of the current and prolonged to a chugging sort of snarl. Tom receded downwards instantly. Ah, well, Polly thought. It wouldn't have worked. She passed the cello, with echoes ebbing out of it, and the bow, floating, and found Tom in front of her.

He was hanging, swaying, with both arms spread out for balance on the very edge of the trench. It was open like a door behind him. And it was nothingness. There were no ripples here, just nothingness. Truly the dead end of nowhere, Polly thought.

"That was a mistake," he said to her. "Wasn't it?"

"Yes," said Polly. The horse was coming. She could feel its hoofbeats in the dying din of the cello, cutting across the rhythm of the ripples above her. She wondered whether to say any more. She could have got it horribly wrong. But the only way to turn that wild strength of the horse to Tom's advantage was to deprive him of it completely. To take everything away, and do it now, because the horse had arrived. When she craned her head in the impossible direction of the garden, back and above, she could see a huge, bent, golden shape racing across the green there. "And it was an even worse mistake," she said, "the way you used me. You took me over as a child to save your own skin."

The golden shape surged above. Polly could feel the beast panic as the current dragged it in. "You're not doing that again," she said.

Tom stared at her incredulously. She could see his eyes behind his glasses, as wide and grey with shock as they were when he first saw the horse. He had been completely sure of her. Polly could hardly blame him. But she had to go on. The horse was on its way down, screaming, lashing, fighting the current, belling echoes against the trench of nothingness, and the large grey shape of Mr. Leroy was tumbling downwards before it.

"Now you know how I felt," Polly said. "Taste of your own medicine. We've nothing in common anyway, and I've got a career to come too."

Then the horse came. It stood above them like a tower of golden flesh and bone, beating the current with its iron hooves and screaming, screaming. Polly saw a big eye tangled in pale horse-hair, and huge, square teeth.

"I never want to see you again!" she screamed at Tom through its screams. The grey lump of Mr. Leroy slid past her into nothingness. Polly turned away as the horse hit them.

CODA
scherzando

CODA

They shaped him in her arms at last
A mother-naked man

TAM LIN

There was an interval of jarring pain, scourging cold and numbing heat. Ages long. After that, the world hardened in jolting stages to pale whiteness. And with it came sadness, such sadness. Polly found herself, shivering and for some reason dripping wet, sitting on the edge of the concrete trough. The grass round it was greyed with the first frost of winter, and greyed further by the rising sun. The grey was as bitter as Polly felt. Water pattered from her clothes and hair. More pattering came from Tom's clothes. Polly could see him in the growing white light, sitting on the opposite edge of the trough, folded up and shivering under the clinging wreck of his suit, trying uselessly to dry his glasses with his soaking jacket.

"You meant that, didn't you?" he said.

"Yes," said Polly. And, thanks to Laurel, had to go on meaning it, or it would all be to do again. To love someone enough to let them go, you had to let them go forever or you did not love them that much. The jet of misery rose in Polly, far higher and stronger than it had ever been at Middleton Fair, but she made herself say, "It was true."

"All right. I did use you. I admit," Tom said, speaking in bursts, between shivers. "All I can say is that I did my best . . . not to hurt you . . . though there was probably no way not to. Are you quite determined . . . never to see me again?"

Polly, shaking all over with cold, held to being stony, and held down the jet of misery behind. "I told you."

"All right. But I want to keep seeing you. I always wanted to keep seeing you." Tom put his blurred glasses on, and took them off with an exclamation of disgust. "It may not work out—between us. But I want to try. At least I can ask now. Won't you change your mind?"

Polly stood up. She saw Tom's head tip to follow her face, trying to make out her reaction. Hunsdon House stood above the uncut lavender bushes, dead and shuttered against the grey-white sky. There were people coming among the bushes, which was probably just as well, or she and Tom would be dying of exposure. And what was her reaction? She looked down at Tom. She thought of Ivy once standing implacably blocking the hallway. She thought of all the things Tom might have said—which Seb *would* have said—just now to change her mind. It was the things not said that showed they might have a great deal in common. And Tom had spent so many years defying Laurel. One of the things he had to be saying, by not saying, was that there had to be some way to get round Laurel's chilly logic. Perhaps there always *was* a way.

The jet of misery died away and became a warm welling of hope. "This is quite impossible," Polly said carefully. "For you, the only way to behave well was to behave badly. For me, the only way to win was to lose. You weren't to know me, and I wasn't to remember you." She saw Tom's head tip again as he began to get her gist. "If two people can't get together anywhere—"

"You think?" Tom said with a shivery laugh. "Nowhere?"

"Yes, and if it's not true nowhere, it has to be somewhere." Polly laughed and held out her hands. "We've got her, either way."

Tom groped, gripped her hand awkwardly, and stood up. "Who's coming? I can't see a thing."

"I think it's the rest of the quartet," Polly said. Sam burst out of the bushes as she said it, and turned to shout that he had found them. We'd better all go to Granny's, Polly thought, gripping Tom's icy hand. Ed followed Sam, carrying Tom's cello, and Ann came behind with Leslie. Even in that early light Polly could tell Leslie had been crying his eyes out. But he had recovered enough to pretend to be normal.

"Hey!" he called out. "That car of yours is sat on top of the roses back there. Squashed them flat!"

Tom leaned his head against Polly's to laugh. "Now, that *is* impossible!" he said.

THE HEROIC IDEAL

In 1989, the academic journal *The Lion and the Unicorn* published the text of a speech by Diana Wynne Jones, "The Heroic Ideal—A Personal Odyssey." In it, she discussed the process and decision-making behind the novel *Fire and Hemlock*, one of the few times she broke down her own personal creative process.

> **This is the first time it has appeared with the book itself.**

THE HEROIC IDEAL—
A Personal Odyssey

I have subtitled this essay "A Personal Odyssey." Hackneyed though this is, I think it is relevant in more than one way. I have never been able to think of heroes or the heroic without taking them to some extent personally—particularly when I was asked to talk about these topics in relation to my book *Fire and Hemlock*.

As a child, I was an expert in heroes. The eccentricity of my parents meant that there were almost no books in the house except learned ones or books they used for teaching—and I was an avid reader. So before I was ten I had read innumerable collections of Greek myths, including Hawthorne's *Tanglewood Tales*, and the unabridged version of the *Morte d'Arthur*, in double columns and tiny print, from which, besides being very puzzled about just what Lancelot was doing in Guinevere's room, I made a mental league

table of the Knights of the Round Table: Galahad went even below
Kay, as a prig—and my favourite was Sir Gawain. I also read *Pil-
grim's Progress* and folk tales innumerable from all over the world,
including all of Grimm—and also a certain amount of Hans Andersen, but as Andersen reputedly made his stories *up*, my parents
only admitted him to their house in limited quantities. I then went
on to the *Odyssey*, which I preferred to the *Iliad*.

In all this, I was saddened to find that as an eldest child and a
girl I was barred from heroism entirely—or was I? I puzzled long
over the story of Hero and Leander. Hero did nothing but let her
lover do all that swimming. Obviously the girl was a wimp. But she
had that *name*. When I was nine, much pleading wrung a frivolous
book from my parents—*The Arabian Nights*, bowdlerized. Scheherazade, I was delighted to find, was an elder sister. So even though
she did nothing but tell stories (literally for dear life), maybe there
was some hope. I found it later in that book, in a tale in which the
Sultana's jealous sisters tell the Sultan that his wife has given birth
to a puppy, a kitten, and a log of wood. The log of wood was a girl,
and she most heroically set things to rights. Good. It was possible
for a girl to be a hero, then.

By this stage, I had acquired a firm mental grasp of what a hero
is. A hero, first, is the one you identify with in the story. (Although
this is not quite intrinsic to heroism, it *is* a fact that keeps flowing
back into the definition and influencing it in all sorts of ways.
When I later read *Paradise Lost*, I saw at once that Milton had made
the mistake of ignoring this.) Otherwise, heroes are brave, physi-
cally strong, never mean or vicious, and possessed of a code of

honor that requires them to come to the aid of the weak or incompetent and the oppressed when no one else will. In addition, most heroes are either related to, or advised by, the gods or other supernatural characters. The gods (even if they only appear in the form of Fate) are important for heroism for two reasons. First, they supply a huge extra set of dimensions that put the hero in touch with the rest of the universe and render his actions significant for the whole of humanity. Second, the fact that the gods are watching over him serves to keep the hero up to his code. If he does chance to behave in a mean or vicious way—or break any of the other rules, for that matter, which are part of the world of that particular story—then he is at once punished and corrected.

But above all, heroes go into action when the odds are against them. They do this knowingly, often knowing they are going to get killed, and for this reason they impinge on a hostile world in a way others don't. When they die, their deaths are glorious and pathetic beyond the average.

Now this probably sums up Hector of Troy, and Hercules, and certainly applies to King Arthur—who has a double supernatural dimension, since he is guided both by Merlin and the Christian God—but I was aware that it did not quite apply to people like Jason of the Golden Fleece; or to Theseus, who coolly abandoned Ariadne on an island; or to the heroes of innumerable folktales who, like the Brave Little Tailor, start their heroic careers with a gross deception; nor, particularly, did it apply to Odysseus. Odysseus, while being billed as every inch a hero, nevertheless conned and tricked and sweet-talked his way all round the Adriatic.

This used to worry me acutely. I was quite aware, of course, that Odysseus belonged to the second type of hero—the foxy, tricksy hero, the hero with a brain—but this being the case, was it proper to regard him as a hero at all? For a long time I felt I only had Homer's word for it—that he was only being a "hero" in the sense of being the person you identified with in the story. Then it dawned on me that the most heroic thing Odysseus does was never properly explained in my translation of the *Odyssey* (maybe Homer doesn't explain it anyway). This was to have himself tied to the mast with his ears open, while his sailors plugged their ears and rowed past the Sirens. My translation represented this simply as a sort of musical curiosity on Odysseus's part; he wanted to hear whatever it was the Sirens did. But if you look at this episode from the point of view of the rules of magic, you see at once that it is a calculated attempt to break the Sirens' spell. Obviously, if a man could hear their irresistible song and yet resist them, this would destroy the power of the Sirens for good. As soon as I saw this, I realized that Odysseus was a *real* hero.

Around this time, my grandmother gave me a book she had won at the age of six as a Sunday School prize (which she confessed she had chosen for its grand and incomprehensible title). It was called *Epics and Romances of the Middle Ages*. It contained almost every heroic legend from Northern Europe that was not part of the Arthurian cycle: the Charlemagne cycle, the stories connected with Dietrich of Berne, the entire Nibelung cycle, including the bits that Wagner did not use, the story of Beowulf and of Wayland Smith, and many more, all illustrated with wonderful woodcuts but otherwise in no way adapted for children. I read it until it fell to pieces. Many of the stories were unutterably sad, particularly those in which the gods took a hand—so much so that, when I later heard the saying, "Those whom the gods love die young," I thought that, though thoroughly unfair, it was probably a profound truth.

Out of all this reading I had by now the basic hero-story well plotted. Your average hero starts out with some accident of birth, parentage, or person which sets him apart from the rest and often, indeed, causes him to be held in contempt. Even if he seems normal, he has at some point to contend with his own physical nature (as when Beowulf fights the dragon as an old man, or when Odysseus listens to the Sirens). Nevertheless he sets out to do a deed which no one else dares to do and/or at which others have horribly failed. The story often does not state the heroic code that demands this. That code only manifests itself when, along the way, the hero's honor, courage, or plain niceness cause him to befriend some being who will later come powerfully to his aid. (This is one of the places where being a hero overlaps with "being the person in the story with whom we identify," because your hero is after all your Goodie.) After this, he may well make some appalling mistake—as Christian strays from the strait and narrow path, or Siegfried forgets Brunhilda—and this lands him deep in trouble. He can then end tragically. Or he can call in the debt from the powerful being he befriended earlier and, with difficulty, prevail.

So much for the male heroes. But it seemed to me the women were a mess. All over the world they were either goaded into taking vengeance, like Medea or Brunhilda in my grandmother's book, or they were passive, like Hero or Andromeda or Christiana. A medievalist I consulted about this opined that Christianity had substantially affected the heroic ideal, especially where women were concerned, by introducing ideas of patience and endurance and the solitary personal struggle against one's fleshly instincts. But you have only to look at the stories I have cited already to see that all these things are there in pre-Christian heroic stories. There seems to have been an overwhelming acceptance that meekness was the lot of a good woman, until she was goaded into turning evil. In the *Odyssey*, Penelope can only stay good by tricksy passive resistance, which doesn't do much to get rid of her suitors. But at least she is using her mind—like her husband.

By this time I was adding the rest of an education to this childhood reading. This involved studying Chaucer's *Canterbury Tales*. And here I found a man writing who was more subtle than Odysseus, *playing* with the kind of narratives I had previously enjoyed, telling them in different styles, delicately deflating the typical hero, altering the balance of the tale with sophisticated touches (not least of which was making some tales almost too appropriate to their tellers, as in the "Clerk's Tale," where he has the ultimate female wimp, Griselda). And most ironical and sophisticated of all, he tells the most truly and obviously heroic story—"Sir Thopas"—pretending it is from his own mouth, and makes it an utter joke, a complete send-up. It was as if a super-Odysseus had passed that way, listening with a delicate and caustic ear to the Siren-song of my childhood stories and breaking their spell entirely. I didn't quite see this at the time, but I *was* left with an uneasy sense that the heroic ideal was awfully banal and naïve and straightforward.

When I got to Oxford as a student I came to see that this was how these stories seemed to *everyone* now that Chaucer had done with them. No respectable writer dared for centuries to write a straightforward heroic narrative. If you wanted to, you had to show that your narrative had a purpose that was not heroic—either to strip the illusions from a naïve hero like Candide or Tom Jones (*Tom Jones,* interestingly enough, being based on the *Odyssey*); or to make a moral and social point aside from the story as, say, Dickens does. And the bad things to be conquered had to be reduced to credible everyday targets, like the Government. Not surprisingly, tricksy, Odysseus-like heroes came to be preferred by the twentieth century (Chandler's Marlowe is typical)—that is, if you still stubbornly wanted any element of heroism or naïve story-telling. And the whole thing reached an apotheosis in a non-heroic non-story by James Joyce called, appropriately enough, *Ulysses.* In the midst of all this I was very grateful to come across Edmund Spenser who had managed to retrieve at least six genuine heroes from this mess and put them in a narrative called *The Faerie Queene.* This is an allegory. Even in Tudor times you couldn't do it straight and be thought serious (I may remind everyone that Shakespeare didn't consider his plays serious; his serious stuff was *Venus and Adonis,* where the decoration almost hides the story).

To my joy, one of Spenser's heroes was a woman. Britomart. Now I haven't space to go into everything I learnt from Spenser—things such as how to organize a complex narrative, or how to implant the far-off supernatural into the here-and-now—but I must pause a bit on what a discovery Britomart was to me. A woman who was a proper hero (this may be a commonplace now, but it certainly was not in the fifties). True, she was also an allegory of Chastity and dressed in armor like a man; but the significant thing to me was that she had a vision of her future lover and set out to do something about it as a hero should. The vision of the future lover is of course a common folktale element. But in *The Faerie Queene* the vision serves as the high ideal, the thing to strive towards, and it is also, in plain human terms, love. And here I began to see just what Christianity had really added to the heroic tradition. It had reinforced the high ideal—for God is love—though heroes have always had that, even if they do not know it when they begin. But, more importantly, Christianity had modified the tradition that a hero is guided by a god or gods. For God watches over everyone. Thanks to Britomart and Spenser, I now knew that every ordinary man or woman *could* be a hero.

But the heroic ideal, I thought, had gone sour. It was not until I had children of my own and through them came to read the children's books I had never had as a child, that I realized that here was the only place where the ideal still existed. It flourished alongside the *story*, since children will not read much without a narrative, in a way that leads me to suspect the two things are closely connected. (Both ideal and story have since begun to flourish again in adult fantasy, but this hardly existed at the time I'm talking of: Tolkien had published only part of *Lord of the Rings*.)

I think the reason that the heroic ideal had, as it were, retreated to children's books is that children do, by nature, status, and instinct, live more in the heroic mode than the rest of humanity. They naturally have the right naïve, straightforward approach. And in every playground there are actual giants to be overcome and the moral issues are usually clearer than they are, say, in politics. I shall never forget the occasion when I was visiting a school as a writer and the whole place suddenly fell into an uproar because the school tomboy—a most splendid Britomart of a girl—had beaten up the school bully. Everything stopped in the staff room while the teachers debated what to do. They wanted to give the tomboy a prize, but decided reluctantly that they had better punish her and the bully too. They knew that if, as a child, you do pluck up courage to hit the bully, it is an act of true heroism—as great as that of Beowulf in his old age. I remember passing the tomboy, sitting in her special place of punishment opposite the bully. She was blazing with her deed, as if she had actually been touched by a god. And I thought that this confirmed all my theories: a child in her position is open to any heroic myth I care to use; she is inward with folktales; she would feel the force of any magical or divine intervention.

On the other hand, it is clear to me that all children don't actually *demand* magical events in their reading. They differ as other people do. But it is a fact that all children's books that *endure* are fantasies of some kind. These do seem to strike the deepest note.

Anyway, you must picture me in the seventies all set to write according to these discoveries. But there was a snag. In 1970 no boy would be seen dead reading a book whose hero was a girl. Children were then—and still are to some extent—rather *too* inward with the heroic tradition that heroes are male and females are either wimps or bad. Girls will read male-hero stories and (wistfully) identify, but not vice versa, not in 1970 anyway. I took this up rather as a challenge: I love a challenge. For instance, I made David in *Eight Days of Luke* a boy, but I put him in a situation with his relations that both sexes could identify with. In *Power of Three*, I provided Gair with a sister with apparently greater gifts, and the same in *Cart and Cwidder*, and I sneaked a female hero past in *Dogsbody* by telling the story from the dog's point of view. But a desire was growing in me to have a real female hero, one with whom all girls could identify and through that, all *persons*—a sort of Everywoman, if you like. This is the reason for the name Polly, when I eventually came to write *Fire and Hemlock*. The Greek *poly* means "more than one; many or much," and this, as we shall see, has more than one significance for the book. Another thing I had also long wanted to do was show children how close to the old heroic ideal they so often are. I'd had a stab at it in *Eight Days of Luke*, by using the days of the week, and the Norse gods they were named after, to indicate that the big things, the stirring events—the heroic ideal—were as much part of modern everyday life as Tuesday, Wednesday, and Thursday are. But I knew that what I wanted to do *really* was write a book in which modern life and heroic mythical events approached one another so closely that they were nearly impossible to separate. I also longed to base something on the ballad "Tam Lin," because that had a real female hero, one of the few Britomart-like heroes in folklore.

Meanwhile, feminism had become a force and was slowly changing the climate of opinion. I looked one day at a picture I own

called *Fire and Hemlock*. It is a very peculiar picture, because sometimes there seem to be people in it and sometimes not. And I realized I was about to unite the book. If anything sparked it off, it was
probably the saying, "Those whom the gods love die young." (I
often find my books are sparked off by a saying or proverb. The
maddest is *Archer's Goon*, which is founded on a dire pun: "urban
gorilla.") But there was another consideration. Janet, the hero of
"Tam Lin," behaves throughout the story like a woman and not like
a pseudo-man. I wanted a narrative structure which did not simply
put a female in a man's place—and, oddly enough, the structure I
came up with was no other than that great twentieth-century
favourite, *The Odyssey*. I think at least part of the reason for this is
Penelope, who, as I said before, is in her way as tricksy as her husband: she clearly has a *mind*. And Odysseus is a thinking hero. I
knew my story was going to be a journey of the *mind* to some extent, both for Polly and Tom.

Now you understand that I came to writing *Fire and Hemlock* not only with the *Odyssey* in mind. My head was awash with
myths and legends, hundreds of them, and they *all* contribute, but
there are three which underlie it principally. The most obvious of
course are the ballads of "Tam Lin" and "Thomas the Rhymer," seen
as parts of a whole. This gives the emotive aspect of the story: that
of a foray into the supernatural world of the imagination to rescue the one you love (and this love is seen in the same way as
Britomart's—as being the same as the heroic ideal). As to the second and third underlay, you must bear with me if I hold the third
up almost to the end. But the second is the *Odyssey*, of course. The

Odyssey accounts for the *shape* of the story, and the way it had largely to be told in flashback. For Homer's *Odyssey* starts in what we have to call present-day Ithaca, and when Odysseus himself finally appears, at least half of *his* story is in flashbacks. We find him disentangling himself from Calypso, a possessive supernatural woman, by telling his story. This gave me several elements. By association with Scheherazade, it made me see that Polly would be telling the story. It gave me Tom's recent divorce from Laurel. And Calypso, when she finally agrees to let Odysseus go, tells him he has to visit Hades first. This could be her way of saying "I'll see you in Hell first!" but, since she is a nymph and semi-divine, it becomes literal truth and means, "You'll have to pass through death first." This ties in wonderfully with the "tithe to hell" that the fairy folk have to pay in "Tam Lin" and gave me the ending of the book. It also gave me an important fact about Laurel: this way she has of bending the truth to her own ends. Put this together with the gift of true-speaking the Queen gives Thomas the Rhymer, and you have Laurel's gift to Tom: that everything he imagines will come true. It is not only a hellish gift from a supernatural female: it is the mark of a particularly terrible type of woman—I'm sure we all know at least one such person—a woman who confuses fact and fiction impartially for her own ends. For Laurel is Circe as well.

At the opening of the book, Polly as well as Tom is in thrall to this woman. She has to perform a strenuous and truthful act of memory to break that thralldom. This is in itself intended to be an act of heroism akin to Odysseus confronting the Sirens. As a girl, one would expect Polly to be in the role of Penelope—and she is, by and large, in that Tom ranges the world, while Polly stays at home. But there is another hero in the *Odyssey*, Odysseus's son, the young, naïve Telemachus. Polly takes the role of Telemachus on herself when she first meets Tom, by naming herself Hero; and this begins a long series of heroic roles both she and Tom take on. (Another reason for her name—she is many people.) Polly does this semi-knowingly at age ten, because she knows instinctively that her only contact with Tom that Laurel cannot break is that of the imagination. At ten, children are good at knowing such things. Polly first expresses this knowledge in the naïve made-up story of Tan Coul and his friends, with herself as assistant hero. As she grows older and recognizes the complexity of life, the naïve make-believe becomes more and more marginal, so that as she searches for her ideal in a new form, she takes on a whole series of heroic roles. She is Gerda in *The Snow Queen*, Snow White, Britomart, St. George, Pierrot, Pandora, Andromeda, Janet from "Tam Lin" and many more, in a sort of overlapping succession.

Tom appears to cling to the role of Odysseus, which he takes on himself with the letter about the giant in the supermarket. Anyone reading that section closely may have noticed that the giant has only one eye, like Polyphemus the Cyclops. But in fact Tom loses that role to Polly around the time he discovers his alter ago in the hardware shop—and becomes in turn Leander, Kay kidnapped by the Snow Queen, the Knight of the Moon, Artegall, Bellerophon, Prometheus/Epimetheus, Harlequin, Perseus, Orpheus, and of course Tam Lin. He and Polly are continually swapping active and passive roles, and, in fact, sharing the part of Odysseus between them.

Now the way I did this was something else I learnt from Spenser.

Spenser's allegory ranges from large overt personifications (Pride is a woman who lives in a palace with a filthy back yard), to correspondences so subtle that it is sometimes hard to call them allegory. And at other times the allegorical role is shared about among many characters, each of whom is some aspect of it. I tried to do the same with the heroic personifications and actions of Polly and Tom. I needed to find some way, you see, to call on the magical or god-guided aspect of all heroic careers. So sometimes I made the action overtly supernatural and sometimes so close to mundane factualness as to be indistinguishable from everyone's ordinary acts. And sometimes halfway between the two.

In order to organize this, I found that the narrative moved in a sort of spiral, with each stage echoing and being supported by the ones that went before. I had to work very hard in the final draft to make sure the echoes were not repetitions, because at the same time I was establishing another set of resonances that had to be hidden in the same spiral. These were *directly* concerned with gods and the supernatural. All the female characters are arranged in threes, with Polly always at the centre. There are Nina (who is silly), Polly (who is learning the whole time), and Fiona (who is sensible); there are Granny, Polly, and Ivy, old, young, and middle-aged respectively. The first threesome may not strike people as significant, but taken along with the second, I hope it begins to suggest the Three-Formed Goddess, *diva triforma*. Towards the end of the book, Granny takes on the role of Fate and Wisdom quite overtly, shearing fish and explaining the riddle of the ballad of "Tam Lin." Laurel is of course an aspect of this Goddess. Consequently, the most important threesome is Laurel, Polly, Ivy. Ivy is the mundane parasitical version of Laurel, evergreen and clinging—Laurel as the Lorelei in Suburbia, if you like. And Polly—make no mistake—is intended to be an aspect of Laurel too—Laurel as Venus and the Fairy Queen. But she is the aspect that appears not in "Tam Lin" but in "Thomas the Rhymer," the good and beloved Queen that Thomas first mistakes for the Virgin Mary and then submits to. The adventures Polly and Tom have together fairly carefully echo this second ballad. I did this not out of perverseness but because of what I had learnt from Spenser, through Britomart, of the Christian contribution to the heroic ideal: that the deity is for everyone. There is God *in* all of us as well as *with* us. It follows that the major part of a hero's quest is to locate that deity within and to live up to its standards. And if the hero is female, it also follows that the deity is likely to be female too, in some sense.

(If anyone wonders about the male characters, yes, they are surreptitiously arranged in the same way.)

You will possibly be thinking by now that I had a rich mix and a complex structure to control. This is true. You are maybe also wondering about the third underlying myth that I mentioned. Before I come to this myth, however, I have to mention another factor. I needed a conscious, organizing *overlay* to this narrative. As you can probably see by now, it could well have run out of control without one. And, unlike the mass of myths and folktales in the story which came surging into the narrative almost unbidden, this *had* to be in my conscious control. The organizing overlay I chose was T. S. Eliot's *Four Quartets*. This, on a purely technical level, gave me a

story divided into four parts and featuring a string quartet. It also
gave me the setting and atmosphere for the funeral Polly gate-
crashes in Hunsdon House:

> *Footfalls echo in the memory*
> *Down the passage which we did not take*
> *Towards the door we never opened*
> *Into the rose garden . . .*
> . . . .
>
> *Quick said the bird, find them, find them,*
> *Round the corner . . . Through the first gate,*
> *Into our first world, shall we follow*
> *The deception of the thrush? . . .*
> . . . .
>
> *So we moved . . .*
> *Along the empty alley, into the box circle,*
> *To look down into the drained pool.*
> *Dry the pool, dry concrete, brown-edged,*
> *And the pool was filled with water out of sunlight,*
> *And the lotus rose, quietly, quietly . . .*

Chapter Two is full of echoes from *Burnt Norton*. The vases
come from here. I chose the poem because it combines static med-
itation with movement in an extraordinary way, to become a quest
of the mind away from the Nothing of spiritual death (Hemlock in
my book), towards the Fire which is imagination and redemption—
the Nowhere of my book. A heroic journey from Nothing to
Nowhere is what Polly takes.

Though I was always aware of Eliot's poem as an overlay, I only, as it were, turned the sound up on it from time to time. I kept it low until the Bristol section after this initial *forte*, where Polly, now in the role of Snow White, Euridice and Britomart—is turned out, lost and looking down into the River Avon.

I think the river is a strong brown god . . .
. . . .

Trying to unweave, unwind, unravel. [Here is Penelope again.]
And piece together the past and the future,
Between midnight and dawn, when the past is all deception.
The future futureless, before the morning watch
When time stops and time is never ending . . .
. . . .

Where is there an end to it, the soundless wailing . . .

I turned the sound down on Eliot again after that, until Polly remembers what it was she did to lose Tom and put them both in Laurel's power. Now here I must remind you of my childhood discovery that all heroes are likely to make one horrible mistake. On the human level, Polly's mistake is to behave like her mother, with possessive curiosity, and spy on Tom. On the mythical level, it throws the story back to the tragedy and failure of Hero and Leander, with which the story started. This unjustified curiosity, which leads the hero to spy on his or her partner, is a motif in dozens of folktales—"East of the Sun and West of the Moon" being the one which is mentioned in the book. Here the young wife sees her husband in his true shape in the night, and loses him. This summary will no doubt remind you all of a much better known story—the story which is, in fact, the third underlying myth in *Fire and Hemlock*—the story of Cupid and Psyche. From long before C. S. Lewis this was a myth of the human soul in search of a beloved ideal, which is what Tom has now become for Polly. Tom in fact has Cupid's attributes, although few people seem to notice. When my British publisher was unable to see this, I simply asked her, "Who is mostly blind and goes to work with a bow?" and she said, "Oh, I *see!*" But, to go back to human terms, and Polly's loss of Tom, people *do* lose sight of their ideals quite often in adolescence and young adulthood; they tend to see life as far too complex and then come up with the idea that things are only real and valid if they are unpleasant or boring. The myth of Cupid and Psyche is certainly about this. Or, as Eliot says, "human kind / Cannot bear very much reality . . ." and the defense is to deny the imagination any reality at all. But the myth of Cupid and Psyche is not mentioned in the book on purpose, because Cupid and Psyche are both in their way gods, not heroes—and anyway, it always seems to me that powerful stories like that one always pull their weight better for only being hinted at.

Once Polly knows she has lost Tom, her quest becomes more urgent. So the narrative moves back to the present time, just as it does in the *Odyssey*, and becomes traditionally heroic in that Polly finds she can call for help on those she has helped in the past. This includes the one she nearly misses because it is too close to her: Fiona. This sort of thing may be a traditional motif, but it does also happen in real life—you can be very blind to people close to you, both for good or evil. Polly has accepted Seb in the same blind way. But at last, having called in her debts and made her heroic act of memory, Polly sets out to retrieve her mistake. Now here I found I had to leave the tradition represented by Janet in "Tam Lin," because it was precisely by hanging on to Tom and being overcurious that Polly had lost him. Anyway she has already done her hanging on as a child. It was clear to me that the only redress she could make was the reverse of possessiveness—complete generosity—generosity so complete that it amounts to rejection. She has to love Tom enough to let him go—hurtfully. This is the only way she can harness Tom's innate strength of character, and only hurting can he summon the full force of the fire—which is to some extent physical passion and to an even greater extent the true strength of the heroic world of the imagination Polly and Tom have built together. But Tom has to do it himself. He has depended on Polly too much.

This is where I turned the sound up again on *The Four Quartets*. Polly has to take the same road that T. S. Eliot describes in his quest:

> *In order to arrive there,*
> *To arrive where you are, to get from where you are not,*
> *You must go by a way wherein there is no ecstasy.*
> *You must go by a way which is the way of ignorance.*
> *In order to possess what you do not possess*
> *You must go by the way of dispossession.*
> *In order to arrive at what you are not*
> *You must go through the way in which you are not.*
> *And what you do not know is the only thing you know*

> *And what you own is what you do not own*
> *And where you are is where you are not.*

Nowhere, you see.

But I was talking about everyday life as much as Eliot was. I was also following the *Odyssey*, where Odysseus does at last come home, to a partnership and a personal relationship. And I wanted to indicate, however briefly, that although a relationship was possible between Polly and Tom, such a relationship is only likely to be maintained through continuing repeated small acts of heroism from both. This is what I tried to do in the Coda, where the structure of the *Odyssey* most remarkably echoes what Eliot has to say:

> *What we call the beginning is often the end*
> *And to make an end is to make a beginning.*
> *The end is where to start from.*

And this is the beginning and the end of my personal version of the *Odyssey*.

Another Diana Wynne Jones classic!

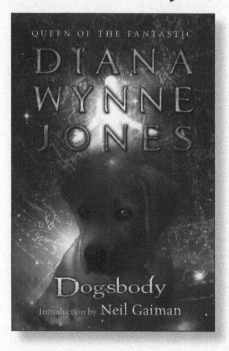

The Dog Star, Sirius, is tried—and found guilty—by his heavenly peers for a murder he did not commit. His sentence: to live on the planet Earth as a dog until such time as he can carry out a seemingly impossible mission—the recovery of a deadly weapon known as the Zoi. The first painful lesson Sirius learns in his lowly earthly form is that humans have all the power. The second is that even though his young mistress loves him, she can't protect either of them from the cruelty of other humans. The third—and worst—is that someone is out there who will do anything to keep Sirius from finding the Zoi. Even if it means destroying Earth itself.

With an introduction by Neil Gaiman

The Dog Star stood beneath the Judgment Seats and raged. The green light of his fury fired the assembled faces viridian. It lit the underside of the rooftrees and turned their moist blue fruit to emerald.

"None of this is *true!*" he shouted. "Why can't you believe *me*, instead of listening to *him*?" He blazed on the chief witness, a blue luminary from the Castor complex, firing him turquoise. The witness backed hastily out of range.

"Sirius," the First Judge rumbled quietly, "we've already found you guilty. Unless you've anything reasonable to say, be quiet and let the Court pass sentence."

"No I will *not* be quiet!" Sirius shouted up at the huge ruddy figure. He was not afraid of Antares. He had often sat beside him as Judge on those same Judgment Seats—that was one of the many miserable things about this trial. "You haven't listened to a word I've said, all through. I did *not* kill that luminary—I only hit him. I was *not* negligent, and I've offered to look for the Zoi. The most you can accuse me of is losing my temper—"

"Once too often, in the opinion of this Court," remarked big crimson Betelgeuse, the Second Judge, in his dry way.

"And I've admitted I lost my temper," said Sirius.

"No one would have believed you if you hadn't," said Betelgeuse.

A long flicker of amusement ran around the assembled luminaries. Sirius glared at them. The hall of blue trees was packed with people from every sphere and all orders of effulgence. It was not often one of the high effulgents was on trial for his life—and there never had been one so notorious for losing his temper.

"That's right—laugh!" Sirius roared. "You're getting what you came for, aren't you? But you're not watching justice done. I tell you I'm not guilty! I don't know who killed that young fool, but it wasn't *me!*"

"The Court is not proposing to go through all that again," Antares said. "We have your Companion's evidence that you often get too angry to know what you're doing."

Sirius saw his Companion look at him warningly. He pretended not to see her. He knew she was trying to warn him not to prove the case against him by raging any more. She had admitted only a little more than anyone knew. She had not really let him down. But he was afraid he would never see her again, and he knew it would make him angrier than ever to look at her. She was so beautiful: small, exquisite and pearly.

"If I were up there, I wouldn't call that evidence," he said.

"No, but it bears out the chief witness," said Antares, "when he says he surprised you with the body and you tried to kill him by throwing the Zoi at him."

"I didn't," said Sirius. He could say nothing more. He could only stand fulminating because his case was so weak. He refused to tell the Court that he had threatened to kill the blue Castor-fellow for hanging around his Companion, or that he had struck out at the young luminary for gossiping about it. None of that proved his innocence anyway.

"Other witnesses saw the Zoi fall," said Antares. "Not to speak of the nova sphere—"

"Oh go to blazes!" said Sirius. "Nobody else saw anything."

"Say that again," Betelgeuse put in, "and we'll add contempt of court to the other charges. Your entire evidence amounts to contempt anyway."

"Have you anything more to say?" asked Antares. "Anything, that is, which isn't a repetition of the nonsense you've given us up to now?"

Rather disconcerted, Sirius looked up at the three Judges, the two red giants and the smaller white Polaris. He could see they all thought he had not told the full story. Perhaps they were hoping for it now. "No, I've nothing else to say," he said. "Except that it was *not* nonsense. I—"

"Then be quiet while our spokesman passes the sentence," said Antares.

Polaris rose, quiet, tall and steadfast. Being a Cepheid, he had a slight stammer, which would have disqualified him as spokesman, had not the other two Judges been of greater effulgence. "D-denizen of S-sirius," he began.

Sirius looked up and tried to compose himself. He had not had much hope all through, and none since they declared him guilty. He had thought he was quite prepared. But now the sentence was actually about to come, he felt sick. This trial had been about whether he, Sirius, lived or died. And it seemed only just to have occurred to him that it was.

"This Court," said Polaris, "has f-found you guilty on three counts, namely: of m-murdering a young luminary s-stationed in Orion; of grossly m-misusing a Zoi to com-m-mit that s-said m-murder; and of culpable negligence, causing t-trepidation, ir-regularity and d-damage in your entire s-sphere of inf-fluence and l-leading t-to the l-loss of the Z-zoi." For the moment, his stammer fazed him, and he had to stop.

Sirius waited. He tried to imagine someone else as denizen of his green sphere, and could not. He looked down, and tried not to think of anything. But that was a mistake. Down there, through the spinning star-motes of the floor, he looked into nothing. He was horrified. It was all he could do not to scream at them not to make him into nothing.

Polaris recovered himself. "In p-passing this s-sentence," he said, "the Court takes into cons-sider-ation your high eff-ffulgency and the s-services you have f-formerly rendered the Court. In view of these, and the f-fact that you are l-liable to rages in which you can-not be s-said to be in your right m-mind, the Court has d-decided to revive an ancient p-prerogative to p-pass a s-special kind of s-susp-pended s-sentence."

What was this? Sirius did not know what to think. He looked at his Companion, and then wished he had not, because of the doubt and consternation he saw in her.

"D-denizen of S-sirius," said Polaris, "you are hereby s-sentenced to be s-stripped of all s-spheres, honors and eff-ffulgences and banished f-from here to the body of a creature native to that s-sphere where the m-missing Z-zoi is thought to have f-fallen. If, d-during the life s-span of that creature, you are able to f-find and retrieve the Z-zoi, the Court will be p-pleased to reinstate you in all your f-former s-spheres and d-dignities. F-failure to retrieve the Z-zoi will carry no f-further p-punishment. In the Court's op-opinion, it is s-sufficient that you s-simply die in the m-manner natural to creatures of that s-sphere."

Slow as Polaris was in giving this extraordinary sentence, Sirius had still barely grasped it when Polaris sat down. It was unheard of. It was worse than nothing, because it condemned him not only to exile but hope—hopeless, brutish hope, over a whole uncertain life span. He flared up again as he realized it.

"But that's the most preposterous sentence I ever heard!"

"Quiet," said Antares. "The Court orders the prisoner taken away and the sentence carried out."

"Try saying *preposterous*, Polaris!" Sirius shouted as they led him away.

The sentence was carried out at once. When he came to himself, Sirius was no longer capable of protesting. He could not see clearly, or speak. Nor did he think much, either. He was very weak and very, very hungry. All his strength had to be spent fighting for food among a warm bundle of creatures like himself. He had just found himself a satisfactory slot and was feeding, when he felt himself plucked off again by a large invincible hand and turned upside down. He made noises in protest, and kicked a little.

A great gruff voice, probably a woman's, said words he did not understand. "That's the sixth beastly dog in this litter. To one bitch. Blast it!"

Sirius was plunked unceremoniously back, and fought his way to his slot again. He did not think much about anything but feeding for quite a while after that. Then he slept, wedged warmly among the other creatures, against a great hairy cliff. It was some days before he thought about anything but food and sleep.

But at length he was seized with an urge to explore. He set off, crawling strenuously on four short legs which seemed far too weak to carry his body. He tripped several times over the folds in the rough cloth he was crawling on. The other creatures were crawling vaguely about, too. More than once, Sirius was bowled over by one. But he kept on, blinking, trying to see where the strong light was coming from a little farther off. He came to cold floor, where crawling was easier.

He was nearly in the strong, warm light, when footsteps clacked toward him. The ground shook. He stopped uncertainly. Once again, he was seized by something ineffably strong and turned upward, kicking and undignified, toward a vaguely looming face. "You're a bold one," remarked the great gruff woman's voice. Then, as Sirius blinked, trying to see what had caught him, the voice said, "I don't like the look of your eyes, fellow. Something tells me Bess has been a naughty girl."

Since he understood none of the sounds the gruff voice made, Sirius felt nothing but exasperation when he was put back in the dark on the rough cloth. Now he would have all that crawling to do again. He waited for the heavy footsteps to clack away, and then set off again.

It did no good. He was put back by someone—either the woman or a being with a hoarse youth's voice—every time he reached the light. He cheeped with frustration. Something in him craved for that light. Why would they not let him have it?

He was in the doorway the next day, when they came—the woman, the hoarse youth and another person. They nearly trod on him. Sirius knew it, and cowered down in terror. The woman, with an exclamation of annoyance, plucked him up from the cold floor into the light.

"Blast this one! It *is* a wanderer." Sirius was quite used to being picked up by this time. He lay quiet. "Well?" said the woman. "What do you think, Mrs. Canning dear? Those markings aren't right, are they? And look at its eyes."

Sirius felt the attention of the other person on him. It felt wrong, somehow. He struggled, and was firmly squeezed for his pains. "No," said a new voice thoughtfully, and it troubled Sirius. It and the smell that went with it set up a ripple that was nearly a memory in his head. "Wrong eyes, wrong color ears. Your bitch must have got out somehow, Mrs. Partridge dear. What are the others like?"

"The same, with variations. Take a look."

There were indignant cheepings that told Sirius that his companions, less used to being handled than he, were being bundled about too. Above the noise, the three voices held a long discussion. And below the cheeping, there was a deeper, anxious whining.

"Shut up, Bess! You've been a bad girl!" said the voice called Mrs. Partridge. "So you don't think these'll fetch any money at all?"

"You might get a pound or so from a pet shop," said the voice called Mrs. Canning. "Otherwise——"

"Much obliged!" Mrs. Partridge said. There was such an unmistakable note of anger in her voice that Sirius cringed and his companions stopped cheeping. They were silent when they were plunked back on the ground, though one or two whimpered plaintively when the big anxious mother licked them. The footsteps went away, but two sets of them returned, briskly and angrily, not long after. All the puppies cringed instinctively.

"Blast you, Bess!" said Mrs. Partridge. "Here I am with a parcel of mongrels, when I might have got nearly a hundred quid for this litter. Got that sack, Brian?"

"Uh-huh." The hoarse youth never used many words. "Brick too. Oughtn't we to leave her one, Mrs. Partridge?"

"Oh, I suppose so," the woman said impatiently. Sirius felt himself seized and lifted. "Not that one!" Mrs. Partridge said sharply. "I don't like its eyes."

"Don't you?" The youth seemed surprised, but he dumped Sirius down again and picked up the next nearest to set beside the mother. The mother whined anxiously, but she did not try to stop him as he seized the other puppies one by one and tossed them into dusty, chaffy darkness. They tumbled in anyhow, cheeping and feebly struggling. Sirius was carried, one of this writhing, squeaking bundle, pressed and clawed by his fellows, jolted by the movement of the sack, until he was nearly frantic. Then a new smell broke through the dust. Even in this distress it interested him. But, the next moment, their bundle swung horribly and dropped, more horribly still, into cold, cold, cold. To his terror, there was nothing to breathe but the cold stuff, and it choked him.

Once he realized it choked him, Sirius had the sense to stop breathing. But there was not much sense to the way he struggled. For as long as he had air and strength in his body, he lashed out with all his short weak legs, tore with his small feeble claws, and fought the darkness and the cold as if it were a live enemy. Some of the other puppies fought too, and got in one another's way. But, one by one, they found the shock and the cold suffocation too much for them. Soon only Sirius was scratching and tearing at the dark, and he only kept on because he had a dim notion that anything was better than cold nothingness.

The darkness opened. Sirius did not care much about anything by then, but he thought he was probably dead. Being dead seemed to mean floating out into a gray-green light. It was not a light he could see by, and it was stronger above him. He had a feeling he was soaring toward the stronger light. Round bubbles, shining yellow, moved up past his eyes and put him in mind of another life he could not quite remember. Then the light was like a silver lid, thick and solid-looking overhead. It surprised him when he broke through the silver without pain or noise into a huge brightness that was blue and green and warm. It was too much for him. He took a gasping breath, choked, and became nothing more than a sodden wisp of life floating down a brisk river.

Behind him, at the bottom of the river, the rotten sack he had torn spread apart in the current and the other sodden wisps floated out. Two were beyond hope and were simply rolled along the mud and stones of the riverbed. But four other wisps rose to the surface and were carried along behind the first. They went bobbing and twisting, one behind the other, around a bend in the river and between the sunny banks of a meadow. Here, the warmth beating from above began to revive Sirius a little. He came to himself enough to know that there was heat somewhere, and that he was helpless in some kind of nightmare. The only good thing in the nightmare was the heat. He came to depend on it.

The river passed hawthorn trees growing on its banks. The current carried Sirius through the shadow of one. He found himself suddenly in deep brown cold. The heat was gone. They had taken his one comfort away now. He was so indignant about it that he opened his eyes and tried to cheep a protest.

He could not manage a noise. But a second later, the river carried him out into sunlight again. Sun struck him full in the eyes and broke into a thousand dazzles on the ripples. Sirius snapped his eyes shut again. The brightness was such a shock that he became a limper wisp than ever and hardly knew that the warmth was back again.

It grew warmer—a golden, searching warmth. "It *is* you, Effulgency!" someone said. "I thought it was!"

This was quite a different order of voice from those Sirius had heard so far. It puzzled him. It was not a voice he knew, though he had a feeling he had heard its kind before. He was not sure he trusted it. All the voices he had heard so far had done him nothing but harm—and he had a notion he had known voices before that, which had done him no good either.

"You aren't dead, are you?" the voice asked. It seemed anxious. It was a warm, golden voice, and, though it sounded anxious, there was a hint of ferocity about it, as if the speaker could be far more dangerous than Mrs. Partridge and her friends if he chose.

Sirius was not sure if he was dead or not. He felt too weak to cope with this strong, fierce voice, so he floated on in silence.

"Can't you answer?" The warmth playing on Sirius's scrap of body grew stronger and hotter, as if the speaker was losing patience. Sirius was too far gone even to be frightened. He simply floated. "I suppose you can't," said the voice. "I think this is just too bad of them! Well, I'll do what I can for you. Just let them try to stop me!"

The warmth stayed, lapping around Sirius, though he sensed that the speaker had gone. He floated a little way farther, until he came up against some things that were long, green and yielding. Here the warmth caught and pinned him, gently rocking. It was almost pleasant. Meanwhile, the other four half-drowned puppies floated on in midstream, around bends, to where the river became wider and dirtier, with houses on its banks.

A shrill voice spoke strange words near Sirius, "Oh, eughky! There's a dead puppy in the rushes!"

"Don't touch it!" said a voice rather older and rougher. And a third voice, gentle and lilting, said, "Let me see!"

"Don't touch it, Kathleen!" said the second voice.

However, there were splashings and rustlings. A pair of hands,

a great deal smaller and much more shaky and nervous than Sirius
was used to, picked him out of the water and held him high in the
air. He did not feel safe. The shakiness of those hands and the cold
air frightened him. He wriggled and managed to utter a faint
squeak of fear. The hands all but dropped him.

"It isn't dead! It's *alive*! Poor thing, it's *frozen*!"

"Someone tried to drown it," said the shrillest voice.

"Throw it back in," said the second voice. "It's too small to lap.
It'll die anyway."

"No it won't." The hands holding Sirius became defiantly steady.
"It can have that old baby bottle. I'm not going to let it die."

"Mum won't let you keep it," the rough voice said nastily.

"She won't. And the cats'll kill it," said the youngest voice.
"Honest, Kathleen."

The girl holding Sirius hugged him defensively to her chest and
began to walk—bump, jerk, bump—away from the river across the
meadow. "Poor little thing," she said. The two boys followed, arguing with her. Their clamor hurt Sirius's ears, and the girl kept jerking him by turning around to argue back. But he realized she was
defending him from the other two and was grateful. Her convulsive
hugging was making him feel safer and a great deal warmer. "Oh!"
Kathleen exclaimed, bending over him. "Its tail's wagging!"

Robin, the younger boy, demanded to see. "It's a queer little tail,"
he said doubtfully. "You don't think it's really a rat, do you?"

"No," said Kathleen. "It's a dog."

"It's a rat," said Basil, the elder boy. "An Irish rat. Shamus O'Rat!"

"Shut up," Kathleen said wearily.

And don't forget . . .

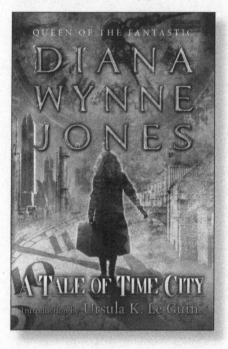

London, 1939. Vivian Smith thinks she is being evacuated to the countryside because of the war. But she is being kidnapped—out of her own time. Her kidnappers are Jonathan and Sam, two boys her own age, from a place called Time City. Built eons ago on a patch of space outside time, Time City was designed especially to oversee history. But now history is going critical, and Jonathan and Sam are convinced that Time City's impending doom can only be averted by a Twenty Century girl named Vivian Smith. Too bad they have the wrong girl. . . .

With an introduction by Ursula K. Le Guin

1

KIDNAPPED

The train journey was horrible. There was a heatwave that September in 1939, and the railway authorities had fastened all the windows shut so that none of the children packed on to the train could fall out. There were several hundred of them and nearly all of them screamed when they saw a cow. They were all being sent away from London from the bombing and most of them had no idea where milk came from. Each child carried a square brown gas mask box. All of them had a label with their name and address on it, and the littlest ones (who cried and wet themselves rather often) had the label tied round their necks with string.

Vivian, being one of the bigger ones, had her label tied to the string bag Mum had found to take the things that refused to fit into her suitcase. That meant that Vivian did not dare let go of the string bag. When your surname is Smith, you need to make very sure everyone knows just which Smith you are. Vivian had carefully written Cousin Marty's name and address on the back of the label, to show that she was not just being sent into the country, like most of the children, to be taken in by anyone who would have her. Cousin Marty, after a long delay, had promised to meet the train and have Vivian to stay with her until the danger of bombs was over. But Vivian had never met Cousin Marty and she was terrified that they would somehow miss each other. So she hung on to the string bag until its handles were wet with sweat and the plaited pattern was stamped in red on her hands.

Half of the children never stayed still for a moment. Sometimes the carriage where Vivian was filled with small boys in grey shorts, whose skinny legs were in thick grey socks and whose heads, each in a grey school cap, seemed too big for their bare, skinny necks. Sometimes a mob of little girls in dresses too long for them crowded in from the corridor. All of them screamed. There were always about three labels saying *Smith* on each fresh crowd. Vivian sat where she was and worried that Cousin Marty would meet the wrong Smith, or meet the wrong train, or that she herself would mistake someone else for Cousin Marty, or get adopted by some- one who thought she had nowhere to go. She was afraid she would get out at the wrong station, or find out that the train had taken her to Scotland instead of the West of England. Or she would get out but Cousin Marty would not be there.

Mum had packed some sandwiches in the string bag, but none of the other evacuees seemed to have any food. Vivian did not quite like to eat when she was the only one, and there were too many children for her to share with. Nor did she dare take off her school coat and hat for fear they got lost. The floor of the train was soon littered with lost coats and caps—and some labels—and there was even a lost, squashed gas mask. So Vivian sat and sweltered and worried. By the time the train chuffed its crowded hot fighting screaming crying laughing way into the station at last, it was early evening and Vivian had thought of every single thing that could possibly go wrong except the one that actually did.

The name of the station was painted out to confuse the enemy, but porters undid the doors, letting in gusts of cool air and shouting in deep country voices. "All get out here! The train stops here!"

The screaming stopped. All the children were stunned to find they had arrived in a real new place. Hesitantly at first, then crowding one another's heels, they scrambled down.

Vivian was among the last to get off. Her suitcase stuck in the strings of the luggage rack and she had to climb on the seat to get it down. With her gas mask giving her square, jumbling bangs and her hands full of suitcase and string bag, she went down on to the platform with a flump, shivering in the cool air. It was all strange. She could see yellow fields beyond the station buildings. The wind smelt of cow dung and chaff.

There was a long muddled crowd of adults up at the other end of the platform. The porters and some people with official arm bands were trying to line the children up in front of them and get them shared out to foster homes. Vivian heard shouts of "Mrs. Miller, you can take two. One for you, Mr. Parker. Oh, you're brother and sister, are you? Mr. Parker, can you take two?"

I'd better not get mixed up in that, Vivian thought. That was one worry she could avoid. She hung back in the middle of the platform, hoping Cousin Marty would realise. But none of the waiting crowd looked at her. "I'm not having all the dirty ones!" someone was saying, and this seemed to be taking everyone's attention. "Give me two clean and I'll take two dirty to make four. Otherwise I'm leaving."

Vivian began to suspect that her worry about her Cousin Marty not being there was going to be the right one. She pressed her mouth against her teeth in order not to cry—or not to cry *yet*.

A hand reached round Vivian and spread out the label on the string bag. "*Ah!*" said someone. "Vivian Smith!"

Vivian whirled round. She found herself facing a lordly-looking dark boy in glasses. He was taller than she was and old enough to wear long trousers, which meant he must be at least a year older than she was. He smiled at her, which made his eyes under his glasses fold in a funny way along the eyelids. "Vivian Smith," he said, "you may not realise this, but I am your long-lost cousin."

Well, Vivian thought, I suppose Marty *is* a boy's name. "Are you sure?" she said. "Cousin Marty?"

"No, my name's Jonathan Walker," said the boy. "Jonathan *Lee* Walker."

The way he put in that *Lee* made it clear he was very proud of it for some reason. But Vivian knew there was something peculiar about this boy, something not as it should be that she could not pin down, and she was far too worried to wonder about his name. "It's a mistake!" she said frantically. "I was supposed to meet Cousin Marty!"

"Cousin Marty's waiting, outside," Jonathan Lee Walker said soothingly. "Let me take your bag." He put out his hand. Vivian snatched the string bag out of his way and he picked up her suitcase from the platform instead and marched away with it across the station.

Vivian hurried after him, with her gas mask banging at her back, to rescue her suitcase. He strode straight to the Waiting Room and opened the door. "Where are you going?" Vivian panted.

"Short cut, my dear V.S.," he said, holding the door open with a soothing smile.

"Give me my suitcase!" Vivian said, grabbing for it. Now she was sure he was a robber. But as soon as she was through the door, Jonathan Lee Walker went galloping noisily across the bare boards of the little room towards the blank back wall.

"Bring us back, Sam!" he shouted, so that the room rang. Vivian decided he was mad, and grabbed for her suitcase again. And suddenly everything turned silvery.

"Where is this?" Vivian said. They were crowding one another in a narrow silvery space like a very smooth telephone booth. Vivian turned desperately to get out again and knocked a piece of what seemed to be the telephone off the wall. Jonathan whirled round like lightning and slammed the piece back. Vivian felt her gas mask dig into him and hoped it hurt. There was nothing but a bare silvery wall behind her.

In front of Jonathan, the smooth silvery surface slid away sideways. A small boy with longish nearly red hair looked anxiously in at them. When he saw Vivian, his face relaxed into a fierce grin with two large teeth in it. "You got her!" he said, and he took what may have been an earphone out of his left ear. It was not much bigger than a pea, but it had a silvery wire connecting it to the side of the silver booth, so Vivian supposed it *was* an earphone. "This works," he said, coiling the wire into one rather plump hand. "I heard you easily."

"And I got her, Sam!" Jonathan answered jubilantly, stepping out of the silver booth. "I recognised her and I got her, right from under their noses!"

"Great!" said the small boy. He said to Vivian, "And now we're going to torture you until you tell us what we want to know!"

Vivian stood in the booth, clutching her string bag, staring at him with a mixture of dislike and amazement. Sam was the sort of small boy Mum called "rough"—the kind with a loud voice and heavy shoes whose shoelaces were always undone. Her eyes went to his shoes—such shoes!—puffy white footgear with red dots. Sure enough, one of the red and white ties of those shoes was trailing on the marble floor. Above that, Sam seemed to be wearing pyjamas. That was the only way Vivian could describe his baggy all-over suit with its one red stripe from his right shoulder to his left ankle. The red clashed with his hair, to Vivian's mind, and she had never seen a boy so much in need of a haircut.

"I told you, Sam," Jonathan said, dumping Vivian's suitcase on a low table Vivian could dimly see behind Sam, "that it's no good thinking of torture. She probably knows enough to torture us instead. We're going to try gentle persuasion. Do please come out of the booth, V.S., and take a seat while I get out of this disguise."

Vivian took another look at the blank, shiny back wall of the booth. Since there seemed no way out that way, she went forward. Sam backed away from her looking just a mite scared, and that made her feel better, until the door of the booth slid shut behind her with a quiet hushing sound and cut out most of the light in the room beyond. It seemed to be night out there, which was probably what had given her the idea that Sam was running around in pyjamas.

What dim light there was came from some kind of streetlights shining through a peculiar-shaped window, but there was enough of it for Vivian to see she was in some kind of ultra-modern office. There was a vast half-circle of desk at the far end, surrounded by things that reminded Vivian of a telephone-exchange. But the odd thing was that the desk, instead of being of steel or chromium as she would have expected a modern desk to be, was made of beautifully carved wood that looked very old and gave off silky reflections in the low bluish light. Vivian looked at it doubtfully as she sat in an odd-shaped chair near the booth. And she nearly leaped straight up again when the chair moved around her, settling into the same shape that she was.

But Jonathan started tearing off his clothes then, right in front of her. Vivian sat stiffly in the form-fitting chair wondering if she was mad, or if Jonathan was, or if she ought to look away, or what. He flung off his grey flannel jacket first. Then he undid his striped tie and threw that down. Then—Vivian's face turned half away sideways—he climbed out of his long grey flannel trousers. But it was all right. Underneath, Jonathan was wearing the same kind of suit as Sam, except that his had dark-coloured diamonds down the legs and sleeves.

"Great Time!" he said, as he dropped the trousers on top of the jacket, "These clothes are vile! They prickle me even through my suit. How do Twenty Century people bear it? Or these?" He plucked his glasses off his nose and pressed a knob on the belt that went round his suit. A flicker sprang into being across his eyes, shifting queerly in the blue light. The fold in his eyelids was much plainer to see like that. Vivian saw that Sam had the same fold. "A sight-function is so much simpler," Jonathan said. He pulled the striped school cap off his head and let about a foot of plaited hair tumble out of it across his shoulder. "That's better!" he said as he hurled the cap down too and rubbed his neck under the pigtail to loosen the tight hair there.

Vivian stared. Never had she seen a boy with such long hair! In fact, she had a vague notion that boys were born with their hair short back and sides and that only girls had hair that grew long. But Jonathan had twice as much hair as she had. Perhaps he was Chinese and she had been spirited away to the Orient. But Sam was not Chinese. Whoever heard of a red-haired Chinaman?

"Who are you?" she said. "Where *is* this?"

Jonathan turned to her, looking very lordly and solemn—and not particularly Chinese. "We are Jonathan Lee Walker and Samuel Lee Donegal," he said. "We're both Lees. My father is the thousandth Sempitern. The Sempitern is the head of Time Council in Chronologue, in case you didn't have those in your day. And Sam's father is Chief of Time Patrol. We feel this qualifies us to talk to you. Welcome back. You have just come through Sam's father's private time-lock and you are now once more in Time City."

A mistake has happened, Vivian thought miserably. And it seemed to be a mistake ten thousand times wilder than any of the mistakes she had imagined on the train. She pressed her lips together. I will *not* cry! she told herself. "I don't understand a word you're saying. What do you mean, 'Welcome back'? Where *is* Time City?"

"Come, come now, V.S.," Jonathan leant one hand on the back of the peculiar chair, in the way Inquisitors did in the kind of films Mum preferred Vivian not to see. "Time City is unique. It is built on a small patch of time and space that exists outside time and history. You know all about Time City, V.S."

"No I don't," said Vivian.

"Yes you do. Your husband built the City," Jonathan said, with his flicker-covered folded eyes staring eerily into Vivian's. "We want you to tell us how to wake Faber John, V.S. Or if he isn't sleeping under the City, tell us how to find him."

"I haven't *got* a husband!" Vivian said. "Oh, this is *mad!*"

Sam, who was breathing noisily and rustily on the other side of Vivian, said, "She looks awfully stupid. Do you think she had her brain damaged in the Mind Wars?"

Vivian sighed and looked rather desperately round the strange dark office. Was it really outside time? Or were they both mad? Both of them seemed to have it fixed in their heads that she was some other Vivian Smith. So how was she going to convince them that she was not?

"Her brain's all right," Jonathan said confidently. "She's just acting stupid so we'll think we've made a mistake." He leant over Vivian again. "See here, V.S.," he said persuasively, "we're not asking for ourselves. It's for Time City. This patch of time and space here is almost worn out. The City is going to crumble away unless you tell us how to find Faber John so that he can renew the City. Or if you hate him too much, you could tell us where the polarities are and how to renew those. That isn't too much to ask, is it, V.S.?"

"Don't keep calling me Vee-Ess!" Vivian almost shrieked. "I'm not—"

"Yes you are, V.S.," said Jonathan. "You were spotted coming up the First Unstable Era in a wave of chronons. We heard Chronologue discussing it. We *know* you are. So how do we wake Faber John, V.S.?"

"I don't *know!*" Vivian screamed at him. "I don't know who you think I am, but I'm not *her*! I don't know you and you don't know me! I was being evacuated from London to stay with Cousin Marty because of the War, and you can just take me back! You're a kidnapper!" Tears came streaming down her face. She scrabbled to get her handkerchief out of the string bag. "And so are you!" she added to Sam.

Sam leaned forward and breathily inspected her face. "She's crying. She means it. You got the wrong one by mistake."

"Of course I didn't!" Jonathan said scornfully. But when Vivian found her handkerchief and looked at him with her face mostly hidden in it, she could tell he was beginning to have doubts.

Vivian did her best to strengthen those doubts. "I've never ever heard of Faber John, or Time City either," she said, trying to stop herself sobbing. "And you can *see* I'm too young to have a husband. I won't be twelve until just after Christmas. We're not in the Middle Ages, you know."

Sam nodded knowingly. "She is. She's just an ordinary Twenty Century native," he pronounced.

"But I recognised her!" Jonathan said. He wandered uneasily across the office. A sort of darkening to his flickering face told Vivian that he was beginning to suspect that he had been a fool—and he was the sort of boy who would do anything not to look a fool. Vivian knew he would take her straight back to the station and try to forget about her if she could convince him properly.

So she sniffed away what she hoped were the last of her tears and said, "I know it says Vivian Smith on my label, but Smith's a very common name. And Vivian's quite common too. Look at Vivien Leigh."

This misfired a little. Jonathan turned and stared at her. "How do you know her? he said suspiciously.

"I don't. I mean—she's a film star," Vivian explained.

She could see this meant nothing to Jonathan. He shrugged. "We could go through her luggage," he suggested to Sam. "That might prove something."

Vivian would have liked to go and sit on her suitcase and clutch the string bag to her and refuse indignantly, but she said with desperate bravery, "Do what you like. Only you're to take me back to the station if you don't find anything."

"I might," said Jonathan. Vivian was fairly sure that meant that he would. She tried not to mind too much when Jonathan dragged the suitcase over into a beam of light from the odd-shaped window, where he began briskly unpacking it. Sam attended to the string bag. Vivian spread it out on her knee for him, because that took her mind off Jonathan going into all her new winter underwear, and wished Sam would not breathe so heavily. The first thing Sam found was her sandwiches.

"Can I eat these?" he said.

"No," said Vivian. "I'm hungry."

"I'll give you half," Sam said, plainly thinking he was being generous.

Jonathan stood up holding Vivian's new liberty bodice with suspenders attached to hold up her winter stockings. "Whatever do you use this for?" he asked, really puzzled by it.

Vivian's face went fiery hot. "Put that down!" she said.

"Corsets," Sam suggested with his mouth full.

There was a sort of buzzing from outside somewhere. Light came on and swiftly grew bright from all the corners of the room. It showed Jonathan standing frozen by the window with the liberty bodice in one hand and Vivian's best jumper in the other. Vivian saw that the flicker over his eyes hardly showed in bright light, and that the diamonds on his suit were dark purple. Sam was frozen too, with a third sandwich in his hand.

"Someone's coming!" Jonathan whispered. "They must have heard her yelling."

"They make regular rounds," Sam whispered back hoarsely.

"Then why didn't you *tell* me? Quick!" Jonathan whispered. He bundled everything back into the suitcase and shoved the lid down. Sam seized the string bag and a handful of Vivian's skirt with it and dragged. It was clear to Vivian that something frightening was about to happen. She let Sam tow her across the marble floor and round behind the huge carved desk.

"Hide!" he said. "Come *on!*"

There was a deep hollow inside the half-circle of desk, so that a person's knees could swivel this way and that to reach the banks of switches. Sam pushed Vivian into it and dived in after her. Before Vivian had a chance even to sit up properly, Jonathan came scrambling into the space too, dragging the suitcase behind him. Vivian ended up half-lying on her side with a clear view through the space at the bottom of the desk. She could see her last sandwich in its paper lying in the middle of the marble floor, and the heap of Jonathan's grey flannel suit beside it.

Jonathan saw them too. "*Damn!*" he whispered, and he was off after them and back again while Vivian was still being shocked to hear him swear. "Don't make a sound!" he said to her breathlessly. "If they find us, they might even shoot you!"

Vivian looked from his face to Sam's, not sure if she believed this. They both had that tense look people have in films when gangsters are looking for them with guns. This made everything completely unreal to Vivian, like a film. She reached out and took her last sandwich from Jonathan before Sam's stretching hand quite got to it. She bit into it. It made her feel better to chew bread she had watched Mum butter and sardines she had helped Mum mash. It told her that real life was still there somewhere.

She was still eating when a door rumbled and the light grew stronger. Two sets of heavy, clacking boots marched into view across the grey-veined white floor. Vivian watched them under the desk, clumping hither and thither, as the people wearing them checked the room. Beside her, she could feel Jonathan beginning to shake and Sam puffing little tiny snorts in an effort to breathe quietly, but she could not believe in any of it and she went on calmly eating her sandwich.

"Seems all right in here," the owner of one pair of boots said, in a rumbling murmur.

"Funny though," murmured the other. This one sounded like a woman. "I can smell fish—sardines. Can you smell sardines?"

Vivian stuffed the rest of the sandwich into her mouth and held both hands across it in order not to giggle. Jonathan's face was white and the lordly look had somehow crumpled away from it entirely. Vivian saw that he had gone from being the Inquisitor to being a scared boy in bad trouble. Sam was holding his breath. His face was going a steadily darker red and his eyes were rolling at Vivian and the sandwich, quite horrified. She could tell they were both very frightened indeed, but she still wanted to laugh.

"No," said the rumbling man's voice. "Don't smell a thing."

"Then I'll blame you," said the woman, "if the Chief gets attacked by a mad sardine tomorrow." They both laughed. Then the woman said, "Come on," and the boots clacked away.

The door rumbled. After a while the lights dimmed. As soon as they did, Sam let out his breath in a near roar and threw himself on his face, gasping. "I'm dying!" he panted.

"No you're not," Jonathan said. His voice had gone shrill and quavering. "Shut up and sit up. We've got to think what to *do*!"

Vivian knew Jonathan's nerve had broken. It was time for her to be firm. "I'll tell you what to do," she said. "Open that silver booth again and put me back in it and send me back to the station to meet Cousin Marty."

"No, we absolutely won't," Jonathan said. "We can't. If we use it again that will make three times and the computer will register it. It always checks the odd numbers anyway, in case an agent goes out and gets lost. And they'll find out we've broken the law. They'll be on to us at once. We're right in the middle of Time Patrol building here. Don't you understand?"